McNEIL'S
Match

McNEIL'S MATCH

ESSENCE BESTSELLING AUTHOR

GWYNNE FORSTER

HARLEQUIN® KIMANI ARABESQUE®

Recycling programs
for this product may
not exist in your area.

MCNEIL'S MATCH

ISBN-13: 978-0-373-09159-1

Copyright © 2006 by Gwendolyn Johnson-Acsadi

For questions and comments about the quality of this book,
please contact us at CustomerService@Harlequin.com.

HARLEQUIN®
www.Harlequin.com

Printed in U.S.A.

Acknowledgments

To my dear friend Ingrid Kasper, whose dry wit and sagacious humor have eased me through some difficult times. Moreover, there seems to be no end to Ingrid's kindness, of which I have been the receipent countless times.

Chapter 1

On the second day of January, Lynne Thurston walked out of municipal court in Ellicott City, Maryland, a free woman after years of psychological abuse intended to break her will. She had not and would not cry about all she had given up for a man, who swore before the world to love, care for and cherish her. He was a man of God, who proved to be a master of self-righteousness, self-ishness and mental cruelty. He hadn't broken her, and no man ever would.

Six years earlier, when she was twenty-three and the number two tennis player in the world, she had walked away from it, because her new husband hadn't thought it proper for a minister's wife to be such a public person engaged in a "nonredeeming" pastime. After six years of fighting to be her own self and not the shell of a person her husband and the brothers and sisters of his church wanted her to be, she ended the charade.

"What are you planning to do now?" her lawyer asked, wiping his forehead with a handkerchief dampened from his fear that his adversary would win the case. "You're lucky, Lynne. It's hard to win any kind of case against a preacher."

"I know. Even that born-again judge knew I couldn't make up all those things. Willard is Dr. Jekyll and Mr. Hyde. Five minutes after smiling and blessing his parishioners, he would treat me as if I wasn't human."

"It's over now," the lawyer said. "What are your plans?"

She hadn't thought much about her future; she had only wanted to change the present, to be a free, independent woman no longer subjected to daily, and sometimes hourly, vicious verbal attacks and scornful criticism.

"Look, Harry. I'm only twenty-nine, and I'm strong and healthy. If I work hard and discipline myself, I can regain my old form. I've never stopped wanting that number one ranking. When I quit to marry Willard, I was the world's number two tennis player, and only eighty-nine points separated me from number one."

They walked side by side down the gray-stone steps of the courthouse. "You were my favorite player, men included. Why'd you quit?"

"Willard said it wasn't proper for a minister's wife to be a professional tennis player."

"You mean he couldn't stand the competition. Well, if you're willing to take the punishment and make the sacrifice to get back to the top, I say go for it. You'll never be satisfied until you try."

"Thanks, Harry. For everything."

She walked to the taxi stand nearby, got into a cab and went to her brother's house where she was staying temporarily. Yes. She would work herself into shape and get back on the tour. Once more, the women tennis players would fear her as they did before she left the sport, and she didn't plan to stop until she was the number one tennis player in the world, the title that would have been hers if she hadn't foolishly fallen in love with the reverend Willard Marsh.

"How'd it go?" her brother asked. "I expected that the divorce would be granted, but what about the terms?"

She adored Bradford, but at times he could be so cut-and-dried that she'd wanted to shake him. Right then, what she needed was a hug, a feeling that somebody somewhere loved her. "There were no terms and no stipulations. I left with what I brought, and he did the same. I didn't want any alimony."

His eyes rounded. "You mean you got nothing for six long years with that rotten excuse for a man?"

She lifted her shoulders in a shrug. "I got plenty. I'm a free woman, and I got a lesson I won't have to learn again. Don't you think that's something?"

"If you say so. Have you made any plans? You can stay here as long as you like. I know you don't need money, but you need some way of passing the time."

She didn't look at him. "I'm giving myself two years to win the US Open tennis tournament."

He jerked around to face her, his mouth agape. "What? What did you say?"

She didn't repeat it. "You heard me."

"Are you out of your mind? You're almost thirty years old, and the hottest player on the tour is eighteen."

"I know how old she is, and I also know how well she plays, but within two years, I'll beat her."

"Look, sis, I hate to say this, but you're setting yourself up for a dreadful disappointment. Why don't you start a tennis clinic or a tennis academy if you want to stay close to the game. But don't do this to yourself."

"Did I hear you saying that Lynne's planning to resume playing professional tennis?"

Lynne glanced to her left and saw Debra, her sister-in-law, rubbing her eyes as she entered the living room.

"That's exactly what you heard," Lynne said. "I want it badly. I need to show myself and Willard Marsh that he can't stop me. And before I've finished, I'll be number one."

Debra dropped herself into a big overstuffed chair. "Well, saints be praised. Girl, that's just like counting stars when the sky's full of 'em. How you gon' do that?"

"Hard work and skill. When I quit, they were saying I was the best there ever was. They'll say it again. Trust me."

Bradford shook his head from side to side and spoke softly, almost a murmur. "I don't believe this is happening. Lynne, you were always so levelheaded."

"And I was always determined, too. Right? I've got what it takes. And another thing: Wasn't Andre Agassi about my age when he went from number one hundred and forty-seven to number one in two seasons? Well, if he did it, so can I."

"You can't compare yourself to—"

"Agassi is the best role model I can think of, and one of the greatest."

* * *

The next day, Lynne sat in the middle of her bed surrounded by maps and travel videos, choosing the place she hoped to live for at least the next five years. She loved to be close to water, but what she needed more was a climate that was dry and warm for most of the year. And she didn't want to live in Florida with its stifling humidity.

"Why not south Texas?" Debra asked at dinner that evening. "It's hot most of the year."

"Yes, indeed!" Lynne said. "San Antonio, here I come. I was there with Willard at a church convention for two days, and I fell in love with the place."

Within three weeks she had leased a house on the outskirts of San Antonio, moved and bought a BMW. "I need a coach and a trainer," she told Bradford during one of their phone conversations, "and if I like this house, I'll buy it."

"What about tennis courts? Where will you practice?" he asked her.

"I'll have a couple put right here, one hard court and one clay court. I don't need a grass court, because I take to grass the way a mouse takes to cheese."

His laughter floated to her ear through the wire— warm, friendly and indulgent. "If you'd said you take to grass the way *you* take to cheese, you'd have been just as accurate. Gotta go. Bye."

She phoned Gary Hines, a recently retired former number one tennis player and told him her goal and that she needed a coach. "You're on," he told her. "But you haven't played for a while, so I'd get a trainer first for, say, about six weeks. Try Max Jergens. He'll get on your last nerve, but he's the best. You and I can start six weeks after you begin your training."

In her rush to begin her comeback, she didn't want to hear that, but she knew he was right, and she agreed.

Building the first tennis court didn't create any problems with her neighbors, whose houses were set a considerable distance from hers. But when they saw the clay court, several complained that she was commercializing the area and ruining property values.

"My presence here can only enhance the value of your property," she told one woman who she had already decided might not like having her live nearby. "I'm building these courts for my own use, so I'll be able to practice at my own house," she said.

"Are you a black tennis player?" the woman asked.

Lynne couldn't help laughing. "I'm a tennis player, and I'm black. Does that answer your question?"

"I don't believe you," the woman said. "I remember one black tennis player, a great one, but she got married and quit."

"Well, I'm living proof that she got a divorce about six weeks ago, and she's trying to make a comeback. I'm Lynne Thurston, and I'm glad to meet you."

"As I live and breathe. Who would have thought it? You never looked this tall out there on the court, but the way you ran I guess you never straightened up to your full height. I'm Thelma MacLendon. I hope you make it back, 'cause I sure did love to see you play."

"There are some other good black female tennis players, Ms. MacLendon."

"If I can call you Lynne, you call me Thelma. Yeah, there're some others, but they don't play like you did. None of those women do. I gotta get back home now. I live in that two-story redbrick across the way. When you get settled, maybe we can have tea or something. Being an athlete, I don't suppose you drink coffee." The woman raised her hand to wave goodbye and started off.

"I appreciate the neighborly gesture," Lynne said.

"'Twasn't anything," the woman said. "You come see me."

One week later, Max Jergens arrived at Lynne's house in a berry-red Mercedes convertible coupe, skintight black T-shirt and skintight black pants. "Hi, I'm Max," he said when she opened the door. "Let's get started."

When she managed to close her mouth, Lynne said, "I thought we were going to work out in a gym."

He stared at her. "Sometimes we will, and sometimes we won't. Today, we're going to work out on your clay court. You *do* have a clay court, don't you?"

I don't like you, buddy, she thought to herself, and pointed to the courts. "Of course I have one."

"Tomorrow, we work out in the gym, but right now, I want to see how bad a shape you're in."

Gritting her teeth, she narrowed her eyes. "Why don't you just ask me? I haven't had a serious workout in six years. And I haven't played a serious game of tennis in just as long, so I am not ready for any kind of strenuous exercise. But since you're the expert, I suppose you know that."

"No point in getting testy with me, honey. I'm here to get you into shape, and that's what I'll do."

"I'm not paying you to kill me," she retorted.

"No, but if you wanted a wet nurse, I'm the last person you'd send for. You gonna exercise in that?" He pointed to her jeans and sweatshirt. "Or are you gonna put on something suitable?"

"Come on in out of the heat and have a seat while I change," she said. "Would you like something to drink?"

He raised an eyebrow. "Like what?"

Both hands went to her hips. "Since I don't have any hemlock, water or ginger ale will have to do."

For a minute, she thought he would laugh, and she had hoped that he would. Instead he said, "Two or three glasses of cold water. I'm parched."

She brought a pitcher of ice water and a glass. "Be back in a minute."

After she changed into shorts, a T-shirt and tennis shoes, she followed him to the clay court and, for the next hour, he put her through some strenuous paces, stretching, jumping and running. "That's enough for now. See you tomorrow at one o'clock sharp." He handed her a list of what she should and should not eat and drink. "Remember. No alcohol."

She nodded, dragged herself into the house and fell onto the living room sofa, exhausted. If what she had just experienced was his nonstrenuous workout, she was in for it. She swung her feet up on the sofa, locked her hands behind her head and smiled a smile that seemed to sweep over her entire body. She had a long journey ahead, but she was on her way.

The following afternoon at twelve-thirty, she turned into Route 35 en route to the gym and, almost immediately, the car stopped. And she could not move it. Cars honked all around her, passing drivers shook their fists at her, and some gave her the finger. She looked at her watch. A quarter of one, and Max would be in a snit. She dialed his cellular phone.

"What do you mean you're stuck on Route 35? I just drove along there, and I didn't see you."

"Listen, Max. Don't give me any stuff. I'm mad enough sitting here in a brand-new car that I've had less than a month, a car that won't move. I'll have to call AAA."

"If you can't get here by one-thirty, let's forget it, and I'll see you here tomorrow same time. If this happens again, honey, I'm out of this contract. My time is valuable."

Thoroughly irritated at him, she said, "So is mine, and it's a pity that you are the only physical trainer in this area. See you tomorrow." She hung up. Let him chew on that.

She called AAA, took a deep breath and waited. After about twenty minutes, a tow truck arrived bearing the inscription, McNeil Motor Service. A big man, somewhere around six feet five inches tall, took his time getting out of the truck, pushed back his navy-blue baseball cap, ran his fingers through his hair and walked around the car as if perplexed.

"I'm sorry to rush you, but I have to keep an appointment, and I have to be there no later than one-thirty."

He didn't answer, merely raised the hood of her car and began fiddling around, screwing and unscrewing things, as far as she could tell.

"Well," she said, becoming increasingly irritated at him. "How long will this take you? I'm serious. I have to be someplace no later that one-thirty."

"Too bad. This car has to go to the shop."

"But it's brand-new. I've only had it a month."

"Uh-huh. I can see that. You want me to take it to the shop, or do you want to call another service?"

"If you take it to the shop, will you lend me a car? Where I live, it's impossible to get around without a car. Now just look! It's twenty-five minutes after one, and I've missed my appointment. Can't you do something?"

"I can take this car to the shop and repair it. I feel for you, lady, but I wouldn't lend you a car of mine if I had one to spare."

"What?"

He checked the tires, took a last look beneath the hood and closed it. "You heard me. I wouldn't trust you with a car of mine. Don't you know to have a new car properly serviced before you drive it? You ought to take it back to the pumpkin head who sold it to you and make him fix it." She hated it when people talked to her without looking at her and especially when they talked down to her.

"If you're going to drive a car, you should make certain that it has a full tank of gas, window washing liquid, motor oil and a well-charged battery," he told her. "Driving without motor oil can cost you the price of a new car."

She tuned out his deep baritone voice, a musical timbre that, in vastly different circumstances, she would have enjoyed hearing. But anger surged within her. Hadn't she listened to a continuous litany of her faults from her ex-husband and several of his parishioners for six long years? She'd taken it from Willard, but that was in the past.

"Who's paying you to lecture to me? You've got a lot of nerve, mister. And you could use a few tips yourself. You walked up here and didn't even say hi, cat, dog or anything. If you're not pleased with me and how I treat my car, I'm not pleased with you, either."

His head snapped up, and she knew she had his attention. He looked at her, really looked at her, as if seeing her for the first time. A fire flickered in his light brown eyes—beautiful eyes—unsettling her.

Down, girl. I am definitely not susceptible to a guy

*who's wearing a navy-blue T-shirt with McNeil embroi-
dered in red above the breast pocket, navy-blue pants
with grease splashed across one thigh, dirty brogans and
a navy-blue baseball cap. Oh, but his eyes!*

She stared at him, and he stared right back at her, until
suddenly, he removed his McNeil baseball cap, ran his
hands through his hair and grinned. "Behave yourself,
miss. I'm not the least bit reliable when it comes to dealing with a smart-ass."

She told herself not to let him ring her bell, but as she
took deep breaths and counted to ten, his grin spread
wider and wider until it became a laugh that transformed
his face into something beautiful.

"It was silly of me to let you get the better of me like
that," she said, her irritation dissolving into laughter.

"Yeah, it was. I do that to people. Come on and get
into the truck." He hooked her car to the tow truck and
drove with her to McNeil Motor Service where he jacked
up the car and began to inspect it.

She didn't want to give Max an excuse to act out, as
she knew he would, given a chance. His temperamen-
tal character was the first trait she'd observed in him,
and she'd never had much tolerance for that in men. The
mechanic who drove her to the service station slid out
from under her car, stood and cleaned his hands with
a cloth that hung against the nearby wall. She walked
over to him.

"How soon can I get my car?"

A slight frown creased his brow, and his eyes projected an expression of sympathy. She took a deep breath,
fearing the worst, reached toward him and gripped his
forearm.

"Please, mister. I need my car."

He gazed down at her, his demeanor serious, but his eyes warm and kind. "I promise you I'll do my best, but I don't see how you can get it before Saturday."

"But—"

He interrupted her. "I'll see that you get to your appointment okay, and as soon as your car is ready, we'll bring it to you."

She could see that the man was honest. Indeed, he wore integrity the way a robin wears his feathers. "All right, but I've already missed my appointment."

"Then, I'll see that you get home." He beckoned to a man who was dressed in a uniform similar to his. "Take this lady home." He looked at her. "I need your name, address, phone number and driver's license." She gave them to him, and he took a pad from his back trouser pocket, wrote something on it and handed her a receipt for her car.

She stared first at the piece of paper that represented her car and then at him. Wordless. No doubt her feelings were mirrored on her face, for he smiled in an obvious attempt to comfort her.

"Don't worry. If I tell you you'll have it Saturday, you'll have it Saturday. I keep my word." He turned from her. "Take her home, Bill, and use one of the sedans." Then, he tipped the bill of his baseball cap and went into the office.

The man named Bill opened the front passenger door of a Lincoln Town Car for her, reached across her and fastened her seat belt before closing the door. *Hmm. Courteousness must be the hallmark of this place.*

"Who's the mechanic who towed my car to the station?" she asked Bill a few minutes after he turned onto Route 10.

He threw her a quizzical glance. "Mechanic? That was Sloan. Sloan McNeil. He owns McNeil Motor Service. Great guy to work with."

"You mean he's the owner, and he does the same work that his mechanics do?"

"He wouldn't like to know you asked that question. Anyway, he's the best mechanic among us."

"I didn't mean that the way it sounded. I hope he has my car ready by Saturday."

He drove up to 2791 Corpus Christi Lane and parked. "If Sloan said you'll get your car Saturday, that's when you'll get it."

"Thanks for the assurance, and thanks for bringing me home."

"My pleasure."

He drove off, and somehow, if didn't worry her one bit that all she had to show for the more than thirty grand she'd spent was a piece of paper. She telephoned Max. "My car is in the shop, and I won't have it till Saturday afternoon."

"What'd you do, buy a lemon?"

Naturally he assumed that she was incompetent. "No. The seller didn't service it properly. I'll deal with him later."

"Okay. Be at the gym at nine o'clock Monday morning. If you feel like it, jog a few miles before you get there."

If she felt like it! "All right. See you Monday morning."

Lynne strolled through the living room and dining room, running her hands over the furnishings as she walked, slowly making up her mind. She entered the solarium, a large room with floor-to-ceiling, wall-to-wall windows situated to the right of the dining room, a large airy place that invited her to linger. *Yes, I'm going to buy this place. It will be splendid with my choice of furnishings and the colors I love. It's big for one person, but I like it. Besides, it won't seem so big when I get a housekeeper...that is, if I ever do.* She got up and walked to the wide center staircase. *When I furnish it, it won't look so overdone. I prefer quality and simplicity.*

Before she married, she put the bulk of her considerable tennis earnings into a retirement trust, and she was reasonably certain that Willard never forgave her for it. When he learned that he wouldn't have access to her money, he showed her a side of himself that she preferred not to remember. "Thank God, it's over," she said to herself.

Saturday morning at 11:43, she headed to the tennis court to knock some balls, and as she stopped on the front lawn to pull a dandelion weed out of the grass, her BMW rolled to a stop in front of her door. She removed her wide-brim straw hat, got up and walked to the car just as Sloan McNeil got out of the driver's seat.

"Hi. I didn't expect you to bring it back yourself."

"Why not?"

"Well, Bill said you're the boss, so—"

My Lord, this is a serious man, she thought, as he glued his gaze to her. "I don't ask or expect the men who work for me to do anything that I wouldn't do."

Best not to reply to that. "Thanks so much for getting it to me today."

"I finished it less than half an hour ago, and I don't mind telling you that I had to put your car ahead of several. I don't usually do that, because it isn't fair."

She decided not to ask him why he did that, because

she had a feeling that she didn't want to know. But he had no compunctions about telling her. "You haven't asked why *I* brought your car, but I'll tell anyway. I wanted to see you again. You interest me."

"Oh."

He stepped closer, but not close enough to touch. "Is that all you have to say? In case you're worried, I don't always wear navy blue. In fact, I wear it so much when I'm working that I never wear it any other time."

She bit her lip when the words, you look great in navy blue, nearly fell out of her mouth. "Uh…you made a statement. If you had asked me a question, I'd have answered it."

A grin spread over his face, lighting his remarkable eyes, softening them and putting ideas into her head. "You left yourself wide open with that comment. Be careful you don't trip yourself up."

"I'm not in the habit of doing that," she said, trying without success to shift her gaze from his. The man had such a commanding presence that he almost unnerved her. So he thought she didn't have the nerve to ask him why he brought the car himself. She'd show him. She leaned her head to one side. "Why didn't you send my car by Bill or one of your other employees? Why did *you* bring it?"

His right eyebrow shot up. "I just told you. I wanted to see you again."

"Yes. So you did." Somehow, his mechanic's uniform in no way diminished him, and she noticed that he'd taken the time to clean his hands. Beautifully tapered fingers. Powerful hands.

His gaze swept over her. "You're wearing a tennis outfit. Does that mean you're Lynne Thurston, the tennis great?" Taken aback at his abrupt question, she hardly knew how to answer or whether she should. "I wondered about it yesterday when you gave me your name. Surely there aren't two of you."

"I stopped playing tennis when I married, because my husband didn't think it proper for a minister to have a professional tennis player for a wife." He looked as if he'd had the wind knocked out of him, and without questioning or understanding why she did so, she hastened to add, "I divorced him about four months ago after six years of pure hell."

As if her words gave him new life, he exhaled a long breath. "I'm sorry."

"Thanks, but all I feel now is joy."

As if he'd decided against asking another direct question, he took a different tactic. "This is a very big house for one person."

"I know," she said, her face wreathed in smiles. "Isn't it wonderful?"

He moved his head from side to side. "Seems to me you should at least have a guard dog."

"I'd love to have a dog, but if I start traveling again, who'll take care of him? Anyway, all the windows and doors are wired. I'm protected."

He shoved his hands into his back pockets and looked into the distance. "If you decide to get a dog, I'll be glad to look after him for you when you're not here. You need a dog." Suddenly he shrugged his right shoulder. "Just a thought. Say, would you play a game with me sometime?"

She hadn't played a game in six years, because Willard didn't want her to practice. He'd said it was like giving up smoking; when you quit, you shouldn't even associate with anyone who smokes lest you fall back into the habit. "I'm about as rusty as a player can be, but if you don't mind being a guinea pig, I'd love a match with you."

"Didn't you play at all while you were married?"

She shook her head and tried not to appear sad, although remembering how she'd pleaded with Willard not to oppose the one thing she enjoyed doing depressed her. "Not once."

"Whew! How about tomorrow morning before it gets hot?"

"Eight o'clock? Or maybe you'd rather sleep a bit longer."

"Eight's fine. I've enjoyed talking with you. See you in the morning."

"Goodbye, Sloan, and don't forget to send the bill. Many thanks."

"You're more than welcome."

She turned, then stopped in her tracks. "Sloan, how are you getting back to the service station? Wait a minute. I'll get my driver's license and drive you."

His teeth sparkled white and his color heightened against his light olive complexion. "Thanks, Lynne. I was going to walk out to the highway and hitch a ride. You're a gracious woman."

Maybe she was, and maybe she was just off her rocker. She had a goal, a tough one, and it didn't include getting involved with a man. She got her driver's license and pocketbook, locked the front door and headed across the lawn. He hadn't moved.

"Who's going to drive?" she asked him. "You or me?" *My Lord,* she thought when he grinned. *I don't need to get involved, and especially not with a guy who's got grease splashed across one pant leg and grime on his brogans. But Lord, this man is a looker.*

"It's your car," he said, still grinning. "I sure wouldn't deign to tell you you couldn't drive your own car."

She handed him the car keys. "Oh, yes, you would. You definitely would. If you had a mind to, you'd tell the president what he couldn't do."

He closed the passenger door, went around and folded his six-foot-five-inch frame into the driver's seat. "I've told him many times but, unfortunately, he didn't hear me."

They rode in silence for a few minutes, and suddenly she heard him release a long sigh. "This is a perfect day for camping, swimming in a river or a lake and fishing for supper."

"You love the outdoors, Sloan?"

"Oh, yes. It's where I feel most at home."

"Me, too, but I'm not going to have much time to enjoy it."

He glanced quickly in her direction before focusing on the road ahead of him. "How's that?"

"I've given myself two years to make it to number one, and that means working hard. I'm twenty-nine, and the top players hadn't reached puberty when I quit playing. It won't be easy."

"Not one of them is as good as you were. You'll get there."

That was what she needed to hear. Not even the coach she hired had said that, and her brother thought she'd lost her mind. "You really think so? Thank you. I need to hear that. My brother thinks I'm out of my mind."

"Don't let that bother you. Get out there and show 'em." He stopped the car in front of his service station, leaned against the door, rested his arm on the back of the seat and looked at her. Did she move closer to him? Something in her seemed to gravitate to him, and it wasn't until she pulled herself back, increasing the distance between them, that she realized she hadn't moved closer. Her gaze shifted to his face, and a gasp escaped her at the naked passion in his eyes.

"See you tomorrow morning at eight," he said and got out of the car before she could answer. He didn't have to tell her that his quick exit was aimed at preventing her from breaking their date to play tennis. She slid over to the driver's seat, waved at him, backed up and headed home. He needn't worry; she didn't want to break the date with him. She told herself that she needed to test her ability, to know if her ground strokes were as far off as her serve. Suddenly she couldn't help laughing at herself. Serving a tennis ball and hitting ground strokes had nothing to do with her eagerness to keep the date with Sloan McNeil.

Sloan went into his office, showered, changed into a business suit, dress shirt and tie, got into his Buick and headed for town. He'd moved to San Antonio because he liked the city's slow pace, peaceful atmosphere and tidy character. Most of the people he knew there were born and grew up somewhere else, as was the case with him. He'd had many setbacks in his life, but none deterred him from pursuing his goal, and nothing would. He meant to own and operate a string of automobile repair stations throughout Texas. He didn't fear competition, because he gave his customers honest service of the highest quality and at reasonable cost. He turned into Route 10, slowed down and told himself that what he had to do in the next hour was not as complicated or as difficult as brain surgery.

"I can see where I'm headed, and I don't want to be carrying any baggage." He parked in front of a house on Potranco Road, got out and rang the bell.

"Oh, how nice. I wasn't expecting to see you this evening, but I'm glad you're here," the tall, self-possessed woman said. "Why am I so lucky today? I'll get us some snacks and drinks."

"Hello, Vickie. No. No. Don't go to any trouble. I won't be staying long."

She folded her arms across her chest, inclined her head to the side and looked at him. "Any special reason?"

"Yes. You and I have been seeing each other occasionally, and I want you to know that, although I've enjoyed your company, we won't see each other in the future."

"I see. Well, you couldn't make it clearer. I admit that we haven't had a romantic…that we aren't lovers…but I've always hoped."

"I'm sorry. I thought I'd been careful not to mislead you."

"Oh, you have been, but these things have a habit of going their own way. Who is she?"

Just like her to cut to the chase. "I've met someone, but nothing has happened. Not a single thing."

"Then, why—"

He interrupted her. "Because I know where it's headed, and I believe in keeping my house in order."

Her smile wavered slightly. "You've always been a straight shooter, Sloan, and I wish you nothing but happiness. I hope she knows how lucky she is."

"Thank you for the compliment. Goodbye." She extended her hand, and he shook it. A first-class woman.

He hoped she found the man she needed. He'd been planning to break that tie for some time, for he knew that they could become a habit with each other and fall into the trap that said he'd taken up so much of her time, he should marry her. Relieved that their talk had been without bitterness, he decided to go home, swim for a while, have a local restaurant deliver his dinner, eat and go to bed. He did not intend to miss his date with Lynne Thurston, and he was not going to let her beat him.

After having tossed in bed most of the night, Lynne crawled out of bed at six-thirty and stumbled into the bathroom. Her shower refreshed her, and she dressed in a white tennis dress, white socks and pink sneakers, went downstairs and made coffee.

"The least I can do is offer him a cup of coffee and a glass of orange juice," she said aloud. As hungry as she was, she didn't dare eat the pancakes and sausage that had been her favorite breakfast in the days when she played tennis at least four hours every day and didn't have to worry about gaining weight. Maybe she'd have that for breakfast Monday.

At eight o'clock, a tan-colored Buick LeSabre stopped in front of her house, and Sloan McNeil got out of it, walked up to her front door and rang the bell. She didn't know what she had expected, but it hadn't occurred to her that he'd be wearing a white, collared T-shirt, white shorts, white socks and white sneakers. She gaped at him until he laughed.

"Hi. Like what you see?"

"Yes, indeed. I had to make certain that it's you. Want a cup of coffee?"

"I already had two cups, but I'll have a glass of orange

juice if you have any. I'll be starving after the match. If you don't mind, we could drive over to Laredo and get some breakfast."

"Good idea," she said, still reeling from the shock of seeing him in that tennis outfit. *My Lord, what a body, and what a pair of legs!*

After he drank the juice, she went to the hall closet, selected a racket and looked at him. "Ready?"

"As I'll ever be. Let's go. Are we playing on the clay court or the hard court? I prefer the hard court."

"I'll be equally bad on both," she said. "You want to serve first?"

He braced his hips with his knuckles. "Oh, no, you don't, miss. We're tossing for this." He showed her a quarter. "Heads I win, tails you lose."

"Oka— *What did you say?* I heard that. I may be groggy, but I'm not asleep."

He favored her with a grin. "Just testing."

She won the toss and served first. It didn't have her old snap and power, but it didn't shame her, either. She knew at once that Sloan played tennis well, and she delighted in being able to keep pace with him. After an hour they were tied at 6–6, and neither could break the other's serve.

"We'll never finish this game," she told him later, when the ten o'clock sun began to burn them.

"We can finish it one evening," he said, then looked around and saw that she didn't have lights. "If you ever want to light one of these courts, buy the equipment and I'll install it for you."

"I've been thinking about that, but I thought I'd need an electrician."

"Not to worry. Every mechanical engineer has training in electronics."

"Is that what you are? A mechanical engineer?"

He lifted his shoulder in a gesture of nonchalance, but she wasn't fooled. "Yeah. That's what it says on the piece of paper, but I'm an automobile mechanic. I don't need a fancy title to tell me who I am."

Better get off that subject. "You said you'd be starved. Are you?"

"How about the Cracker Barrel? I can almost taste the pancakes oozing with butter and syrup, fried apples and bacon," he said, patting his stomach and smiling with sparkling eyes, as if talking about the food was a joy.

She realized that she stared at him. *This guy is sensuous, and it's natural to him.* Nobody was going to make her believe that he wasn't married. Men like him did not run around loose.

"Are you married?" she blurted out.

At first he seemed taken aback at the abruptness of her question. "No, I'm not. If I were, I wouldn't be here with you. I am not, and I never have been married."

"I know you're telling the truth, but, I don't see how it's possible." When he frowned, she added, "I mean, I do…but I don't." Best to change the subject. "Want to wash up before we go to breakfast? Come on, I'll show you the powder room."

"Hey, wait a minute. *Powder room.* What would I do in *there?*"

She lowered her right eyelid in a slow wink. "Powder your nose. Meet you here in five minutes."

He stared at her, and the heat in his eyes had nothing to do with the morning sun. "I thought I told you that when it comes to dealing with a smart-ass, I'm not reliable. I tend to lose it when imps get fresh with me, too."

She didn't know when, if ever, she had enjoyed joshing with a man so much. "I suppose that, since there doesn't seem to be either a smart-ass or an imp anywhere around here, you'll be on your good behavior, and I can relax."

He took her hand and began walking to the car, and she liked the feel of it. There was something strong and reassuring about this man, and his height had nothing to do with it. When they were seated in the car, he turned to her. "You're a delightful woman. Fresh, sassy and provocative, but not one bit boring. When may I see you again?"

"Sloan, this is moving too fast."

He put the key in the ignition, turned it and drove off. "Yeah, and the scary thing is that it's moving of its own accord. Neither of us is pushing it. Relationships go forward or backward, Lynne. They seldom stand still. You want to see me again?"

The exit he took had a one-hundred-and-eighty-degree curve, and as he leaned with the car, his naked thigh pressed against her own bare flesh. Her nipples hardened, and she sucked in her breath.

"What's the matter?" he asked. "You needn't be afraid. I'm a careful driver and a good one. Whatever I do, I do it properly and thoroughly. Remember that." *And he wasn't speaking about driving.*

He parked at the Cracker Barrel, but she was buried in her thoughts and was hardly aware that the car was no longer moving. He wanted to see her again, and she wanted to see him. But she had a difficult road ahead, and she didn't see how she could concentrate on regaining her tennis form if she got involved with him. He was like no man she had ever known. If she had any sense, she would call it off right then. He walked around the car, opened her door and took her hand. She grasped it and held it.

Chapter 2

"You'll be sore tomorrow," Max told Lynne at the end of her workout that Monday, "so maybe you want to soak in a hot tub when you get home."

If he was trying to soften her up after his harsh treatment for the past three hours, he'd missed the mark. "You mean to tell me that you care whether I'm sore?"

He gave her a withering look, leaned against the wall of the gym and folded his arms. "If you want me to treat you like you're a baby, fine, but six weeks from now your muscles will still be flabby, and Gary won't touch you. You gotta prove you're serious, honey."

"If I'm dead, he won't touch me, either. See you tomorrow."

"Yeah," he yelled after her, as she slung her gym bag over her shoulder and walked out of the gym, "and run about four miles before you get here to loosen up."

She went home, soaked in a tub of hot water and made a note to install a Jacuzzi. The phone rang as she was about to take a nap and, thinking that the caller was most likely Bradford, her brother, she sat up in bed anticipating his voice.

"Hello,"

"Hello back at you." Her heartbeat accelerated. That wasn't Brad's voice. "This is Sloan McNeil. Feel like a movie this evening?" She rested her back against the headboard and gripped the telephone as if that would steady her nerves. "If you don't want to see a movie," he began without waiting for her answer, "maybe we could go to a concert. You like jazz? Bettye Gamble's at the Down Beat."

She closed her eyes and rested her head against the headboard. "Sloan, I ache. I just finished the first real workout I've had in six years. I just want to sleep."

"I give great massages."

She had to laugh at his antics. "I won't ask where or how you learned that."

"We know you're chicken, Lynne, but you shouldn't fear my answer. When I was a teenager, my dad ran a health spa. He said I had to learn how to be a masseuse, because the ones he hired usually had such outrageous temperaments that he fired 'em within a month. My work as a masseuse paid my way through college. I'm pretty good."

"I'm sure you are, but I'll take a rain check on that service." His laughter thrilled her, and she realized that she would go to great lengths to keep him laughing.

"I don't know why I mentioned it," he said, almost as if in afterthought, "since I'm sure you wouldn't dare let me put my hands on you."

Talk about a leading statement! "Really? Oh, I don't know. As Fats Waller used to sing, 'One never knows, *do* one?'"

"Wait a minute, woman. Are you leading me on?"

She stretched from head to foot as best she could, considering the knot in her shoulder. "Me? You think I'd do something like that?"

"Hmm. I wonder. No movie, no concert and no massage. You wound me."

She rolled over in order to get more comfortable. "You poor baby."

"Well, what about a walk? Anyplace will do."

"Walk? Sloan, my legs are killing me."

"A smart woman would take me up on my offer of a massage."

"You want to see me at my worst, hobbling around like an invalid?"

After what seemed to her too long a silence, he said, "You want me to see you at your best? Mind telling me why?"

"Sloan, will you stop asking those kinds of questions. You do not have hayseed in your hair, so stop acting like a country bumpkin."

Laughter roared out of him, delighting her and making her wish she was with him.

"Country bumpkin, eh? Now you've really wounded me, and you're going to make amends."

She wanted to see him. All of a sudden, talking with him seemed as natural as breathing. Usually a cautious person, she pondered her next move. *I am definitely not getting involved, but I'll go out with him. After all these years of misery, I need to be with somebody who makes me laugh.*

"What's the name of the movie?" she asked him.

"Uh—"

She interrupted him. "You don't have a movie in mind, do you?"

"Truth? No. I just want to see you."

Honesty was to be valued, and especially when it was practiced at a risk. "We could go to El Mercado and look around."

"We could, but what about your legs? If my memory serves me, they're really something nice to look at. I wouldn't like you to abuse them."

She stifled a laugh. "A minute ago, you were ahead."

"Well, let me get back there. Tell you what. Let's have a nice dinner in an attractive, relaxing place. Dress somewhere between up and down, and I'll pick you up at six-thirty. Okay?"

"Okay. Will you wear a jacket?"

"You bet. See you at six-thirty."

She hugged the pillow to her chest, rolled over, kicked up her heels and laughed. Suddenly she sat up. *I don't know one thing about this man. I don't even know anybody who knows him. Am I crazy?*

She dressed slowly for their date, less at ease than she would have liked. Who was he, and why was she so drawn to him? Why did she respond to him as a flower unfolds to the sun? She wasn't a snob. That was her brother's domain. But to literally pick up a mechanic and start a relationship with him just because he had his own business and a mesmerizing personality didn't make sense. She was brushing her hair when the phone rang. *Maybe he changed his mind.*

"Hello."

"Hi, sis. Next Saturday is Debra's birthday, and I

thought I'd give her a dinner party. I can't decide between a small party in a top restaurant and a big party in a, say, four-star restaurant. What do you think?"

"For me, small would be better, but I need to think about this. Debra likes to make a splash. I was just about to leave home. Call you when I get back. Oh, there's the bell."

"Who is he? You got a guy down there *al*ready?"

"Just someone I met when my car broke down on the highway. Gotta go."

"Just somebody you… Are you out of your mind? A passerby who—"

She blew out a long breath. "He wasn't a passerby. He's the guy who towed my car to the service station and fixed it."

"*What? Jeez!* A baby would know better than to hook up with a… Don't go anywhere with that guy, and don't let him inside your house."

"He's already been in here. I gotta go. See you." She hung up and sprinted down the stairs, unmindful of her aching limbs. In telling Brad about Sloan, she had created a problem that she didn't need. She dashed to the door and flung it open.

"Hi." She was certain that her eyes rounded to twice their normal size. In a light tan-colored linen suit, pale green shirt, pale green and tan necktie, Sloan McNeil looked like an advertisement for *Esquire Magazine*. She blinked a few times. "Sorry I kept you waiting. My brother called a minute before you rang the doorbell."

His smile was obviously intended to absolve her, and it did, for she felt as if she floated on air. "It was worth the wait," he said. "You look so lovely."

She was glad she'd chosen the sleeveless, canary-yellow georgette dress that had a flared skirt with a flounce and barely touched her knees. It was soft and feminine, and she had thrown the matching stole across her shoulders. Large gold hoops hung from her ears, and her hair hung straight to her shoulders.

"Beautiful." He breathed the word as if it were itself precious.

"You look nice, too, Sloan. What kind of food are we going to eat?"

She closed the door and handed him the key. He took it, locked the front door, handed it back to her and took her hand. "I reserved a table at Michael's. They serve American and continental foods. Does that suit you?"

"I'd love to go to Michael's. I've heard it's the best in this region. Thanks for choosing it."

He headed out Route 35 to San Antonio. "Why did you change your mind about going out with me this evening?"

She decided to tell the truth. "Because you made me laugh. I spent the past six years in self-defense, listening to a continuous stream of criticism. You brightened my world."

He drove at least five miles before replying. "I hope that means you like me, because if you don't, I'm in trouble."

"Sloan, you just met me."

"I know, but apparently that's all it takes."

She had no answer for that, because she was also drawn to him, and had been from the minute he'd grinned, pushed back his blue McNeil baseball cap and called her a smart-ass. But she knew that her brother would test the powers of heaven and hell in an effort to push Sloan out of her life. She leaned back and rested her head against the comfortable leather seat.

"Aw, Sloan. If only life were so simple!"

"It's as complicated as we make it, Lynne. No more and no less. I do my best to keep my house in order. That way, I don't have to keep track of lies, women or bad debts."

"Speaks well for you," she said to herself. Although she didn't know why, she believed him. He parked in front of a hotel, got out and gave the parking attendant his ticket. "Are we going in here?" she asked him, taken aback because the place didn't look like Michael's.

"Oh, no. This is the easiest way to get a parking place. He gets a tip and I get the convenience of parking three doors from the restaurant."

She wondered why he took her hand whenever they walked side by side as he did then, but she didn't consider it prudent to ask him. She could also ask herself why she allowed it, but she didn't, and she didn't think her behavior with Sloan would bear close examination. She was not and never had been careless about her choice of associates, and she had no intention of ascribing to fate her strong attraction to Sloan. She accepted that she felt comfortable with him and that, however strange it seemed—and it was very strange—he made her happy.

"You're quiet," he said as they entered the restaurant. "Mind if I ask why?"

"Nothing special. I was trying to figure me out."

He waited until the maître d' seated them before saying, "Don't worry about why you're with me. If we continue to enjoy each other's company, this will only be the beginning. I have to tell you, though, that I expect us to be tight years from now."

She frowned and didn't care if he noticed. "Do you have extrasensory perception? I don't like it when someone seems to read my mind."

A grin spread over his face, a face that she liked more and more. "Nothing of the sort. I figured it was logical for you to ask yourself why you came with me tonight when you were tired and wanted to rest. No point in wondering about it, though, Lynne. We like each other."

She looked at him from beneath half-lowered lashes. "I suppose saying whatever you think is a mark of honesty, but couldn't you occasionally store your wisdom in the recesses of your mind till some future date?"

"I could, but I want to be sure you know where I'm heading."

Lynne stopped herself just before she sucked her teeth. "I'm twenty-nine, and I know where you're headed."

He treated her to a withering look. "I'll give you six... no, three months in which to eat those words."

With eyes wide and lips parted, she fixed an expression of innocence on her face. "What on earth do you mean?"

He leaned back in his chair, his facial expression unreadable. "I thought you said you're twenty-nine. Sure you want to know?"

She lowered her gaze. "All right. I'm sorry."

He leaned forward and grasped the hand that rested on the white tablecloth. "It's fun matching wits, but I was serious. Get to know me before you decide that I'm not worthy of your time."

Stunned that he had such an opinion concerning her reservation about a relationship with him and fearing that she had hurt him, she reached for his other hand.

"Please don't ever say anything like that to me again. It was uncalled for and unfounded."

His smile barely reached his eyes. "I hope you're right. Now, tell me why your trainer pushed you to work out until you ached. He ought to begin more slowly, or so it seems to me."

"Max has an exaggerated opinion of himself. He's much sought after by sports professionals, and I think that's gone to his head."

"There must be other good trainers."

"There are, but my coach told me to work with Max for six weeks before I begin practicing. I think Max has a mean streak."

He glanced at her. "If you think he's sadistic, get rid of him regardless of what your coach says. Enough about Max. Who's your coach?"

"Gary Hines."

"If he's as good a coach as he was a player, he's the best."

"I hope so." He still held both of her hands, and his gaze bore into her, causing little shimmers throughout her body. "Sloan," she said, "please don't move so fast."

He stroked her finger in a loving caress. "You aren't getting that feeling from me but from yourself, from what's happening inside of *you*."

The waiter took their orders, and she couldn't help noticing that the man's attentiveness to her had nothing to do with the restaurant's service policy, and a glance at Sloan's narrowed eyes told her that he was vexed.

"I'd like a bottle of Châteauneuf-du-Pape. That will be *all.*" He emphasized the word *all*. And as if he hadn't just reprimanded the waiter, he said, "This place becomes you. It has just the right amount of elegance to go with its beauty. You're like that."

"Thank you. I've never thought of myself in those terms."

He leaned back in the gold-leaf chair, its seat and back embroidered in antique-gold brocade, comfortable in his surroundings, a conundrum if she'd ever met one. "And that's a good thing," he said in response to her comment. "Vanity has buried a lot of fools." Before she could digest that, he said, "Can I take up all of your weekends? I'm off Saturday afternoon and Sunday."

"Sloan—"

"And don't tell me I'm moving too fast. I haven't made one bit of headway since we sat down here."

She couldn't help laughing at him, at the merriment that twinkled in his eyes and the roguish smile that lit up his face. *Little did he know.* "If you haven't made any headway, why would I tell you that you're moving too fast?"

His long, tapered fingers punished his scalp, and she had the pleasure of seeing him as perplexed as she felt. The waiter brought their dinner, and Sloan locked his gaze on the man who, having had his comeuppance earlier, managed not to look at her.

When she thought Sloan had forgotten her question, he said, "Looks as if what's fast to you is a snail's pace to me. I want to see some evidence."

She changed the subject. "I got used to saying grace before I eat, so—"

"I say it, too. When did you get used to it?"

"When I was married to the reverend Willard Marsh. He preached and he prayed, and he was as cruel as a person could be."

Sloan fingered his chin in a way that suggested he didn't know he was doing it. "I suppose anyone who had an unpleasant marriage would be reluctant to develop a liaison of any kind. But I'm asking you, Lynne, don't make me pay for your ex-husband's sins."

She put her knife and fork on her plate, rested her hands in her lap and looked into his eyes. "I already know that you are nothing like him, and if I seem reluctant, it's because I am. I don't see how I can focus on my goal so long as you are a distraction."

"Woman, I am not a distraction. I'm the man you're going to wrap your life around."

Be careful, girl. That's a leading statement. "I'm not going near that one," she said.

"I enjoyed dinner with you," he said as they walked hand in hand to the hotel to get his car. "But I almost wish we'd gone to El Mercado. It's too early to leave you."

"Exploring El Mercado with you would be fun, Sloan, but right now, my body is telling me to go home and give it a chance to rest. How about Saturday?"

He thought his heart would dance out of his chest, as joy suffused him. "All right."

She was as cautious as he, and that was one of the things he liked about her, but he needed the taste of her lips, the sensation of her skin heating his. Maybe he *was* moving too fast, but he longed to know the feel of her in his arms, sweet, loving and pliant. Would she be the soul mate of his dreams? Intuition told him not to rush her, and at her door, as much as he wanted to kiss her, he merely brushed her right cheek with his hungry lips.

"I'll call you tomorrow," he said after checking her

house for intruders and finding none. "And if you'd like me to help you pick out a dog, we can do that."

He didn't recall ever having been so flustered as when she stood on tiptoe, reached up and brushed his lips with hers, then dashed into the house, closed the door and locked it.

He stood there for a while staring at the door. "Well I'll be damned. Whatta you know?"

"You gotta get with it, honey," Max told Lynne several mornings later. "You're sluggish, but you're not going to give Max Jergens a bad name. By the end of the week, I want you to be doing fifty push-ups, fifty sit-ups, forty minutes of stretches and weight lifts, and I want you to do it all in the space of two hours. You also gotta run eight miles every morning."

"I ran ten miles this morning, and it's a wonder I can move."

He waved his hand as if to say, that's nothing. "If I don't have you into shape within the next three weeks, Gary Hines will dump me. I've trained all of his players, and you're not going to be a fly in this ointment."

She fastened her knuckles to her hips and glared at him. "Stuff it, Max. I'm in as good a shape this minute as I was when I was eighteen. I run faster, can lift heavier weights and do more sit-ups. You may be doing this to please Gary, but I'm doing it for myself. In less than two years from now, I'll be number one. Who has the greater incentive? You or me?"

Max glared right back at her. "I don't give a rat's behind for your reasons, honey. When I finish with you, you'll be able to play three sets in one-hundred-degree heat without getting tired. And beginning next week, you'll work out in the afternoon on your clay court. So get me a couple of straw mats."

She tolerated Max's bossiness because she could see that, with every workout, she made progress. She had begun to serve with the power for which she was once famous, though she lacked consistency. But she couldn't see Sloan as frequently as she would like, and she wondered if he had begun to develop other interests.

"What do you mean you wouldn't want to see me if I was bringing you a billion dollars?" Sloan asked her during one of their nightly telephone chats. "I want you to know that I do not appreciate that."

Barely able to move her neck, she whispered, "I'm worn out. Please understand and don't be annoyed. I want to see you, but I have to rest."

"Thanks for that much. Sleep well."

She fell asleep, and the next morning, she didn't remember telling him good-night.

"I'm glad you dropped that mechanic," her brother Brad said during their conversation later that morning. She swallowed her coffee, and in a sharper voice than she intended, she asked him, "Why do you think I've dropped him?"

"Because you haven't mentioned him lately."

"Really? When you see Sloan McNeil, you won't envisage anybody dropping him." A note of amusement colored her words. "He hasn't done anything to make me curtail our friendship. He's nice, Brad."

"But he's a friggin' mechanic. Dammit. How do you know *what* he'll turn out to be?"

"That's worth a laugh, brother. I married a minister of the gospel, and look what *he* turned out to be. Don't be such a snob. I've never met anyone like Sloan."

"You bet your life you haven't. Are you willing to let that guy escort you to the Grammy Awards or to the Academy Awards? Are you?"

Laughter rolled out of her. "If he looks as good in a tux as he did in that tan linen suit a couple of Saturdays ago, he can take me to the White House or anywhere else."

"Lynne, I'm serious. Didn't it occur to you that he could be after your money?"

She spoke forcefully now, no longer amused by her brother's antics. "I'm serious, too, and no such thing has occurred to me. Besides, the bulk of my money is in a retirement trust, safe even from me, and learning that made Willard so mad that I'm sure he'd counted on spending a lot of it."

"Well, you be careful. You hear?"

"Brad, I am not rushing into anything with anybody, including Sloan."

"Glad to hear it."

Brad might have relaxed a little if he had known that Sloan never rushed into anything, that he charted his course carefully after considerable thought. At that moment, Sloan was digging into himself. He questioned the wisdom of an involvement with a world-famous woman whose drive to reach the pinnacle of her sport might cost her heartbreak, injury and disappointment, and who might experience adversity when he was thousands of miles away and unable to help or to comfort her. Gloomily he signed the weekly paychecks for his employees, closed the service station and locked it.

"See you Monday," he called to Bill. "It's shaping up to be a great weekend for sailing. Enjoy it."

"Do my best, Sloan. The kids always love it. You have a good one, too."

"Now what do I do with myself from one o'clock Saturday until Monday morning?" he said aloud. "If I were luckier, Lynne would be waiting for me with open arms." He leaned against the door, ruminating about his options. "What the hell!"

He went home, showered, dressed in a pair of white trousers, a yellow, collared T-shirt, yellow socks and white shoes and headed for the barber shop. An hour later, after getting a haircut, shave and manicure, he stepped out into the blazing sunlight. The thought of calling a woman he knew would gladly meet his needs occurred to him, but after pondering it, he thought better of the idea. It wasn't what he wanted or needed.

If I want Lynne, I have to fight for her. If she cares for me, she'll be glad to see me, if only for a few minutes, no matter how tired she is.

He got into his Buick LeSabre, pointed it toward 2791 Corpus Christi Lane and parked it in front of Lynne's house at about three-thirty. When she didn't answer her doorbell, he walked out to the tennis court and saw her running in place on the clay court.

"Raise your knees. Higher. Higher, I said. Higher," Max screamed at her. "Come on. Faster. I said faster."

Suddenly she groped her way to the bench behind the baseline, nearly fell onto it, folded her forearms across her knees and rested her head there.

"Get up, for Pete's sake. You'll never get anywhere folding up in a little heat. If you can't stand this, you can't play tennis in one-hundred-degree heat. Move it," Max yelled.

Infuriated, Sloan rushed to Lynne, sat beside her and,

with one arm around her, rested her head on his shoulder. "How do you feel?"

She raised her head, glanced at him and returned to the comfort of his shoulder. "Oh, it's you. I'm so glad to see you. Dizzy. I could hardly stand up straight. Real dizzy."

He looked at Max who stood nearby, akimbo and belligerent, his legs widespread. "Leave her alone. She doesn't need to be babied," Max said to Sloan, who glared at him.

"You're not talking to me," Sloan growled. "You wouldn't have the nerve. I say she's finished for today, and it may as well be carved in stone. In the future, try to be a little more human. And it wouldn't hurt you to remember that she doesn't work for you—you work for her."

He looked down at her, fragile and limp, her head on his shoulder and her right hand clutching his T-shirt. "Where's the key to your front door? We need to lock the house. I'm taking you to the clinic." He intended to take her to hospital emergency, but he didn't say so for fear of alarming her.

"The key's on the table in the foyer."

"Sit here. I'll be right back." After securing the house, be went back to her and encouraged her to stand, but when she sagged against him, he lifted her and carried her to his car. He put her in the front seat and fastened her seat belt, aware that Max was still on the clay court smarting for having been outdone.

"We'll be there in a few minutes," he said after driving several miles, and from a glance in the rearview mirror, he realized that Max was no longer behind them, but had taken his red convertible in a different direction. He had concluded that the man was either sadistic, unfeeling or stupid. He turned into Houston Street and headed for Santa Rosa Hospital at the corner of Santa Rosa Street. Never had eight miles seemed so long, he thought, as he drove into the hospital's emergency zone and parked. With his arm holding Lynne tight to his side, he spoke to the guard at the desk.

"She all but passed out in the sun, and she's too weak to walk alone. She needs to see a doctor."

"In a minute." The guard relayed the information via intercom, and a doctor arrived at once. "This way, please." No one asked him whether he had a right to stay with her, so he didn't leave her.

"Are you her husband?" the doctor asked him in the examining room as he prepared to examine Lynne.

When he said that he wasn't, the doctor asked him to step outside while he examined her.

"I'll call you in a few minutes," he said.

After what seemed like an hour, but was only eighteen minutes by his watch, he was allowed to reenter the examining room. "What's the problem, doctor? Is she going to be all right?" Lynne reached for his hand, held it and smiled, but he wasn't satisfied. "Well?" He glowered at the doctor.

"She's dehydrated and exhausted. I've told her to rest, and I've given her fluid, but she must drink a lot of water and any nonalcoholic liquid." He looked down at Lynne. "You must rest. That's crucial."

She nodded. "Yes, sir."

"And that's what she'll get, Doctor," Sloan said. He sat beside the bed holding her hand, uneasy because she seemed so sleepy at four-thirty in the afternoon.

After about an hour, the doctor returned. "You may

go home now, but I want to impress upon you the need to rest. You've got a strong guy to look after you, so do as I say, and don't forget to drink plenty of water. The hospital will send you a bill."

"I don't know how to thank you, Sloan," she said when he parked in front of her house.

"I don't need thanks. I'm grateful that I ignored your insistence that you were too busy to spend a few minutes with me." He took her hand and walked with her to her front door, judging her ability to navigate properly.

"It's been like that every day, and on Sundays, I've hardly been able to move. I wanted to see you, but I didn't think you would enjoy being with a woman who was tired and worn out."

I want to be with this woman every possible minute. He took her door key out of his pocket and handed it to her, and from her inquiring look, it was clear to him that she didn't remember how he happened to have it. She opened the door, stood beside it, half leaning, and waited.

It was his move. "You're supposed to rest, and I want to see that you do, so this evening, I'll be your cook and bottle washer." He smiled in the hope of reassuring her. "I need to do this, Lynne."

"Uh…okay, but can you cook?"

He suppressed a sigh of relief thinking that such an expression might unsettle her. "Of course I can cook. I'm single. I live alone, and I eat." She reached behind him and closed the door, and he said a silent word of thanks. He had needed evidence that she trusted him.

"Park yourself on the living room sofa," he said, affecting an air of jocularity meant to put her at ease. He went into the kitchen and checked the refrigerator. Carrots, celery, spinach and tomatoes. Nothing there that he wanted to cook or eat.

"I'm going to the supermarket. Be back shortly." He bought shrimp, filet mignon, bib lettuce, Idaho potatoes, asparagus, orange juice, cranberry juice and ice cream. Ordinarily he'd want wine with the meal he planned to cook, but she couldn't drink it, so neither would he.

He returned to find her asleep on the sofa, and began to wonder if that doctor did his job well. He put an ice cube into a tall glass, poured cranberry juice over it and took it to her.

"Lynne, wake up. Wake up, baby, and drink this. You need to drink."

She sat up slowly. "Why am I so sleepy?"

"The doctor told you that you're exhausted. Could that be the reason? I brought you some cranberry juice. Drink up. And before you nod off again, where do I find the table linen?" She told him. "Maybe if you turn on the TV, you'll wake up. I'll be in the kitchen."

"Dinner's ready."

The voice came from far away, but it was a voice that she liked and she wanted to get closer to it. She tucked the cover to her body and hugged the pillow.

"Sweetheart, dinner's ready."

Sweetheart? Willard never called her names of endearment. Where was she?

"Aren't you hungry? If we don't eat, the food will spoil."

She dragged herself upright, rubbed her eyes and looked around. Her gaze fell on Sloan, who hunkered beside the sofa with a kind and indulgent smile on his face.

Her right hand stroked his left cheek. "You're so

sweet. When did you put this bedding over me? And this pillow? I was sleeping so good." She stood, and for a second, it seemed that she floated, but he was there with a hand on her arm.

"This food is wonderful," she told him later, savoring the shrimp diablo. "How'd you cook all this without getting a spot on those white trousers?"

"I'm a genius. Also, I tucked a towel in my belt."

"Are we having dessert, too?" she asked him when he took their dishes to the kitchen. "I love dessert."

His right hand went to the left side of his chest. "You wound me. Would I feed my best girl and not give her dessert? Horrors."

He served the ice cream with two tablespoons of coffee liqueur poured over it. "It isn't much, so you're not disobeying the doctor. After I clean up, I'll bring us some coffee and we can talk."

She ate the last spoonful of ice cream, wondering if the man facing her was real or imagined. "You're a wonderful man, Sloan," she said before realizing that the words would slip from her mouth.

He got up to collect the dessert bowls, stopped and regarded her. "I'll be happy if you still feel that way six months from now."

"Why do you say that?"

"By then, you should know what I mean to you and whether I suit you in every way. Then, if you tell me I'm wonderful, I'll welcome it."

Not every comment demanded a response. He was counseling caution, and he may as well have told her that he was being careful where she was concerned. She sat in the living room, thoroughly awake after the best home-cooked meal she'd had in a long time. He brought the coffee and a bowl of the grapes he found in the refrigerator. *I could really get used to being with this man.*

"Tell me about yourself, Sloan. I mean…tell me who you are down deep where it counts."

He rubbed the square chin that set off his lean, longish face and gave him the appearance of one in command. "My parents aren't poor, and they aren't rich. I'm an only child, but I worked my way through college because they wanted me to appreciate my education. I'm glad for that. After working for an unscrupulous man, I started my own business, the McNeil Motor Service. I bought the plant from a man who had decided to retire. At the beginning, I paid my employees when I couldn't afford to buy myself a decent meal. They knew I was hurting, and they went the extra mile for me, so to speak. I'm solvent now, debt free, and by the first of the year, I hope to open my second service station in Castle Hills. My goal is to have a chain of them throughout Texas.

"I don't have to support my parents, Lynne, but I'm careful to know their needs, and I check regularly and often to be sure they are comfortable. I'm prepared to take care of them, if that ever becomes necessary."

In other words, she said to herself, *any woman who takes me must accept my commitment to my parents. He wouldn't be much of a man if he felt otherwise.*

"I contribute to a boys' club and volunteer there regularly," he went on. "When I was a teenager, I could have benefited from the counsel of a wise man other than my father, a man who didn't see me as a reflection of himself, and who appreciated that I had to fumble my way."

She assimilated his words, concluding that she already knew him, that he was a man of compassion and honor, kind and generous.

"Why did you decide to divorce your husband? Is the decree final?"

"It's legally final. During the year that we courted, Willard was not controlling and certainly not abusive—if he had been, I wouldn't have married him. But within a month of our marriage, he became verbally abusive. Nothing I did, wore or cooked pleased him. He wouldn't allow me to work or to have a cleaning woman, not to speak of a housekeeper, and he didn't mind littering the house with his parishioners and expecting me to feed and serve them.

"If he was at home, I couldn't even watch a tennis match on the television set, and he wouldn't let me play or practice. Even when I begged, he said that part of my life was over. I couldn't see how a man who had been warm, loving and full of smiles could have changed so drastically."

"It was there, Lynne, but you somehow failed to detect it."

"I'm sure you're right. I married as a virgin, and I've regretted that. He is a cold man, and I learned it the hard way. One day I realized that I no longer loved him or cared for him, and probably never had loved him, that I had grown to dislike him. He didn't want a divorce and fought it, but the judge believed me. No one could make up the tales I told. It's over, Sloan, and if I've seemed skittish, I had good reason."

Quiet for a time and with both hands cupping his knees, he half turned and looked at her. "I hope I never meet that man. I don't believe in settling matters in a violent way, and he'd test my resolve, believe me." And as if he had to touch her, but didn't consider it prudent, he patted the back of her hand, unaware that the gentle touch sent tremors racing through her. "Since we're speaking about intimate things, I've been wondering why you were married for six years and didn't have any children. Was there a reason?"

She rested her head against the back of the sofa and closed her eyes. "Yes, there were reasons. We were… uh…intimate infrequently and, after the second year I decided not to have a child with him until our relationship improved. It got worse. He browbeat me about that and everything else."

They talked until almost midnight. "Is he the reason why you're working so hard to get back on top of your game?"

"No. I want to do it for myself. I was the best, on my way to robbing Williams of her crown. If I'm number one for one day only, I'll be happy. I want the title, because I would have had it if I had played one more tournament. When I quit to marry Willard—and at his request—I was only eighty-nine points behind Williams."

"You'll get there. I have no doubt of it."

They had talked for hours at a level that she had never managed to achieve with her husband. "Sloan, I can't help wondering why a man who behaves as you do, looks as you do and is as successful as you are is single. I know I don't understand Texas women, but the more I see of you and the better I get to know you, the less sense it makes." She held his hand, hoping to tell him without words that whatever he said would be all right with her.

"I've taken my lumps from women, Lynne. From the one who, I discovered, considered me a grease monkey who could be toyed with, and from another, the one I cared about, who thought it natural for me to join her coterie of lovers and to do so without complaining. I didn't know I was one of five until she forgot to lock her apartment door one evening when we had a date. I found her making it with the superintendent of the building in which she lived. It hurt. You can't imagine how it hurt. After that, I had women friends, some of them lovers and some merely movie, dinner or opera partners, but I always let them know that neither marriage nor shacking up was on my mind. I have never misled a woman, and don't intend to.

"The day after you and I played tennis together, I went to the woman who I'd spent the most time with and told her that I would not be seeing her again, that I'd met someone, and I wanted to begin the relationship with a clean slate. We had never been lovers, but I knew she wanted us to be more intimate, although I had discouraged that."

Her lower lip dropped. "You were talking about me?"

"Oh, yes. I knew the day I met you that something good could happen between us." He looked at his watch. "Good grief, it's midnight, and you should have been resting in bed long ago. Sure you can get upstairs all right?"

She nodded, looking up at him standing before her big, strong and so masculine, his face wreathed in a smile that tore at her heart. "I'm sure."

"May I come to see you tomorrow?"

She didn't want him to leave her, but it wasn't appropriate for him to stay. Her gaze locked on his full bottom lip, and a restlessness suffused her. What was wrong with her? She crossed her arms and rubbed her shoulders, unaware of its telltale meaning.

"May I?" he asked again.

He extended his hand, and with his touch a sweet

and terrible hunger stirred in her. "If you want to," she managed to say.

He tugged at her hand, encouraging her to stand, and when she looked into his eyes, their expression nearly unglued her. "I want to," he said, "and I'll call you first. Walk me to the door?"

After all they had shared, wasn't he even going to… He stood at the door holding her hand, his back against the wall that faced the guest closet, and stared down at her. His eyes projected a simmering gleam, and when she moistened her lips with the tip of her tongue, that gleam became a raging storm.

Why didn't he hold her, love her? She tried but couldn't tear her gaze from his as his eyes possessed her.

"Sloan…I—"

"What is it?" The urgency in his voice bespoke the storm in his eyes.

"Nothing. I…" She gripped his right arm. "Can't you…k…kiss me? Hold me?"

His eyes widened as he continued to stare down at her. "Do you know what you're asking? I've spent the last eight hours struggling to keep my hands off you and—"

"I want you to hold me. I need to know how it feels to be in your arms."

He sucked in his breath, and then she felt his hands on her, powerful and possessive as he wrapped her to him. His fingers sent fiery ripples spiraling down her arms as she stared into the dark desire of his mesmerizing eyes. Her right hand went to his nape, and he lifted her from the floor and let her feel his tongue plunge into her open, waiting mouth. At last she had him inside of her where he belonged.

With a hand on her buttock and the other at the back

of her head, not even air could get between them as he tested every crevice, every centimeter of her mouth. Fire shot through her, and she thought that marbles fought for space in the pit of her belly. When she pulled his tongue deeper into her mouth and with her hands on his hips, pressed his body to her, contractions in her womb and a tightening in her vagina brought moans from her lips. He seemed to break the kiss, but she tightened her hold on him.

His moans echoed through the foyer, and she twisted against him until her nipples erected and she raised one leg, longing to have his bulk inside of her vagina. Without thought as to its effect upon him, she leaned into him, taking the loving that she had needed for so long. Maybe she should stop it, but she'd never had that feeling, and when the warm tightening became a swelling, she heard her own keening cry and undulated against him because she couldn't help herself.

He stopped kissing her and gazed into her eyes, but she took no heed, grabbed his right hand and rubbed it across her left breast.

"Kiss me," she moaned. "I need it. Kiss me."

His hand lifted her T-shirt and pulled up her bra. Still gazing into her eyes, he stroked, teased and pinched her nipple.

"Honey, please."

Abruptly he closed his warm, moist mouth over her nipple and suckled her.

"Oh. My Lord," she cried aloud as the heat of desire spiraled through her. At last, trembling with the need to have him locked deep inside of her, she managed to stop herself and him.

"Sloan. Oh, Sloan. What have I done?" She rested her

head against his chest and his arms went around her. "We can't take this any further…it's too soon for us, but I've been so lonely, so long, and you… You're so sweet, and I've never responded to a man, not any man, this way."

He kissed her cheek and stroked her back. "Thank you for telling me that. And you're right…it *is* too soon, but it's also not the right time for this, because you're not up to snuff."

"I'm not sorry, Sloan."

"I certainly am not. You couldn't kiss me that way if you didn't care for me. You may think it's too soon to care, but it only takes a minute. Remember that."

She slipped her arms around him and hugged him as tightly as she could. "It's a good thing I have long arms. You're big. See you around noon."

"Ten is better. You have to eat breakfast." He kissed her nose. "Good night, sweetheart. Lock the door."

She stood in the foyer shaking her head and marveling at what had just transpired. What would Sloan Mc-Neil say if she told him that, in her lifetime, he had just given her her first physical urge to make love? Until then, desire had been in her head, never in her vagina. She turned out the light and plodded up the stairs. Seven or eight hours with Sloan McNeil were enough to convince her that she had never before been truly adored. But only time would tell what their being together meant to them.

Chapter 3

Sloan got into his car, drove a quarter of a mile from Lynne's house and stopped; he hadn't wanted to linger in front of her place, and he wasn't fit to drive. Every atom in his body wanted him to turn that car around and go back to her.

He'd spent almost eight hours with her, wanting her, starving for her and not daring to touch her, for he had to teach her to trust him. And then she rocked him out of his senses. Warm, sweet and giving. And how she could give! She'd set him afire and hadn't known how close he'd come to losing control. Loving. Pure loving. There was no other name for it. How could she have been married for six years and remained so innocent? Even before he tasted her sweet nipple, he should have been inside of her. A more experienced woman would have demanded it.

With his arms on the stirring wheel, he rested his head on them. She cared, but she had some strange notions that a certain amount of time had to elapse before she learned to care for a man. He had to go slow with her, but how could he if she heated him to the boiling point and let him know she wanted him as she did earlier? Hot. Passionate.

"My God," he said aloud. "I could love that woman!"

He put the car in Drive and headed home. One thing was certain: he'd be there Monday afternoon at three o'clock to check on that monster of a trainer. Lynne didn't know it yet, but she had equal priority with McNeil Motor Service, and he took care of his own. He parked in the garage that joined his beige, green-shuttered town house and walked around to the front door. Looking up at the full moon and the millions of stars surrounding it, he thought of the pleasure he'd get walking through a moonlit night with Lynne beside him. Did she entertain such notions about him? He hoped so.

Sunday morning at nine o'clock found him in the supermarket shopping for groceries for breakfast, lunch and dinner. He had never seen a refrigerator as empty as the one in Lynne's kitchen, unless it was on display in a store. How could she expect to have energy if she ate like a rabbit?

When she opened the door after he rang enough times to become concerned, she looked as if she had barely awakened. Warm, sweet and…lovable. Just the way he liked a woman, sleepy, cuddly and pliable. *Straighten out your head, buddy. Right now, she's untouchable.*

"Hi. I meant to get up early, but you can see I didn't make it."

He leaned down and kissed her cheek. "There was no

need. I hope you're hungry, because I eat a big breakfast, and I plan to cook a lot of food." It pleased him that she ate heartily, devouring second helpings of the fruit, pancakes and sausage.

"I thought men were messy in the kitchen. How can you cook and keep the place so tidy?"

"Easily. I make as little mess as possible, because I'm not fond of cleaning up." He hadn't imagined what their day together would be like. Certainly he hadn't envisaged them sitting outside on the deck surrounded by flowers, trees and birds, conversing leisurely or not talking at all. Comfortable and content with each other. Deeply touched by the serenity, he moved from the chaise on which he reclined, sat beside her and clasped her hand in his.

"Is this surreal to you, or are you feeling peaceful and happy as I am?"

For what seemed like ages, she didn't reply. Then, she squeezed his hand. "I don't know why, Sloan, and I am not trying to understand it, but this seems so right. I know my drive to become the world's number one tennis player could derail our friendship. I hope not. But right now, I'm happy."

He slid his right arm around her, and she laid her head on his chest. "Seems right to me, too," he said, "and I don't question it. Let's spend as much time together as possible."

When she took a deep breath and let it out slowly, he suspected that he wouldn't like what came next. "Monday after next, I start practicing with my coach, and in all I'll have two hours of training and four hours of tennis every day except Sunday."

If that was going to be her excuse, he wasn't buying

it. "There are twenty-four hours in the day, Lynne, so let's plan the time we'll be together."

She looked as if he'd disarmed her, and he hadn't meant to, so he sought to appease her. "We can adjust it as need be, but I want to be able to look forward to the time I'll be with you. If it's a week, so be it. But at least at Saturday noon, I'll know that you'll be with me the next day."

"Okay. Sundays—" she paused "—and evenings when I'm not half-dead."

"Even then, we can be together for half an hour. I can bring a couple of cones of ice cream, and we can sit together somewhere and eat them."

She frowned. It was ever so slight, but he caught it. "Are you asking for a commitment?"

He hadn't expected that question, and he wasn't sure he wanted to address it. "Not in a formal sense. I want to give this a chance to bloom, because I'm confident that it will."

"All right. Sundays when I'm in town and any evening that suits us."

"Isn't that your doorbell?" he asked her. "I'll see who it is."

He opened the front door and looked down into the face of a petite and aged white woman who carried a pie with both hands.

"And who would you be?" she asked him. "Lynne doesn't have a husband."

A local busybody, huh? He grinned at her. "No, she doesn't. Who would you be, ma'am?" he asked, mimicking her.

"I'm Thelma MacLendon, and I'm just paying my neighbor a visit. I hope you like pecan pie, because mine is the best in Bexar County, and I don't like to think of it being wasted. Where's Lynne?"

"Out back on the deck. Come with me."

"Ms. MacLendon is here to see you, Lynne," he called to her as they neared the deck, "and she brought you something nice."

Lynne stood to greet her neighbor. "You brought this for me? How nice of you. Thanks so much. Have a seat while I put it in the kitchen. Would you like some?"

"Thanks, but I left one at home. I won't stay, since you've got this charmer here. At least you know how to pick a man. How's your tennis coming along?"

"I haven't started practicing yet. I'm working with a trainer to get into shape."

"You mean that ugly little man who always wears black and drives that red sports car? I was worried at first thinking he was your man, but after the way he drove you in that hot sun the other day, I knew you had more sense than to hook up with him. Is he any good?"

"Supposed to be the best."

"Well, at least he's got *some*thing going for him. You come see me, now, and bring…" She let it hang.

"Oh, I'm so sorry, Thelma. This is Sloan McNeil."

"How do you do, ma'am?"

"Fine for my age. Glad to meet you. Always did like tall men. You come see me now." She headed back through the house, and he raced to see her out.

"Whew! Is she always like that?"

"Couldn't say," Lynne replied. "This is only the second time I've seen her. I like her."

"I'm glad you have a good neighbor. I think I'll make us hamburgers, and we can have pie for dessert. I can't wait to get my teeth into it. I love pecan pie."

"I've never tasted it, but I have an open mind."

"Good. I hope you'll give us as much of a chance as you're willing to give that pie."

Her eyelids lowered slowly and she settled more deeply into the swing's cushion, and stretched in a cat-like fashion. "Don't think for a minute, honey, that a pie rates with you."

He gazed down at her, so sexy and so tempting. "You be grateful that I'm a disciplined man."

She slanted him a quick glance and closed her eyes again. "Discipline has its virtues and its moments of decadence."

He hunkered in front of her and shocked himself by bracing his hands on her uncovered knees. "You've got a rapid-fire tongue, and I suspect it can be sharp. Some-day, you'll explain to me how to be disciplined is to be immoral, but not right now, because I have to cook us some hamburgers."

"I'd do that if you didn't insist that I rest."

"Don't get off the subject, and don't tell me criminals are disciplined. That's not what we're talking about."

"You're introducing complications," she said.

He looked up at her, relaxed, comfortable and beautiful, and shook his head. If he'd had his thinking cap on, he would have urged Thelma MacLendon to stay. He and Lynne should spend time around other people so he could think of something other than making love to her.

"After we eat, would you like me to drive us to Hemisphere Park, site of the 1968 World's Fair? We can sit in the park and talk. I go there a lot, because it's so peaceful. We could stay an hour or so and then come back and get dinner."

Her face wrinkled into a frown. "Are you bored? Tell me."

He laughed, although he wasn't amused. "Quite the opposite. You're so interesting that I could use a distraction."

She covered his hands with hers. "We can stay here, Sloan. I'll keep it between the lines."

He looked into her eyes for evidence of mischief or even insincerity and found none. "All right. Be back in a few minutes."

Later, after eating his hamburger as fast as good sense would allow, he could finally bite into the pecan pie. "That woman wasn't lying. I've eaten a lot of pecan pie in my life, and this is supreme. I'm going to make friends with that lady."

"You're not bad yourself. This is one delicious hamburger. Mind telling me what's in it?"

Remembering how she'd teased him earlier, he said, "No, I don't mind."

"Then—" She began to laugh, a big belly laugh. He got caught up in it and laughed with her until, unable to do otherwise, he wiped his mouth, picked her up, settled her in his lap and pressed his lips to hers in a sweet and gentle kiss. "Hold it, Sloan. I said I'd keep it between the lines, and I'm good as my word, but, honey, I need your help."

"Yeah," he said, putting her down. "I planned us a nice lobster dinner, but I suggest you keep the lobsters in your freezer, and we eat out. There's a nice little Mom and Pop restaurant not far that serves good home-cooked food. I'm enjoying cooking for us, but this togetherness is getting to me."

As if affronted, she sat forward and looked hard at him. "What exactly do you mean?"

Might as well call a spade a spade and keep the wires from getting tangled later on. "Lynne, I am a man, and I am strongly attracted to you, emotionally as well as physically. A man wants to express what he feels for a woman by making love with her, and it's getting more and more difficult for me to sit here with you and keep my hands off you. And this setting doesn't help."

He moved back to the chaise and settled himself on it. "On one hand, this is one of the most relaxing days I've had in years. Maybe the most relaxing. I don't think I've ever before taken the time to hear the birds twittering among themselves. Just listen to them. And to the wind, whispering so softly that I can barely hear it. Every day, I pass flowers along the roads and highways, in the markets and flower shops, and I don't even look at them. But sitting out here with you, I sense an almost spiritual kinship with these bluebonnets and yellow roses. I feel a part of everything around me, the trees, the flowers, the wind…and you, Lynne.

"On the other hand, it's frustrating being so close to you and…" What the hell, he wasn't going to dump that on her. Being with her showed him how barren his life had been, what he'd missed in companionship with a woman he cared for.

"I've learned a lot about you these past two days, Sloan, and a lot more, perhaps, about myself. Stop worrying about what I think of you, and whether I trust you." She threw up her hands. "Oh, yes, I'm not full of experience where men are concerned, but I know that's been worrying you. I would not fall asleep in this house alone with you, as I did yesterday, if I didn't trust you."

"Thanks for that, Lynne. What are you getting at?"

"I love lobster."

The mirth that began somewhere in the pit of him slowly expelled itself in a big belly laugh. What a precious woman! "All right. All right. I get the message." She went inside, and minutes later, he heard the music of Count Basie storming out of Kansas City, Missouri, in the 1937 rendition of "One O'clock Jump."

"Where did you get that recording?" he asked when she returned to the deck.

"I've had it since…gee, I don't know when. I have a large collection of jazz recordings, and I figured something not very sentimental would straighten things out here."

"Just don't play 'Every Day I Have the Blues.' The way Joe Williams sings that song is enough to send a man into shock."

"Okay, I won't play it. Let's walk along Corpus Christi Lane for a while before sunset. You know, someday I want to have a house near a large body of water, large enough so that I can see the daybreak and the sunset. I miss the sunset here."

"You can see it from my place, and I hope one day you will. I'd like a walk. Let's go." He wanted to observe her walking, to know whether she would be able to return to her routine Monday morning.

As they walked, the entire environment along Corpus Christi Lane struck him as being idyllic, though he had not noticed it on his earlier visits. Willow trees interspersed with flowering crepe myrtles, the eternal bluebonnets and rose trees decorated the properties that they passed.

"What are those flowers?" he asked of the white pointed blooms that flanked an imposing redbrick home.

"Calla lilies. They're my favorites, and if I ever marry again, I am going to carry a bunch of those. I'm also going to wear a white bridal gown and veil, though that's considered appropriate only for a first marriage. Willard thought formal weddings were an endorsement of fashion and therefore sinful, but I later learned that he was concerned about the expense. Anyway, as far as I'm concerned, I never had a real marriage."

"Hmm. How much older is he than you?"

She looked up at him. "How'd you guess? Twelve years. I was twenty-three, and he was thirty-five. That didn't seem like much of a difference when we were dating, but it was, and if you add that to his being a minister, the basis for conflict is obvious."

"Who lives over there?" he asked, pointing to a redbrick colonial that sat far back from the street and had a beautiful rose garden in front of it.

"Thelma MacLendon. All by herself."

"She said we should come see her. Let's see if she meant it. I want to thank her for that great pie."

A grin spread over her face and when she looked at him, her right eye closed slowly in a wink. "Okay. I see you want to make certain that you get some more of that pie. My guess is that she likes to cook and doesn't have anybody to cook for other than herself. Grin your best grin, and maybe she'll adopt you."

He stopped walking and turned her to face him. "You are a wicked woman." She wrinkled her nose and appeared wistful. "But I absolutely adore you."

"You're sweet, too," she said, grasped his hand and turned toward Thelma MacLendon's house.

"Who is it?" a voice asked from behind the door.

"Lynne Thurston and Sloan McNeil. We came to—"

The door was flung open, and Thelma rushed out. "Come on in. Come on in. I didn't expect you to come so soon, but I was hoping you would." She looked up at Sloan. "And you brought this nice young man with you. Don't get many visitors anymore. Y'all come right on in."

She ushered them into the large and airy living room, its windows adorned with white lace curtains and vertical white venetian blinds, the parquet floors warmed with scattered oriental carpets and the walls brightened with original paintings of Texas scenes and beautiful landscapes. The breeze brought to them the scent of roses, sweet and sensuous. Delicate like the woman beside him. What a time to have his hormones activated!

"Make yourselves comfortable. I just made some iced tea," she said, and left the room.

Lynne looked at him, and he thought she seemed a little embarrassed. "I should have visited her earlier. She asked me to come see her, but I thought she was only saying what was expected of her. I think she's lonely."

"I was thinking the same. We'll see."

"Did you like the pie? There's plenty more." She placed a tray containing a crystal pitcher and three Waterford iced tea glasses, three porcelain plates on which she'd put slices of pie, three silver forks and three white linen napkins. "Don't get much chance to use my nice things. When my husband was living, we entertained a lot. But this is a world for couples, and after he died, I didn't get invitations to people's homes, and I had to stop inviting them here. It's a pity, 'cause I love having people around me."

He took a slice of pie, savored it and the scent of fresh

caramel, and knew that his face gave her the answer she wanted, but he told her nonetheless. "Mrs. MacLendon, I'm a connoisseur of pecan pie, and yours is the best I've ever tasted. I can't tell you how much I enjoyed that pie."

"My name's Thelma. I'm glad. I love to make 'em. Anytime you drop by, I'll have one for you."

"Be careful," he said. "I spoil easily."

"Don't worry. I got sense enough not to get on Lynne's left side. Still…" For a moment, she seemed pensive. "My son would have been a little older than you, Sloan, but he went to Afghanistan and didn't make it back. He was my only child."

He reached for the thin, blue-veined white hand that trembled unsteadily and held it. "I'm so sorry. I can't tell you how sorry I am."

She locked him in her gaze for long seconds. "You're a strong man, but you're gentle. Lynne is lucky to have you in her life."

"Thanks. I think I'm lucky that I found her."

"And I hope you continue to feel that way after she goes back to playing tennis. I used to watch her and marvel at the way she played—she was the swiftest, the best server, and I used to jump out of my seat when those line drives of hers would hit the very corner every time." She looked at Lynne. "Do you think you'll get back to where you were? Frankly, I thought you were crazy to quit, but…" She threw up her hands. "I figured I didn't know everything."

"I'm trying, Thelma. My serve isn't trustworthy yet, and I won't know how my ground strokes are until I begin working with my coach. I had to get into shape first."

Thelma MacLendon looked directly at him. "Do you think you can handle being the man in a celebrity's life?"

"Why not? I'm sure it would entail surprises and some disappointments, but if a woman loved me and let me know it, and if she was always straight with me, her being famous wouldn't bother me at all. I'd be proud of her."

"I hope so. It took my husband a while to accept that, as a champion swimmer, I traveled a lot, but after he decided to accompany me whenever he could, our marriage and my swimming became a joint project. You're welcome to swim in my pool anytime you want to, Lynne."

"Thanks. If I decide to buy that house, I'll put one in behind my tennis courts. Maybe you could give me some advice about that."

"Sure thing." They talked for a long time, with Thelma leading the conversation. A glance at his watch told him that they had spent over two hours as uninvited guests in the woman's home.

He stood. "We didn't plan to stay more than a few minutes, Thelma. Thanks for your kindness."

Lynne walked over to the woman and took her hand. "Yes," she said. "I have enjoyed this time with you, Thelma, and I'll expect a visit anytime you get the notion."

"I want us to be neighborly," Thelma said, "and I like to know I have a friend nearby. Don't let that trainer push you around now. I watched him. He's mean."

"Don't worry about him," Sloan said. "There are other good trainers, and I aim to remind him of that fact."

"Good for you," Thelma said as they started for the door. "Wait a minute." She returned with what he knew would be the remainder of the pie and handed it to him.

"Now you remember where you got this. It takes me less than an hour to make it."

He couldn't help smiling, for she seemed so eager, and no one had ever needed to beg him to eat pecan pie. "What's your phone number?" he asked her. She hurried off and returned with the number written on a piece of paper along with her name and address. "Thanks. I'll see you."

"Don't make it too long."

At the end of the long walkway leading from her house, he looked back and, as he expected, she was standing in the door and raised her hand to wave them goodbye. He would think about her for a long time.

"I'm glad we went to see her, because I think she's lonely," Lynne said. "Loneliness is a terrible thing."

"You sound as if you've had some experience with it. When were you lonely, if you don't mind telling me?"

"While I was married. I didn't have any friends, no one with whom to communicate except my brother, and I had to be careful about what I said to him because he is very protective. I'm not a milquetoast, Sloan, but I took those vows seriously, and I did everything I could to keep the marriage together. Have you ever been lonely?"

"Oh, yes. I know all about it. As I told you, I've taken a few lumps."

"I'm sorry, but I suspect you're stronger because of it. Look. Fireflies. I love them."

He let his gaze sweep over her. "I have yet to hear you say that you disliked anything or anyone."

"That's because you haven't mentioned snakes or mosquitoes. I guarantee you I despise both."

He turned on the foyer lights as they entered the

house. "Considering your affection for mosquitoes, I think we'd better stay in here. Tomorrow, I'll bring you some outdoor candles that will keep them away from the deck."

When she didn't object to his coming to see her the following afternoon, he seemed to relax, to accept her acquiescence as evidence that she intended to abide by their agreement. He needn't have worried; she hadn't spent so happy a day since she won her first grand slam tournament ten years earlier.

"Dinner will be ready as soon as these little potatoes steam," he said, tucking a towel into his belt.

"What about the lobster?"

He tweaked her nose. "Ten minutes at best. Now sit down somewhere. You're supposed to be resting."

"But I'm not a bit tired."

"I don't want you to *get* tired, either."

She set the table while he cooked their dinner, rejecting thoughts of domesticity as she did so. Suddenly, wanting him to see her at her best, she walked out to the garden, quickly snipped some bluebonnets and got back inside before he missed her. She put the flowers into a small vase, placed them in the center of the table, got two crystal candleholders and looked for some candles. She let out a deep breath when she found some twelve-inch white candles. After finishing setting the table, she went into the living room and sat down as if she'd been there the entire time.

"Dinner's read... When did you... You were supposed to be resting."

She met him at the door between the dining and living rooms. "A lobster dinner deserves flowers and candles, and so do you. Don't worry. I'm rested."

He put the food on the table, and after sitting down, held her hand while he said the grace. She waited for him to begin eating, since he was the cook, but he merely sat there looking at her.

"I don't care what you say or how you say it, one day, you and I will embrace this world together. I've never before had the feeling that I was in my proper place." He leaned forward. "Lynne, I feel as if I could touch the moon if you were with me. While I was putting the food into serving plates, I wished I had flowers and candles for the table, but didn't mention that to you because I didn't want you to bestir yourself. The table is beautiful. I'm sorry you can't have wine."

She lowered her head and glanced up at him. "I bet I could have a wine and soda spritzer. What do you think?"

He jumped up from the table. "I bet you could, too."

After dipping a chunk of lobster into the butter and lemon sauce, she tasted it first, closed her eyes and shook her head slowly. "Hmm. I've died and gone to heaven. Sloan, this is fantastic. No wonder you're single. Any woman who cooks for you commits romantic suicide, because you're so much better at it."

"Thanks for the compliment, but I do not plan to let you use that as an excuse not to invite me to breakfast, lunch and dinner many times."

She tasted the potato fluff and threw up her hands. "This settles it. Will you marry me?"

He stopped eating, and she knew at once that she'd made a big mistake. "I will, and I want an engagement ring, and I am *not* joking."

The seriousness of his facial expression disconcerted her, and she got up from the table, went to him and put an arm around his shoulder. "Forgive me if I got carried away. I didn't intend to demean the relationship between us with what seemed like a joke. I'm so sorry." She hugged him because she needed to feel him close to her.

"I was surprised, but it was just a bump in the road. Don't worry about it."

"Does that mean you forgive me?" she insisted.

"Of course. But in the future, remember that it's just as binding if you say it as it would be if I said it. All right?"

"Thanks." She finished the meal, relishing every bite, and she measured each word carefully. She didn't remember having been loose with words, but after liberating herself from Willard Marsh, she seemed to have relaxed her tongue as well as her guard. Four months after a divorce, she was slowly but definitely falling in love with a man she had known less than one month.

He cleaned the kitchen and brought coffee to the living room. "I'm going to leave in a few minutes, but before I go, I want to tell you something. This has been one of the most pleasant days of my life. I don't remember enjoying anyone's company as much as I've enjoyed yours. I've never believed in fate, but get this—I don't usually answer afternoon service calls. Along with one of my men, I take calls between seven and twelve. Bill, whom you met, and another man take afternoon calls. For some reason, I said to Bill, 'Finish your lunch. I'll take it.' Ordinarily he'd have finished his lunch, rested for the remainder of his lunch hour and then gone on the call. If this is fate or what God wants, as my mother would say, I'm willing to go along with his program. What about you?"

"Me? I suppose he knows what he's doing."

"Woman, you have evasiveness down to a fine art. I repeat. What about you?"

"When you kissed me senseless last night, you didn't leave me with a bag of options."

"Good. I was hoping I left you with none. Is the answer to my question yes or no?"

"Yes."

He stood. "Walk me to the door?"

"Not unless you promise to behave better than you did last night."

Merriment danced in his warm brown eyes, eyes that darkened to a mahogany when passion gripped him. "I promise."

With the wall supporting his back, he gripped her hips with one hand, held the back of her head with the other one, lifted her to fit him and searched the seams of her lips with his tongue. Frantic for the taste of him, she parted her lips and took him in. Nothing had prepared her for the force of his passion, as he locked her to his body and, with the dance of his tongue, simulated the act of love. His pectorals pressed against her nipples, and she knew he could feel it, that it heated him the same way that it made fire spiral through her body. The blood raced to her loins, and she raised her knees, pressed them beside him against the wall and felt him rise hard and powerfully against her center. He attempted to move her away from him, but she refused to give place. She wanted him inside of her, and she didn't care if he knew it. Sucking the sweet ambrosia from his swirling tongue, she moved against him, her hips undulating in a wild and unrestrained rhythm, demanding, until he gripped her body and set her from him. He stared down at her with eyes of liquid fire, and sensation rioted throughout her body.

Frustrated, she poked him in the chest with her fist, and still he stared, the silence so pregnant with tension that it spoke with a voice of its own.

"Oh Lord," she moaned, wrapped her arms around him and rested her head on his chest. "Go now, or stay. I can't handle any more of this."

His arms eased around her. "When we make love, it will be very special. I'll see you around three tomorrow. Good night, love."

Hours later, Lynne twisted, kicked and turned until the bedding bound her as wrappings bind a mummy. She rolled over and over until she could extricate herself and sit on the side of the bed. She switched on the lamp beside her bed, stared at the scene around her and thought how strange it appeared. The moon shone brightly from beyond her window, and she thought of the cold, loveless nights she'd lived for six long years of her life. What would she find if she linked her life with Sloan McNeil's? Would it be her second gargantuan error?

It wasn't amusing, nothing was right then, but nonetheless, she began to laugh at herself. Sloan McNeil hadn't said a word about linking himself to her, except in bed, and making love didn't imply commitment. Commitment or not, a fire burned inside of her, and it burned for him, wild and almost out of control. If he was half the man he seemed to be and purported himself to be, she meant to have him at least once. She deserved to know her feminine self and her potential as a woman, and Sloan McNeil would help her realize it. She crawled back into bed, pulled the covers up to her neck and went to sleep.

At seven the next morning, she locked her front door, ran down Corpus Christi Lane and headed for the bikers' trail. After jogging to the end and back, she sat beside a pond about half a mile from her house and watched a frog jump from water lily to water lily, snapping at flies and other bugs. If only she could get in a few laps in an Olympic-size pool. Buying and furnishing a house was more she should tackle at the moment, she knew, because she needed to focus on sharpening her tennis game, but she wanted a swimming pool. She went home and telephoned her brother.

"This is Lynne," she said when Brad answered. "How are you? I'm thinking of buying this house, and I need some advice. Do you know anyone in San Antonio who can be trusted to give me an honest appraisal?"

"Sure. What's up? Don't tell me your mechanic is urging you to buy a house."

"For goodness' sake, Bradford—" he knew she only called him that when he annoyed her "—the man has his own house. I haven't seen it, but I know he has one."

"Damned if you're not hooked on that guy. Lynne, listen to me. It won't do your career one bit of good to be tied to a grease monkey. I—"

She interrupted him. "Brad, how could you? You know nothing about him. He's as well educated as you are, and he carries himself as well as you do. Put the two of you in a room together and no one would be able to guess which of you was the automobile mechanic."

"Well, if he's such a hotshot, ask him to work in his office and let his employees do the greasy work. I don't want my sister hanging out with a beer-drinking mechanic."

"Really? When we had dinner at Michael's, the best restaurant anywhere near here, he ordered Châteauneuf-du-Pape with the meal."

"I didn't know you were so easily impressed. Tell him to take a desk job."

"What about someone to appraise this house?"

"Oh, yes. Breckenridge and Breckenridge, and tell them I sent you. Now, you—"

"I'm hanging up, Brad, before you make me really mad. Bye and thanks."

If only Brad would get off her case about Sloan. She loved her brother, and she wanted him at least to be friendly toward the man she cared for. Anyone would think that, after her six-year trial with Willard Marsh, her brother would be glad if she found a gentle, caring man. "Oh well, I'll worry about that some other time."

She ate a hearty breakfast of oatmeal, melon, toast, bacon and coffee, showered and dressed in her gym suit in preparation for her "battle" with Max, who arrived promptly at ten-thirty.

"I hope you've sent lover boy packing," he said, in place of good morning. "You tell him that I do not permit interference between me and my clients. Where my clients are concerned, I am the boss." He pointed to his chest. "Me."

"You tell him that the first chance you get. I'm not going to tell him any such thing. Let's get started."

He put her through some difficult paces, as she'd known he would. "I'm tired," she told him at noon. "Let's take an hour for lunch and rest. I can make you a ham sandwich or I'll meet you here at about one-fifteen."

He glared at her, but she knew he remembered Sloan's words: "You work for her." *I should have told him that myself, and from now on, whether it's trainer or coach, I am the boss.*

"I'll meet you here at one-fifteen, and don't eat too much. Strenuous exercise is not good on a full stomach." She let him have the last word.

He'd saved the stretches for the last, and it occurred to her that he did that to test her, because for her, it was the most demanding. When, at last, she walked over to the bench and put on her sweatshirt, he yelled, "You got twenty more minutes."

"You sent me to the hospital emergency room Friday," she told him, "but today, I'm using my common sense. I'm tired, and I'll see you at ten-thirty tomorrow morning."

Her head snapped around at the sound of applause. "Good going," Sloan said. "You want to rest a few minutes? I've got something to show you." As if Max wasn't there, he brushed her lips with his and then hunkered before her. "How do you feel?"

"Fine, considering how little sleep I got. Most of the night, you fooled around in my head. What you did was criminal."

"At least I only fooled around in your head."

She looked at a point past his shoulder. "I'm not going there. What do you want to show me?"

He straightened up and grasped her hand. "Come. It's in the truck."

She looked at his pristine white trousers, white shoes and white short-sleeved shirt. "You drove the truck?"

He nodded, seemingly overflowing with joy. "I had to. You'll see."

As they walked from the tennis court across the lawn
to the side of the house that had a walkway leading to
the street, he dropped her hand and slung his arm loosely
around her waist. She didn't object, because it seemed
to belong there.

"You didn't even speak to Max."

"I would have if I hadn't focused on you. Anyhow,
I'm still a little vexed with him."

Her lower lip dropped when her gaze caught the truck
and the big red doll's house, or what seemed like one,
that loomed in the back of it. "What's this?"

He went around the truck and came back to her carrying a four-month-old German shepherd. "He's a beauty."

She looked from Sloan to the puppy, who seemed so
comfortable in Sloan's arms. "You brought him for me?"
He nodded. "But where will he sleep?"

"That's his house in the truck. He'll take good care
of you, if you take care of him. I promise. Feed him in
front of his house, never inside your house. Take him
for a walk mornings and evenings, and don't let people
pet him or play with him. He's a guard dog." He took
her hands and let the puppy sniff them. "He's getting
heavy, but I think you can hold him while I put his house
on your deck. When he's full grown, it might be a good
idea to put his house in the yard. Can you hold him?"

Overwhelmed and, she realized, excited, she took
the puppy and cradled him in her arms, stroking and
hugging him. "He's so cute and cuddly," she said as she
looked up to find Sloan staring at her, and nearly dropped
the animal. Passion heated his dazzling gaze, and she
stood immobile as tension danced between them like
an unharnessed electric current, wild and dangerous.

"You're a born nurturer," he said in a voice so soft

that she strained to hear it. "And you'll be a wonderful, loving mother."

"If I ever get the chance. I…uh…I know what it means to need love," she said, then turned and walked away from him toward the back side of the house, holding the puppy, who made no effort to move out of her arms. The man was a living magnet.

"He needs a name, a strong name," Sloan said, carrying the doghouse. "He's a purebred German shepherd, and his name should reflect his nobility."

She laughed. "A nobleman, eh? Then I guess I can't name him Wimbledon. I'll call him Caesar. What do you think?"

"Sounds right. I'll register it tomorrow, and I'll bring you a copy of his papers. You sure you want to keep him? I know I took a chance, but if you like having him, that's all I want. It will take a load from my mind."

"Were you worried about me? Caesar won't be a guard dog till he's grown, will he?"

"Acquaint him with the premises, walk him around—" he handed her a leash that would hook to the dog's collar "—so he'll know his territory. In a couple of weeks, he'll growl at any trespasser."

"I don't want him to growl at you."

He put Caesar's house on the deck, flush against the wall of Lynne's back porch. "Not to worry. He'll get used to me after a while." He put the dog in his new house, got the bag of dog biscuits and the plate that he had taped to the top and handed them to her. "You feed him, and then get him some water for this bowl. Always feed him right here."

"Caesar," she called to the dog, but getting no answer, she hunkered before the door and held a biscuit so that the dog could smell it. He poked his head out, looked first at Sloan, then at her before deciding to come out and eat.

"Now he knows who feeds him," Sloan said. "Dogs are like children, they love the person who nurtures them."

When the dog finished eating she gave him water, patted his head and hooked the leash to his collar. "Come, Caesar, we're going for a walk." She hadn't fully appreciated the size of her property until she'd walked the length and breadth of it with Caesar. She walked back to the deck intending to put Caesar in his house and found Sloan working on it.

"What's that you're putting on it?" she asked him.

"I made a window on the side, but it's glass, and he needs air, so I'm putting in this window screen. When he's inside and you don't want him to get out, slide that other screen across the door. He'll be comfortable and happy."

She backed away and moved around him in order to see the other side of the doghouse. "You *made* this?"

"One of my workers is a pretty good carpenter, and he set the frame up for me. I can't lay out anything this complicated. All I had to do was saw the boards and nail them to the frame. We started working on it last week."

He straightened up. "Want to ride into San Antonio? I'll stop past the service station, get my car and we can have what's left of the afternoon. What do you say?"

His tone and the smile upon his face beguiled her. *I will not be putty in this man's hands,* she said to herself, but to him she said, "Give me a few minutes to change. I want to be home by eight-thirty so I can take Caesar for a walk and be in bed by ten."

"You'll be back by then. I promised I'd dance to your

rhythm, and I keep my word. Remember, though, that on Sundays we please each other."

"That's what we'll always do." She looked at the doghouse. "Suppose he gets lonely while I'm gone?"

"He'll be that much happier to see you when you get back."

She went inside, showered, dabbed a bit of Miss Dior perfume in strategic places and slipped on a pale green, short-sleeve linen dress. "Ready when you are."

"You're lovelier every time I see you." He leaned down and kissed her cheek. "Good as you look, I sure hate to ask you to ride in this truck, but it's all I have just now. When we get to the service station, I'll make amends."

He drove along Route 35 with the windows down and the breeze dancing through her hair. She leaned back and perused the countryside that she was beginning to love. The Texans adored their bluebonnets, but she adored the yellow daisies and multicolored calla lilies that bloomed on the roadside. Although the sun shone brightly, sprinkles of rain, like hesitant teardrops, landed occasionally on the window, cooling the atmosphere. But suddenly, as if the heavens opened and poured out its sorrows of the ages, a torrent of rain obscured their vision. Sloan quickly closed the windows,

"I hope you didn't get wet," he said. "Maybe it's a passing shower." He pulled into the service station. "Wait here. I have an umbrella in my office."

Her hand on his arm detained him. "I don't want to be dry and comfortable at your expense. Can't we sit here for a while until the rain slacks?"

He frowned deeply, and his gaze seemed to penetrate her, to search inside of her, but his otherwise casual demeanor belied his intenseness as he let his arm rest on the back of her seat. "For a minute there, I almost wished I was Caesar. You're going to love him and take care of him, and he's going to be one lucky bastard."

She wasn't sure as to what her reaction to that statement should be, so she expressed her true feelings. "I would take good care of anything you gave me."

A grin spread over his face, and the light in his eyes sparkled and danced its mischievous dance. "Sweetheart, I am not going to touch that one, because I would definitely incriminate myself."

"Not more than you just did. It's stopped raining."

"Right. I'll be back in a few minutes." He returned wearing a beige jacket and, with an umbrella hanging on his arm, opened her door and said, "I'll help you out. This truck is high, and your skirt is narrow." She swung her feet to the side and looked up at him. "I'll use any excuse to get my hands on you," he said, lifting her and carrying her to a black Lincoln Town Car.

"I'm still able to walk, Sloan."

"I know, but I didn't want you to get your shoes muddy."

"Muddy? We're not on a farm, we're standing on concrete."

He rubbed the back of his neck with his fingers and affected an air of innocence. "Well, I was honest. I told you I'd use any excuse to—"

"Put me down. If you need an excuse, we're both in trouble."

"What did you say?"

She slid into the car and fastened her seat belt. "You heard me correctly."

He got in, fastened his seat belt and glanced at her.

"If I don't need an excuse, that means I can put my arms around you whenever I like." She didn't respond. "Well, what do you say to that?"

"You do that already."

He ignited the engine and headed the car toward the center of the city. "Oh, no, I don't. There are times, like last night, when I practically come unglued because I can't have my arms around you."

"I hope you're not suggesting that that's my fault."

"Whose fault is it? It isn't mine."

She snapped her finger. "I knew it was something. I just knew it. The little people are at it again."

"I wish they'd mind their own business."

"No," she said, feeling her oats. "You're the one who isn't minding yours. You sat there with me fifteen minutes while the rain beat out a rhythm on the hood of your truck, the most romantic kind of setting, and I don't remember your having put your arms around me or kissing me, either." She nudged him in his side. "Do you?"

"Did you want me to kiss you?"

"We're not talking about what I wanted…we're discussing your wants and how lackadaisically you handle them. If I wanted—"

"Don't say it. Nothing's to prevent my pulling over to the curb and giving the citizens of San Antonio a little show."

"You would need my cooperation."

"And if I really wanted to do that, I'd get your cooperation," he said without an inkling of a smile. "Oh, you'd make me pay later, but just as I remember with the clarity of clear, clean glass how I feel when you let yourself go in my arms, I know you recall what it's like when I heat you up. That said, let's stop the one-upmanship and enjoy being together."

"What one-upmanship? I don't mind if you win. Nothing gives me more pleasure than being close to you when you're on fire. Of course, if I start daydreaming about you, I won't be able to focus on my tennis game, and you wouldn't want that. Would you?"

"You're the one who thinks we haven't known each other long enough to…to care for each other. I don't subscribe to that, and if you face the facts, neither will you."

"How can you be so sure?"

"I don't believe it. A parking place." He parked, cut the engine and turned to face her. "I understand myself and my reactions to you and to other people, and I know when what a woman expresses to me is deep feeling and when it's only sexual desire. I wouldn't be much of a man if I didn't know the difference." His hand caressed the side of her face and stroked her shoulder. "You and I are on the same tract, sweetheart, and I think you know it."

Chapter 4

A week later, exhausted from her workout with Max, Lynne opened her front door and welcomed Gary Hines into her home and her life. She wasn't used to hearing her teeth chatter, but for the several minutes before Gary was due to arrive, that and the trembling of her fingers gave her reason to wonder whether she was ready for the opinions of one of the greatest tennis players of all time.

"Hi. Come in," she said. "We met briefly years back when I was climbing up the ranks, so I don't expect you to remember meeting me."

His smile set her at ease. "I don't remember that, but I sure remember that blistering backhand of yours. How'd you get along with Max?"

She led Gary through the house to the deck where she had laid out lemonade and sandwiches. "It's enough to endure four hours with Max. I'd as soon not spend time

talking about him. He's a great trainer, especially if you
happen to be a horse."

Gary's roar of laughter told her that he understood
well what she hadn't said. "He is that, but he's a hard pill
to swallow. If you're still with him, that tells me you're
in good shape."

"Have a seat. I thought we'd eat lunch out here. Would
you rather have iced tea?"

He shook his head and reached for the lemonade.
"This hits the spot. How are you feeling? Mentally, I
mean."

"I'm giving myself two years in which to become
number one. That's my goal. If I make it sooner, so much
the better."

"If you're fit, there's no reason why you shouldn't
get there."

"But I'm twelve years older than the current champion, and that's the only thing that worries me."

He stopped eating, leaned back in the chair and looked
hard at her. "No woman playing tennis today is as good
at it as you were when you left the game. You still hold
the record for serves. I don't want to hear any talk like
that." He picked up his sandwich. "I'm here to see that
you win. If you jog five miles a day and spend an hour
with Max, that will keep you in shape. Two hours with
him and four with me will wear you out."

Thank the Lord for a reasonable coach. "Who's going
to tell Max, you or me?"

Gary's laugh sounded a bit hollow. "I will. Max
doesn't show me his ugly side."

After their lunch, they walked out to the tennis courts.
"I'm thinking of putting lights over the hard court so
I'll get used to playing at night. I figure I don't need a

grass court here, because grass was always an easy surface for me."

He walked over to the bench beside the hard court
and selected two tennis balls from the container filled
with them. "I'd like to see you serve."

She tossed up the ball and let it fall to the ground,
picked it up, tossed again and drove it with all her
strength. *Not bad,* she thought, served again and watched
the ball streak down the center line for an ace.

"Change over and serve from the other side."

She did it well, though less perfectly. "That's my weak
side," she explained.

"I wouldn't call it weak. Are you ambidextrous?" She
shook her head. "Then, it was a good serve. Not as powerful as it's going to be, mind you, but a good one. Let's
play a game. You serve first."

At the end of their two sets, which she lost 6–2, 6–3
to a man still capable of winning tough matches on the
men's tour, she sat down on the bench and said a word
of thanks. If she worked hard, she'd make it. Gary hadn't
forced her to run from one side of the court to another
like a puppy chasing a Frisbee disk, because his thirty-
six years had taken their toll, but one of the younger female players would, so she didn't think she had anything
to preen about.

"How'd I do, Gary?"

"Your second serve needs some work, but I think
that's only a matter of confidence. You're reasonably
accurate, but you want to add power, and you need to
get those drives to the corners down as perfect as they
used to be. That's what we'll work on first. When you're
satisfied that you can hit those corners, you'll be on
your way. For today, I'm pleased. See you tomorrow at

eleven-thirty. We'll work for two hours, rest for an hour and work two more hours. Okay?"

She remembered her pledge to Sloan. "I'd like Saturday afternoon and Sunday off. I don't work out on Saturday."

"Good. Then you and I will work out Saturday mornings from eight to twelve with half an hour for rest. See you tomorrow."

After a shower, she put on a yellow sundress and a pair of espadrilles, went out on the deck—shaded by the huge willows and pine trees—and after hooking a chain to Caesar's collar, tethered him to the railing beside her chair. The pup settled beside her feet and went to sleep. Using her cellular phone, she telephoned her brother at his office.

"Thurston speaking. What may I do for you?" She enjoyed the authority with which Brad answered the phone and, indeed, with which he carried himself. He didn't allow anyone to guess whether he meant what he said or whether he was in command, traits she knew he had learned from their late father.

"Hi, Thurston," she teased. "This is Thurston calling." Simultaneously with the sound of a car stopping in front of her house, Caesar growled and jumped up with his tail straight out.

"What was that? Was that a dog?" Brad asked her.

"That was Caesar. Let me see if anyone's coming to the house." She listened, heard the automobile drive off and looked down at Caesar. The dog relaxed his guard, returned to his place beside her chair and closed his eyes as if asleep.

"A car stopped and that got Caesar's attention, but

it continued down Corpus Christi Lane, and Caesar's ready to go back to sleep."

"When did you get a dog and what kind is he?"

"He's a purebred German shepherd, and I've had him about ten days. Sloan gave him to me. He said I should have a guard dog, and even though Caesar is a little less than five months, he's already conscious of his territory and his job."

"If it was *his* dog, who's going to protect you from Sloan?"

She was going to enjoy this. Rarely did she get a chance to put her uppity brother in his place. "Brad, I don't want anybody to protect me from Sloan. He does that well enough himself. Beside, Sloan got that dog from a kennel and brought him straight to me."

"Are you out of your mind? The guy's a complete stranger."

"He was. But I'm getting to know him, and I'm discovering that he reminds me a lot of Daddy. Brad, this man is as straight as the crow flies, and I'd bet my life on it."

"How did he react when you asked him to work in his office and leave servicing automobiles to his employees?"

"I…uh…I didn't mention it to him yet."

"Well, you'll be on the tour soon, and you want to be able to introduce him to your associates."

"And whether he works at a desk or under a car will determine how he shakes hands? Give me a break, Brad."

"Look, sis, don't be too clever. I'm right, and you know it. If you insist on seeing this guy, protect your money, your virtue and your status. I know what I'm

talking about. Did you call Breckenridge and Breckenridge?"

"Not yet. I'll do that tomorrow. Do you think they
could find the deed specifying the perimeters of my
property?"

"Sure. They have experts on every aspect of property
buying and selling, and they won't mislead you."

She thanked him and made a mental note to telephone
Thelma about the pool she hoped to install if her house
proved to be a sound buy.

Sloan wanted to see Lynne that evening, but he didn't
intend to make a nuisance of himself. He wanted proof
that what he felt for her was mutual, and that meant she
had to acknowledge it at least to herself. At about six
o'clock, when he knew that she had finished her tennis
lessons, he sat on his back porch, braced his feet against
the railing and crossed his ankles. Maybe he'd call her.
He usually liked the sound of his neighbor's young children playing, laughing and enjoying their childhood, but
that afternoon, he wanted peace and to be as much alone
as possible. If he couldn't be with Lynne, he didn't want
human company. He reached down and got the bottle of
beer that rested on the floor beside him, twisted off its
top and drank half of it, guaranteeing that when he went
to bed, he'd fall asleep. He wanted to know how she was
and how she was faring with Caesar, but those were ex-
cuses, and he refused to indulge himself.

"Hello," he said after allowing the mobile phone to
ring half a dozen times.

"Hi. This is Lynne. Where were you?"

For a minute, his breath seemed trapped in his throat,
and he couldn't utter a word. "Sloan?"

"Sorry. Hello, Lynne. What a pleasant surprise. How are you and how was your first day with your coach?"

"I like working with him. We played two sets and he beat me 6–2, 6–3. I'm not sure he played his best, but he sure gave me a tough game. He identified the weakest elements of my game, and that's what we'll work on first. Also, Sloan, he's far more gentle than Max will ever be, and he reduced my training schedule with Max to one hour daily Monday through Friday. So I'm feeling good right now."

"I imagine you are. And if you scored five points in two sets with Gary Hines, you really played well. Remember, this is his first year in retirement, and he's probably the best ever. How's Caesar?"

"Caesar is lying here at my feet, pretending to doze. A car stopped in front of the house a while ago, and he growled, jumped up, cocked his ears and seemed ready to spring. The car drove on, and he lay down again and closed his eyes. I patted his head, and he seemed to like that."

"Do you have any idea why that car stopped or who it was?" He'd bet she hadn't bothered to check.

"We're on the deck, and I didn't go to the front of the house."

"Hmm. Do you think you deserve a cone of ice cream?"

"I sure do, but I also deserve some supper before I eat dessert. If you promise to be good, I'll treat you to deviled shrimp."

"You're on. Woman, I'm always good, and I love shrimp. What time shall I get there?"

"If you want to, you may leave home now, and we can take Caesar for a walk."

"I'll be there in forty-five minutes."

He changed his T-shirt for a short-sleeve dress shirt, decided that his light gray trousers were adequate, slipped on a pair of black loafers, threw a black dress jacket over his right shoulder and locked his house. After checking his tires, as he usually did before driving, he got into the Buick and headed for Lynne's house. She answered the door wearing a green scooped-neck blouse, a beige broomstick skirt and white espadrilles. Her welcoming smile kicked his heart into a gallop, and he sucked in his breath.

"You are so beautiful. It doesn't matter whether you're dressed up or dressed down. You're always lovely. At least to me." He handed her a bag that contained the ice cream.

She seemed taken aback, and he couldn't figure out why. With her gaze on the floor, she said, "You look good, too." Then she looked up and smiled. "Real good."

"I could love you senseless." He stared at her, realizing that he'd voiced his thoughts although he hadn't meant to. "I…uh…didn't plan to say that. It…" He gave up. "Let's take Caesar for a walk before it gets too dark. By the way, I didn't notice anything untoward when I looked around out there."

She left him, put the ice cream in the freezer and strode back to him, her face a blanket of smiles.

"Did you think anything could be wrong?"

"Not necessarily, but I leave nothing to chance." He grinned at her, though he didn't feel like it. "Don't you think you should kiss me?" he asked. "I mean, if I have to be on my best behavior, you have to do the kissing."

She gaped at him, as would one who was dumbstruck.

And suddenly, laughter pealed out of her and her body shook with it until she leaned against him and clung.

"Lynne, something must be funny, or you wouldn't laugh this way. But, sweetheart, you shouldn't laugh at a guy who's trying to do the right thing." She clapped her hands, spread her arms and exploded with laughter, and he realized that she wasn't laughing at him, but that she was truly joyous.

She confirmed that when she collected her composure and said, "You're so precious. So sweet and so precious. I wouldn't take anything for you. Oh, Sloan, you're so dear."

He was ahead, and he planned to stay there. "If that's true, why don't you kiss me?"

Playing his game, she took both his hands, locked them behind him and held them there, stood on tiptoe with parted lips and said, "Bend down, please." His lips touched hers, and she flicked her tongue over them, sending fiery shocks throughout his body. She pressed herself to him, and a sweet and terrible longing spread over him as she kissed his eyes, his cheeks, his nose, forehead and lips. Then, she released his hands and gripped him in a fierce hug.

"Want to go now? I'll get Caesar."

She turned to go, but he detained her with an arm across her shoulder. He had to do something, anything, to show her how the tenderness with which she had adored him affected him. Careful not to start a fire, he hugged her tightly and set her away from him.

"Go ahead. I'll be hungry any minute."

She walked away from him, tall and willowy, her beautifully rounded hips swaying as she went. Surely the Lord wouldn't bring this woman into his life for the purpose of teasing and punishing him. Yet, he knew there was much he didn't know about her, and that he wanted and needed to know. She returned with Caesar leashed, his tail wagging in a friendly greeting. He resisted patting the dog, because he thought that Lynne alone should exercise that familiarity with him. He was, after all, not a pet but a guard dog.

"He's grown a lot in such a short time," he told her, taking her key and locking the door.

"Yes, and he's so intelligent. I walk him around the edges of my property, but when we're leaving here to walk down the lane, I bring him through the front door. He knows the difference, and he knows where he lives."

He allowed a smile to envelop his face. "Would I give you anything that wasn't perfect?"

She looked up at him and winked. "Not if you could help it."

"Best not to comment on that," he said to himself, and didn't.

Caesar ran along in front of them to the extent that his leash would allow, but when the reached the corner, he stopped and looked at Lynne.

"Let's wait for the light," she said. "I'm trying to teach him not to cross on the red light, to cross when traffic is going in his direction. I don't know if it makes sense, but I'd just die if he got hurt. I'm going to fence the property so that he can enjoy roving around without a leash."

"I think you've become attached to him."

"I am. He's wonderful company. When I'm on the deck, he always puts himself down beside my feet."

He grinned, although he didn't feel much like it. "God forbid I should be jealous of a dog. What are your plans for the Thanksgiving and Christmas holidays? I imagine my parents will be distraught if I don't spend those holidays with them, but I'd also like to be with you."

"I usually spend Christmas with my brother and his wife, and I'd invite you to join us, but I envision you and Brad at loggerheads. He'll get on your nerves, and you'll put him in his place."

"Well," he said, seeing an out, "in that case, you come to Galveston with me, and visit with my parents. That way, you'll learn as much about me as you need to know, and you'll enjoy it. They're right on the Gulf. My father has a boat, and—"

"But what would I do with Caesar? I wouldn't want to leave him alone for three days, and you wouldn't be home to take care of him."

"We would board him in the same kennel that I got him from. That's not an excuse."

"I'll keep that under advisement, but if I don't go to Frederick for Christmas, I can see Brad going up in smoke. Anyway, it's too soon to be thinking about Christmas."

So brother Brad was a troublemaker, was he? He'd gotten over worse hurdles. "Did you spend Christmas with him and his wife when you were married?"

"Why, no, and he didn't come to us, either, though I suppose he might have if I had invited him. As I think of it, I didn't invite one person to my home the entire six years of that marital debacle. He visited me on several occasions for periods of an hour or so. A little of Willard tested him to his limit."

"Think we should head back?" he asked. If he told her that he came to her because he wanted to find out the reason, if any, why an automobile would stop in front of her house for a minute or so and then move on, she wouldn't like it. If he'd learned anything about her, it was that she cherished her independence, that she would tolerate protectiveness so long as she didn't feel controlled or smothered.

Lynne fed Caesar, patted him in the way that he loved, led him to his house and shut his gate. Then she went to the kitchen, washed her hands and got busy cooking the dinner.

"When did you cook all this?" he asked when they sat down to eat half an hour later.

"A few minutes ago. I made the jalapeño corn bread and the salad while you were on your way here. Rice takes seventeen minutes from the time the water boils, broccoli in the microwave takes four and a half minutes, and the sorrel soup was left over. Shrimp is done almost the minute it hits a hot pan."

"This is gourmet fare. I like the wine, too."

"Thanks. It isn't much. Someday I'll cook you something nice."

She thought his face registered surprise. "If this indicates the quality of your culinary efforts, I can't wait, but then, from the minute I met you I've received one surprise after another. Who would have dreamed that the great Lynne Thurston was such a down to earth, gentle and lovable woman, devoid of arrogance and conceit?"

Her laugh was self-deprecating, and she was aware that he knew it. "If I ever had any conceit, Willard Marsh promptly rid me of it while the words 'I do' were still warm from the heat of his breath."

"What is it that causes you to refer to him so often? Is it a sense of failure, is it hatred, or a way of reminding yourself to be…uh, more cautious?"

Lynne loved his voice, and when he spoke softly, as he did then, he gave her a warm, comfortable feeling and a desire to curl into him with his arms tight around her. "I haven't thought much about why I can't forget the horror of those years, although I realize that I hold myself responsible for staying with him when I knew the marriage was a farce. But I've stopped beating on myself about it."

She put her fork down and looked at him, for what she would say was as important as anything she had ever said to him. "Sloan, that weekend you spent taking care of me, including the way we kissed each other when you were leaving, confirmed for me that no man had ever loved me and that I had never loved a man."

He gulped loudly enough for her to hear it, and she could see his Adam's apple move rapidly. "And you still won't admit that we care for each other? That doesn't mean we're ready to swear eternal love, Lynne, but that we're there for each other. I'm not asking you not to see other men, but if I'm honest, I'll tell you that I'd rather you didn't. As for me, I can't imagine relating to any other woman. I told you what to expect the day we played tennis together?"

"You knew it then? You'd only met me three or four days earlier."

His laugh bore no mirth. "Really? I knew the day I met you that it would be a while, if ever, before I got you out of my blood. So don't tell me about how long it takes."

She got up from the table, took their dishes to the kitchen and prepared the dessert. Ice cream cones made of praline cookies. She set them in tall, slim tea glasses, put the glasses into colorful plates and took them to the table. "What kind of ice cream is this?"

"Praline-pecan. I think it's delicious, and I hope you concur."

She licked her tongue over it and looked up to find him gazing at her. What the heck! That was the way people ate ice cream, wasn't it? She savored it a second before allowing it to slide down her throat.

"Hmm. It *is* delicious."

"You are one sensuous woman. It's the most natural thing about you."

She heard what he didn't say, and her nerve ends fired up, sending rivulets of heat from her scalp to her toes. This time, she made certain not to catch his gaze, for she knew he could read her emotions. He surprised her when he suggested that they clean the kitchen together, and after they finished, he gave her another reason to gape at him.

"I haven't been to any affair given by the local chapter of the Howard University Alumni since I've been in San Antonio, but I'll go if you'll go with me. It's a fund-raiser for homeless children. Will you go with me?"

"Why, yes, I will. But why haven't you attended these functions before?"

He leaned against the wall in a lazy and relaxed manner, comfortable with himself and with the answer he would give. "I've never regarded such affairs as a social occasion, as many of my fellow alumni do. I mail a contribution, but I don't attend. I consider them humanitarian functions, not an occasion to show off wealth in designer clothes while donating a measly couple a hundred bucks to help the less fortunate, and I think you'd view it the same way."

She couldn't resist a laugh. "Sloan, I do not own any high-fashion designer clothes, and I never have. I belong to the look-good-for-less society. It's formal, right?"

"Yes, of course."

"When?"

"A week from Saturday. Black tie."

"I'll enjoy going with you." And she would. For six years, her recreation had consisted of after-morning-church-service coffee hours, annual church suppers and Christmas and Easter choir concerts. She enjoyed the concerts, but she hoped never to see another piece of bread pudding as long as she lived. She wouldn't buy an expensive designer's dress, but if this man was going to wear a tux, he could bet she'd dress to make him and a few other men look at least twice.

"Say, that's Saturday after the Fourth of July, which is on Thursday this year," she said. When his left eyebrow shot up, she added, "I'd planned to spend that weekend with my brother in Frederick, but I can come back here that Friday and see you on Saturday."

"Good. Thanks for the really delightful dinner. I'd... uh, better get going. It's getting late, and you have a rough day ahead."

"I'm glad you came. I don't think ice cream is on the list Max gave me, but I can cheat once in a while."

When he eased his arm around her and started for the front door, she rested her head against his shoulder as if she'd done that all of her life. As they reached the door, he said, "You may not realize it, but we made a lot of progress this afternoon and evening. I care for you. Do you think you can tell me that it's mutual?"

She didn't hesitate, for there was no point in lying

either by word or action. "Yes," she said, "I do care for you. Now, kiss me and…scat."

A grin began around his lower lip and slowly spread over his face, lighting his eyes and causing them to sparkle. "Yeah. I guess we'd better not build a fire tonight." And then, with lightning speed, she was in his arms, held tightly to his body, but when his lips touched hers, they were soft and gentle, sweet and tender, sending shock waves all through her.

"Good night, love," he said, then opened the door and was gone.

She watched from the window as he drove off. So he had punished his libido until he reached his limit, had he? If so, it suited her, because another passionate exchange with him might result in something neither of them seemed prepared for at the present time. She was more than reluctant to make love with him so early in their relationship, and she didn't doubt that he wouldn't want her unless she was both eager and willing.

"Our day will come," she said aloud. "If it doesn't, what a pity that would be."

They settled into a comfortable relationship, one fueled less by passion than by a growing understanding of and need for each other. Relaxed and, she had to admit, happier than she had ever been, her tennis game progressed faster than she or her coach had hoped.

"That bloom on your face has taken hold of your game," Gary told her one afternoon, when she sent three consecutive aces past him on the clay court.

"Thanks, but my ground strokes still seem too slow on this clay court."

"Not to worry. Your game is best suited to hard courts and grass. You know that. What I want you to do is lean your whole body into your shots. Power. Make every shot a power shot, and that requires concentration. Whoever the guy is, don't think about him when you're playing tennis. Got it? Now show me some line drives that cut the corners."

After making several points that way, without giving it a thought, she used a technique that had once been one of her specialties and, catching Gary flat-footed behind the baseline, she looped a drop shop right over the net.

He stood in the spot, his right hand on his hipbone, and looked hard at her. Then he began to laugh. "Right on, girl. That's just what you should have done. Your instincts are kicking in. If you continue this way, I'd like to enter you in a small tournament late this summer. What do you say?" The racquet fell from her hand, and when she bent to retrieve it, she dropped the ball. "A small tournament is nothing for you to be nervous about, Lynne."

"All r-right." That couldn't be her teeth chattering. "I'll play whenever you think I'm ready."

"That's what I like to hear." He glanced up toward the sky, and frowned. "Looks like rain. Feels like it, too, and I smell a thunderstorm coming up, so perhaps we'd better knock off for today. Close your windows, and take your dog inside. Those clouds are getting darker by the minute."

She skipped to the house and danced from one window to another, closing them as Gary suggested. She couldn't wait to tell Sloan that Gary wanted her to enter a tournament before summer's end. Bubbling with enthusiasm, she went outside to the deck to check on Caesar and was startled by his whimpers. Thinking that he might be ill, she telephoned Sloan and asked him what she should do.

"Take him inside. Dogs dislike thunderstorms, and he knows one is coming." After assuring Sloan that she had closed all of the windows in her house, she told him of Gary's plan for her.

"Congratulations. This is great news. Are you willing to play a match with me? I'd love to see what progress you've made. I'll bet we won't play to a tie this time."

"Don't be so sure. You're a good player." When Caesar's whimpers became louder and more persistent, she said, "Caesar's really agitated now. I'd better take him inside and call you back. Okay?"

"Okay, but if you call after the storm hits, use your cell phone. It doesn't conduct electricity. Okay? Kiss me?"

She made the sound of a kiss. "I'm not any more fond of these storms than Caesar is, so he and I will huddle together." She laughed, but she was far from amused.

"Want me to come keep you company?"

"I don't want you to drive in a bad storm. I'm not that scared. Bye."

She hung up, took Caesar into the den and settled him on the dog bed that she'd bought the previous week. From his facial expression, she'd swear that he offered humble thanks. "I hope this storm passes quickly," she said to the dog, "because I am not going to feed you here in the house."

She dialed Sloan's home phone number, but didn't get an answer. "Maybe the lines are already down," she said to herself, noting that the wind had strengthened considerably, and that although it was only six o'clock, outside it seemed almost as black as a moonless night. She found some candles, matches and a flashlight and put them on the table beside her chair, in the event that her house should lose power.

Caesar's growl startled her, and when he sprang up and barked, her nerves seemed to reassemble themselves. She patted him on the head and started toward the foyer and, to her surprise, he dashed ahead of her and waited at the door. She looked out of the window, saw the beige Buick Le Sabre parked in front of her house, rushed to the door and flung it open. However, when she opened her arms to him, he merely leaned down and kissed her cheek. She stepped back, her face blanked by an inquiring expression.

"Don't want to teach Caesar bad habits," he said as the dog wagged his tail in welcome.

But she wasn't placated. "What do you mean?"

"If he sees me hugging you, he may get the mistaken idea that it's all right for a man to put his arms around you, and he might fail to protect you from a guy out to harm you."

She sucked air through her front teeth. "My dog isn't stupid."

He showed his teeth in a devilish grin. "Maybe not, but I'm not taking chances. Dogs learn what their masters and mistresses teach them. Can I come in?"

With her hands fastened to her hips, she made an effort to glare at him, but he'd covered his face with a mask of innocence, and she soon joined him in the laughter that he had obviously struggled to contain.

"I won't ask if anybody's ever called you a smart-ass," she said, taking his hand and walking with him to the den. He was about to sit in the chair she had previously occupied when Caesar growled.

"What's with him?" he asked.

"He likes to lie beside my feet, and his bed's right beside that chair."

"Just as I expected. I'm taking a back seat to a dog." He sat in the Shaker rocker on the opposite side of the fireplace. "Come over here and sit on my knee. I want some recognition." She did and was rewarded with a warm and loving kiss, but when she moved away from him, she noticed that Caesar watched them intently.

She had forgotten the storm until a loud crack of thunder and a sharp flash of lightning reminded her. But it was the sudden sound of the wind howling with a fierce intensity that unsettled her, and made her doubly glad for Sloan's presence.

"I've never been in a hurricane," she said.

"This is just one of our summer storms. If it was a hurricane, we'd have had plenty of notice to board up the windows and store water and food supplies, maybe even go to a safe place."

"How long will it last? Caesar and I haven't had dinner. Have you?"

"It should be over in an hour at best, and then you can feed Caesar. You and I can go someplace nearby and eat. I wonder how Thelma's doing."

The thunder roared, and flash after flash of lightning lit up the room. "You don't know how glad I am that you're here," she said.

"I'll always be here for you when you need me. If you reach out to me, Lynne, I'll never let you down."

"What was that?" She almost screamed it. "It sounded like a bomb."

He went to the living room, looked out the window and turned to her. "That big crab apple tree split wide open. Did you close the garage door?" She nodded. "Thank goodness. I wish Thelma had given me a cell phone number—I'd like to call her. This is a bad storm." He brought the rocker and placed it beside the chair in which she sat, reached over, wrapped her hand in his and gently rocked. "Thunderstorms have always fascinated me. We think we're busy with a thousand things to do and not enough time to stop and live, to visit with a friend or to be a good neighbor, and then we get a bad electrical storm, and no matter what we were doing, we stop, become quiet and thoughtful. Maybe this is nature's way of bringing us to heel."

"But it's frightening, because it's out of our hands… we're at the mercy of the storm."

He shrugged. "Not really. We're always warned and given enough time to take precautions." He pushed back his sleeve and looked at his wristwatch. "It's been almost ten minutes since the last streak of lightning. Stay here. I'm going to dash over to Thelma's and see if she's all right."

"But—"

"Not to worry. I've lived with these Texas storms for thirty-six years. Be right back."

"At least take an umbrella."

"Wouldn't last a minute in this wind."

She couldn't ask him not to go, for he wouldn't appreciate it, and moreover, Thelma might need him. She watched as he sprinted across the street and down the road to Thelma's house, uneasy at the sight of fallen trees and broken tree limbs. "Lord, please don't let anything happen to him," she whispered.

He wiped the water from his face and pounded on the door. "Who is it?" the frail and unsteady voice demanded.

"Sloan McNeil. Are you all right?"

She flung open the door, and a draft literally sucked him inside. He closed the door as quickly as possible and looked down at the frightened woman.

"What's open?"

"The kitchen window's stuck, and I can't close it. My kitchen is a river. Thank God you came."

"Where's the kitchen? I was over at Lynne's, and you wouldn't get out of my head." He closed the window. "Do you have a mop and a bucket?"

"Thanks for closing the window. I don't want you to mop that up. I'll do it tomorrow."

He ignored her. "Give me the mop. It won't take me but a few minutes." When she hesitated, he found the broom and storage closet and got busy mopping up the water. "I wanted to telephone you, but talking on phones during an electrical storm is too risky. You need a cellular phone for occasions like this and in case of electricity failure."

"I guess you're right, but aren't they difficult to master?"

"No. Get one, and I'll teach you in two minutes."

"I will. I'll do it tomorrow. I don't have to tell you that I was scared to death. Who knows how long this thing will last?"

He emptied the water into the commode, put the bucket and mop back into the closet and looked at the tiny woman whose face had been chalk-white with fear. "The thunder and lightning has about passed, but there's no telling how long this rain will last. Do you have food essentials in the house?"

She grasped his hand. "I keep the place well stocked, so I'm not likely to run out of anything but fresh milk, and I can do without that. Can you sit down for a minute? I know you're wet, but the kitchen chair won't be uncomfortable, and we can take that to the living room."

The plaintiveness in her voice affected him strangely, bringing to his mind the thought that, if his parents were in need and he wasn't with them, hopefully someone would be kind to them.

He sat down, took out his cell phone and called Lynne on hers. "You don't know how glad I am that I came." He explained what he'd found. "She asked me to stay a minute, and I will for about half an hour. See you then." When she sent him a kiss, he relaxed. Another point in her favor.

"I made some drip coffee," Thelma said, "and I had just a little piece of pecan pie left, so I split it. You eat this and take this other little piece to Lynne."

He resisted hugging her because he wasn't sure their friendship had progressed that far. "Lynne and I are going out to dinner when this wind dies down. Want to come with us? We aren't going to a fancy place. We can't because even if I dry, my clothes will look as if I slept in them."

Her spoon clattered in the saucer. "You serious? You don't think Lynne would mind?"

He stifled a laugh and let the mirth surface as a grin. "Why should she mind? We're only going to eat."

She stared at him for a minute, and then whooped. "You're a wicked man, but I wouldn't exchange you for anything. Thanks. I'll be glad to enjoy a meal in good company." She rested the cup in its saucer and placed them on the table beside her. "I hadn't ever thought about this, Sloan, but it has just occurred to me how lucky I am that I'm not a bigot. If I hadn't gone over and introduced myself to Lynne, I wouldn't know you. In my heart, I feel that you're both a blessing to me."

"Maybe we're a blessing to each other. I'd better go. We'll let you know when we're ready to leave, and I'll come over for you."

"Don't you want an umbrella?"

"Thanks, but it would be a quarter of a mile from here almost as soon as I opened it. Not to worry. I'll be fine." He wasn't given to premonitions, but he'd surely had one about her. He wondered whether he was entering a new cycle of his life.

"You're soaked," Lynne told him when he walked into her house. "I think you'd better put on my old paisley robe while I put your clothes in the drier."

"Don't make jokes. It won't fit me."

"It will. It's a one-size-fits-all man's robe that once belonged to my brother. But I liked it so much that he gave it to me. Come on upstairs." He followed her, and when they reached the landing, she turned to him and said, "You can stay up here until your clothes dry."

He laughed. It spilled out of him like water gushing over a dam. "Why do I have to stay up here? I can be a gentleman downstairs, too."

She didn't look at him. "You can also keep such

thoughts to yourself. Here's the robe. I'll be back in a
minute to get your things. And will you please stop grinning?"

The scene embarrassed her, and that surprised him.
After all, she wasn't a teenager. "I'll put them beside
the door. Okay?"

"Uh-huh," she said, then left the room and closed
the door.

He liked the room, although he realized that she
hadn't furnished it. But surely that was her lavender-
peach silk cover on the bed. He undressed quickly. "I
don't see the advantage of wet shorts under dry pants,"
he said to himself, unwilling to let her dry his underwear. Besides, he didn't think it polite to give them to
her. He put his shirt and trousers outside, took a seat in
the flowered, chintz chair—he hated chintz—and waited
for her knock. When it came, he realized he had enjoyed
a short and peaceful nap.

"I was asleep," he told her when he came downstairs, dry and much more comfortable. He went into
the kitchen, got a piece of paper towel and wrapped his
Jockey shorts in it.

The rain and wind slackened around seven o'clock and
he telephoned Thelma. "We're ready, if you are," he said.

"I'm ready. This is exciting. I haven't had a dinner
invitation in so long I forgot the last time."

He waited while Lynne fed Caesar and put him in his
house. "He knows where he lives now, so I think you can
leave his door open. He won't stray."

He drove up the street to Thelma's house, parked and
knocked on her door. She opened it at once, as if she had
been waiting beside it. "You look lovely," he said of her
beige and white checkered linen dress.

"Thank you. I won't ask how you got dry," she drawled.

He realized that he liked her brand of humor, told her as much and added, "She locked me in the room while she dried them, and since I was practically handcuffed, I caught up on my sleep."

They strolled down the cobblestone walk from her house to the car. "I knew she was smart. Nothing like the power of suggestion to get a woman into trouble. A man, too, maybe, but I can only speak from experience."

What an enjoyable woman! When he was with her, he didn't remember her age unless he was looking at her. He opened the back door, helped her into the car and fastened her seat belt. They ate at a roadside restaurant, and although he'd had better food, he enjoyed the occasion.

"Next time, we'll do this at my house," Lynne said.

"Well, if you have time," Thelma said. "With your coach planning to start you in tournaments, you might not have much time for a social life, and if you don't, I'll understand."

The comment reminded him that she might not have time for him, either, but he knew that if she wanted to see him and spend time with him, she would find a way. He walked with Thelma to her door, opened it, kissed her cheek and went back to the woman who lived inside of him.

"I'm not going inside," he told her, "because I have to finish working out my payroll before I sleep. A couple of the men are due for a raise. I intend to promote one of them to manager of the station I'll build in Clinton Hills. If I go inside with you, there's no telling when I'll come out of there."

She reached over and tweaked his nose. "Don't let

when you'll leave worry you—concern yourself with getting home *after* you leave me."

"Now wait a minute here!"

She threw up both hands. "Don't get riled. No offense intended. What I said makes sense. I'll see that you leave here, and your job is to drive home carefully."

"Sorry. After an evening of matching wits with Thelma, I guess I'm keyed up." He took her key and opened the door. "Give me a kiss, and please don't pour it on."

"Okay. I won't." She stepped close, pressed her body—her soft, luscious body—to him, and the minute he put his hands on her, he could feel the tension in her breasts, arms and belly as she rocked into him. Without counting the cost, his hands went to her buttocks, the rounded, soft and sexy part of her that made him think all kind of things, and he pressed her to him.

My Lord, he thought, *I haven't even kissed her, and I'm about to explode.* He backed away sufficiently to get a grip on his libido. "I'll see you in a couple of days but, in the meantime, I'll call you, and you can call me."

"You didn't kiss me," she said, and he realized that it was a serious complaint.

"I asked you not to pour it on but you waded into me, and in less than two minutes, I was ready to break out of my skin."

"Sorry, but you invite that kind of behavior on my part."

"Yeah," he growled, grabbed her and spread kisses over her face, neck and ears. *No more,* he thought. *If I get my tongue in her mouth, I won't leave here tonight.* She hugged him and pushed him toward the door. "Bye, love."

After he left, she wandered around the house, tidying the den, dusting the living room, washing Caesar's food containers and strolling aimlessly from one place to another. Finally, with nothing else to occupy her time, she telephoned her brother. "Gary wants to enter me in the Western Tournament in Cincinnati, July 18. He says I'm making great progress."

"Sure. You're paying him to say that. Why're you going into such a small tournament?"

"Davenport's the reigning champion. If it isn't too small for her, it isn't too small for me."

"Well. All right, but I think the whole thing's crazy. I don't want you to be disappointed, sis."

"Brad, I want you to understand that I'm going to make it to the top, and I'm giving myself two years in which to do it."

"What did Tom Breckenridge say about the house?"

"He said if the title is clear, I should buy it, and I will. After the closing, I'll start collecting furniture, and I'm going to put in a swimming pool. This is hot country."

"Swimming pool's a good idea. By the way, has your boyfriend stopped greasing cars?"

She bristled at that. "Brad, for goodness' sake, don't be so disrespectful. You don't know Sloan. And no, I haven't mentioned it to him."

"You'll be sorry if you don't. Mark my word. Are you going to ask him? It's a little thing to do for you if he cares about you."

"Yes, I'll ask him, but the idea doesn't sit too well with me."

"Trust me. I know what I'm talking about."

"I'll see you this weekend, and we'll talk."

After a restful night, she rose early, fed Caesar,

hooked his leash to his collar and by seven o'clock she headed up the street with him, deciding to combine her jogging with Caesar's morning walk, much to the dog's delight. He didn't dally among the shrubs and flowers, as he did when they walked, but seemed to relish the brisk run. Back home by seven-thirty, she ate a breakfast of orange juice, oatmeal and coffee, and prepared herself mentally for her trial with Max as she walked around the property, deciding where to put her swimming pool and cabana.

"I'm on my way," she said to herself and had begun to practice deep breathing when Max drove up in his red convertible and sauntered toward her.

"You're not supposed to do that unless I'm here to make sure you do it right," he said, and for the first time, she realized that scolding her was his method of control.

"Are you saying the only time I should breathe is when you're looking at me?" she asked him, though she knew the question would irritate him.

"You're too smart for your own good. Two years from now, you'll still be number three hundred on the tour. I'm wasting my time."

"Really? How inconsiderate of me! I suggest that beginning this minute, you not waste any more of it. How much do I owe you?"

His face was ashen suddenly, and his knees seemed to nearly buckle. He'd overplayed his hand, and he knew it. "Oh, come on, Lynne, you and I have these…uh, settos all the time. What's the problem?"

"You are. And I'm fed up with you. How much do I owe you?"

He glowered at her. "You think you're hot stuff because you got Gary Hines for a coach. Well, you're not.

You're a has-been, and that's all you'll ever be. I'll send you a bill."

"Thanks. And don't forget that I can multiply and add."

"These heifers make me sick," she heard him say as he headed for his car.

She phoned Gary and gave him an account of the incident. "You fired Max?" he asked in a tone of bewilderment. "Really?" Then he laughed. "He must be in shock. The guy treats the players like dirt, and his clients accept it from him because he's supposed to be the best. Bully for you."

"Thanks," she said. "I think Max's main problem is that he doesn't like women."

"That's for sure. I think Clive Roberts is free, and he's about as good as Max. I'll call him. See you at eleven."

She didn't usually telephone Sloan before noon, because he took emergency calls during that period, so she called Thelma and invited her over for coffee. "This is a hoot," she said to herself. "My closest female friend is seventy-five if she's a day." She thought about that for a minute and concluded that she enjoyed the woman's company, age notwithstanding.

"I'll be right over," Thelma said. "I just made some scones, and they're still hot."

She made the coffee, set the table on the deck, cut a cantaloupe and gave each of them half. Minutes later, Thelma rang the doorbell. "I hope you're planning to marry Sloan," she said without preliminaries. "He's about the nicest, most considerate and most decent man I ever got to know. If you let him slip through your fingers, you will live to regret it. That kind of man is hard to find."

Lynne blinked at her. "I only met him three months ago."

"So? I knew my dear Lloyd exactly six weeks before we married, and we lived together happily for fifty-one years. I thanked God for him every day of those fifty-one years. You'd better wake up. You hear me?"

"Yes, ma'am. I hear you."

"What're you going to do about it?"

"Uh…I'll think of something," she said, barely aware of her words.

Chapter 5

Thursday morning, July 3, Lynne flew to Baltimore and, because both her brother and her sister-in-law were at work, traveled the fifteen miles to Ellicott City by airport shuttle bus. She let herself into the house, called her brother and then undressed and crawled into bed, but she couldn't sleep.

Thelma's words lashed at her. Was she so immature that she didn't understand her feelings for a man? She adored Sloan, but was that the same as caring for him, the kind of caring that developed into love? Admittedly she was happier with him than she remembered being at any time in her life, and until he had her in his arms, she hadn't known what it was to need a man; she'd only thought she did. He'd said he was patient, and he was. She wasn't ready for sex with him, and he didn't pressure her. Thelma said a man like him was hard to find, and she believed her. But what was she to do? If she fell in love with Sloan, her thoughts would be on him, and not on her goal. She didn't see the fairness in it, if indeed there was any. She suspected that, if Sloan walked out of her life, she'd be too depressed to focus on her tennis game. *I'm damned if I do and damned if I don't.*

Lynne sat up in bed, stunned, as realization hit her. Was she reluctant to make love with Sloan because she had never succeeded at it? Because six years of disappointments with her husband had conditioned her to a life without sexual fulfillment?

She got up, put on a blue knee-skimming sundress and her espadrilles, went out on the back porch and sat in the swing. She'd been cheated in more ways than one, and one of these days, she would confront Willard Marsh with his inadequacies. And Lord, how she was going to enjoy that moment!

"Hey, girl," Debra called from the hall as she headed for the back porch. "I got stuff for a barbecue or a boring ordinary meal. Which do you prefer for dinner tonight?" Debra seldom provided preliminaries to any action or question. She seemed to assume that you followed her thinking, whatever that was. The only woman she knew who wore gloves and a hat as a fashion statement; not even the debilitating heat deigned to wilt Debra Thurston, who always looked as if she had just finished dressing. Lynne listened to the clicking of her sister-in-law's spike heels on the beige tile hallway and shuddered at the thought of what they did to the woman's feet. Still, she had to admit that Debra—tall, willowy and always elegant—was perfect for Brad.

"Don't you barbecue tomorrow, July Fourth?" she asked Debra.

"Good heavens, no. Brad will be up before daylight to go fishing in the Patapsco River, which means we'll have some good old catfish fried right over the fire in a black skillet, corn and potatoes wrapped in foil and roasted on the grill and I'll cook down some collards with smoked pig knuckles. Naturally we'll have blueberries or blueberry cobbler for dessert. You know, this is the blueberry season. Honey, tomorrow we'll get down with some serious eating."

She tossed her hat onto the chaise nearby, pulled off her white gloves, sat down beside Lynne, crossed her knees and, in a conspiratorial tone, said, "Now, tell me about this mechanic before Brad gets here. You know how he can be. For some reason, he's decided the man is worthless."

With a deep sigh, Lynne turned and looked straight at her sister-in law. "Sloan McNeil holds a master's degree in mechanical engineering from Howard University. He owns McNeil's Motor Service, and he's planning to open a second station in a matter of months. He is a kind, gracious and considerate man, and I am getting tired of Brad's nastiness about a man he doesn't know and has never seen."

"Seems you like him a lot."

"You bet I do, and I have no reason to apologize for it. If Brad ever meets Sloan with the attitude he has now, he's subject to get the surprise of his life."

"Hmm. What does he look like? Do you have a picture?"

Lynne let a shrug indicate what she thought of that question. "No, I don't. He's about six feet five inches tall, well proportioned, fair complexion about the color of shelled pecans, light brown eyes, and what eyes. The man is stunningly good-looking. In terms of personality and behavior, he's everything Willard isn't."

"A charmer, eh?"

"Not to me," she said with her head higher and her tone haughty.

"Well 'scuse me," Debra said. "Don't let Brad discourage you. After what you went through, you deserve a man who makes you laugh."

"And he does that, all the time."

"Where's everybody?"

Debra glanced at Lynne. "Oh-oh. Out here on the porch, honey. I was just telling Lynne how you like to go fishing on July Fourth."

Her tall and handsome brother walked out onto the porch, dropped his Louis Vuitton briefcase by the door and opened his arms to her for a big hug. "My baby sis is looking great." He stepped back and observed her closely. "Hmm. Looks like all that exercise you're getting is putting a glow on you. Hope you had a good nap. How was your flight?"

She sat back in the swing, crossed her knees and prepared for Brad's onslaught. Whether it was a disarming mechanism he'd developed as an attorney, she didn't know, but he usually engaged in senseless banalities and small talk just before he aimed for the jugular, as if that was his way of throwing his adversary off guard. She decided to preempt the attack.

"What's your point, Brad? If I'm glowing, I must be getting a fever. My physical training sessions have made me more supple, caused me a lot of pain and pulled me into shape. Period."

"Hey, wait a minute. Somebody jerk your chain?"

"I was merely beating you to the draw."

"Look, everybody can tell when a woman gets a new…er…love interest, misguided or not. By the way—" Here it comes, she thought, and he didn't disappoint her. "Did you speak to him yet about running his business from his office? If he's a Howard grad, it would suit him a hell of a lot better than fooling around beneath automobiles."

Brad enjoyed talking to her as if she were a teenager. He knew everything better and let her know it. She had always accepted his assumption that, being three years older and a man, he was better informed than she. Perhaps it was the way that Sloan treated her, his respect for her opinions and ideas that gave her the courage to stand up to Brad. Or maybe it was the strength she gained when she sued the reverend Willard Marsh for a divorce and won. Whatever. She'd found her tongue and she meant to use it.

"Brad, the next time you mention that to me while I'm here these two days, I'll start packing."

He raised his hands as if in surrender. "All right. All right. I'll shut up, but—"

"I meant what I said, Brad."

His shoulders slumped in defeat, and he walked over to his wife and kissed her. "What are we doing for dinner, babe?"

The short visit ended quickly, for which she was grateful. The current of tension between her brother and herself banished the warmth and camaraderie that usually attended their times together.

"I'm sorry Brad had to spoil your visit," Debra said to Lynne as they cleaned the kitchen that Friday night. "I guess you know he was waiting for the opportunity to tell you what he thought of your friendship with a mechanic. I tried to talk some sense into him, but he wouldn't hear it. He doesn't want you involved with a man who is a laborer. You're the one living your life. If I was in your place, I'd ignore Brad."

"The problem is that he's frequently right," Lynne said, "but I think I should go with my feelings."

"Well, I'm not going to make the same mistake as Brad. You have to decide for yourself. When will you see Sloan again?"

"Tomorrow night. He invited me to go to the local Howard University alumni club dance with him."

"Go for broke, honey. If the guy's as good-looking as you say, look your best, because every woman there— married or single—will be able to see the same thing you can see, and they will look."

That Saturday morning, Brad drove her to Baltimore to get a seven o'clock flight to San Antonio. It seemed as if years had passed since she saw Sloan, although it had only been three days. "Something's happening to me," she said to herself, "and I'd better be careful."

"Why so quiet?" he asked as they neared the airport. "You and I were always able to communicate, but you're in a world of your own these days."

"Do you realize that you never once tried to dissuade me from getting involved with Willard and marrying him? Not once. He made me miserable for six intermin-able years. I've been happier in Sloan's company than I ever remember being, and I'm the only person who can make up my mind about him. Do you understand?"

"You're telling me that if you have to choose, it's this guy over your blood brother?"

Her gaze took in his Gucci loafers and moved up to the gold Rolex watch on his wrist. Of course he wouldn't understand her affection for a man who repaired auto-mobiles. "It's not you or him, Brad. It's my decision to run my life as I see fit, and after six years of having somebody tell me I can't wear any color underwear but white, I'm going to enjoy the freedom to do as I please."

"All right. But remember what I said. You'll be happier with him if he's got an office job, because he'll feel better about himself. My last word on the subject…for now."

She walked into her house at eleven-thirty that morning, went out on the deck and remembered that Caesar was with Sloan. "I guess I'll go jogging by myself," she said, having become accustomed to running with her dog. After the five-mile run, she took her mobile phone from the table in the foyer, threw off her clothes and shoes and stretched out on the chaise longue on her deck. With the warm breeze refreshing her, she let her naked pores breathe in the invigorating air.

"When I have my pool, I'm going to fence in this place and swim nude," she said to herself, thinking how shocked Willard would be if he saw her right then.

The ringing of the telephone interrupted her dozing. "Hello."

"Were you asleep? What happened to you? I waited in the terminal for an hour and a half after the plane landed. Didn't you check luggage?"

"Sloan! I was half asleep. I never check luggage if I can avoid it. I went directly to the taxi stand. Honey, I'm sorry I missed you. Thank you so much for making the effort." As if he could see her, she crossed her legs and covered her breasts with her left arm.

"Did you think I wouldn't meet you?"

"I guess I just didn't think. Am I forgiven?"

"I'll think about it." Would there ever come a time when his voice didn't make her tingle all over? "Want me to bring Caesar when I come for you this evening?"

"Yes, if you don't mind. I miss him."

"I'll see you at seven-thirty."

No point in trying to sleep. She went upstairs, checked her melon-red evening gown for imperfections and examined her black silk shoes and bag and rolled up her hair to give it shape, as she planned to wear it down around her shoulders. The day passed so slowly. For lunch, she managed, by forcing them down, to consume four shrimp, two lettuce leaves and a handful of cherry tomatoes. She measured the living room windows for blinds and forgot to record the measurements, made a list of the changes she wanted in her kitchen and lost the paper. Disgusted, she attempted to contact a painter for an estimate, remembered that the day was Saturday and gave up after the phone rang half a dozen times.

Five-thirty finally came, and she took a leisurely bubble bath. After drying off, she pampered her skin with Fendi lotion, slipped on red bikini panties, red garters and sheer off-black stockings and enjoyed the wickedness she felt. At six-fifteen, she combed out her hair, applied Fendi perfume where it counted, stepped into the sleek, figure-flattering red dress and zipped it. After slipping into her shoes, she put on her diamond earrings, the only extravagant purchase she made during her former tennis successes, grabbed a black lace stole and reached the bottom of the stairs as the doorbell rang.

When she opened the door, his eyes widened. "You look… Hi." His arms opened, and she walked into them making room with her own to clasp him in her embrace.

"You're so beautiful," he said, "and I can't even kiss you."

"Just look at you. I can't kiss you, either. All you need is for me to get powder or lipstick on this white tuxedo. My! What a figure you make in it. Where's Caesar?"

"I decided not to bring him. He's not as considerate as I am. The minute you opened the door, he would have been all over you, and your dress would be a mess."

That hadn't occurred to her. "Thanks. I hadn't thought of that. Can you bring him tomorrow?" The look of surprise on his face told her much, and it occurred to her that he might not have planned to return to San Antonio after bringing her home.

He handed her a bunch of purple and yellow calla lilies, and without thinking, she reached up and kissed his cheek. "Oh, dear, let me get that lipstick off you."

His eyes sparkled with lights. "How do you know I don't want all those guys at the reception to know you kissed me?"

She looked at him from beneath lowered lashes. "In that case, maybe I should kiss your mouth so they'll see that I know how to do it properly."

When his bottom lip curved into a devilish grin, she expected an example of his piercing wit, but he said, "It's enough that *I* know it."

She put the flowers in water, turned off the lights and handed him her key. As they strolled together down the cobblestone walk to his car, she wondered if she was living in dreamland. The willow trees facing her house swayed in the breeze, fireflies danced as they blinked on her lawn and even the yellow dandelions that peeped up from between the stones of her walkway appeared to her as flowers and not weeds. She looked up at the blanket of stars that twinkled around the moon, so bright and arrogant in its majesty. Unaware that she squeezed Sloan's hand, she missed a step when his arm went around her. As they reached his car, he paused. "It's breathtaking, isn't it?"

"I've never known a night like this," she said. And she hadn't, for she had never looked and felt as she did then in the company of a man like Sloan McNeil, a man capable of turning any woman's head. "I even missed my high school prom because I had what they called 'the grip.' And this night… It's so perfect."

Forty minutes later, he handed his car keys to the bellboy at the Hyatt Regency Hotel situated on the River Walk, took her hand and walked with her into the hotel and on to its grand ballroom. He presented their tickets at the door, and as he walked with Lynne into the glittering room he gave thanks for his foresight in straightening things out with Vickie Moore as soon as he realized he wanted Lynne. In a black sequined gown and alone, Vickie strolled toward them.

"Hello, Sloan," she said. "How nice to see you. Perfect as usual."

From the corner of his eye, he saw that Lynne watched him, and he allowed himself a broad smile. "How are you, Vickie. This is Lynne Thurston. Lynne, this is Victoria Moore. I spoke to you about her, though I didn't identify her."

That ought to set things straight here. I'm not going to allow anything to spoil my first real date with Lynne. I want this evening to remain perfect for her.

Lynne extended her hand to the woman, her face radiant with a smile. "How are you, Vickie? I'm glad to meet you."

"I'm fine," Vickie said. "Sloan didn't tell me about you, only that there was a *you*. The alumni gala is one of my favorite social occasions. I hope you both enjoy the evening. It was good to see you, Sloan. Goodbye."

He told her goodbye and marveled at the way in which she carried off her obvious disappointment. Obvious to him, at least.

"She's a gracious woman," Lynne said.

"She has no reason to be otherwise. We had a lot of fun together, but I never led her to believe that anything would develop between us. As I told you, we were never lovers, or even close to it."

"But she wanted it." It wasn't a question, but a statement of fact.

"So she said when I told her goodbye."

"I wouldn't be that sanguine about it."

Her back was bare almost down to the curve of her hips, giving him plenty of room in which to press his hand to her naked flesh and he did so with relish. "I didn't go as far with her as I've gone with you."

"Sloan, you're not playing fair right now."

He rubbed her back, though not enough for an on-looker to realize what he was doing. "Where do you want me to put my hand? If I put it on the back of your *dress,* I'll disgrace you, so—"

She interrupted him. "When I get even, I do it with a vengeance. You watch."

He imagined the danger of laughing at her, so he con-trolled as much of the laughter as he could, and let it spill out in a big grin. "I have to claim rights. Here comes a brother ready to horn in on my territory right now." He could see her priming herself to get some of her own, but he didn't plan to let it happen.

"It's been a while, Jacques," he said, extending his hand to the man. "How are you, and how's Melanie? Haven't seen her for ages." He nearly collapsed in laughter as the man seemed to shrink as a balloon shrivels when the air seeps out of it.

"Uh, Melanie's good. Who's…uh…this American beauty rose you've got here?"

"The lady is Miss Lynne Thurston. I heard you'd gone monogamous, and that you and Melanie moved in together."

"How'd you know? Man, news sure travels fast. That happened last week." He wanted Jacques to move on so that he could introduce Lynne to a couple of his friends.

"Well, nice running into you, man," he said. "See you around."

She pinched his arm. "You brushed him off."

"You bet I did. You were just about to begin your vengeance, and he's one guy who wouldn't let you get away with playing up to him. Jacques is not a man of principle. He's living with Melanie, but he'd date you tomorrow if he got a chance. Let's find our table."

"Sloan McNeil! It's great to see you, man. I always wondered why you never came to any of the alumni gatherings. I'm down here in San Antonio because my bride-to-be is from around here, and her cousin, Magnus Cooper, invited me to his annual gala. Come, I'll introduce you. This is Pamela Langford. Pamela, meet a classmate and good friend, Sloan McNeil."

"Hello, Pamela. I'm delighted to meet the woman who brought Drake Harrington to heel. Pamela and Drake, this is Lynne Thurston." He knew his arm draped around her in a gesture of possessiveness, but what the heck! If she wasn't his then, she soon would be.

"What a pleasure," she said, extending her hand first to Pamela and then to Drake. "I wish you both as much happiness as a human being can bear." Her comment brought a laugh from both Drake and Pamela, and they thanked her in unison. They made plans to meet after the reception, and Sloan continued to his table.

"They are a good-looking couple," Lynne said. "I liked them at once."

"Drake's got the charm to sell saltwater to ocean fishermen, but he's a serious man, and I hear he's very successful as an architectural engineer."

"I'm glad to hear it," she said. "It would be a pity if a man with his looks and presence was trifling."

"He certainly isn't that. Here's our table. I apologize if the menu consists of mashed potatoes, peas, chicken à la king and either chocolate or coconut cake. We have to remember that this is a fund-raiser."

She looked around at the women who helped support the French, Italian and American fashion designers in a style to which the women themselves couldn't even aspire and, as if he read her thoughts, Sloan said, "You put most of the women here to shame. Lady, you are one elegant woman."

She blinked back a tear. "What is it? What's the matter?" he asked her, leaning forward and grasping her hand.

"Nothing's wrong. It's just…so wonderful to be complimented rather than berated."

He leaned closer and spoke to her ear. "I like everything about you, and every time I'm with you, I'm more impressed with the kind of person you are. And if we were alone, I'd have you in my arms this minute."

She bit her lip to stop its trembling. "And that's where I'd want to be." She looked away from him so that he couldn't read her thoughts. If they were alone in her house, she wouldn't let him leave there without making love with her.

"Look at me." She dragged her gaze to his face, aware that her own reflected the desire that churned within her, and stared into his dark and fiery mesmerizing eyes. Eyes that burned with hot desire. He swallowed again and again as if trying to rid himself of an unwanted taste.

"Sloan, I want you to meet my wife," a voice to his left said.

Saved from the passion that threatened to engulf him, he turned to the man. "Bill Jones. I'm glad to see you."

"Me, too, man. It's been a while. I'm club president now, and I'd love for you to attend the meetings. We need some sensible voices."

"I'll give it some thought. Thanks for seating me at the head table. This is Lynne Thurston."

"Glad to meet you, Ms. Thurston. Encourage him to be active in—" His head snapped around toward Sloan. "Did you say Lynne Thurston? Not the tennis player!"

"Former tennis player," Lynne said. "I'm happy to meet you."

"Our chaplain will now lead us in saying the grace," a voice intoned over the microphone, and a hush fell over the large crowd. The chaplain said the brief prayer, and immediately, the waiters began serving the food.

"Chicken à la king must be out of style," Bill said, "or maybe we just got lucky. Give me roast beef any day."

"It isn't roast beef," Bill's wife said. "It's filet mignon."

"So what," Bill said with a hint of impatience in his voice. "It's still beef."

"The difference between roast beef and filet mignon is like the difference between a Chevrolet and a Rolls-Royce," she insisted, "and you of all people should know that."

"I don't give a damn as long as it's edible," he said. "Now, cut the racket and eat."

"I won't have you talking to me this way in front of people," the woman said. At that point, Lynne tuned them out, but when she let herself look toward Sloan, she saw that he had stopped eating.

"Don't let it bother you," she whispered.

"Conflict is something that I have no tolerance for. If you ever want to disagree with me about anything, tell me you want to discuss it, and we will. But I can't stand bickering."

It seemed to her that most of the affair bored Sloan, or perhaps the argument between Bill and his wife had ruined the occasion. She hoped not, because he had seemed so happy when they arrived.

"Are we meeting Drake and Pamela?" she asked him as he thanked Bill again and stood to leave.

"Yes. I'll stop by their table."

"We want you and Lynne to come to our wedding September 10," Pamela said. She handed Sloan a small card. "Please write your address and phone number here."

He complied. "Wouldn't miss it." He patted Drake's shoulder. "You've chosen a real winner, man."

Drake's face seemed to bloom in a charismatic grin.

"You're traveling first class yourself, brother. See you in September."

As they said their goodbyes, she wondered how the Howard University women handled the presence of Drake Harrington and Sloan McNeil. More handsome men she hadn't seen. No wonder they were friends; they needed each other for company.

A man approached wearing a black tuxedo, black shirt and black tie, and he wore a diamond stud in his right earlobe. Although he was a bigger man, he reminded her of Max. Max. Her right hand flew to her mouth.

"What's wrong?" Sloan asked her. "Did you forget something?"

She had, indeed. "I can't believe I never told you that I fired Max two days before I left for Ellicott City."

He stopped walking and stared down at her. "You fired him? And you didn't tell me?"

"I had a reason for not calling you that morning right after I... Oh, yes. I make it a point not to call you during mornings because I know you may be busy, and when we talked that night, I was focused on going to Ellicott City."

"I see. Well, good riddance. When will you get another one?"

"Gary got Clive Roberts for me, and we start Monday morning."

"That's a good choice. If I remember well, Roberts is reputed to be a gentleman."

She could see that he was not pleased, and she appreciated his not making an issue of it. Yet, although he held her hand as they waited for the bellhop to bring his car, she sensed that by forgetting to tell him that she fired Max, a step so important to her, she had hurt him.

The oneness she felt with him when they arrived at the gala was missing.

"Want to come in?" she asked him after he opened her door.

Without answering, he walked in with her, but stood near the door. "Sloan, please don't read anything into my lapse in not telling you about Max. After it happened, you were the first person I thought of. I even asked myself when you became more important to me than my brother, who I have always looked up to and almost worshiped. I can see that we've lost what we had earlier this evening."

"You said you care for me. Do you or don't you? And if you do, I come first with you as you come first with me."

She caught herself rubbing her arms as if they were cold, and inside of her, she was cold.

"Lynne, do you want my arms around you?"

"Yes. Oh, yes!"

He picked her up, carried her into the living room and sat with her in his lap. "This evening isn't going to end as I had hoped it would," he said, "because I'm doing more thinking than feeling. No woman has ever meant as much to me as you do. Don't forget that."

So he had intended for them to make love. Her disappointment shocked her, for she hadn't realized that she was ready to cross that threshold. When she said, "You're precious to me," he held her away from him and, in the dimly lighted room let her see in his eyes all that he felt for her.

"I'd better go now. I'll bring Caesar tomorrow evening, and perhaps…" He paused. "We'll take it from there."

She brushed his lips with her own, but didn't part her lips, for she understood him well enough now to know that he wasn't in the mood for romance. Sloan McNeil was not pretentious. At the door with his hands stuffed in his pockets, he looked down at her. "It's just as well that I get to bed early. Bill and Gerald were both off today, and I had almost more calls than I could handle, plus the work that came into the station."

Without thinking it over first, she said, "Why don't you give up that work, let the men do it and you take care of the business from your office. I mean, life would be so much easier and—"

"You mean I should work in the office, keeping books and that sort of thing, and let my employees do the dirty work?"

"Yes, and that way, you won't be tired, and you'll feel better about yourself," she said, parroting Brad and happy that Sloan understood her.

His eyes, suddenly cold and penetrating, seemed to dissect her. He put one hand on the doorknob and saluted her with the other one. "See you around."

Her bottom lip dropped as she watched, transfixed, when he stepped out of the door and, she realized, out of her life. *What have I done?* With her head back and her face toward the ceiling, she wrapped her arms around her waist and groped through the darkness to the living room, where she fell onto the sofa and cried tearless tears until her body's every muscle ached and her heart seemed to settle at the bottom of her belly.

He warned me that he and his work were one, that he enjoyed what he did and was good at it. How could I have been so wrong?

She went up the stairs to her bedroom, took off the

dress and threw it across the chintz boudoir chair. She hated chintz and stopped her foot just before it collided with the offensive furniture. She had never looked as beautiful as she did that night, but if she never saw the dress again, she wouldn't care. With effort, she dragged herself to the bathroom, washed her face and then crawled into bed. She didn't expect to sleep and, at daybreak, she was still awake.

Sloan walked with heavy steps to his car, got into it and headed home. He hadn't glanced back, because he never looked back. Another woman who saw him as a grease monkey, who liked him in a tuxedo, but couldn't stand the idea of having a man who got his hands dirty when he worked. He wanted nothing to do with a woman who wasn't proud of him, who was only satisfied with the way he looked. As far as he was concerned, she was history. He didn't underestimate what he was up against because he loved her, and he knew it would hurt, but damned if he was going to let it kill him.

Now what? As he entered his house, he remembered that he still had Caesar, and that meant he had to see her again. With a shrug, he shook off the implications of that. After checking on the dog, who he had leashed on his back porch, he undressed, went to bed and to sleep.

That Sunday morning was unlike any he'd spent in the past three months. He looked forward to nothing, not even to a phone call. As he sat on his porch eating a breakfast of cantaloupe, cold cereal and coffee, it occurred to him that the beauty of his surroundings left him unmoved, that the sound of birds chirping seemed less joyful, and that the feel of the early morning breeze on his bare skin failed to invigorate him. He didn't open the service station on Sundays, but he wished he had some grueling work to distract him. He didn't want to think of Lynne and of what could have been.

After breakfast, he put his dishes in the dishwasher, donned a pair of jeans, a shirt and a McNeil jacket and took Caesar for a walk, though the dog indicated a preference for running. "You're going home, buddy. I don't need you around to remind me of her."

He procrastinated for roughly an hour and then he telephoned Lynne. "Hello, Lynne. This is Sloan." He heard the catch in her breath, but he wasn't going to respond to that or any other indication that she might have regrets. "If you'll be at home around one today, I'll bring Caesar home."

Her voice seemed small and uncertain, but he closed his mind and his heart. "I'll be here."

"See you then," he said, and hung up. He couldn't do better, because he was not a liar, and he had no intention of pretending what he didn't feel.

He hung up and called Thelma. "This is Sloan. If you'll be home around one, I'll fix your kitchen window so you can close it the next time there's a storm."

"Oh, Sloan. God bless you. I'll be here."

Caesar enjoyed riding in the front seat of the Buick LeSabre, but he didn't like being strapped in. "Sorry, buddy, but any being—human or otherwise—who rides up here with me wears this strap, and you are not an exception." As if he understood, the dog settled down and allowed the offense.

He headed up the walk to Lynne's house with Caesar straining at the leash, wagging his tail and barking as if with joy. Almost as soon as he rang the doorbell, she opened the door and gazed up at him with a look of expectancy on her that sent his heart into a tumble.

"He's been fed, and he had his morning walk," he said, without preliminaries, and handed her the leash.

"Thanks. Uh...won't you come in?"

He stared down into her large, luminous eyes and saw the pain reflected in them, but he didn't allow it to move him. "No, thanks. Be seeing you."

He hurried down the steps out of the way of temptation, strode down the walkway to his car and got into it feeling that he had just escaped something more powerful than he. He drove to the end of the block, parked and went to Thelma's house. Pity stole over him when the old woman opened the door before he reached the house, for she had been waiting for what was probably her only guest since he was last in her house.

"You're a dear," she said. "I haven't opened that window since you closed it."

"This may take a while," he told her, "so you get comfortable somewhere and let me see what I can do with it." He dropped his bag of tools on the floor beneath the window and got busy. Seeing that it was hung crooked, he removed it and rehung it.

"Can you come here?" he called to her. The tiny woman appeared, her face all smiles, and looked up at him. "See if you can raise it now."

She did and it went up with ease. "What did you do to it?"

"It was crooked. When it gets wet or the humidity is high, wood tends to swell. I took the window out and hung it properly. You won't have any problems with it now."

"You don't know how grateful I am, Sloan. You go in

the bathroom there and wash your hands. I've got something nice for you."

"Yes, ma'am. You couldn't have picked a better time. I can use some pampering."

"Hmm." An inquiring expression flashed over her face, and she patted his arm. "Go ahead. I'll be in the living room. Sit over here in front of the coffee table," she said when he walked into the living room. "It's nice and fresh." She cut a wedge of the pie and served it to him on what he recognized as her best porcelain and poured coffee into a matching cup. "If you'd rather have iced tea, I have some made."

"This is perfect, Thelma. I don't have to tell you what I think of this pie."

Her smile rewarded his graciousness. "Now you tell me why you need pampering from an old woman like me. Aren't you going back to Lynne's place when you leave here?"

He shook his head, chewed the pie and swallowed it. "Hadn't planned to."

"But you didn't stay there more than a minute. What's going on?"

"It isn't going to work, Thelma, and I'm glad I know it now."

"Now look, the two of you are in love with each other. I could actually feel it. What the devil happened?"

"It's simple. I'm not what she thought, and—"

She interrupted him. "And she's not what you thought. Hogwash!! You had a misunderstanding, and one of you's not willing to forgive." She looked straight at him, and he didn't duck her perusal. "Or—" she waved her fork at him "—she did something you don't like, and you're not willing to forgive her or even to discuss it. So don't tell me you aren't what she thought you were. There isn't a thing wrong with you that less stubbornness wouldn't cure. I'm right and you know it."

Sloan ate the last piece of pie on his plate, sipped his coffee a few times and sat back in his chair. "I fell in love with Lynne practically on sight, and the more I saw of her the more solid the feeling became. But, Thelma, I need a woman who appreciates me just as I am, and that means accepting the fact that I crawl under automobiles, that when I'm working, my hands, shoes, clothing and sometimes my face are filthy. If I wanted to sit in my office, keep books and hand out assignments to the men who work for me, I wouldn't need my degrees in mechanical engineering."

Thelma sat forward, the hand in which she held the cup of coffee trembling. "And what makes you think all that matters to her?"

"She told me as much last night when she advised me to confine my work to the office, and I'd, 'feel better about myself,' was the way she put it."

"Here. Have some more pie," she said as she put another hefty slice on his plate. "Seems to me like she's using somebody's head other than her own. She adores you, and I imagine she's miserable."

He knew she was, but he had to cut his losses. "I know, but I'm not going that route again. She's a celebrity, and she will be an even bigger one, so I suppose she's concerned with her image."

"She's not that kind of person. If she was, she wouldn't spend time with an old woman like me. I've lived a long time, and I know the real thing when I see it. This isn't the end of it, and if I live another year and you don't fall out with *me,* I expect to be present at your wedding."

He felt a grin spreading over his face. "If you prove to be right, I won't get angry with you. I'd better go." He started to get up and paused. "At this rate, I ought to send you a sack of pecans."

"Don't you dare! I've got two pecan trees in the back of my house, and I haven't used up half of last year's harvest." She walked with him to the door. "You come see me again soon now. You hear?"

"You bet. If you need me, call me. All right?" He turned at the sight of her tears. "None of that. I'll see you soon."

She grasped his hand to detain him. "If Lynne wants to talk with you, listen to what she has to say. Promise me you'll give your relationship with her one more chance. You're two wonderful people, and I...well you know what I mean."

"If she convinces me, I'll be happy," he said, but he didn't plan to create the opportunity for that to happen.

He told her goodbye and jogged to his car without a glance toward Lynne's house. What was done was done.

Returning from a jaunt around the block with Caesar, Lynne reached Thelma's house at about the same time that Sloan's Buick shot away from the curb and headed down the street. She had planned to stop by Thelma's house with Caesar in the hope that her neighbor and the dog could become friends, and that eventually Thelma would be willing to keep the dog for her when she traveled. She gave silent thanks that she hadn't gotten that far while Sloan was visiting Thelma; she had no desire to encounter him. She turned back to her house as a man left her front door and headed down her walk. Caesar jumped forward with such strength that he dragged her along with him, and she could hardly control the dog as he growled and jumped at the man.

"You'd better get out of the way," she said to the stranger. "He's my guard dog and that's my house. What were you doing there?"

Caesar continued to strain at his leash and to bark ferociously, and with a look of horror on his face, the man backed away, but was reluctant to miss an opportunity to hawk his wares. "I was canvassing votes for the independent party in the coming election," he said. "I'll come back another time."

When he turned to go, she screamed at him, "Don't run, for goodness' sake. You'll make my dog more excited."

He slowed down so quickly that she almost laughed. The experience was sufficient to divest her of the notion that Thelma might occasionally take care of Caesar: with his strength, the dog could injure her if she attempted to restrain him. She patted Caesar, went inside, fed him and prepared to spend Sunday evening alone. Almost at once, her phone rang, and she grabbed her chest, as excitement raced through her. Could it be…?

"Hello."

"Hi, sis. What's up?" She didn't want to talk with Brad. She'd had enough of his wisdom.

"Nothing," she said. "How's Debra?"

"Deb's fine. She went shopping with one of her cronies. You sound as if you lost your best friend. Say, did you tell your boyfriend to quit the dirty work and get himself an office?"

She gasped for breath, stood up and stamped her right foot. "I did indeed," she said between clenched teeth. "Would you like to know what he said?"

"Uh…what?" he asked in a subdued tone, so unlike himself.

"He said, 'See you around.' So, Mr. All Wise, thanks for ruining my life."

But the stridency quickly returned. "Say! You're better off. Find a guy with enough savvy to get a white-collar job."

Her lips quivered, and she walked to the other end of the living room and back, shaking with anger. "All you care about is your Gucci shoes, Hugo Boss suits and Louis Vuitton luggage. He doesn't give a damn about any of that, and even if he doesn't work for somebody's law firm, he works for himself in his own business and hires five adult males."

"Hey, calm down. I hear you, but I still think I gave you the right advice."

"I'm hanging up, Brad." And she did.

Sloan had made his position clear. She'd overstepped the bounds with him, and he wouldn't forgive her. She stopped examining her old tennis outfits, sat down in the middle of the bedroom floor and wrapped her arms around her raised knees. Hadn't he told her that he was a mechanic and didn't need the fancy term "mechanical engineer" to legitimatize himself? Why had she let Brad persuade her to do something guaranteed to hurt Sloan and cause him to turn his back on her?

"It's time I charted my own course and planned my own strategies," she said, rising both literally and figuratively. She chose four white sets, for their style was as modern as when she bought them a decade earlier, and she'd as soon not remind tennis fans of her passion for yellow outfits. She put the yellow ones in a sack to be deposited at a thrift shop somewhere.

During the coming week, she intended to work out with Clive and practice with Gary every minute that they would let her, for she didn't intend to go out in the first round or the second. She meant to let everybody know that she was back and that the women tennis players had to reckon with her.

Chapter 6

For the next two weeks, Lynne worked with Clive to make herself as fit as possible for what would probably be grueling matches in the rapidly approaching tournament. Oddly, she felt better about her game than she did about withstanding what could be hours of combat in the Cincinnati heat. Moreover, she had to win a lot of pretournament matches in order to qualify for the tournament. *I'm on the bottom,* she reminded herself, *but not for long.* No media hype attended her qualifying matches, and she thanked Gary for that.

"You ought to be feeling pretty good," he told her. "You didn't lose a set."

"I do," she said, "but the real test comes Monday. I'll be facing a tough player in the first round."

He draped an arm around her shoulder. "You can beat her. She's good on clay, but you'll be playing on a hard court, and that's your best surface. You'll eat her alive."

She laughed at the idea. "Just pray. I don't want to disgrace myself."

"You won't."

Shivers raced down her spine that Monday afternoon when she heard the announcer say, "Ladies and gentlemen, Lorrie Payne and Lynne Thurston." Like a race car revving to go, her adrenaline began pumping, and she had an urge to run onto the tennis court. With restraint, she followed Payne, waving as she entered the comparatively small arena and enjoying the applause and cheers. This was what she had worked so hard for. She won the toss and served first, a blistering ace down the middle.

Encouraged, she told herself, *I'm going for broke,* and won the first set with a score of 6–2. Then, her opponent seemed to grasp Lynne's strategy and began to anticipate her shots, and Lynne tried desperately to break the woman, but without success. Finally Payne double faulted, losing a point, near the end of the second and final set, and Lynne won the set with a score of 6–4, and the match was hers. At the applause and cheers, tears streamed from Lynne's eyes as she ran to the net to shake hands with her fallen opponent.

"With that level of play," Gary told her as they drove to her hotel, "you'll go a long way in this tournament. You took some unbelievable risks out there, though. When you sent up that last lob, I thought Lorrie would clobber you, but you got away with it."

She wondered if the smile would ever leave her face. The impulse to jump and shout for joy crowded out every negative thought except one. "I had to play as if I had nothing to lose," she said, "because if I lost that one, not even you would have continued to take me seriously. If only—"

"If only what? This is a time for joy, not... Say, what happened to that tall fellow who used to come over to your place every day at about the time we finished practicing? Is he off somewhere? I thought he seemed like a good guy."

"I messed up, and he took a walk."

"What'd you do?"

Her right shoulder flexed in a quick shrug. "I followed my know-it-all brother's advice and meddled in Sloan's business. I underrated him."

"Oops. Can't you patch it up with him?"

"He's not going to give me a chance."

Gary sucked air through his front teeth. "You're kidding. That guy's nuts about you. Trouble is you don't know how to handle him. If he won't come to you, you go to him. The phone won't do it. Get him alone, and let him see what he's giving up. Get busy."

Somehow, she felt better. In many ways, Gary behaved as an ordinary man, not the corporate achiever that her brother either was or aspired to be, and he expressed sympathy for those less fortunate than he.

"All right, Gary. I'll try. A man's opinion got me into this, maybe another man's opinion will get me out of it."

With her first four matches under her belt, Lynne should have felt expansive, but when she awakened that morning, her first and depressing thought was that she had to face the tournament's number one player.

I'll give it my best, she promised herself. *Any way I look at it, this tournament has been a success for me. There's only one top-five player here, and I'll meet her today, but the players I've beaten were tough tests for me, and no matter what else happens, I can leave here with my head high.*

Ana du Pree strolled over to Lynne in the locker room and shook hands. "It's great to see you back on the tour."

Her eyes widened at the unusual gesture. "Thanks. You're the first player who's welcomed me. I appreciate your kindness."

Ana grinned. "The rest are probably scared to death, not that I blame them. I figure I'll always get what's coming to me. See you on the court."

Lynne's heartbeat accelerated, and her nerves unsettled her after she won the first set with a score of 6–4, and she lost the second 3–6. *Get your act together, girl. You can beat this chick.* Though she fought as hard as she ever had, she lost the third-set tiebreaker, 13–15, after battling for it an hour and a half. She sprinted to the net and embraced the victorious Ana du Pree.

"If I had to lose," she told the woman, "I'm glad the loss was to you. You played a great match."

"Thanks," Ana said. "You're back in a big way, and everybody had better look out."

"What went wrong in that second set?" Lynne asked Gary at her first practice after returning home.

"Your second serve didn't work, and you have to realize that you won't lose any power by standing five inches from the serving line. You lost some points by stepping on the line and especially during the second serve."

"All right, let's do it," she said and twirled her racquet in anticipation of her match with him.

"No game. You're going to serve until you get sick of it."

By three o'clock that afternoon, she felt as if she never

wanted to see another tennis ball. "You think I made any progress, Gary?"

"Some, but what counts is how you do when the chips are down. Incidentally I entered you in the Stanford classic next week."

"You *what?*"

"What's wrong?" he asked, flashing a grin. "You're playing tennis now."

When could she make an opportunity to see Sloan if she was playing in a tournament practically every week? "Okay. Okay. When do we leave?" He told her, and she spent the next two hours sorting out what she'd wear on the court starting three days hence.

Around six o'clock, she telephoned Thelma. "I'm making some bean soup and a salad for supper. Want to come over at about seven-thirty?" She needed to share her success with a friend. She needed to share it with Sloan, but there was no Sloan. "I won't let it get to me," she swore.

"I sure will, and I'll bring some corn bread. I sure missed you, and I want to hear all about it. I saw in the *Sun Times* that you almost beat du Pree. How exciting! See you later."

"Have you seen Sloan?" she asked Thelma during their supper when she could no longer bear not knowing.

"A couple of times. He told me why you two split up. He's a proud man, and I guess you didn't count on that." Thelma stirred sour cream into her bean soup, tasted it and added some more. "The soup is delicious. I bet you put some ham hocks in it."

"Of course I did. You want some of it?" Thelma nodded, and Lynne went to the stove, shredded a ham hock and brought it to the table. "All right now, Thelma. What else did he say?"

Thelma served herself some of the meat. "Nothing much except that he'd been there before, and didn't plan to go through it again. Something like that. I told him I expected to be present when he marries you."

Lynne's spoon fell to the table. "What did he say?"

"Well, that was very interesting. Just exactly like a man. He grinned. Now that is one good-looking man, and when he grins... Even at my old age I can see that."

"Thelma!"

"Oh. He said if it worked out like that, he wouldn't be angry. At least, I think that's what he said." She tilted the bowl and spooned up the last bit of soup. "Tell me. Are you sitting on your behind doing nothing about this and that man is running around loose? You think you're the only woman who can see? Get busy. He loves you."

"What am I supposed to do? He froze me out."

Thelma laughed. "I see you've never been to bed with him. If you had, you'd figure something out. That is a sweet, generous and loving man, plus he loves you, and if you don't know how to get next to him, something's lacking in your raising. Take your car to get if fixed, for goodness' sake. If nothing's wrong with it, kick the door in."

Laughter bubbled up in Lynne's throat, and she let it pour out. Girl talk with a septuagenarian. How sweet it was! "Kick the car door in, huh? Better still I'll tell him it chokes on me, and ask him to repair it. It'll take him a while to figure out that nothing's wrong with it, then he'll give me what for, and I'll get a chance to... I'll just hug him."

"I'm not sure I'd go about it that way, but it's your program."

The more Lynne pondered the idea, the more she liked it, but it needed a foolproof strategy and, in two days, she'd be leaving for Stanford, California. "Living out of a suitcase is the aspect of tennis playing that I forgot I hated," she said to herself.

However, two days later, she took Caesar back to the kennel, parked her car at the airport and headed for California. "The field is heavier with top players than the Cincinnati Western was, but you can handle them," Gary said. "Go for it…you've got everything to win."

At the end of the week, despondent because she lost in the quarter finals, Gary assured her, "You should be happy. You beat two top-five players, and the one who barely beat you won her last seventeen matches."

"I guess you're right, but I'm playing to win. Oh, well. The next time I play, I'll make it to the finals."

"Your next one will be the Pilot Penn in New Haven the end of August, and every top player will be there. You've got a month, so let's get busy."

Her mind wasn't on tennis, but on Sloan and the possibility that in a month's time, she could patch things up with him. She glanced toward the sky in a silent prayer. "Lord, my heart aches."

"What did you say?" Gary asked.

"I'm going to put everything into polishing my serves these next weeks, Gary. I'm not an also-ran, so I've got to make a statement."

"I didn't think you'd move along so fast. Stop worrying about winning and focus on polishing your game."

She knew it was good advice, but how was she going to temper her impatient nature?

* * *

Sloan leaned against the hood of the car on which he was working and took out his cell phone. "McNeil Motor Service. McNeil speaking." His heartbeat accelerated at the silence. Could it be…?

"Sloan, this is Lynne. If I bring my car in, will you look at it, please?"

He held the phone away from his ear and stared at the receiver. "How are you, Lynne? Of course, I'll look at it. What seems to be wrong?"

'I don't know. It…stops all of a sudden with no notice. I guess you'd say it chokes up."

"How often has this happened?"

"Three times. Once when I was pulling out of my garage, but the other times, I was on a highway."

"Hmm. In that case, you shouldn't drive it. I'll send someone to pick it up. When will you be home?"

"Anytime after nine in the morning will be fine, though I'll be on the tennis court. I finish practicing at three."

"Ben and someone else will be there around three tomorrow."

"Thanks so much. I don't want to entrust my car to just anybody. Bye."

"See you," he said. He didn't like the feeling that he'd been emptied of something precious to him, but he couldn't shake it. Why hadn't she phoned AAA? He hooked the cell phone to his belt and returned to the damage that a flood caused to the carburetor in a 1981 Cadillac. "It wouldn't hurt this brother to buy a new car," he said to no one in particular. Twenty-five minutes later, after having bent over the engine until his head seemed to swim, he threw the wrench to the ground, straightened up and wiped the sweat from his face and neck.

Maybe an elegant woman like Lynne deserved a man who would come home at night with his hands looking as if they'd just been manicured. He spread out his hands, turned them over and gazed at them for a long minute. What the hell! He was who he was, and he was damned if he would remake himself to satisfy a frivolous whim. He leaned against the old Cadillac, and released a strong expletive. Lord, but he needed her!

Ben returned to the shop with an SUV that he towed off Route 10. "What's the problem with that one?" he asked his assistant manager.

"Looks to me like transmission problems."

"I see a lot of transmission failure with that line. Ben, do you remember where Lynne Thurston lives?"

"Sure do. I think it's the twenty-seven hundred block of Corpus Christi Lane. Why?"

"Take Jasper with you tomorrow around three and pick up her car. She said it chokes, and I don't think she should drive it."

"Chokes? That car? I'd be surprised."

"Me, too, but that's what she said."

"Uh, Sloan, I was planning to ask if I could be off tomorrow afternoon. My boy's choir is going on a picnic, and I can't let him play around in the Atascosa or the San Antonio River—I don't know which one they're going to—chaperoned by somebody I hardly know. I want to encourage him to stay in the choir because he has a great voice, so I'm letting him go."

Sloan blew out a long breath. "You're right, man. First things first. Don't worry. I'll manage it." Precisely what he had intended to avoid. He didn't want to go to Lynne's house. Caesar would greet him enthusiastically, she'd be gracious and he would have to be courteous if nothing else.

He didn't feel like extending himself. He had been on air, so to speak, dreaming dreams of forever, so full of her and his feeling for her that, apart from his work, he thought of little else. And then with two short sentences, she pitched him back to earth. Flat on his face. If she knew how she hurt him. Oh, the hell with it!

And that Sunday morning when he brought her dog back to her, her eyes had sparkled with unshed tears, and if he hadn't gotten a tight grip on himself, he'd have grabbed her and kissed her senseless. He ran his fingers through his hair, punishing his scalp. "I've got to stop thinking about her."

The following afternoon at two-thirty, he quit work on the old Cadillac, went into his office and stopped as if he'd been hit by a bolt of lightning. What was he thinking? "I'm going to pick up a car that needs work, dammit, and that means I wear my work clothes. I'm working, so she'll see me in my work clothes." He washed his hands, scrubbed them with a nail brush and dried them. He always cleaned his hands before leaving the shop, he assured himself. It had nothing to do with her.

He stepped out of his office and called to Jasper. "I need you to go with me to pick up a car. I'm taking the truck. If the car will run, I'll drive it back. If not, we'll tow it."

"Whenever you're ready."

Just before he reached Lynne's house, a smile broke out on his face. With Jasper along to chaperone him, he wasn't likely to do anything stupid. Suddenly he laughed aloud. He'd be thirty-six before the end of the year, and he needed a chaperone?

"What's funny, Sloan? I could use a good laugh myself."

"You don't want to know, man, but I'm here to tell you, it's funny as hell." He parked in front of Lynne's house, got out of the truck and walked around to the tennis court where he expected to find her practicing with her coach.

"Hi."

He spun around when her voice came from behind him. "Hi." He thought he'd prepared himself for seeing her, but he hadn't reckoned on the effect of her smile, and he'd forgotten that Lynne Thurston in a pair of short shorts could make a ninety-year-old man's mouth water.

While he stared at her, Jasper came to his rescue. "Where's your car, Miss Thurston?"

She didn't look at Jasper, but kept her gaze glued to Sloan's face. "In the garage.

"Thank you for coming," she said in that low voice that always brought carnal thoughts to his mind. "I played in two tournaments since I saw you. Unfortunately I lost each time in the fourth round."

"I know," he said. "You did surprisingly well."

She kicked at a tuft of grass. "That's what my coach says, but I hate losing. I really hate it."

He hadn't wanted to get into a conversation with her, hadn't wanted to involve himself in her life, hadn't wanted to empathize with her, to want to hold her so badly that he ached.

Somewhere, as if from a great distance, he heard Jasper say, "Can I have the keys, Miss Thurston? I mean, you want me to look at your car, don't you?"

Shape up, man, he told himself. Nobody had to tell him that Jasper had detected the hot tension between Lynne and himself, for none of his employees would ordinarily take over if he were present. Caesar's whimpers—a signal that the dog knew he was there—gave him an excuse to get away from Lynne, and he dashed over to the deck.

"You're one person he'll never protect me from," he heard her say and realized that she followed him. Ignoring her as best he could, he stroked and patted the dog, who greeted him joyfully. But Lynne didn't let up.

"At least you got a decent greeting, Caesar," she said. "Anyone would think Sloan cares more for you than he does for me."

His head snapped up. "Did you tell Caesar to let his hair grow long, that you preferred poodles to German shepherds? No, because you don't think a poodle would defend you."

"Sloan, I'm sorry. You don't know what I would give to—"

With his hands up, palms out, he interrupted her. "I'm not here to talk about that or anything else. You want your car repaired, and that's what I'll do, provided I find anything wrong with it." A hole opened up in his gut when he released the dog and walked away from her. When he hurt her, he injured himself, but he couldn't help it. After days and weeks of immersion in her warmth and sweetness, and after the loving she promised with every kiss and every caress, he hadn't been prepared for the damning knowledge that he wasn't good enough for her.

He walked over to where Jasper sat in Lynne's car racing the engine. "What do you think?"

"I don't know, Sloan. Maybe something happens after it's been running a while, but damned if I can imagine what that could be. Let's take it in and see what we find."

He balanced himself on his haunches and listened to the motor. The thing was as regular as sunrise in the desert. Across the lawn past the clay court, Lynne stood facing him with her folded arms pressed to her middle.

"All right, Jasper. I was going to drive it, but I think we'll tow it. Hook it up while I let her know she'll be without her car for a few days."

"I...uh...I guess I'll rent one. It's impossible to get along here without a car."

He knew that, and in normal circumstances he'd lend her one, but he'd become suspicious of her car problems, and he didn't plan to make it easy for her to manipulate him and do it with impunity.

"That's a good idea." He opened his wallet, extracted a business card and handed it to her. "This company will deliver a rental to you. We'll let you know when your car is ready."

She stepped closer, and the scent that he knew and loved so well filled his nostrils, tantalizing him. Yes, and sending a surge of pain through his body. His hands itched to hold and caress her, but he had never settled for second best, and he wouldn't do it then. If a woman wasn't proud of him, he wanted her out of his life, pain or no pain.

With his emotions sheltered, he gazed down at her. "Be seeing you." Without waiting for her response, he strode to the truck and hopped in.

He hadn't driven a mile before Jasper, a man ten years his senior, said to him, "Look, Sloan, it ain't my business, but nothing's wrong with this engine. It's as smooth as a baby's bottom. If you ask me, she wanted to see you again. Period." Jasper knocked his McNeil baseball cap back and scratched his head. "Pretty clever, though."

He had already considered that possibility, but he had to give her the benefit of the doubt. "We'll jack it and you examine it thoroughly. McNeil Motor Service doesn't give anybody a botched job." From the corner of his eye, he could see Jasper's raised eyebrows, and if he had been in the man's place, he would have certainly done the same.

"Work it out, man," Jasper said, proving that he knew the issue was a personal one. "Sometimes we get a lot just by giving a little."

"Yeah," he said, hoping to put an end to the discussion of Lynne and himself. He knew that Jasper and his other workers cared about him beyond their work relationship for they had demonstrated that on more than one occasion, so he spoke gently to Jasper.

"I know you're right, but that depends on what you're willing to trade. She's a fine woman, and if she manages to change my mind, I'll be grateful to her."

"Well, if you weren't tough, you wouldn't be where you are. Still, from what I saw back there, I think you ought to give it a chance, man. I've known you and your parents since you were ten years old, and I wouldn't steer you wrong. Nobody's head is harder than mine, but if I hadn't listened to my father—and I usually didn't—I wouldn't have Ellie, and you know I practically worship the ground she walks on."

"I'm listening, Jasper, but I'd like us to let it go for now."

"All right, but did you happen to catch her match in Stanford last week? Man, she was brilliant for four

matches before Costa got the better of her. I think she's
headed back to the top."

"I didn't see her matches in that tournament, but I
read a report of the last one." He hadn't known she'd
be playing in the Stanford Classic, and he didn't know
her future program. *But you'll find out,* his conscience
jeered at him.

While Sloan pondered Jasper's words, Lynne sat at
home musing over Sloan's behavior. Right in her presence, he'd fought a battle with himself and won it. He
probably suspected that her car was in perfect working
order, but he took it to the shop because, as he'd told
her several times, he wasn't a man to leave anything to
chance. He hadn't wanted to hear her apology, or so he'd
implied. But his pain had radiated from him like bees
swarming outward from their hive.

"He was mine, and he will be again," she vowed. "He
can't shut me out of his life. I won't let him." With that
determination, she went inside her house, loped up the
stairs to the sitting room beside her bedroom and got a
pen and sheet of writing paper from her desk.

Dear Sloan,
I made a terrible mistake when I followed my
brother's advice and said words that insulted you.
I knew better. For days, I had resisted saying that
to you, because it didn't feel right. I had defended
each of his snobbish attacks on you, but understand
that I love my brother and have always followed his
advice. He was so certain that you would be receptive to the idea. What I didn't count on was that I
would hurt you. I had told him that if the two of

you were in the same room together, no one would
be able to discern which of you was the mechanic.
And that is true. You mean more to me than winning a grand slam, becoming number one or anything or anybody that I can think of. I don't have
words to tell you how much I miss you.
Love, Lynne

She addressed it to him at McNeil Motor Service,
stamped it and put it in her mailbox with the flag up so
that the mailman would take it the next morning. If that
didn't work, she'd think of something else.

"I'll give it two months," she promised herself, "and
if he doesn't budge, I'm going to that shop and make him
reject me in the presence of his employees."

As always, when she took action to solve a problem,
her spirits rose, and she hooked Caesar to his leash and
went for a run. On the way home, a few sprinkles caused
her to slow down so as to avoid sliding over the wet pave-
ment. The raindrops thickened, bringing to her mind the
day Sloan returned to her house soaking wet, and she
dried his clothes in her drier while, clothed in her brother's old robe, he waited in her bedroom.

*Why on earth didn't I stop to think of Sloan's person-
ality and his outlook on life before I made that ridiculous mistake? And on an evening when we were both so
happy? I don't blame him. It's unforgivable.*

She wondered why Caesar repeatedly turned back and
looked at her as if he expected a command. She picked
her way carefully among some broken branches as she
passed the yellow house, a big rambling structure with
five great gables, the only wooden building in the block
and an example of how the well-to-do lived in late-nine-

teenth-century, post–Civil War Texas. It was said that the original owner wanted the gables so as to keep his five wives separate. Thelma claimed that the tale had no foundation in fact.

After a while, she realized that, in her musings about Sloan and herself, her pace had slowed almost to a crawl, and Caesar wanted to run. She jogged the remainder of the way, careful of her footing, fed Caesar and then sat alone in her living room contemplating her future. Never had she been so grateful for a phone call as when she answered and heard her sister-in-law's voice.

"Say, girl, where've you been all afternoon? I must have called you half a dozen times."

"I was outside. How's Brad?"

"He thinks you're mad at him because you haven't called recently. What's up?"

She looked toward the ceiling and blew out a long and impatient breath. "Debra, I am not in the mood to deal with Brad's antics. He told me to do something stupid. I did it, and I'm suffering the consequences. What should I do, call him and thank him? Tell him that from now on, I keep my own counsel."

"Then you *are* angry with him."

"No, Debra. I'm angry with myself, because I knew it was wrong. Now let's get off the subject."

"Whew! You're straining at the bit. Brad loves you dearly. You know that."

"Yes, Debra, I know it. I also know that he thinks he knows best, and the fact that his advice messed up my life won't prevent his giving me more of it the next time we talk."

"I'm sorry, Lynne. I can see that you care a lot for the guy, but don't cut us out of your life."

"Oh, for goodness' sake, don't be so melodramatic. You and Brad are all the family I have. Why would I do that? Give Brad a kiss for me. I have to look after my dinner, Debra, before it burns up. Bye."

She didn't remember previously having lost her temper with her sister-in-law, but at least now Debra would know that she wasn't a sponge that absorbed every foolish thing said to her. She warmed up a pot of lima beans, okra and smoked ham hocks, ate enough of it to banish the hunger cramps and went to bed.

"It's a hard lesson," she told herself, "but at least I've learned it, and all future advice will be examined under a magnifying glass, even if a preacher volunteers it."

She slept peacefully and awoke the next morning resolved not to allow her unhappiness in her relationship with Sloan to derail her progress toward becoming the world's number one tennis player. It wouldn't be easy, but with her first two tournaments, she'd moved up from number three hundred and fifty to number one hundred and seven. That was as much encouragement as she needed.

Nearly a week later, Sloan thumbed through the pile of mail on his desk, tossing catalogs and other junk mail into the wastebasket. "What was that?" he said of an envelope that he'd pitched into the basket. He retrieved it, studied the handwriting, turned the envelope over and the air seeped out of him when he saw that it came from Lynne. Misgivings quickly replaced his eagerness, and he put the letter, unopened, in his top desk drawer.

"I don't want to deal with that right now." Although that was what he told himself, he knew that—in his stubbornness—he wanted to deal with Lynne on his terms and not hers, for if she even hinted that she loved him, he would capitulate.

He wanted to visit his parents the coming weekend, but he also needed to spend time in Clinton Hills with the builder of the shop he was locating there, and his mind told him to drop by Thelma's house. He telephoned Thelma.

"This is Sloan," he said when she answered. "I've been wondering how your window is holding up in all this rain we've been having."

"It's perfect," she said, "and I finally broke down and had the place air-conditioned. What a difference. The heat got so bad I couldn't sleep, and the doctor told me to put an air conditioner in my bedroom. Lynne told me that to air-condition the house made more sense, so I did it. Sloan, I was just thinking of all the years I was miserable because I was too stubborn to cool this place off."

A chuckle escaped him without warning, spoiling his plan to give her a good lecture. "That little anecdote is supposed to lead to a lecture about my stubbornness with Lynne. Right? I know you, now, so you can't fool me. How is she?" he asked, using it for his own purpose.

"I don't see too much of her because she's getting ready for a tournament in Connecticut, and I think she said her coach entered her in the US Open."

"Is he crazy? She can't possibly be ready for that," he said, appalled at the thought.

"I 'spect she'd make better progress if she didn't have all these…uh…personal things on her mind," Thelma said, rubbing salt into his open wound, as it were. "A gentleman answers his personal mail."

"I always answer my mai… She told you about that letter? I haven't read it yet."

"For goodness' sake, aren't you going to?"

"Eventually I suppose. You know, Thelma, you take liberties with me that my mother wouldn't consider, and I tolerate it."

"That means I'm good for you. Everybody needs a Thelma, a person who cares deeply, who'll listen to whatever you say, and who'll tell you the unbiased truth. Your mother's biased because anybody who hurts her precious boy is a bad person. Right?"

"Yeah, but if her precious boy does something wrong, he'll definitely hear from her. If you're going to be home tomorrow afternoon, I'll check your trees. The wind must have weakened a few limbs. If so, that can pose a danger when you're in your back garden."

"I sure would appreciate that, but I'm smelling these buttermilk biscuits I just put in the oven. Can you come over this afternoon or maybe this evening?"

"Woman, you definitely know how to treat a bachelor. I'll be over there around six."

Afterward he mused over his purpose in conjuring up a reason to visit Thelma, but when he faced the truth, he knew he wanted to be near Lynne and hoped Thelma would invite her to join them.

However, Thelma let him know that the idea hadn't occurred to her. "When you two get together," she told him over their supper of fried chicken, string beans, ham, boiled potatoes and buttermilk biscuits, "it will be because you both put forth the effort. I'm not going to butt in and make it easy for either one of you. When you both hurt badly enough, you'll put an end to this foolishness."

"I hadn't planned to eat up your dinner, but thanks for inviting me. I enjoyed it."

"I see you're avoiding answering me. You're a stub-

born man, Sloan. Here. Take this pie home with you."
She cut a slice from another pie and put it on a plate and
handed it to him. "You're a good man, and you're good
to me. I know my son is smiling down on you right this
minute."

She sat down, folded her hands and began to twist
them. "Read Lynne's letter, Sloan. I don't think you'll
be sorry you did."

He got up, put the dishes in the dishwasher and took
the bag that contained his pie. "You're spoiling me, but
I like it." She walked with him to the door and he leaned
down and kissed her cheek. Then he gazed down at her,
waiting for her reaction, and it shocked him when tears
streamed down her cheeks.

She didn't wipe them away, and she didn't smile.
"You're so dear to me, and now I know I mean something to you," was all she said. He told her he'd be in
touch and, when he left her, he walked with slow, delib-
erate steps. When had that old woman come to mean so
much to him? She cared about him, too, and she wanted
what she thought was best for him.

Instead of going home, he went back to the shop, unlocked it and opened his desk drawer. Since writing that
letter, Lynne had made no effort to contact him, and he
wondered if by not answering, he would write finis to
their friendship. Jasper's words pounded his head. He
picked up a silver letter opener that a client gave him
one Christmas and slit the envelope. Maybe she wasn't
asking for reconciliation. Maybe she was telling him she
intended to get on with her life. His fingers trembled as
he pulled the folded sheet from its envelope, opened it
and began to read.

"I don't have the words to tell you how much I miss

you." He read that sentence over and over. It contained no genuine surprises, but it made him wonder why she hadn't told him that she loved him. He remained there for more than an hour, thinking about her and about himself. He wasn't a Solomon whose wisdom was sufficient for the ages, and hadn't he done things that he regretted? He folded the letter and put it in his breast pocket.

"I've learned a lot about myself these past weeks. Some of it I like, and some I don't." He locked the shop and went home, and although he wanted to telephone Lynne, he resisted doing so, for what could he say? *I read your letter, and I'm glad you feel that way. Let's have lunch?* He wasn't pretentious and didn't know how to start. He missed Lynne probably as much as she missed him, but he wasn't ready for that step.

Lynne checked into the Omni New Haven Hotel on Temple Street, unpacked her bags, pressed the wrinkled tennis suits and fell across the bed. This was it. If she did well in the Pilot Pen, she would definitely be on her way.

"I want you to relax and have fun," Gary Hines said when he called her. "You're stuck with a helluva draw, but you're playing well, and you'll get through it. Remember that the fans will be rooting for you. See you on court for practice in about an hour."

On Monday morning, after fighting for two long hours, she won her first match in three sets from a woman who, in the old days, she beat easily, but who now held the fourth-highest ranking. Happy, but exhausted, she returned to her hotel as quickly as traffic allowed, showered and collapsed into bed. Two days later, she prevailed after a similar, but more grueling experience that depleted her energy. This was the highest-level tournament she had entered, and every top player was there to feed off the misfortunes of lesser, struggling players. *And to think that, when I was near the top, I never concerned myself with how the losers felt.*

She ordered dinner in her room and was preparing to eat when the phone rang. "Hello," she said, expecting either her brother or a member of the press.

"Hello. This is Sloan. You really let it all hang out today, better even than yesterday. How do you feel?"

"Sloan! Oh, I'm so glad you called me. I'm... How did you know I was here? Oh, Sloan, this is... I'm so happy that you called."

"So am I. I read that you had entered, and I wanted to wish you good luck tomorrow in your match with Davenport."

"Thanks. I'll need it."

"She's been known to lose, you know, and you two have a similar game, so you can figure out her moves."

"I certainly hope so."

"I won't keep you because you need to rest. Bye for now."

"Goodbye, Sloan. Your call was the medicine I needed."

She hung up, and tried to eat her dinner, but the food held little interest. Had anything changed? Did he read her letter, and if he did, had he forgiven her? At least he'd shown her that he was not intractable, that he'd bend. He called. That was really something. Not one affectionate word, but it was better than nothing.

The next morning, unwilling to play the roll of the underdog, she donned her new yellow tennis dress and yellow sneakers, put a yellow sweat band above her forehead, packed yellow handled racquets and headed for the stadium. "Nobody can say I don't look great."

She shook hands with the tennis great, loss the toss and the right to serve first, and lost the first set to Davenport with a score of 4–6. However, she quickly got on a roll and won the second set 6–3. So the lady could be had, she thought, and began the third and final set with her hopes high. However, Davenport loved the hard court as much as Lynne did, and at the end of the tenth game they were tied at five games each. It was then that Davenport raised the level of her game and poured it on, taking the set seven games to five, and winning the match.

Lynne made her way to the net, shook hands with her famous opponent, plastered a smile on her face and bowed to the crowd, but the tears streamed down her insides. Victory had been within her reach, but in her overeagerness, she'd lost it and her opponent had played like the champion she was. She put her racquets, towels and soda water in her duffel bag, and almost ran to the locker room, where she dressed as fast as she could and headed out of the stadium complex.

"Sloan," she murmured to herself. "Where are you now that I need you so badly?" She had her duffel bag slung over her shoulder and her head down when someone yelled, "Great game, Lynne. We're glad you're back." She looked up, waved and walked out of the building. *Why am I looking as if I lost my best friend? I played a first-class game, and I lost to the number one player.*

She turned the corner to go to the car that awaited her thirty feet away and stopped. Her heart seemed to fly out of her chest, and the duffel bag slid from her shoulder to the ground. She stood there. How could it be? It was. Oh, it was! Sloan leaned against the limousine that awaited her. Her feet moved, and she sprinted to him as fast as her legs would carry her and launched herself into his open arms. He locked her body to his, lifted her and swung around with her, his head thrown back as if joy suffused him. When several clicking sounds were heard, he settled her on her feet.

"Who's the gentleman, Miss Thurston?" a reporter asked, and handed her the duffel bag.

With an arm around Sloan's waist, she told the reporter, "His name is Sloan McNeil. Thanks so much for retrieving my bag."

"Ready to go, Miss Thurston?" the limousine driver asked her.

She looked at Sloan. "Did you drive?" He shook his head. "Ready, and Mr. McNeil is coming with me," she said.

In the back of the stretch limousine, she sat close to Sloan and rested her head on his shoulder. Maybe it was only for the moment, but her heart seemed to overflow with happiness at the knowledge that his arm was around her. His free hand tipped up her chin, and the bottom dropped out of her belly when his lips brushed over hers and then she felt the pressure, parted her own lips and took his sweet tongue into her mouth.

"Did you read my letter?" she asked him when he broke the kiss.

He reached into his pocket, withdrew the letter and showed it to her. "I didn't right away, but after I read it, I had to come here because I knew you needed me, and I'm glad I did. Today, you played like a champion. I'll bet anything that by this time next year, you'll be on top."

"You think so?"

"I know it. You came close to banishing the number

one, but she knows how to close out a match, and she put everything into it. I'm so proud of you."

She hated to cry, but the tears that had been building up inside of her like stagnant water refused to be contained any longer and spilled out of her, down her cheeks, over her chin and onto her blouse.

"What… You're crying," he said. "Stop. Please. I can't bear it."

"I'm…it's all…everything that's gone on for the past weeks. It's been awful. I managed to train and to practice, but looking back, I don't know how I did it. My heart wasn't in it."

"It's all right, love. It wasn't easy for me, either, but we're together now."

The limousine arrived at the Omni and the driver got out, took her bag from the trunk, reached for the handle of the passengers' door and discovered that Sloan had opened it and was getting out of the car. "No need for that," he told the man and handed him a folded bill. *Shame on me,* she thought, for she hadn't remembered the tip.

In the hotel's lobby, Sloan's hand on her shoulder detained her. "When are you leaving?"

"Gary will get my ticket. I haven't spoken with him since I—"

He interrupted her. "Since the end of the match? I don't suppose he'll suggest that you fly out tonight. Can we see each other this evening?"

"I…uh, thought we might spend the rest of the day together. Want to come up while I shower and change?"

Both of his eyebrows shot up. "Definitely not. I'll wait down here."

At her shocked expression, he treated her to an elec-

trifying smile. "To the best of my knowledge and judgment, I haven't yet achieved sainthood, and if I go up
there with you right now, I never will."

If a potential for wildness was holding him back, he
needn't be demure on her account; she wouldn't mind
having him wild in her arms. She suppressed a sigh.
What did she know about a man in the heat of passion?
Willard had no idea what passion was.

"I'll be down in half an hour," she told him, "and I'm
already starved." As if to insure his being there when
she returned, she reached up and pressed a quick kiss
to his mouth and was rewarded with a blaze of desire
in his eyes.

"I'll be here."

Lynne didn't know what to think of Sloan's change
of heart. Many questions roamed around in her mind
as she showered and dressed as quickly as she could.
He'd be there, because he'd said he would, but she could
barely wait to get back to him. When she saw him leaning against the limousine with his hands stuffed into
his pockets and his ankles crossed, seemingly casual
and laid-back, she had thought her heart would burst
open. She'd soon know whether he wanted to resume
their friendship.

Since he was wearing a beige linen suit with an open
collared shirt, she dressed casually in a white pantsuit,
yellow tank top and white loafers. She sprayed Fendi
perfume at her pulsepoints, picked up a white shoulder
bag and headed for the elevator.

Standing to greet her, he appeared taller than she remembered. "Right on the minute," he said, "and you
look…" He seemed to search for the word. "Lovely."

"Thanks. Where're we going?"

He appeared to relish that question, for a grin lit his face. "To my lair, madam."

"Aren't you going to feed me first?"

"Whoa. If you're joking, let me know it, and fast."

Genuinely perplexed, she stared up at him. "Joking about what?"

His left hand went to the back of his neck where he rubbed furiously, a habit that she knew signaled frustration. "I'd better get us to a place where we can eat," he said as if he were speaking to himself alone.

"What did you say?" she asked him, unsure that she'd heard properly.

"Would you call a taxi?" he asked the doorman.

"Nine sixty-four Chapel Street," he told the taxi driver.

"Yes, sir. Around here, mister, you just say Zinc. That's all a cabbie needs to hear. They serve the best."

"Glad to know it," Sloan said. "A friend recommended it to me."

"Your friend steered you right. You not from this part of the country, I take it."

The driver monopolized Sloan until they reached the restaurant. "Many thanks, brother," Sloan said when he paid the driver. "We're from Texas, and this is my first visit to New Haven."

"Thank you, sir," the driver said, his face wreathed in a smile. "Here's my card. If you need transportation to the airport or anyplace else, just give me a call. Yes, sir. I sure do thank you." She imagined that the man received a tip commensurate with Sloan's usual generosity.

"Did you telephone Gary?" he asked her after the waiter took their order.

"Good Lord, I forgot all about Gary. The man probably thinks I'm someplace crying my heart out because I lost. I'll call him as soon as we leave here." She gazed up at him. "I thought you were going to take me to your lair."

When he leaned back and studied her, his whole demeanor tense and serious, she remembered that she shouldn't joke with him about their relationship, at least not until they repaired it.

"That's where I'd like to take you, but I think you'll agree that we ought to iron out whatever wrinkles remain in our relationship, and that we ought to have the comfort of either your home or mine."

"I do, and I'd like us to get started on it."

"I saw a sitting area on the second floor of your hotel that offers a bit of privacy," he told her. "Let's sit there and talk, but first, call your coach."

As soon as she got into the taxi, she dialed Gary's cellular phone number. "Hi, Gary, this is Lynne. Oh, I'm fine, but Sloan met me as I left the stadium, and I didn't know he was in town. I forgot everything else. Huh? Yes, you could say that. What time am I leaving tomorrow? Eleven o'clock? Which airline?

"Delta at eleven, nonstop. Thanks a lot. I'll meet you at the door. Have a pleasant evening."

"If I can't change my ticket, let's meet at the airport," Sloan said. "But I'll hate not flying back with you."

When she got out of the taxi in front of the hotel, a glance at the darkening clouds told her that their decision to return to the hotel and talk there was the right one and, as they entered the elevator to go to the second floor, she said as much to Sloan.

He reached for her hand and held it. "Let's talk, and I

mean talk. I won't hold back, and you shouldn't. We need to know and understand each other. I can't continue this unless I know you will open up to me. Okay?"

"You're right, and I'm willing to try."

He found two comfortable chairs in a remote corner, turned them so that their backs partly faced passersby and suggested that they sit there, facing each other. As soon as they sat down, he took her letter from his pocket and read it aloud:

"You must know that I love you, Lynne. Why couldn't you tell me that you love me? Did you think that information would give me an edge of some kind? I need to love and to receive love just as you do."

"The truth? I suppose I didn't tell you because I had never heard you say the words, and I've experienced so much rejection that I—"

"Don't compare me to Willard Marsh, Lynne. Put that part of your life behind you. I don't deserve to pay for his transgressions." He folded the letter and returned it to his pocket. "I'll keep this always."

"Thank you. I'm glad I wrote it. Have you forgiven me? That's what I need to know."

"I couldn't have held you and kissed you if I hadn't forgiven you. Your words hurt because they told me that the real Sloan McNeil wasn't good enough for you. I love what I do, and I hope I never have to do anything else. If I get a chain of fifty shops, I'll hire a manager, and I will work where I'm working now, doing the same thing I do now." He stretched his left leg and then crossed his knees. "If you brought one of your fans or an author friend to the shop and found me lying beneath a car that I was repairing, how would you introduce me?"

She wasn't sure he was being fair, but she would

examine that question more thoroughly later on. "I'd say this is my friend, Sloan McNeil, the best mechanic anywhere around here. If I had the right to say more, I would."

He leaned forward, pressing her hand. "Are you sure? I'm never going to change, Lynne."

"I don't want you to change."

"All right. What do you need from me that I'm not giving you?"

She struggled to snuff out the urge to laugh but couldn't quite master it, and a grin spread over her face. He couldn't possibly be serious.

Like a flash of lightning, his gaze quickened, and desire blazed in his eyes. For a long minute, he stared at her. "It's a damned good thing we're not upstairs in your room. I believe in being prudent, but push me hard and I'll say the hell with prudence. I owe you one for that." They talked until it was time to eat dinner and then shared a meal in the hotel's main restaurant, but she didn't want to leave him.

"I'll walk you to your door," he told her, "but I'm not going in. My plane leaves at ten-fifty, so if your coach doesn't mind, I'd like to travel with you to the airport."

At her room door, his kiss was brief, but she didn't ask for more. Their time would come, and very soon.

She endured the seemingly endless flight with Gary sleeping beside her. When she reached the baggage carousel, Sloan leaned against the wall waiting for her.

"Our flight left late. How long have you waited?" she asked him.

"About an hour."

"And before you sleep this night, I mean to make it worth your while," she said out loud. "If he needs me as much as I need him, it's past time."

Chapter 7

"You want to travel with me?" she asked Sloan. "Or, did you drive? I reserved a rental car."

"I took a taxi here, so I'll ride with you."

She found the car keys and gave them to him. He put their bags in the trunk of the Chevrolet and, within minutes, headed toward the city. "There was nothing wrong with your car, Lynne. Did you know that?"

"Yes, I knew it, but when I was trying to figure out a way to see you, Thelma suggested that I kick in the car door, leaving a dent, and ask you to repair it, but I didn't think you'd pick up my car for anything as simple as that."

"Thelma's a real piece of work when she puts herself to it. I've developed a true affection for her."

"Me, too."

He glanced at her and returned his focus to the

crowded highway. "The best and surest way to get my attention is to go straight to the point. You should have called me and told me you wanted to talk with me. I know how I acted, but I also know that I wanted badly to have some assurance that you didn't mean what your words implied and that you deeply regretted them."

"I hope you didn't spend too much time trying to locate a problem with my car."

"That's behind me."

She let herself relax as a plan for the evening began to form in her mind. "Would you please stop by one of the malls that has a supermarket or a gourmet grocer. I don't even have milk in the house."

He waited in the car while she bought snacks and what she needed for dinner and breakfast. "Looks as if you did a week's grocery shopping," he said when he put the food in the back seat to take advantage of the air-conditioning.

"Do you need to stop at home?" she asked him, aware of the boldness that her question implied.

Both of his eyebrows shot up. "For a few minutes, if you don't mind. Say, aren't you picking up Caesar from the kennel?"

She had hoped he wouldn't remember Caesar until they'd reached her house. "Uh...no. I'll get him tomorrow." The evening forming in her mind held no room for the frisky dog who would want to take off immediately on a romp down the street or wherever she would run with him, leaving Sloan either to tag along or to wait alone for her. Sloan drove to his town house and parked.

"Would you like to come in?"

"Thanks, but you'll move faster if I stay in the car."

A grin spread over his face and bloomed into a smile

that electrified her. "Truer words were never spoken." He leaned over and kissed her mouth. "Be back in about fifteen minutes."

Hmm. Just time enough to take a shower. I'm way ahead of you, sweetheart.

He was back in fifteen minutes as promised, and it didn't escape her that he wore different clothes and carried a small leather pouch. When he drove into her garage, the day had almost spent itself.

He unloaded her purchases and took them into the kitchen. "I'll check around the house to see if everything's in order." After putting the food in the refrigerator, she set the table. "What's wrong with me?" she asked herself. "I don't seem to care that I lost in the third round, although I know I do. Maybe I'm just happy that he still loves me in spite of the hurt I caused him."

She peeled half a dozen waxy red potatoes, sliced them in the food processor, placed them in a casserole dish, seasoned them with salt and pepper and poured light cream until it covered the potatoes. She lit the oven, placed the dish inside and looked at her watch. Next, she trimmed the beef filet, seasoned it and placed it in a roasting pan. She spent the next fifteen minutes cleaning asparagus, and putting together a green salad. Broiled grapefruit would have to do for a first course. After cutting one into halves and paring them, she set them in a baking pan, sprinkled them with generous amounts of brown sugar and, to each, she added several jiggers of cognac. Later, she would broil them. She eyed the bottle of Napoleon VSOP cognac and saw that she had plenty to pour over the raspberry ice cream that she'd bought for dessert.

Sloan hadn't come into the house, so she went outside

and found him cutting away a wild vine that had begun to choke one of her rosebushes. "I'd like to disappear for about thirty minutes," she said. "Would you excuse me?"

He folded the Swiss Army Knife and put it in his pocket. "Sure. Should I keep an eye on whatever's happening in the kitchen?"

"Thanks, but I've got it covered. Would you like a drink before I go upstairs?"

He walked toward her, his gait lazy and his body swinging in a sexy rhythm. "You know I don't drink when I have to drive, and I'm taking the rental car back for you, aren't I?"

She looked him in the eye. "Would you like a drink or wouldn't you?"

Like the sun suddenly popping out from behind a storm cloud, the fire of sexual desire radiated from his eyes, drawing her into him the way a lightbulb seduces a moth. She caught herself as she moved to him and stopped, for within minutes he'd have had her in bed, and her plans called for a much different scenario.

"Scotch, bourbon or vodka?" she asked him

The heat of his gaze seemed to burn her. "I'll take anything you give me."

Never having seen him drink hard liquor, she was temporarily stymied. "Well," she said, "I can handle a double entendre as well as the next person. Vodka and tonic it is, and with plenty of ice to water it down."

With a frown and narrowed eyes, he asked her, "Woman, are you suggesting I can't hold my liquor?"

"Not at all. Just making sure the drink won't sap your energy." She whirled around and headed for the kitchen, but he made certain she heard him when he said, "If that's the effect, you may wish you'd made it a triple."

He followed her into the kitchen, walked over to where she was removing ice cubes from an ice tray and tweaked her nose. "Pretty fresh today, aren't you. Be prepared to back it up."

She moved out of his reach, made a vodka Collins and handed it to him. "As you said, I'll take anything you can give me... Oops. I mean...anything you give me."

The joy of his laughter wrapped around her as she fled up the stairs. "Lord, he's got me so excited that I probably won't be able to eat a thing." She showered, oiled and perfumed her body, put on a pair of green bikini panties and stepped into a green halter-top silk jumpsuit, and after combing out her hair and putting a lip gloss on her lips, she streaked down the stairs to him with a minute to spare.

She noticed that his drink remained untouched. "What's the matter? Too much ice?"

She loved the mischievous glint in his eyes. *Lord, but this man is sexy.*

"I wouldn't drink without you." As if cataloging the treasures before him, his gaze traveled from her toes to the top of her head, lingering here and there, and his Adam's apple bobbed when he swallowed as he seemed to anticipate what he knew was to come. She didn't imagine the shivers that shot through her. "You're one lovely woman."

"Thanks. I'll get a glass of wine, and I've got a bag of roasted almonds and some cheese sticks while we wait for those potatoes to cook." She looked at her watch. "Remind me in fifteen minutes to put the meat in the oven." *Why am I nervous? I'm chattering like a ten-year-old at her first overnight pajama party. Calm down, girl.*

At last she could serve the dinner, but as she removed the broiled grapefruit from the broiler, the telephone rang.

"Hello."

"Hi, sis. What's happening? I figured you'd be home by now. You really planning to continue wearing yourself out on the tour?"

"Hello, Brad. Thanks for the encouragement. I can't talk with you right now, because I've just begun to serve dinner."

"Oh, yeah? Who's your guest?"

"Sloan McNeil, and my dinner's getting cold."

"Now look. It's time you came to your senses about—"

She interrupted him. "I'm hanging up, Brad, and I won't answer the phone again tonight. I don't feel like being harassed. Goodbye."

"I don't like coming between you and your brother," Sloan said. She hadn't realized that he'd heard her side of the conversation.

She answered him indirectly. "As many times as I let Brad know how miserable Willard made my life, he never suggested I get out of that situation. Nor did he tell me to avoid it in the first place. Where you are concerned, I'm taking no more advice from him. Let's forget that interruption. I won't let anything or anybody spoil my evening with you."

He jumped up from the table, put his arms around her and said, "Smile for me."

When she did, his lips parted above hers, and when she opened to him, his tongue dipped into her mouth. "This is what matters right now, Lynne. You and I. That's all."

After saying the grace, he tasted the broiled grapefruit. "Mmm. This is different...and delicious."

She didn't remember having cooked a more perfect meal. It was as if Providence was on her side. He took the dishes from the table, put them in the dishwasher and cleaned the kitchen. When she insisted that she'd do them the next morning, he said, "I don't believe in that. I straighten up when I finish eating. Find some interesting music."

She took a bottle of Tia Maria and aperitif glasses to the living room, put on Buddy Guy's recording of "It Looks Like Rain," sat down and waited for Sloan, but a restlessness suffused her.

When she heard his footsteps, chills plowed through her, she crossed and uncrossed her knees and when, with trembling fingers, she reached for the empty glass, he said, "What's the matter, sweetheart? Are you afraid?"

She shook her head. "I...so much is riding on this evening."

"You're wrong. Nothing is riding on it. We'll take it as it comes. Why do you say that? Remember," he admonished, just before she made light of it, "we've pledged honesty with each other, and if there is one thing we have to be frank about, it's this. Tell me what's bothering you."

Thank God she could tell him. "I've never had any success at it, and I'm scared you'll be disappointed."

He poured each of them a glass of the liqueur. "Get rid of that notion right now. Don't even think it. Why did you choose this particular recording?"

"Because I wouldn't care how many times it played over and over."

"Neither would I. Buddy Guy is a great singer, and nobody is better than he at playing that guitar. A real genius. Do you know the words? Let's sing it."

After the first two bars, she stopped singing and listened to his rich, velvet baritone caress the words, "And I feel you reaching out to me."

Either the liqueur or his voice—she didn't know which—warmed her insides and set her blood to racing, and thoughts of that moment when he would plunge into her blotted out all else.

"Kiss me," he whispered.

For a minute, she stared into his hypnotic gaze, and then she parted her lips and sucked his tongue into her mouth. His big hand roamed over her naked back, claiming, stroking and possessing while he showed her with his tongue what he would do to her later. Her nerves began to tingle with exhilaration, drowning her in a pool of sensuality. She wanted his hands all over her. She wanted…

His fingers teased her nipple, and she pressed his hand to her body. "Kiss me. Honey, kiss me."

He untied the strings at the back of her neck, and when he had exposed her breasts to him, she trembled in anticipation, and he sucked in his breath. "Sloan, kiss me."

"If I do that, baby, I'm gone. I want you so badly I can hardly breathe. If I—"

She grasped the back of his head. "Take me in your mouth. I want to feel your mouth on me."

When his warm, moist mouth covered her nipple, she let out a cry that reverberated throughout the house, and he began to suck, stroking and pulling her other nipple as he did so. Contractions at the mouth of her womb and heat at the bottom of her feet nearly unraveled her as he dragged her into a ravishing need, a sensation that she hadn't previously known. Her blood seemed to churn and, with no experience at it, she did the natural thing and began to stroke and fondle him.

"No. No," he groaned, but covered her hand the better to enjoy the pleasure of it. But when she squeezed, he stopped her.

"Look at me, Lynne. I want us to make love. I need to love you right now more than I need air. If you don't want that, let me know this minute."

She buried her face in his shoulder. "I want you to make love with me. I want it so badly." He lifted her into his arms and carried her up the stairs to her bedroom, where he unzipped her dress, and she stepped out of it.

His whistle split the air as she stood before him, bare but for the tiniest of bikini panties. "You are... Sweetheart, you take my breath away. You're so beautiful." The hunger in his eyes made her cover her breasts with her hands, and as if sensitive to her embarrassment, he quickly threw back the covers and put her in the bed.

He flung off his clothes, stepped out of his shoes and yanked off his socks. When he looked at her lying nude in that bed with her arms stretched out to him, the blood pooled in his groin. He told himself to take it slow, that she needed his skill, patience and his love. But she lay there, arms outstretched and smiling at him, and he had to control the urge to run to her, and as he reached the edge of the bed, she stretched out her hand and stroked him.

"Let me," she said, and he stood before her while she dropped his shorts to the floor and caressed him. Knowing his limits, he prayed for control as he sprang hard and heavy into her hands. Oh, the feel of her unschooled fingers stroking, teasing and toying with his rigid flesh, making his senses whirl dizzily. He had to stop her, but it had been so long since warm and loving hands had paid tribute to his manhood.

"My God, stop it," he yelled, when her lips closed over him and she caressed him with the tip of her tongue. Aware of the certain consequences, he moved her from him, climbed into the bed and brought her body to his, breast to chest and thigh to thigh. In his lifetime, he hadn't known such gentle sweetness as she gave him in that kiss. He couldn't control the trembling of his body when her arms went around him and she threw her right leg across his hip telling him without words that she was his.

Liquid accumulated in her mouth when she felt his penis rubbing against her thigh, and she reached down to capture the organ and put it inside of her. But he moved from her.

"You're not nearly ready, love." His lips brushed over her eyes, her ears and her throat.

"Oh, Sloan, kiss me. I want to feel you inside of me."

"Let's not rush this, sweetheart. We've got all night." His lips spread kisses over her shoulders, and her nerves rioted through her body as she waited for the feel of her nipple in his mouth. At last he began to suckle her, and her groan of passion echoed through the room. If only he would get in her. He eased her to her back, and when he began kissing her belly, hot darts seemed to pummel her vagina.

"I can't stand this," she moaned.

His fingers opened her vaginal folds, and she bucked beneath him. When he hooked her knees over his shoulders and kissed her, she let out a loud cry and then...

Oh Lord, the feel of his tongue dancing in her and of his lips sucking and kissing. She thought she would die from the pleasure of it. And then, contractions in her vagina startled her.

"Honey, what is happing to me? Oh Lord. I think I want to burst. Get in me. *Get in me!*"

He moved up her body, slipped on a condom and kissed her. "Relax now and look at me."

She opened her eyes and stared into the face of the man she loved as he pressed against her. Her eyes widened at the discomfort, but she pressed her body up to him and he slowly sank into her. His fingers inched between them and he massaged her, his talented fingers sending spirals of unbearable tension to her vagina. As if powered by a magical force, her body took over, and she began to move against him.

"Tell me you're mine," he said. "Mine and no one else's."

"I am. I'm yours. Just love me. That's all I want," she said. And then he began to thrust in and out of her.

"Tell me when I'm in the right place, when it's so good you can't stand it," he said.

"I want to burst. I feel as if... Oh Lord. I'm swelling inside. I'm—"

"That's good. Oh, yes." He increased the pace, and now she was going to die if he didn't... The pumping and squeezing began, and her thighs started to quiver. She was dying, sinking. She couldn't stand it. He flung her into a whirlpool, and she grabbed his hips. "Sloan! Honey, I'm...I'm dying."

"You're not. You're loving me."

"I'm..." Screams erupted from her as he flung her

into ecstasy, and she spread her arms and gave herself to him. "I'm...I love you. I love you."

He pumped furiously, and shouted his release as he lost himself in her and he fell apart in her arms. "I'll always love you."

They lay entwined for a long time without speaking, holding each other. "Are you all right?" he asked her.

"Me? I'm fine."

"This is important, Lynne. Did you have an orgasm? Tell me."

"I guess I did. I don't know what else it could have been. If there's something better, believe me, I want it."

"Then you don't feel as if there's something else that wants to be released, something lacking."

"No. I don't. Of course, I wouldn't mind feeling like that again, if you can manage it. How do *you* feel?"

He hugged and kissed her. "Like a crowned king. The wonderful thing about this is that practice makes perfect. The better we know each other, the more pleasure we can give each other." He sat up in bed and looked at his watch. "Do I have to go home tonight?"

With her hands above her head, she stretched long and lazily. "Honey, don't even let that cross your mind."

"Then, I think I'll go see what I can find to eat. Sex makes me hungry as the devil."

It occurred to her to follow him down the stairs and help him find something to eat, but lethargic as she was after the workout he'd given her, she yielded to the demands of her sated body and fell asleep.

"Where do I turn off this light?" His voice reached her from a great distance. She put the pillow over her head, removed it and sat up as the scent of their lovemaking brought her from her dream world to reality.

"Sloan? Did you find anything to eat? I meant to go down and help you." She covered her mouth to enjoy a yawn. "But it looks like I fell off to sleep. I'm sorry."

"I found plenty to eat and, trust me, I ate it. Aren't you hungry?"

"I don't think so. I'm still half asleep. You wanna kiss me? Huh?"

"I'm not in a habit of taking advantage of women, and I'm not sure you're awake."

"Then wake me up. You sure have what it takes." She slumped against him. "I want to feel the way I felt when you were inside me. Lord, if I ever have anything better than that, I know it will kill me. How'd you learn all that? You should give classes. You'd be a millionaire in no time. And you're sweet, too, but you can't teach that. Can you? I mean…"

"Lynne, wake up and show me where the light switch is. Come on, baby."

Lynne sat up straighter, rubbed her eyes and looked at him. "It's on the cord." She leaned across him in an attempt to find it, and her breasts rubbed over his chest. She turned slowly and stared at him.

"I didn't do a thing," he said.

As if he hadn't spoken, she kept her gaze glued to his face as she wondered about protocol for lovers when they were already in the bed together, and had made love. Within a minute, his eyes darkened with unmistakable desire and, more certain of her ground now, she leaned down and twirled her tongue around his pectoral. If it worked with her, shouldn't it excite him, too? Immediately, as fiery need blazed in his eyes, she crawled over, mounted him and took him into her body. He shifted until he lay flat on his back. As she bent over him, he pulled her nipple into his mouth and suckled her.

Wide awake now, Lynne moved her body as Sloan directed until she could feel him quivering inside of her. He quickened the pace and she thought she would die from the feeling. Suddenly, she forgot about finesse and went after what she wanted and needed, telling him what she wanted him to do to her and how she wanted it done. The contractions, pumping and squeezing began, and she erupted around him, holding him prisoner until they both shouted the hymn of lovers in climax. Depleted of energy, she collapsed on him, suddenly aware of her wild behavior and unwillingness to look at him.

He held her face in his hands, forcing her to meet his gaze. "You're my woman, and any man who attempts to tamper with that fact will deal with me. Understand?"

"Fine," she said, "provided you understand that you're not free to associate with other women."

"No sweat. You're the only woman who interests me." He turned out the light, wrapped her in his arms and went to sleep. She listened to his breathing, aware that she had just committed herself to Sloan McNeil. *But I love him, and he loves me, and I have everything to gain by it.*

Two weeks before the beginning of the US Open—the tournament that Lynne coveted most—Sloan slid out from beneath an SUV, and a crowbar fell on his left foot, damaging his big toe. After a visit to the hospital emergency room, he was obliged to wear a cast.

"I can't get over to your place this afternoon," he told Lynne. "This foot is in pain, and I don't dare drive."

"I'll go to your place," she told him. "What do you want to eat for supper?"

"I don't want you to cook. I want you to conserve your energy. In two weeks, you'll need all of it that you can get."

"I don't get tired playing tennis—it's after the game is over that I'm ready to collapse. I'll see you about six-thirty."

He expected that she would be loyal to him, that she'd be there for him if he needed her, but he did not expect her to cook for him. He could easily send out for his meals. However, her willingness to help him touched his heart, and he wouldn't forget it.

"Here, you take Sloan this pecan pie," Thelma said to Lynne when she stopped to see her en route to Sloan's house. "Tomorrow, I'll fix him some chicken and dumplings. Never saw a man who didn't love chicken and dumplings. I want you to come over about this time and get it. Okay?"

"All right. He'll love it, Thelma, and I appreciate it, too. By the time I finish practicing, I'm too beat to cook."

"Sure you are. That's why you have friends."

She knew she wouldn't be able to visit him every day, and he let her know that he didn't expect it.

That evening, they ate dinner together at Sloan's house, enjoying the baked pork chops with gravy, mashed potatoes, string beans and broiled mushrooms that Lynne cooked at home, and Thelma's pecan pie. "I love your kitchen," she told him after she straightened up and put the dishes in the dishwasher. "When I remodel mine, I'm going to use this one as an example."

He propped his lame foot on an ottoman and stared into her face. "Why would you need two kitchens?"

"What?"

"You heard me. Think about it before you invest time and money in the house you're renting." And as if he hadn't just handed her a live hand grenade, he leaned back and closed his eyes.

"All right," she said to herself, "I'll think about it, but I definitely will not comment."

Later that night, after she returned home, finished her ablutions and prepared for bed, she was startled by the ringing of the telephone. Her brother never called that late, and she doubted Sloan would, knowing that she arose early. She considered not answering it until it occurred to her that Thelma might be in distress.

"Hello," she said, so softly that her own voice nearly startled her.

"Hello. You mighty late getting home. Where've you been?"

At the sound of Willard Marsh's voice, she dropped the telephone as if it were a hot poker, and it landed on her bed. When she didn't answer what she regarded as his insolent question, his voice rose as it had always done in his angry or otherwise excited state during their marriage, and although she stood at her full height, she heard his every word.

"What God has joined, no man should sever," he said, putting his own twist on the famous edict. "I want us to get back together. We set a poor example for my congregation, and to tell you the truth, none of my flock can understand it—we were the ideal couple."

Willard remembered her as a docile and obedient wife, but when she shed his name, she rid herself simultaneously of his influence, and it was time he knew it. "I'm trying hard not to laugh, Willard, because I'm sure this is your idea of a joke. I've gotten on with my life, I'm happier than I've ever been and I don't have time for your nonsense. Please don't call me again."

"How dare you speak to me that way and in that tone?" he said, reverting to his real self.

She hung up. If he needed proof that he was shaking a barren tree, she'd be glad to provide it. Thank God, her divorce was final. She got in bed and enjoyed a refreshing night's sleep. However, a call interrupted her breakfast the next morning, and she answered it to hear a high-pitched female voice.

"May I please speak with Mrs. Marsh?"

Lynne suppressed an epithet. "Who is this?"

"This is Mrs. Hand from Reverend Marsh's church. I'm calling to offer a prayer with Mrs. Marsh."

Lynne had the feeling that she might swell until she popped. "There is no such person here, and please don't call here again."

"Mrs. Marsh? I thought that was you. Our entire congregation is praying that you'll see the error of your ways and return to your husband and to the church."

Lynne blew out a deep breath. "I remember you, and you're so fascinated with Willard Marsh that you believe every damned thing he tells you. I am legally divorced from that man, and I never want to hear his name called again. Mind your own business, and leave me alone."

"You left him so you could go back to playing tennis. That's the devil's work, and you—" Lynne hung up. Then, she called the telephone company, asked that her phone number be changed and unlisted. "Don't give it out to anyone unless you get my permission."

"Yes, ma'am. I'll call in about half an hour and give you your new number. Please be prepared to write it down. Your old number will be retired."

She thanked the woman, made a list of the people to whom she would have to give her new number, and as soon as she received it, she phoned Sloan.

"You mean he's seeking a reconciliation?" he asked after she told him about Willard's call.

"I don't see how he can be serious. I suspect his naïve parishioners are behind this."

"Does he have a chance? Tell me now."

"Does the sun rise in the north? How can you ask such a question? He didn't have a chance before I met you. Do you think he has a chance *now*? Let's talk about something that makes sense. How's your foot?"

"My foot's fine, except that the cast is hot, but my toe is not happy."

"Did the doctor give you a painkiller?"

"Aspirin. All that did for my toe was insult it."

Giggles rolled out of her. "I'm coming over this afternoon and singing it a lullaby." She remembered that Thelma wanted to send Sloan a supper of chicken and dumplings, and she knew he would enjoy having that evidence of the woman's affection for him.

"I shouldn't encourage you, because I know you need to focus on your tennis right now, but I want to see you if you can make it."

"I'll make it. Uh, I'll be in Toronto next week for the Canadian Open. Gary only told me today that he'd registered me for it. He said he waited until he thought I was ready. I'm not sure it's the right move, but I have to accept his judgment."

"Who says you do? If you don't agree with him, tell

him. I'm not even sure you should enter the US Open, but you've acquitted yourself well so far. Why do you want to go to Toronto?"

"I'm playing well with my coach, Sloan, but I'm not battle-tough. I don't have practice at slugging it out when it's too hot, when I hurt, when I'm losing, when the crowd's against me, when the chips are down. I need experience at digging into my last reserves and coming up with a winner."

"And you'll have one week between that and the US Open. Maybe the Canadian tournament is a good thing, but I have my doubts about the US Open at this time. It's always scalding hot out there, and they're not likely to give you night games unless you're playing a top-ten player. I don't want to discourage you, but I want what's best for you. I want you to be happy."

"I know you do. I'd better do my five miles. See you this evening. Kisses."

"Love you, sweetheart."

Her heart thumped wildly in her chest, and she had to pause for breath before she could say, "I love you, too. Bye."

Just his luck to be confined to his house at a time when Lynne needed his support. She'd made it to the quarter finals in all but the last tournament she entered, but those were minor competitions compared to what she could expect at the US Open, where every professional female tennis player worth her salt would compete. Not that he doubted Lynne's fitness; he didn't. But she had been a champion, a great one, and he wanted her to return a champion. Maybe it was unrealistic, but he didn't want her to hurt.

He answered his cell phone and got a report from Ben on the previous day's problems and activities. "Would you mind going over to Castle Hills and checking the work on that ceiling? I want to be sure it's properly insulated. The fact that it's an automobile service center doesn't mean it shouldn't be comfortable."

"Right. The foreman said you wanted the ATM machine built into the outside wall to cut down traffic into the station. Is that right?"

"Yeah. Don't you think it makes sense? Tell Jasper to get a longer hose for that air pump."

"I think he did that yesterday. How's your foot?"

"Painful. I'm not supposed to put any pressure on it. Otherwise, I'd be at work."

"Don't even think it, Sloan. That toe is completely exposed, and if anything fell on it or if you stumped it on something, you really would have a problem."

"I know. I should be able to get out of here sometime next week, or so I hope. Thanks."

He passed the day reading, a pleasure for which, in his struggle to get ahead, he'd never had enough time. A biography of Thomas Jefferson perplexed him, and he wondered if the enigmatic man even understood himself. How could he have considered himself a champion of freedom and liberty while his own children and the woman who bore them toiled for him on his lands as his slaves?

"Put your money where your mouth is, man," he said aloud, tossed the book aside and, with a marking pencil in his hand, began reading W.E.B. duBois's masterpiece, *The Souls of Black Folks*.

Every few minutes, he looked at his watch. "I didn't know time could crawl so slowly. She won't be here for another three hours at the least." He hobbled over to his music center and looked through the CDs. He wanted to hear some blues but, deciding that he didn't want to be in the mood that the blues would create, he settled for a collection of Mozart piano concertos. "Nothing sentimental about these," he told himself, and was listening to the set for the third time when he heard Caesar's bark.

He opened the door and, without a word, she reached up and singed his lips with a fleeting kiss. He was so hungry for her, but he merely looked down at her face, open and expectant. The thumping of Caesar's tail reminded him that he had ignored his other visitor, and he braced himself against the door, leaned down and patted the big German shepherd on his head. Caesar rewarded him with a wag of his tail.

"Come on in," he said to Lynne. "From the time you hung up until now, a week seems to have passed. I spent the day waiting for you. Oh, I read this and that, and I listened to music, but they were ways of surviving until I could feel your lips on mine."

"I did some counting, too, and the hours took their time passing."

"What's in there?" he asked of the package she carried.

"Our supper. Thelma sent you something good. She also thinks you need somebody to look after you, and if you think the same, she wants to volunteer for the job."

"I wouldn't mind seeing her, but I don't want her to play nursemaid, though I'm sure she's good at it. If you come back before you go to Toronto, would you bring her?" By any description, the expression on her face was a dressing down. "Did I say something wrong?"

She brushed past him and headed for the kitchen.

"Any other man would expect us to have some private moments before I go away," she said without looking back.

His left hand went to the back of his neck and began rubbing, a certain sign of his frustration. If he lived to be a thousand, he'd never understand women. She didn't want them to have an affair, so why was she suggesting that she expected them to make love before she left town?

"Hell. I sure am not going to complain," he said to himself, digging his fingers into his scalp. "She can't possibly want me any more than I want her."

Caesar gazed up at him with an expression of pity on his face, and Sloan couldn't help laughing. "I guess you've been there, too, boy," he said and headed to his favorite lounge chair with Caesar right behind him. The dog made himself comfortable on the floor beside the chair, and Sloan reached down and rubbed his back.

The telephone rang, and he was about to let the answering machine take the call when he saw his parents' telephone number in the viewing box. "Hello. Mom? Dad? What's up?"

"How's your toe, son?" his mother asked. "I've been worried that you can't get around and you don't have anybody to do things for you."

"Hi, Mom. My toe's improving. I'm away from work because the doctor doesn't want me to take chances on hurting it again. And don't worry about how I'm getting along. An absolutely beautiful woman is in my kitchen at this moment."

"Really? Wonderful. When are you going to bring her home? If she knows you well enough to cook for you—"

"Slow down, Mom. I didn't say she was cooking, but she might be. I intend to ask her to go home with me sometime this autumn. Right now, our schedules don't permit it."

"Are you…uh…happy, son?"

"Yes. I think she's the one for me, but as you always say, 'there's many a slip between the cup and the lip.'"

"I hope there won't be any slips this time, son, and I'll be praying that it works out. You deserve something wonderful in your life."

"Thanks. Where's Dad?"

"Out on his boat, fishing. I'll tell him you asked about him."

"Love you. Bye."

He looked up as Lynne walked toward him with a scowl marring the beauty of her face. "If that wasn't your mother on the phone, I'm out of here."

He didn't bother trying to stifle the laugh that wanted to come out, but gave it free expression. When he could, he said, "That was my mother, and here is her phone number, so you may verify it." He wrote the number on the pad beside the phone and handed it to her. "My mother's name is Lucille McNeil, and if you want to talk to my dad, his name is Connor McNeil." He threw up his hands. "I'm an honest man."

With both hands on her hips, she stared down at him, and suddenly without a warning, she grasped the back of his chair and seated herself in his lap. He didn't doubt that she detected his surprise for he could feel his bottom lip drop and his eyes widen. He was glad to have her there, but he would have appreciated the opportunity to collect himself and stave off what he feared would be a full erection. He knew he was in for it when she put her hands behind his head and her parted lips to his mouth.

He kissed her quickly, and tried harder to avoid the

inevitable. "You're taking advantage of my invalidness," he told her, seeking levity.

She leaned away from him. "Invalidness? I thought it was just your toe. I didn't know it was...uh..." She wiggled suggestively, and he threw up his hands.

"Now you've done it!" he said.

A smile transformed the contours of her face. "It's a heck of a lot better than what I was thinking. Can it wait awhile? Dinner's getting cold."

He wanted to tell her hell, no, that he needed relief right then and that she could reheat the supper, but what he said was, "You were a little smart-ass at the start, and nothing's changed. Go on to the dining room. I'll be there in a minute."

Her smile seemed to widen, and she jumped up from his lap. "Okay, as long as you've got an inflator around here somewhere."

"You bet I have, and I'm looking at her."

"I don't know when I've had such good chicken and dumplings," he said as they ate supper. "This is one of my favorite meals. I'm going to call Thelma and tell her that, with these dumplings, she's stuck in my heart like a leaf fossilized in rock. She's wonderful."

"Guess what she sent you for dessert?"

"I did already."

"Would you look in the pantry on the top shelf and get that box of dog food, please," he asked Lynne after they finished supper. "I don't want Caesar to think I have bad manners. There's a dish for him right outside the back door, and tie him up out there. He doesn't need to know everything."

While she fed the dog and straightened up the dining room and the kitchen, he put on a CD of blues music and waited for her. "Let's sit in the dining room," he said when she came back to him.

Her face bore an inquiring look, but she said nothing. In the dining room, he sat in a straight-back, armless chair. "Come here, Lynne."

The jersey top that she wore betrayed to his eyes the hardening of her nipples, and he knew she was ready for him. "Sit here, facing me. It won't be what it could be, but I'll make it as pleasant as I can."

She straddled him and within seconds, he had his tongue in her mouth. The fingers of his right hand teased her left nipple and with his left, he toyed and teased at the entrance to her vagina. He was hard and hurting, and he had to bring her to climax quickly. She began moving against him, pulling on his tongue and moaning her need.

"Shh," he said. "I don't want Caesar to get the idea that I'm hurting you." He slipped the blouse over her head, unfastened her bra, sucked her nipple into his mouth, and when she undulated frantically against him, he raised her, slipped off his Bermuda shorts, dispensed with her bikini panties, shielded himself and, after testing her for readiness, slipped into her. He tried not to take pride in her gasp of momentary discomfort, for he knew he suited her. With one nipple in his mouth, he pressed her buttocks to him, and she threw back her head and moved against him in a rapid rhythm searching for her own orgasm. She bucked, twisted and changed her pace at will, and he rode with her, praying for the strength to hang on until she exploded all around him as she did their first time.

"Is it all right, baby?" he asked her. "Am I hitting the right spot?"

"Yes. Yes."

The ripples began, and as if he were being suctioned into a vacuum, she clutched and squeezed him, sending hot needles of unspeakable pleasure careening through his body, dragging him into a vortex of ecstasy, until he flung wide his arms and gave her the essence of himself as he shouted, "You're mine! Mine, do you hear me? Mine!" She bucked against him, let out a keening cry and went limp in his arms.

He held her that way for a long time. Finally he said, "I won't ask if you're satisfied, because I know your pattern now, and I felt your powerful eruption on me, in me, around me and all over me." He let his fingers stroke her back, tenderly and with all the love he felt. "What I want to know is whether you've thought about what you'd do with two houses?" Maybe it wasn't the time to ask that, but he couldn't help it. He needed to know. He couldn't ask her to marry him because it wasn't time for that, either, although he knew that if nothing went wrong between them, he would someday do exactly that.

She captured his lips in a long and drugging kiss. "We'll talk about it when I'm able to think. Right now, with you locked inside of me, my brain is in recess. All I know is that I want you in my life."

"And I want to be there. What I'm concerned about are the terms."

"You have as much control over that as I do."

"Really? I'm not so sure."

Chapter 8

Lynne unpacked her bags in Toronto's Grand hotel, un-dressed, put on her bathing suit and the white terry robe she found in the closet and headed for the swimming pool. Refreshed after two laps in the Olympic-size pool, she went to her room, showered and got in bed for a nap. The flight from San Antonio to Toronto took longer than a trip from New York to London. "I have to call Sloan," she said to herself just before she fell off to sleep. Two hours later, the ringing telephone awakened her and a glance at the window told her that darkness encroached.

"Hello."

"Hello, sweetheart. Just checking to know if you got to your hotel safely, and if you're comfortable."

"I am. It's a lovely hotel. Worth the money. I meant to call you, but as soon as I unpacked, I did two laps in that enormous pool and that made me sleepy. Your call woke me up. I wish I'd stayed awake long enough to call you. How's your toe?"

"Much less painful than it was yesterday, but I have to keep my weight off it. When do you begin practicing?"

"Tomorrow morning. The tournament starts day after tomorrow."

They spoke at length about nothing significant, but each word told of their deep caring for each other. "I really don't have anything special to say to you," he admitted. "I just called to...to let you know I care deeply for you."

"I know, and it's such a welcome and wonderful feeling to have this loving relationship with a man who feels this way about me and lets me know it. I care for you, too, hon."

"If I could walk, I'd be there with you, but I'm with you in spirit."

"I know. Send me a blessing."

"I'll do that. Blow me a kiss and say goodbye."

She made the sound of a kiss. "Goodbye, love."

He also made the sound of a kiss. "Goodbye, sweetheart."

Lynne struggled out of bed, barely able to resist getting back into it and daydreaming about Sloan. She dressed and went down to the lounge to look around. She didn't want to eat alone, but she did it for most of the six years of her marriage, so she could do it now.

A woman walked past her, stopped and looked at her more closely. "You're Lynne Thurston? I'm Ingrid Lund from Sweden. Do you have a dinner companion?"

"No, I don't, and I'd love to have company."

They entered the dining room together and, as they followed the maître d' to their table, men who they passed eyed them with frank appreciation. "Have you seen the draw?" Ingrid asked Lynne. "I doubt I'll get past the first round. Imagine starting with Sharapova!"

"I don't envy you," Lynne said. "I don't even want to know who I've got."

They talked tennis talk, because that was what they knew they had in common, exchanged phone numbers and home addresses and promised to stay in touch.

"I'm glad you've rejoined the tour," Ingrid told her. "You were a great player, and you will be again."

Lynne thanked her and retired early, for she had to meet Gary at eight o'clock for practice. On the opening day of the tournament, she dispensed with Ida Craig in fifty minutes of play in a businesslike fashion, and moved on to the second round.

"You were almost like your old self out there," Gary told her, "cutting those corners like you were cutting paper with a pair of sharp scissors. Don't forget that the play gets harder with each round. Rest and early to bed tonight."

She headed for her hotel, did two laps in the pool and went to her room. After dialing Sloan's number, she dumped herself on the bed and waited for him to answer.

"McNeil."

"Hi. How's your toe?"

"Somewhat better, but my foot has to remain in a cast. Congratulations. You made mush out of that girl, and I was surprised at her poor showing; she's usually better than that. Either she couldn't figure out your game or you're on a roll."

"I hope I can get past Langley. She can be dangerous."

"She's not the player that you are. I don't think she'll take a set from you."

And she didn't. Lynne breezed into the fourth round having hardly broken a sweat, but once more, she was denied a berth in the semifinals.

"This time it was my own fault," she told Sloan. "I got overanxious and began reacting to her rather than playing my game. But it taught me something. I have to stick to my game plan."

"Do what you have to do in order to win honorably. I'm proud of you."

Hearing him say those words lessened the pain of losing. She wondered if he knew it, if he knew how important to her he had become.

"What do you think, Gary?" she asked her coach at dinner that evening. "Am I ever going to get past the fourth round?"

"You'd have done that today if you hadn't stayed at the baseline and traded ground strokes with her. You're a serve and volley player, and you didn't play your game."

He was right, and she didn't dispute him. "All right, when we practice, see if you can challenge me the way she did. I don't want to get into that habit."

"You've climbed from the bottom up to number twenty-eight in what's probably the shortest time on record. You done good, girl."

Praise from Gary came rarely, and she allowed herself a moment to bask in it. A peculiar thought occurred to her, and it wasn't until she'd said good-night to Gary and was alone in her room that she understood it. "I hope I see Davenport in the clubhouse tomorrow. I want to ask her if playing is easier when you're married or when you're single. She's playing better than ever, and she's married. Maybe I shouldn't look askance at the institution of marriage just because I did a stupid thing and hooked myself up to Willard. Sloan is nothing like him." She did sit-ups for twenty minutes. "But I love my house. Why can't we have two?" She thought for a minute. "I'm not going to try having my cake and eating it, too. Nobody's ever succeeded at that."

She answered her cell phone and considered changing the tune of its ring from "Frère Jacques" to something more romantic. "Hello."

"Hi. This is your brother. Remember me?"

"Hi, Brad. What's up?"

"Are you still in Canada? I happened to catch your last two matches. You should have won that last one. What happened to you? I got the feeling you didn't want it badly enough. You can't win like that."

"Brad, I've been through the postmortem with my coach. How's Debra?"

"Deb's her usual self. You still hanging out with that mechanic?"

"I'm still seeing Sloan McNeil, if that's the person to whom you're referring. And I'm not hanging out with him, Brad. He lives at least ten miles from me." Anger began to unfurl in her, and she took a few deep breaths in the hope of controlling it.

"Brad, you're dear to me, and I love you, but I am not going to tolerate your berating a man you don't know, have never seen and never spoken with just because he works with his hands and gets them dirty while he does it. And if you can't talk to me without doing that, then don't talk to me."

"Are you saying you'd choose that stranger over your own flesh and blood?"

"It's been a while since he was a stranger, Brad. My dog doesn't even bark at him." She laughed when she mentioned Caesar, because she knew the comment was guaranteed to infuriate Brad.

"Does he have a key to your house?"

"You are definitely not lacking in temerity, brother. He doesn't need a key because I make it my business to be home when he's coming there." She soon tired of provoking him, but she refused to concede him the right to exercise his prejudice at Sloan's expense. "My plane to San Antonio leaves early tomorrow, so I'd better get some sleep."

"Sure," he said in a voice tinged with sarcasm. "You don't want to get back to your mechanic one minute later than you have to."

She didn't pick up the gauntlet. For Brad, winning was everything. She let him bask in the meaningless victory. Suddenly a thought occurred to her that she didn't like, and she had to clear up the matter. "Brad, I received a call from Willard last week. Did you give him my phone number?"

"Well…yeah. He said he had to straighten out something in the divorce papers."

"He lied. The divorce is final, and nothing in the decree can be changed. He wants me to go back to him. A woman member of his church called to badger me. That's why I changed my phone number. Please don't give it to anyone."

"Sorry. What a nerd! As much trouble as you went to in order to get rid of him, how could he possibly think you'd take him back?"

"Willard doesn't do a lot of thinking, Brad. Gotta sleep. Good night, bro."

How could Brad have been so gullible? After all she'd told him about Willard, why would he believe anything the man said? Bradford Thurston gullible? Not in a million years! All kinds of thoughts frolicked around in her mind, and one of them was the idea that Brad would do anything to prevent her from marrying a laborer. If he only knew how wrong he was!

The day after Lynne's return from Canada, Sloan waited impatiently for the moment when she would step into his house and into his arms again. He'd asked her to bring Thelma with her because he wanted to see his friend and especially to thank her for her kindness to him. But he also didn't want to be alone with Lynne, lest he give her the impression that he expected sex every time they were alone together. He wanted it, but he knew that if he suggested it by word or deed, she would begin to doubt his professed feelings and his intentions.

He heard Caesar's bark, hobbled to the door and opened it. The dog demanded to be recognized, and he complied. That done, he looked down into her face, bright and happy with a smile that said he was special. He reached for her, lifted her and hugged her, then did the same with Thelma.

"I've been looking forward to your visit," he told the older woman. "And yours," he said to Lynne in a voice that was warm and intimate.

"I see you two have made some real progress," Thelma said as she walked into the living room and sat down. He hadn't realized how big that room really was until the petite woman seemed frailer, even smaller than usual and lost in her surrounding. She got up, walked to the stone fireplace that took up much of the wall at the long end of the room, stood there for a minute and then walked back to him.

"My dear husband loved fireplaces, and we always had one in at least one room of the house. You know, there's something to be said for these modern town houses. They're so efficient, and there's nothing to hide. Look at these big windows, not a curtain, and the room is still elegant. Plenty of space for paintings on nice smooth walls. And I'll bet your kitchen is a dream." She looked at Lynne. "If you decide to settle here, give some thought to a modern house. I love your house, but when the wind blows hard, I'll bet the noise from those crooked windows scares you to death."

He wondered whether Lynne had mentioned to Thelma his suggestion that she wouldn't need two houses. In any case, he hoped Lynne was paying close attention to what the woman said.

He followed Lynne's gaze around the large, elegant living room, saw her take note of the picture windows that received the magic of the setting sun as it mated with the dark amber carpet, the beige walls, the tan leather chairs and sofas and the modern walnut furniture scattered around.

Lynne glanced up and caught him looking at her, and the smile that formed on her face said she liked his attention. "Knowing you," she said, "I'm sure you didn't use a decorator for this room. I think it's magnificent."

"No," he said, walking toward her as if drawn by a magnet. "I shopped for and arranged everything in here, though I confess I consulted my mother about whether I could leave the windows bare. She's a great believer in pleasing oneself whenever possible."

Thelma looked at Lynne, and from her expression, it was clear that she knew she might be fomenting trouble but that she also didn't care. "Do you like the up-stairs, too?"

But Lynne wasn't taken in by Thelma's deviltry. "Haven't been up there yet, but when I do, I'll let you know what I think." When Thelma's lower lip dropped, Lynne added, "I'll tell you what Sloan told me: 'If you want an answer, ask me a direct question.'"

Thelma's hands went to the bones that passed for her hips. "I'm afraid of what you'll tell me. Anyhow, it looks to me like he's got your number, so I'm not going to worry." She paused and seemed thoughtful. "Still…no point in wasting time—life's short."

"Let's eat," Lynne said. "I want to see what Thelma cooked this time."

He did, too. He had planned to phone for their sup-per, but when he saw that Lynne carried a large insulated bag, he knew he was getting a home-cooked meal. Sup-per consisted of minestrone, an antipasto, Sicilian-style lasagna and pecan pie.

"I made enough for a couple more meals," Thelma said. "We can freeze it."

He stared at her. "Freeze it? Won't it last in the refrig-erator for two days?"

Thelma laughed, obviously pleased. "I can make lasa-gna blindfolded, so you can have some anytime Lynne's coming to see you."

They chatted convivially through the meal. Dining at his table with Lynne serving the food and Thelma keep-ing them laughing with her odd, but candid, wit seemed as natural as breathing. He was getting the feeling that Thelma was not an accident in his life, but that she some-how belonged there—it didn't seem strange that Lynne had chosen a septuagenarian for a buddy.

He wondered how Thelma had lived as a widow before Lynne moved into the house on Corpus Christi Lane. What a lonely woman she must have been. He'd always known that most vital, sophisticated young people had no time for senior citizens, but he hadn't guessed the effect of isolation on the aged. He moved over to Thelma, and when he put an arm around her shoulder, she snuggled closer to him.

"How'd you like to spend a couple of weeks down at Galveston on the Gulf? My mother loves company and my father's always out on his boat fishing. Since you were an Olympic swimmer, you ought to have a ball down there. The water is fantastic all year. I'm going down there for Thanksgiving, and I want you and Lynne to go with me."

She leaned back and looked up at him. "You can invite a stranger to spend two weeks at your parents' house without asking them first?"

It probably did seem strange to her, but not to him. "Of course," he said. "My friends have always been welcome in my parents' home. Besides, you and my mother will love each other, and my dad will have one more woman to show off for. How about it?"

"You ask them, and if they say it's all right, I'll start packing."

He looked at Lynne for evidence that she understood his need to do something special for the woman who had practically adopted him, and when she smiled through glistening tears, he pulled her into his arms, pressed his lips to hers and let her feel the strength of the emotion that plowed through him. She parted her lips, and he slipped his tongue between them for a fleeting kiss.

"Yep," Thelma said. "Just like I told you, Sloan. I'll

be at your wedding. I'm getting too old to dance, but I certainly can clap my hands."

Letting Lynne Thurston out of his life wasn't on his mind.

With the August sun bearing down on her, Lynne shaded her eyes and looked at her coach. She wasn't tired, just drenched with sweat. Gary didn't let up. "You're a champion, and you're going to play like one," he told Lynne after their practice session in Armstrong Stadium. Until the larger and more modern Arthur Ashe Stadium was built a few yards away, Armstrong Stadium had been the center court at Flushing Meadow, home of the US Open tennis tournament.

"What are you doing the rest of the day?" he asked her.

"I'm going to swim, and then, I'm going to sleep until it's time for dinner, as these New Yorkers call it."

"Good idea. I just wanted to be sure you don't have plans to wear yourself out shopping."

The following morning, she gazed longingly at the yellow tennis dress with the pleated skirt, the costume that had been her trademark back in the days when fans clamored for her and players feared her. Then, she stared into the full-length mirror, at the likeness of herself in a prim white dress slit modestly on each side to show white pants. It would take some courage to…

"Oh, what the heck," she said. "If I don't believe in myself, who will?"

She stepped out of the white clothes, slipped on the yellow dress and shorts, yellow socks and tennis shoes and tied a yellow band around her head. The people were expecting the old Lynne and she'd do her best to be that person. In a moment of apprehension, she looked toward the heavens.

"I'm going for it," she said to herself, "and if my best isn't good enough, I'll just work harder, because I intend to be number one at the end of next year."

She slung the handle of the duffel bag containing her racquets, towels and extra shoes, socks and clothing over her shoulder, said a word of prayer and headed downstairs to the hotel's entrance where a limousine awaited her.

She'd hardly sat down before her cell phone rang. "Hello."

"Hi, sweetheart. I'll be watching. If you do your best, you're a winner either way. I love you, and I'm pulling for you."

"I know, and that means everything to me."

That afternoon, at the hottest part of the day, an announcer said, "Ladies and gentlemen, Linda Waters." After the crowd's mild applause, the voice intoned, "The US Open's own champion, Lynne Thurston." She walked onto center court to the prolonged cheers and stomping of the largest crowd she'd seen since she last played in Louis Armstrong stadium six years earlier. She bowed to each section of the arena, and when an usher ran out to present her with a bunch of yellow roses, she was glad that she'd worn her yellow dress.

She won the toss and double-faulted immediately, losing the first point. "To hell with that," she said to herself and, to the crowd's delight, served two aces down the middle. "All right, girl," she said, pumping her fist. "Let's go."

And go she did, winning the first set by a score of six games to one for her opponent. Waters gained strength in the next and last set, but couldn't break Lynne's serve and lost it four games to six.

When Waters's attempt at a passing shot went out of bounds, Lynne tossed her racquet into the air and jumped nearly as high. The crowd roared its appreciation as she raced to the net for the obligatory handshake.

Holding Lynne's hand, Waters said, "Girl, you some shit. I thought I was gonna skate right through this one. Good luck."

"Thanks," Lynne said, keeping her delight in abeyance to show good sportsmanship. She shook hands with the referee, waved once more to the crowd and, after signing the pieces of paper, tennis balls, baseball caps, T-shirts and balloons handed to her, she made her way to the clubhouse.

"How does it feel to be back, Lynne?" a reporter asked. "You think you'll take the championship?"

"I'm not only taking one match at the time," she replied. "I'm only thinking about one play at a time. The lineup consists of the best players in the world, and I wouldn't deign to put myself in that class. At least, not yet."

The reporter stared at her. "You're joking, I assume."

She pulled off one of her shoes in the hopes of sending the message that the interview was over. "Never been more serious. This game didn't stand still waiting for me the six years that I stayed out of it. I have to work my way back up, and that's what I'm going to do. Thanks for the interview." She ducked into the locker room and leaned against the wall. The fans had been wonderful to her, and she had not disgraced herself by losing in the first round.

She won her next two matches and moved to the quarter finals. It would be tough, she knew, because she faced Garner, a top player known for her concentration and her ability to pull rabbits out of a hat, as it were. Whenever one player seemed to have all but won a match, Garner would still find a way to win. Lynne reminded herself that she was playing well and vowed to give it her best shot. If Garner won, she would have to outplay her, because she had no intention of beating herself.

As she was about to leave her room on the morning of her fourth-round match, her cell phone rang. She sat down on the edge of the bed and answered it. "Hello."

"Hi. I just got in," Sloan said, "and I'm on my way to the stadium as we speak. I'll be watching you this time from the stands."

"Sloan! Honey, you're not supposed to be traveling with that busted toe."

"I had to wish you good luck. I know how important this one is to you, and I had to be here."

She wiped the tear that had begun to trickle down her cheek. "You...you're wonderful. I'm so glad you're here. At least I'll have two people, you and Gary, rooting for me."

"Trust me. After the way you've been playing, everybody will be there for you. I'll see you later, sweetheart."

"Bye, love."

She dressed in yellow as she did in her glory days, left the room and headed downstairs for the limousine that would take her to the scene of her triumph or to one more loss in the fourth round.

She lost the first set, won the second and, when Garner got out of trouble with two straight aces, Lynne lost the match. "I was ahead," she said to herself. "How on earth did she sneak past me like that?" But she was damned if she would cry. She'd played a great game, and as she went to the net to shake hands with Garner, shouts of "Lynne, Lynne" pummeled her ears.

"You gave me a tough match," Garner told her. "I'm lucky to have won."

"You earned it," Lynne told her. "Congratulations."

When Lynne waved at the crowd, everyone stood and applauded her. She covered her immense disappointment with smiles, but it hurt. Oh, how it hurt! One point had separated her from a berth in the semifinals, and she'd lost the point and the game. As hard as she'd fought, Garner had, nevertheless, taken that final game and the match. One stroke. If only she had hit a lob instead of attempting one of her famous drives down the line, she'd be in the semifinals. The tears didn't fall until she saw Sloan at the gate waiting to take her to the hotel.

"It's all right, baby," he said as his arms went around her. "You played fantastically, and I'm proud of you. There's no doubt that you're headed for the top. Garner was lucky—her second ace could have been in or out, depending on how you looked at it."

"It was in…by a hair. Where're you staying?"

"At the Hilton on Sixth Avenue, but I haven't checked in yet. I went from the airport directly to the stadium."

She looked down at the bag beside his foot. "I have limousine service, so you can ride with me." Should she suggest that he stay with her? After thinking about it for a bit, she decided to let him make the first move.

"Let me check in first," he said. "Then you go to your hotel and dress, after which we can spend the evening together."

That wasn't good enough. He'd said where his luggage would be, but not where he'd sleep. "How are we getting together tomorrow morning?" she asked him. "I mean, are we having breakfast together, flying together? What?"

"I'll be at your hotel by eight o'clock, and we can have breakfast together and then leave for the airport. We're on the same flight."

He took her to the 21 Club for dinner, and she was glad that she'd worn a short evening dress because the female patrons at that restaurant all looked as if they were either fashion models or well-paid actresses.

"You're treating me as if I won the tournament," she said when he ordered an expensive vintage champagne to accompany their dessert. "You're a man who enjoys even the simplest things that are seemingly incompatible with vintage champagne and fine French desserts. Where did you cultivate such expensive—and I might say exquisite—taste?"

He didn't seem to think the question odd, nor did he take offense. "When you meet my mother, you'll understand the conflicts you see in me." He didn't elaborate further, and she didn't press him. Looking around at the elegant restaurant, a setting that would have been more fitting if she had won, she vowed that after next year's US Open, the celebration would honor her triumph. *I'll have to work hard,* she told herself, *but it will be worth it.*

"You've drifted away from me," Sloan said as he raised his glass to her. "Next year in this same restaurant, we will celebrate your victory." He linked arms with her and sipped the champagne.

"I was telling myself the same thing, Sloan. I don't think I will ever be able to make you understand what your being here with me this day means to me. It…means more to me than…" She looked for the words. "It's made me happier than if I had won that match, because I can imagine what you went through to get here."

He looked at her for a long time, his expression soft and loving, and when she thought he had decided not to answer or to comment on her remark, he said, "I'll kiss you for that, and I'll love you for it, too."

She must have seemed perplexed, for he added, "Yes, I went through a lot to get here, and it wasn't all pleasant, but I'd do it again in a second to hear you tell me you love me in those same words." He leaned toward her, staring her in the face, his expression stern and purposeful. "I hope you're not thinking that this is a temporary fling with me, because it isn't. Your name will be the last word I utter. You're my woman. Your brother and your ex are a couple of human termites burrowing at our relationship. They can root as much as they like and for as long as they can, but baby, I am not giving you up. Never. And you can tell both of them that. You're mine."

She couldn't imagine what had brought that on. "I'm with you because I want to be, because there's no other place I'd rather be and no person whose company I prefer to yours. Willard is just proving that he never knew me. His pride is suffering, and he wants a chance for revenge. Most days, I don't remember that he exists. As for Brad, I am learning that he is a bigot and arrogant to boot, but he's my brother and I love him. That doesn't mean that he can influence me as he once did. I've grown up."

He relaxed and leaned back in the chair. "I just wanted to make sure that you and I are on the same page."

She reached across the table and caressed his fingers. "We are."

* * *

Bradford Thurston was a corporate lawyer who considered his achievements, as a black man, exceptional. He worked and frequently traveled in a white-shirted, white man's world of conference-room decisions, happy-hour friendships and margarita lunches. He bought his sports attire at the Princeton Shop, his shirts, suits, ties and loafers at Gucci, his leather goods at Louis Vuitton and his slim bank account reflected his taste. Any man who lived, dressed and carried himself differently was not worth Bradford's time. Women thought him good-looking, and he was, with an intimidating six-feet-four-inch height to support his handsome face. Brad had rejoiced when Lynne married Willard Marsh, for he thought that guaranteed her an upper-middle-class life-style and status in the community in which she lived. Domestic abuse was the last crime he had expected a minister to be guilty of, and he wondered whether and how much of it Lynne provoked. Not fair, maybe, but he had to consider both sides. He walked into the offices of Jain, Feldman and Sharp, took the seat shown him and dropped his Louis Vuitton–initialed briefcase on the floor beside the chair.

He handed Rupert Sharp a slip of paper on which he had written the name and occupation of Sloan McNeil. "He lives in San Antonio or thereabouts. I want you to find out everything about this man, where he works, what he does there, his age, marital—"

Sharp interrupted him. "You said you wanted to know everything about him. That's all you need to say. I know my job, Mr. Thurston. I'll get you the goods on him, but I need a retainer of five hundred dollars, cash or credit

card. You'll hear from me in a week, and I'll need another five hundred when I give you my report."

Brad didn't like giving up a thousand dollars that easily, but he couldn't think of another way to put an end
to Lynne's stupidity. He'd bet his eyetooth that the man
was a gold digger. Everybody knew that Lynne made
millions before she married, and she seemed headed
for more of the same, now that tennis prize money had
doubled in the last few years.

He opened his wallet and counted out five hundred
dollars for the advance payment. Sharp raised an eyebrow. "Why cash? Is this deal on the up-and-up? Why
is finding out about this McNeil fellow so important to
you? I don't get involved in anything that's unsavory,
buddy."

"My sister is famous, and she's gone nuts over this
guy. I don't want her ever to know about this, so I'm
covering my tracks by paying you cash."

Sharp flexed his right shoulder in a quick shrug. "As
a lawyer, I suppose you'd think that way. You may be
wasting your money, though. If she's nuts about the guy
as you say, nothing you can do will break it up. Nothing
that's honest and legal, that is. I'll call you in a week."

If McNeil was a businessman, he had to have made
some wrong moves, and he intended to find out what
they were. Nobody was completely honest, and if he
knew Sharp's reputation, the man would find out everything, including the number of hairs on McNeil's
head. He left the private investigator's office, got in his
Mercedes coupe and headed for work. With the windows rolled down and a warm breeze kissing his face, he
thought about his good life. Not many people had what

he had or did what he did for a living. Lynne came from a family that was well respected in Ellicott City, and he didn't intend to see her sink to lower class because she couldn't control her hormones.

He walked into his office at White, White and White, threw his LV briefcase on his desk and went immediately to Edgar White's office. "What have you got for me this morning, Ed?"

Edgar White didn't raise his head from the paper that had his attention. "I'll get to you in a minute."

He camouflaged his displeasure with a smile. "Right on," he said, but he'd give anything to chew out the pompous jerk, but he had to remember his bills and his mortgage. He sat there for half an hour before Edgar looked up at him and smiled.

"See what you can do with the grammar on this brief."

"Right on, man."

"I'd like to enter one or two of those small tournaments in Asia," Lynne told Gary the day after she returned home from New York.

"All right," he said. "I want you to take two weeks off from practice, but not from training. Go out and have a life. Spend some time with McNeil. The happier you are, the more likely you are to win."

After her workout the next morning, she put a leash on Caesar, locked the house and walked over to visit with Thelma. "I've got two weeks to do practically nothing. I'd like to be buying and decorating my house, but—"

"What are you going to do with two houses?" Thelma asked her. "Are you trying to discourage Sloan?"

"He asked me the same question, but I don't have an answer. I'm not going to shack up with him, and he hasn't mentioned marriage. If he's fishing to know what his chances are, he can forget it. I'm not giving him assurances until he gives me some."

Thelma stopped rolling pie crust dough and stared at Lynne. "What would you say to him if he asked you to marry him?"

"Oh, I don't know. I just got out of a marriage less than a year ago."

Thelma treated her to a withering look, and she prepared herself for some of the woman's wisdom. "From what you've told me, I'd say that mess you were in could hardly be called a marriage. When you marry Sloan McNeil, you'll find out what it means to have a man love you and cherish you. You don't know a thing about that."

"No. I don't suppose I do. I wouldn't be happy if Sloan took himself out of my life, but…well, right now, I don't have to answer to anybody."

"Sure," Thelma said. "Independence is great until you find yourself with that and nothing else. You can have your independence with Sloan, because he's self-confident enough not to try to imprison you and to let you fly. Forget about that rotten excuse for a man that you married, and thank God that you have Sloan."

When Caesar swung his tail, whimpered and rubbed against her leg, Lynne patted his head and told Thelma, "Caesar has to go out, so we'll continue this another time. Want to see a movie this evening?"

"Love it, but you'd better check with Sloan. He has some rights, you know."

She returned home, checked her home phone and cellular phone and found that she had three messages from Sloan. "I was over at Thelma's house," she told him, "and

I forgot to take along my cell phone. Gary says I have two weeks off from practice, but what'll I do with myself?"

"I hope to take up a lot of your time. I'm working from seven until three, and after that, you may do with me as you like."

She didn't dare share with him the thoughts that crossed her mind. "You may get tired of my company."

"Really? Which man do you think you're talking to?"

"I was joking. I wouldn't mind seeing you right now, since you offered me the possibility of doing with you as I wish."

His silence reminded her again that he didn't joke about their relationship. "What do you want to do with me?" he growled.

But she refused to let the tenor of his voice intimidate her. "Nothing that I haven't already done."

"Watch what you're saying. I can take a long lunch hour if I want to."

"And I can take the rest of the day, if *I* want to. Why did you call me?"

"Ben has two tickets to the accordion festival tonight, and he can't use them. I was going to ask if you'd like to go, but what you're offering is far more attractive. What do you say I collect some supper someplace and we eat it together at your house around six o'clock?"

She recalled one of Thelma's bits of wisdom: "Not even a prostitute offers what she can't or won't give. Never come on to a man unless you mean what you're suggesting."

"Maybe we can walk through the park over to the waterfall. I love it late in the day."

"I've never seen the waterfall, Lynne, and I'd like it. I have a call. See you around six."

She donned a pair of garden gloves, and set about cleaning out the weeds and overgrown bushes from her garden. She had neglected the garden all summer, and it felt good to work at something other than tennis. She trimmed hedges, clipped low-hanging limbs from a pine tree and stacked the refuse in a corner to be burned later. When she looked at her watch, a gasp escaped her; three o'clock, and she hadn't eaten lunch. She washed her hands, made a salad of lettuce, tomatoes and shredded cold chicken breast, and ate it.

After a leisurely shower, she laid across the bed to rest for a few minutes. Hours later, Caesar's bark awakened her. Still half asleep, she slipped on a cornflower-blue silk kimono and ran down the stairs to find out why the dog barked with such furor.

"Oh m'gosh," she said when she saw Sloan standing at the back door with two shopping bags at his feet. "I was asleep. How long have you been here?"

"A good half hour." He patted Caesar, who wagged his tail and accepted Sloan's gratitude.

"I'm sorry. I worked out here in the garden for hours, took a shower and thought I'd rest for a few minutes. You know the rest. Come on in." She hugged Caesar. "You're a smart dog."

"I'll be back in a minute," she said to Sloan.

"Oh, don't go to any trouble on my account. You're perfect as you are," he threw over his shoulder as he headed toward the kitchen with their food.

"I'll bet," she said and started up the stairs, but he caught her before she reached the third step and, standing behind her, fastened one hand to her belly and slipped his other one through the opening of the robe and clamped it on her naked breast.

As if suddenly aware of his treasure, he untied the robe, pressed his hand to her bare belly and then slid it down until he fastened it between her legs. No longer able to pretend that she was unmoved by his bold caresses, she gripped the hand that massaged her breast, telling him without words that she wanted and needed more. But he ignored her whimpers and the tightening of her thighs against his hands, and she knew she'd have to tell him what she wanted.

"Take me to bed," she whispered.

"You're going to stop playing with me," he said, then turned her around and sucked her nipple into his mouth. He lifted her and carried her up the stairs. "You knew when you teased me this morning that I was on fire for you, didn't you? What you didn't know was that I'm no longer wearing that cast. Nothing that you haven't already done to me, eh? Isn't that what you said?"

She didn't care whether he was angry, annoyed or pretending. He was doing what she wanted him to do. "I don't remember what I said, but if it makes you act as you're doing now, I wish I'd written it down."

He laid her on the bed, and she opened her robe wide and raised her arms to him in a gesture as old as womankind.

The fire that blazed in his eyes sent hot arrows of anticipation shooting through her. Anticipation of what she knew was to come. "You told me that I'm yours," she said, "and I want you to know that you belong to me."

As if her words heated his blood, he threw off his clothes and covered her body with his own. "Kiss me," he said. "Wrap me in your arms and kiss me. You don't know how I need you." She could feel the trem-

ors that passed through his body and the shudders that
shook him.

*This isn't about me. He needs me, and I want to show
him that I'm here for him.* She released her hold on him,
placed a hand on his shoulder and urged him to his back.
The question in his eyes made her heart skip beats. This
man loved her.

She kissed his eyes, his lips, cheeks and neck and,
with nothing to guide her, set out to explore his body.
When the twirling of her tongue around one of his pectorals brought a moan from him, she sucked it into her
mouth and toyed with it until he nearly rolled off the bed.
Emboldened now, she kissed his belly, moved down and
licked the insides of his thighs. And when his hips began
to shift from side to side, she stroked his penis, admiring its firmness and its stunning size. A smile broke out
on her face when it dawned on her that that lovely organ
belonged to her, and she sucked it into her mouth. His
scream of joy shocked her, but only momentarily. She
gripped his thigh with one hand, held his penis with the
other and loved him until he yelled.

"Stop. Stop. For God's sake, *stop!*"

She released him, and he pulled her up, eased her onto
her back and slipped inside of her.

It had never been like that. She had no will of her
own, but submitted to him and took what he gave her.
She didn't drive for her orgasm but enjoyed the feeling of
him inside her, stroking and loving. She asked for nothing, but gave all that was in her. A fire slowly began its
wild journey through her veins, singeing every ounce of
her flesh. Oh, the sweet hell of it as the heat started at
the bottom of her feet, and the tip of his penis anointed

the mouth of her uterus. She threw herself up to him to give him better access to her body, and as if she had injected him with a potion, he began to stroke wildly, moaning her name. Her thighs began a quivering, jerking motion and when she thought she could no longer stand the sinking feeling, the pumping and squeezing began. Her entire vaginal canal clutched him so tightly that his eyes widened, and they screamed simultaneously in release. He collapsed in her arms.

She hadn't the energy to speak. He kissed her shoulder, but said nothing. As she held him, she knew that by thinking only of him and not of herself and what he would give her, she had gained more than she'd ever thought possible. On the two previous times when he'd made love with her, he had given her her woman's birthright. Now, she wondered if any new pleasure remained, for what she had just experienced with him far surpassed anything she had ever known or imagined.

"Are you awake?" he asked.

"Uh-huh. Are you okay?"

He raised himself up and braced on his elbows. "I think so. What happened to you? What you gave me...I never..." He eased up and sat with his back against the headboard of the bed. "I never had such an experience in my entire life. You gave without thought of your own needs."

"You did that each time. For the first time in my life, my needs were not important, Sloan, and what you gave me as a result I will cherish every minute that I live."

He reached over and pulled her into his arms. "Does that mean I should stop worrying about what you'll do with two houses?"

She cut him a side glance. "Some people have half a dozen."

"And some people live in caves, too. Will you ever give me a straight answer?"

She looped her arms around his neck. "When you ask me a straight question. I don't want to shack up with you, Sloan. In my opinion, that's not commitment, that's trying to have your cake and eat it. Is it enough to know that no one on this earth is as important to me as you are?"

His arm tightened around her. "No, Lynne. It isn't, and before long, you will realize it, too."

He served their dinner of deviled shrimp, yellow saffron rice, steamed zucchini and a salad that consisted of spinach, mushrooms, tomatoes and pitted green olives. He'd brought apple pie and vanilla ice cream for dessert.

"I thought this ice cream was going to become vanilla soup while Caesar and I were trying to wake you up. I was becoming alarmed."

"Caesar knew I was at home," she said in a high-handed tone.

"I don't doubt that, but Caesar's a dog, and he can't talk."

With her chin in the air, she said, "Then we'll have to teach him how. My, this pie is delicious."

She kept her gaze diverted from his, got up, went around to her chair and kissed his mouth. "You devil. Woman, you could drive a man mad if you put yourself to it."

She looked at him then, her face shrouded in innocence. "What did I do? Where did you get this food? I'd like a charge account with them."

He couldn't help laughing. Their similarities often

stunned him, and they always pleased him. "You may use mine. I just call them for what I want, and they send me a bill."

Later, he stood at her front door with his arms wrapped tight around her. "I'd rather not leave just now, but I told Thelma I'd check the air-conditioning vent in her bedroom. From what she said, I suspect it gets clogged with ice. She probably needs a good filter. Ever been to SeaWorld?" She shook her head. "It's great entertainment. Want to go tomorrow afternoon around four-thirty?"

"I'd love it."

"All right. I'll be here at four, and you be dressed."

Her throaty laugh sent the blood straight to his loins. "Behave yourself, woman." He had to get away from there before he made a nuisance of himself, and that was not his style. He kissed her nose and left her.

The next morning, Ben walked over to him wearing a quizzical expression. "Look, man, you're not in any trouble, are you?"

"Not that I know of. Why?"

"Well, this guy was sniffing around here after you left yesterday asking all kinds of questions about you, and a few minutes ago the builder in Castle Hills said somebody was over there following him around and asking questions about you. He pinned the man against a wall and wouldn't release him until the guy told him who was paying him. From the description he gave me, I'd say it's the same man who was over here yesterday. He works for...I hate to tell you this, but he said he was working for Thurston."

"What? He said what?"

Ben didn't repeat it. "That's what he said, Sloan."

He whirled around, stormed into his office and dialed Lynne's cell phone number. "Hello?" Her voice, soft, sweet and loving, came to him like a wave washing over his head and sucking him beneath the surface of the water. He hung up. Maybe his number showed on her caller ID screen, and maybe it didn't. He couldn't help it. How could she do that to him? He would give his life for her, and she could… He closed his eyes and fought the pain. For the next hour, he pondered Ben's words. Then he got into his car, drove to Castle Hills and confronted the builder.

"What did that man ask you about me?"

The man recited a list of questions. "He said he was in the pay of someone named Thurston. I didn't get the person's first name."

"Thanks."

As much as he longed to confront her, he resisted doing it because he didn't want to be sucked into the quicksand of her mesmerizing allure. Instead he phoned her at six o'clock that evening. "This is Sloan. I'm canceling our date for this evening, and I think it best that we don't see each other again. I wish you the best."

"What on earth are you talking about?" she screamed.

"You'll figure it out. Goodbye." He hung up, went into the bathroom and put a cold wet washcloth on the back of his neck. An hour later, he lost his supper.

Sitting in the big overstuffed chair that dominated a corner of her living room with Caesar lying at her feet, Lynne did what she swore she would never do. She let the tears gush down her face and pool in her lap. No explanation, no opportunity to clear up whatever misunderstanding caused him to sever relations with her.

Darkness fell, and Caesar demanded to eat. Later, sensing her sadness, the dog didn't want to leave her alone, and she spent the night sitting in the chair with the faithful German shepherd lying at her feet.

"You're pretty lethargic today," Clive, her physical trainer, told her. "You don't want to go to Seoul with your body as weak as a wet rag."

"I'm doing the best I can," she told him.

"Did that big guy do something to upset you? If that's the case, you need to show him that you're not going to fold up. You're made of sturdy stuff, Lynne. Don't let anybody kill your dream."

She looked steadily at Clive, who had never shown her any affection, who maintained a strict employee-employer relationship with her and never showed an interest in any aspect of her well-being other than her fitness.

"You're right, Clive. I've had worse setbacks. I'm going to Seoul, and then I'm going to Tashkent. I'm a tennis player, and I intend to act like it."

"Pretty soon, you'll be bringing home the prizes," Gary told her a week later, "and I'm going to drink a whole bottle of champagne."

She laughed. For the first time in a week, she laughed and enjoyed the feeling. "You'll drink half of it," she said, "because I'll drink the other half. See you at the Omni day after tomorrow."

Chapter 9

Lynne strolled along Seoul's "American Avenue," so nicknamed because the United States dollar was once the only currency that the legion of shops would accept. Smart shopkeepers had begun trading in the euro and the Swiss franc as well. She couldn't help laughing when she walked into the store that carried only top French and Italian designer leather goods, and at prices so low that she examined them to verify their authenticity.

"We make here in Seoul. Big factory," the saleswoman told her. She bought billfolds for Clive and for her brother, Brad, an eyeglass case for Debra and a lined leather "shopping" bag for Thelma. Unable to resist it, she bought an elegant soft leather travel kit for a man's personal items.

I may keep it forever, she said to herself, *but if we're ever friends again, I'll give it to him for old times' sake.*

No matter what happens, he'll always be special, and I'll be forever in his debt, for it was he who taught me what it means to be a happy woman.

"All set?" Gary asked her by telephone that Monday morning before she left her hotel room for the tournament stadium.

"I'm as ready as I can be."

"You shouldn't have any trouble with Lewis. Get your mind on winning, on your game, and keep it there. If you concentrate, you can't miss."

But Lynne was unable to concentrate. Her powerful serve didn't work, and she lost the first set one game to six for her opponent. In the short rest period between sets, she told herself to shape up.

"No one hundred and twenty-fifth ranked player is going to beat me," she told herself, and won the next set six games to none for Lewis. But she struggled through the third and last sets, finally winning it with two aces down the middle."

"I've never played worse," she told Gary. "Even when I lost, I did a lot better than I played today."

"Get McNeil out of your mind," he said. "You've worked too hard to throw this away. This is not a big-time tournament. Half of the top players are over in Germany. This is your chance."

She knew it, and she also knew that she couldn't brush aside the fact that Sloan had removed himself from her life. "Damned if I'll let it throw me."

She won the next match and the next and, once more she faced the number one player in the quarter finals. The crowd's boisterous welcome when she entered center court for the first game buoyed her spirits, but she wanted to kick herself when thoughts of Sloan weighted on her like an ominous cloud.

"I'm beginning to wonder if this is a jinx," she said to Gary after losing in a third set tiebreaker.

"No," he said. "Next week, I'm going to get one of my buddies to play a few practice games with you. You have to get into the habit of closing out a match. There's an art to it, although you have to have confidence, too. Your game is similar to mine, and that may be one of your problems. We'll see."

She didn't go back home, but went directly to Tashkent in the southeastern region of the former Soviet Union. When Gary asked her if she intended to shop, she said, "I'm not nuts about vodka, and I'll have to pay too much duty on caviar to make it worthwhile. I did all the shopping I'm planning to do in Seoul." They practiced for two hours the morning of the day after she arrived, and she spent the remainder of the day lolling around the hotel.

"Would you like some company, or am I being a nuisance?" a well-tanned blond with a northern European accent said, sliding to within an inch of where she sat with her feet dangling in the swimming pool.

"Would you mind getting out of my space?" she asked him. "I don't like strangers touching my flesh."

His shrug said much about him, and he jumped up immediately. "No need to waste my time."

He's either buying or selling, she thought with a glance at the back of his skimpy bathing trunks, and either way, he's out of luck.

She dived into the pool, swam a lap, got out and headed for her room, but not before she realized that the pool served as a meeting place for women and men on the make. "As long as they stay out of my way, I don't care," she muttered to herself. "I'm not giving up swimming here just because some people don't care who they sleep with."

She stepped on the elevator and pushed the number to her floor. "You're a beautiful woman," a low and sexy male voice said. She hadn't looked directly at him in the hope of discouraging conversation. "I'm not stupid enough to assume that you're traveling alone, but if you are, I'd love to have dinner with you this evening."

She looked at him then. The man was a knockout, guaranteed to take a woman's mind off just about anyone and anything. And she didn't have to be told that he would provide lavish fare, an evening certain to make her unfit for anything the next morning other than sleep.

"Thank you," she said, "but I have to work tomorrow morning, and I need to be fresh." She looked up, saw that the elevator had arrived at her floor, smiled and got off. "At least I'm not so besotted with Sloan that another good-looking man can't tempt me," she told herself, although she admitted that the temptation wasn't very strong.

The next morning, in a blistering noonday sun, she strolled onto the court. In the still, dry air she thought she would melt beneath the desertlike sun. Again, she lost the match in the fourth round.

"I was too tired to move another step," she told Gary. "I could hardly breathe. I know it sounds like an excuse, but it's a fact. I was relieved when that final point was over, and I couldn't get to that air-conditioned dressing room fast enough. This is it for me until the Australian Open in January. Nobody's going to knock me out of the fourth round in that one," she said.

"I've got some news for you—getting into the fourth round gives you some points. In June, you were ranked three hundred and fifty. After this match, you're number twenty-six, and for your next tournament, you'll be a seeded player. How's that for five months' work?"

He wasn't waiting for her when the plane landed in San Antonio. She hadn't expected it, but if he had reconsidered his position—whatever that was—and decided he at least owed her an explanation for his abrupt and hurtful action, she would have listened and maybe understood. She collected a rental car at the airport, drove to the kennel to collect Caesar and went on home to her big, empty house. After taking Caesar for a run and feeding him, she walked over to see Thelma and take her the bag she bought for her in Seoul.

"You're spoiling me, but I sure love it. From the time of my husband's last illness, nobody's spoiled me but you and Sloan. People don't pamper old folks. Seems like you were gone a year," Thelma said. "I sure did miss you. Couldn't get Sloan to say one word about you. What happened? The poor man was the picture of gloom. He comes to see me regularly, though."

"He broke off our relationship with no explanation, so you know as much as I do. I hope he realizes how much he hurt me."

"If he did that, he's probably thinking about how much you hurt him. Don't worry. It'll work out. These things always do. He's been in our local papers lately."

Lynne sat forward, practically holding her breath. "What about?"

"I kept the papers for you, and you can take 'em with you when you leave. I saved you some supper in case you came over this evening." She reached up and patted Lynne's shoulder. "I hope you can patch things up with Sloan, Lynne. He's a wonderful man." She raised her hands as if to ward off a coming argument. "Oh, I know he's stubborn and maybe a little bit ornery sometimes, but that man loves you. I'd bet my life on it."

After a meal of roasted chicken, stuffing, string beans and a tomato and red-onion salad, she refused dessert, hugged Thelma and went home to read the papers and find out what Sloan had done to get his name in the local papers.

She heard the sound of thunder in the distance and brought Caesar inside, remembering that electric storms frightened the dog. She sat in her favorite chair with Caesar lying beside her feet, turned on the floor lamp beside her chair and opened the papers. She flipped through the issue of the *San Antonio Star,* saw nothing of interest, and went back to the first page to read it more carefully.

She found it on the second page. "Sloan McNeil, owner of McNeil Motor Service on Bremont Street, opened a new and modern service center in Castle Hills. Mayor Archer cut the ribbon at eleven o'clock yesterday morning and opened the champagne. McNeil served ham and turkey breast sandwiches and coffee to every motorist who stopped at the McNeil Motor Service center between eleven and one."

She read the same story in two other papers. "Why on earth would Thelma have a copy of the *Houston Defender,* a black newspaper?" She went into the kitchen to make coffee and thought better of it when a streak of lightning was followed by a loud clap of thunder that seemed as if it were a few feet above her house. It didn't surprise her to see Caesar standing beside her in the kitchen. She patted his head. "You're supposed to be protecting *me,* not the other way around," she told him.

She found the story easily, because it was accompanied by a color photograph of Sloan in an elegant gray business suit. She read the full-page story and realized that there was much that she didn't know about him, such as his work with young boys who didn't have fathers in their home. She learned that he tutored the boys to improve their schoolwork, gave them tennis lessons and took them on an annual fishing retreat. She also read that his workers recommended him for the NAACP image award and that, after investigating, the organization gave him the award.

Things were happening to Sloan—wonderful things that she longed to share with him. She waited until half an hour had elapsed since she'd heard thunder or seen lightning, and telephoned Sloan.

"McNeil."

"Hello, Sloan, this is Lynne." She imagined that her call surprised him since seconds passed before he responded.

"Hello, Lynne."

The ball was in her court, and she knew he'd let it stay there, so she didn't waste time. "I called to congratulate you on your nomination for an NAACP image award and on the opening of your second service center. You have a lot to be proud of."

"Thank you."

"I had no idea that you mentored young boys. That article in the *Houston Defender* would have impressed anyone. I'm sure your parents must be very proud."

"I imagine they are, at least that's what they said. I wouldn't have thought that anything in that article would surprise you because I told you about the service center in Castle Hills and about my work with teenage boys. And even if I hadn't, I'd like to know why all that you knew about me from my own mouth wasn't sufficient. Why didn't you believe what I've told you, and why did you think it necessary to have a private investigator dig into my background and my affairs?"

"What? Are you out of your mind? I haven't done any such thing."

"According to the man who was prying into my life, Thurston was paying him a thousand dollars for the job."

She jumped up from the chair, startling Caesar. "Get outta here! Nothing like that has even crossed my mind. Is that what this is all about? Dammit, you wait until I see Brad. How could he do such a thing? And you put me through pure hell for something I haven't even contemplated doing. If you had asked me... Oh, what the hell!" She hung up and telephoned her brother.

"Thurston speaking."

"Let me tell you something, Brad. I'm mad enough with you to stop using my maiden name. How could you do such a thing? You wanted to break Sloan and me up? Well, you managed to do that, and I've finished with you."

"The guy's as clean as falling snow, and at least you can thank me for verifying that."

"I already knew it. I've got sense. If you think I'm going to forgive you for this, you're mistaken. Goodbye." She dropped the receiver into its cradle and closed her eyes. She was damned if she'd cry.

The telephone rang persistently, but she refused to answer it. She'd had enough pain for one evening, and neither Brad nor Sloan deserved her courtesy. Thinking that Thelma might need her, she used her cellular phone to call the woman.

"I'm calling to find out whether you had any storm damage. That one was pretty rough."

"Thanks. I think the garage door blew off the hinges, but I don't care about that. There hasn't been a car in the place in thirty-five years, and nothing's stored in there except the garden things. You're a dear, and I love you."

"I love you, too, Thelma."

Lynne flipped on the television and watched Tavis Smiley on PBS. She had always admired Tavis's ability to be equally at ease with rappers and opera singers, rabble rousers and major politicians. Somehow, he managed to get something of relevance, as well as newsworthy, out of all of them.

Caesar sat up and thumped his tail, but didn't growl. Now what? she thought. *I'm not walking the dog this time of night, and after a big storm, too.* She decided to take him out to the garden, but Caesar jumped up and ran to the front door, getting there at about the time the doorbell rang.

A prickling sensation irritated the back of her neck, and when Caesar whimpered in a show of delight, her heart seemed to somersault, and she quickened her steps. She didn't peep through the side window, but asked, "Who is it?"

"Sloan."

Caesar's behavior had already communicated that to her, but at the sound of his voice, confirming his presence, her blood raced. Her fingers shook so badly that she could hardly release the chain on the door. At last, she could open it. Caesar greeted him with a wagging tail, and he bent down, rubbed the dog's head and patted his shoulder, barely removing his gaze from her face.

"May I come in?" he asked her, and she stepped back and closed the door behind him. "I suppose you knew I'd come here if it was humanly possible."

"No, Sloan, I didn't know that. This is the second time that you've convicted me without allowing me to defend myself. I've been through hell. What had I done? Had I made a mistake the night before when I opened my heart and showed you how I love you, giving you all that I had to give? Sloan, did it occur to you that you hurt me?" She sat in her favorite chair, and motioned for Sloan to take the chair opposite her. It didn't escape her that the dog placed himself on the floor between them. "I'm not in a conciliatory mood."

"I imagine you aren't. If I had remembered that you have a brother who thinks I'm not good enough for you, I'd have saved us both some pain. Lynne, I'm sure that I hurt you, and God knows I'm sorry. But I, too, have been living in pure hell. And even though I let myself believe that you did that, I didn't love you any less. I couldn't have if I'd tried." He leaned toward her. "Can you forgive me?"

"I don't control that, Sloan. You're as much a part of me as my arms and legs, but I've proved to myself these past two weeks that no matter how much I miss you, I can get on with my life. Not as successfully as I'd like, perhaps, but I can do it. You have to decide whether you have faith in me. Excuse me."

She got a pitcher of lemonade from the refrigerator and two glasses and went back into the living room. "Oh, I forgot something." She grabbed a handful of the pecan and raisin cookies that she bought in the airport and put a small plate of them on the coffee table. "Lemonade always needs something sweet," she said. "Have some."

"You're right. I have to forget past relations with women. You aren't like any woman I've known, and I'm grateful for that. But, Lynne, I've had my heart broken in more ways than one, and women have used me to escort them places because I looked decent in a suit, but a grease monkey wasn't good enough to take home to their parents or to get serious about." Her eyes widened. "Oh, yes. I think I told you that was the favorite nickname one of them had for me. Up to the time I found out, she was very dear to me, and she let me believe that it was mutual. That doesn't justify my breaking off our relationship summarily and without hearing your side of it."

"That's water under the bridge, but I don't know how long it will take me to forget about that awful pain."

"You did well in Seoul," he said in what she surmised was an attempt to soften their conversation.

"I thought I should have done better, and in Tashkent, I was way off. I struggled for every point and against lesser players. I couldn't wait for that last match to be over."

He walked over to her and knelt before her. "I know. I saw it in your demeanor, and you are right—she was a lesser player. I knew that your mind was elsewhere, and I prayed that it wasn't on me."

"But it was, and it had been every waking minute since I last saw you." For the life of her, she couldn't imagine why her left hand strayed to his head, sending her fingers through his hair and letting them linger at the back of his head.

"Don't tell me. You could have won that match. If not, you would at least have been in the finals."

"Who knows? I'm going to work hard, and I'm going to be number one if only for one day."

"I don't doubt that you'll get there, Lynne, and I want to be with you when you do. Will you go with me to visit my parents Thanksgiving? I told them I was bringing you and Thelma, and I didn't have the heart to let them know you and I were no longer together."

"You told them about me?"

His face creased in a frown. "Of course I did. I can't keep anything important from my mother—she practically reads my mind. 'Who's the girl?' she asked when I was out there last. So I told her. I was happy to tell her, because she's always worrying about my being alone and spending so much time working."

She rubbed her right hand over her face and rested her chin in the palm of her hand. "Do you mind telling me what you told your mother?"

"Not at all. I told her that you're very important to me, but we're still getting to know each other. I believe she said, 'In other words, don't expect anything yet.' Will you go with me? Lynne, give me a chance to make amends."

"Amends? I'm not thinking in those terms. You were hurt, and you put as much distance between yourself and the source of your discomfort as you could."

He shook his head. "It was far more than that. I couldn't get you to say you'd postpone buying this house, and I linked that to the investigation. The thought that you would have me investigated before accepting me made me physically ill. I couldn't eat and keep food down for two days straight." He braced his hands on her knees and looked into her eyes. "I'm deeply in love with you. As you say, I've learned that being without you won't kill me, but it will guarantee me unhappiness."

She didn't want him to ask her a third time to go with him to his parents home, so she tilted his chin up with her right index finger and forced him to smile. "I'd love to have Thanksgiving dinner with you, your parents and Thelma."

He reached toward her with his arms open and an expression of hope on his face. She slid into his arms and oh, the sweet joy of holding him close to her body and of being locked tightly in his arms. They didn't kiss but merely held each other as if enjoying a narrow escape. After some minutes, he heaved himself up while holding her in his arms.

"Do you love me?" he asked her.

"Yes. I love you. But right now, I can't go farther than that."

He tightened his arms around her and released her. "Can we see each other on a regular basis?"

If she punished him, she'd do the same to herself. "Yes. I want that. I'm straight with you, Sloan, and I want you to be sure of it."

"I've always been, and I expect that accounts for my reaction. The man not only questioned my employees here in San Antonio, but at the Castle Hills center as well."

"I'm sorry for that, and I've given my brother a piece of my mind for doing it, not that I made a dent. He said I should be glad to know that you're as clean as…I forget what he said, but he meant that his investigator didn't find out anything negative about you. I told him I had a good mind to drop my maiden name and change it to Marsh."

"Are you still planning to spend Christmas with him? I don't think I want to put a foot across his threshold ever."

She tried to imagine what her facial expression communicated to him when he said, "There isn't much that I wouldn't do for you, and if it would make you happy, I'd control my temper and my attitude and go there."

"Thanks. I've recently come to understand that Brad is frequently wrong, but he's my brother, and the only close blood relative that I have."

"I'd better leave, because it's getting late, and I want to stop by Thelma's and remind her that she promised to go with us to Galveston." He took her hand and walked to the door with Caesar tagging behind them.

He put his hands in his pockets and his back to the wall as he gazed down at her. Frissons of heat shot through her in anticipation of what he'd do next. "I need to kiss you. I need it," he repeated, his voice suggesting that all of the air had swooshed out of him. "And I need *you!*"

Lord, how I love this man! She raised her arms to him and, with a tortured groan, he crushed her to his body.

"Lynne! Lynne!" She parted her lips, and he plunged into her, seeking, anointing, testing and twirling. She took him in. *I shouldn't give all.* But she couldn't help herself, for suddenly, he cooled the passion and gently brushed her eyes, cheeks and lips with his own closed lips as he stroked her back and her hair. His gentleness was a torch to her libido, and her hot blood raced to her loins. But as if he was unaware of it, he pressed a kiss to her lips and whispered, "I'll call you when I get home." A second later, he was out the door and striding down the walk.

You were about to make a mistake, her common sense told her. *He didn't think making love was appropriate, and neither did you.*

She put Caesar in his house, locked the doors and carried the untouched lemonade, cookies and glasses to the kitchen. It wasn't a night for a leisurely bath, so she took a shower, said her prayers and got into bed. *If he calls, I'll wake up and talk to him.*

For the first time in three weeks, she fell asleep as soon as she put her head on the pillow. The ringing of the telephone pulled her out of a deep sleep.

"Hi," she said, and even to her that one word sounded like a sexy come-on.

She heard him suck in his breath, or at least that was what it sounded like to her. "I didn't think you'd be asleep so soon," he said. "I'm sorry that I awakened you. I wanted to tell you good-night."

"Good night, love," she said and hung up.

The next morning, she remembered that he called her, but not that she told him good-night. She finished breakfast and telephoned him. No point in causing a riff when they were trying to patch up one.

"Did I tell you good-night?" she asked him when he answered the phone.

"Hi. You did, indeed, and in the sweetest way. That made up for your hanging up on me and not giving me a chance to reciprocate, but I realized you were asleep."

"I was. Did Thelma agree to go?"

"Yes, and she's taking pecans so she can show my mother how to make pecan pie. She said she'd never given her recipe to anybody.

"Remember that the pastimes down there center

around the Gulf and Galveston Bay. Boating, fishing, swimming and—"

"Go no further. It sounds like paradise to me. Will I ever need a dressy dress down there?"

"One, but not an evening dress. Down there, it's water sports year-round. Bring some slacks. My mother's fussy about short-shorts at the table. Other than that, be as free as a seagull."

"I'm looking forward to it. Gary gave me two weeks off beginning yesterday, and that will include Thanksgiving. Do they have horses down there?"

His laughter warmed her. "Are you serious? Where in Texas are there no horses?"

"Caesar is nagging me to run with him, so I'd better say goodbye."

"Would you like to see a movie this evening? One of the movie houses is showing Humphrey Bogart movies this week, and I never saw *To Have and Have Not.*"

"I haven't seen it, either. I'd love to go with you."

"Then I'll be at your place at six-thirty. Bye for now."

Gradually they resumed their relationship, although Lynne knew that something was missing, and she also knew that she was the reason. Sloan showed her many courtesies, as he'd always done. She couldn't have asked for a more attentive man, but he wasn't subservient and he didn't grovel in order to win her favor. Bootlicking wasn't in him, and if he'd resorted to that, he would have demeaned himself in her eyes.

Shortly after daybreak on Thanksgiving eve, he rang her doorbell. "We're ready when you are," he told her. "But first, I need a kiss. Only the Lord knows when I'll get another one. Just don't turn the flame up too high."

"Why not?" she asked him, aware that Thelma's presence outside in Sloan's car was like a lock on their libidos.

He looked at her for a long time. "Kiss me like you mean it."

He lowered his head, and his hot mouth singed her, draining her of her will. She clutched him and opened her mouth for the plunge of his sweet tongue. Wider. She had to get more of him as she sucked his tongue into her mouth, hungrily, unable to get enough of him. The hot fire of desire snaked through her, and she swayed dizzily until he pulled her so close that air couldn't squeeze between them. Tremors plowed through his body, but they were not only driven by the force of his desire, but by the love in him for her and by the feel of his beloved in his arms again.

"I didn't mean to take it this far," he said, "but I wouldn't have missed this for anything. It's the first time since that chilling evening that you've really opened up to me, that you've given yourself to me. Let's go."

"It's what I felt, what came naturally."

"I know," he said. "It was like pouring gasoline on an open flame. Say, I thought we were going to bring Caesar."

"He's beginning to think he's a pet, and I want him to remember that he's a guard dog." She searched his face to see whether she'd left lipstick on him. If she had, Thelma wouldn't miss it. She didn't see any marks and allowed herself to relax.

"He knows his job, Lynne. Pity the poor Joe who tries to get past him. Those dogs can be vicious."

"I thought I was going to have to go in there and get you," Thelma said when they arrived at her car door, "but

I see you made it. This is the perfect day for an outing, and I plan to sleep all the way to Galveston."

"We'll stop somewhere near Houston and rest for a few minutes," he told her as he put the Lincoln Town Car in Drive and headed for Galveston.

He could hardly wait to get on his father's boat. He loved the water and had been a good swimmer since he was three years old. More than anything, he wanted Lynne to like his parents, and he wanted them to like her. He'd taken some of the pressure off her by inviting Thelma along, but his motive hadn't been selfish because he loved Thelma and wanted her and his mother to become friends.

He looked at Lynne sitting beside him and humming along with the music from his CD as if she had the world in her arms. He wondered if she was as happy right then as he was. "Are you happy?" he asked her.

Her head turned sharply toward him, and she blinked as if he had startled her. "I hadn't thought about it, but I am."

"So am I. Have you entered any of the warm-up tournaments for the Australian Open?"

"Two, both in Australia. I'll get a workout, because the heat in both cities will be oppressive. I want that grand-slam tournament so badly I can taste it."

"Remember, you gave yourself two years to get to the top, and that seems reasonable. So don't stress yourself out if you suddenly smell victory and can't wait for it. I'm convinced that you'll get there."

After a brief stop at a restaurant outside of Houston, he headed for Galveston. The closer he got to Galveston the more difficulty he had staying within the speed limit.

He could smell the briny water miles before he reached the port city, its freshness exhilarating him from head to toe. He wanted to roll down the windows and let the hometown air transport him back to the days when he ran barefoot along the sandy beaches, surfed in waves that were sometimes almost overwhelming and always challenging. And he thought of the hours during which he had fished at his father's side, often from the pier and, when he was older, from the bow of his father's boat.

As the Town Car sped across Galveston Bay, he glanced at his watch and saw that he'd made it in four and a half hours. Most of the time, he'd been alone: both Lynne and Thelma had spent the trip making up for having had to rise at four in the morning in order to leave at five. He headed toward Jasper Avenue near Ferry Road.

"Wake up, you two. We should be there in five minutes."

"Good heavens," Lynne said. "I missed all the sights."

"Me, too," Thelma said, "but I enjoyed my sleep. I hadn't been awake at four o'clock in the morning since my wedding day, and that was because I was so excited I couldn't sleep."

"You'll both see plenty before we leave. Galveston is known as the New Orleans of Texas. It even has its own Mardi Gras, and the food is great. We live on the bay side, but my dad docks his boat on the Gulf Coast." He slowed to a stop and parked. "We're here." He went around to the back door and opened it for Thelma, and by the time he got to the front passenger door, Lynne was standing beside the car pressing the wrinkles from her white pants.

"I thought we agreed that I'd open that door for you,"

he said, aware that his facial expression was one of mild disapproval. "I know you can open it and hop out without my help, but it gives me pleasure to open it for you."

"But I feel silly sitting there waiting for you to walk around and open it. How do I know your foot isn't sore?"

Thelma patted Lynne's shoulder. "Honey, there isn't much that most men can do these days, so let them open the doors. They need the exercise."

"I take it you've excluded me," Sloan said.

"Of course. But I always take sides with you against Lynne, and this was one little thing I could do to let her know I'm not biased." She winked at him. "You can open the door for me anytime it suits you."

He stared down at her, a mite of a woman with an enveloping personality and as feminine as a woman could be. "In your youth, you had many a man spinning, didn't you?"

"Now you stop digging into my secrets. Let's just say I knew a man when I saw one, and I never failed to acknowledge him."

He let the laughter pour out of him. "Come on," he said, taking the arm of each. "My mother is probably in her garden, and I'm sure Dad's around someplace." He was about to ring the bell when the door opened, and Connor McNeil—nearly as tall as his son and just as handsome—stepped out on the front porch, opened his arms and embraced Sloan. Then he looked at their guests.

"Welcome, Thelma," he said, shaking her hand. "Lucille and I want you to enjoy your visit with us, and we're going to do all we can to ensure it." He walked over to Lynne and gazed down at her with eyes so like

Sloan's, and then he smiled and sparkles lit them as they lit Sloan's. "I'm delighted to meet you, and I hope I'll be seeing a lot more of you."

Sloan let himself relax. His father liked Lynne on sight, and he was a man who had confidence in his judgment and rarely changed his opinions. He followed his father and the two women through the house to the garden where his mother was on her knees pulling weeds from among a row of pepper plants.

"Hi, Mom," he called to her as he headed out to the garden to greet her. "The garden's beautiful."

She dropped her tools and gloves and rushed to meet him, and he bent to embrace her. "You got here earlier than I expected," she said. "You didn't speed, did you? Where are Lynne and Thelma?"

He turned her around and pointed to the deck. She cleaned her hands on her slacks and headed toward them, but both women went to meet her. Thelma stood back to give Lynne passage, but Lynne insisted that Thelma move ahead of her. The two women embraced as if they had known each other all of their lives.

"I'm so glad Sloan has you for a friend," she told Thelma. "A motherly figure helps to balance a person." She hugged the woman again. "You're welcome here anytime you feel like swimming in the Gulf."

"She was an Olympic champión, Mom."

"I remember it well. She could dive like a dolphin." Lucille turned to Lynne. "I've been waiting for years to put my arms around a woman who my son loves. Thank you for coming to see us." She embraced Lynne, and Sloan thought his heart would run away from him when Lynne's arms went around his mother and the woman he loved kissed his mother's cheek. They held each other, and he didn't have to be told that, without saying it in words, they shared a bond of singular importance.

"If I'm lucky, my bachelor days are nearing an end," he said to himself out loud. "The problem is that she hasn't given me a single indication that she wants a life with me."

What do you call the way she made love to you the night before you broke it off? And what about the way she related to you this morning? his niggling conscience asked him.

Lucille walked ahead of him toward the deck with one arm around Thelma and the other one around Lynne. "How'd you get to be so lucky?" he asked his father. "Mom is such a tender, loving person."

Connor McNeil stopped walking and eyed his only son. "Lucky? I was blessed by God, but not one bit more than you are. Lynne is a solid woman, and she loves you. I'm sure you can handle that."

"Why are you so sure about her?"

Connor released what could best be described as a snort. "I know a woman when I see one. But it was the way she greeted your mother, almost as if she thanked her for something precious, that told me what I needed to know. Yeah. She loves you."

"She does, but we have to get past this coming year. She wants to regain her form and become the world's number one tennis player, and she can do it. She doesn't care if she's on top for only one day, so long as she gets there."

"And then?"

"She's twenty-nine, and I want a family."

"Then set the stage for it. From your mother's response to her, I know you'll have both our blessings."

"Thanks. That's what I intend to do."

Lynne hadn't allowed herself to envision the weekend
with Sloan's family, and if she had, she wouldn't have
dreamed how comfortable she would be with them. She
sat on a stool in the kitchen and cracked and shelled the
pecans that Thelma brought for the pecan pies.

"You can make two of 'em in an hour," she told Lucille, "and if Connor's anything like Sloan, he'll love
'em."

She looked up to see Sloan slouched in the doorway
between the kitchen and the dining room. "When you
finish those, we could go over to the Gulf. If Dad will
go with us, we might get a ride in his boat."

"You're not going without Lucille and me," Thelma
said, "so go someplace and keep each other company.
After we make these pies, we have to start on the stuffing
for the turkey." She looked at Lucille. "I haven't stuffed
a turkey in thirty-five years—not since my husband
passed—but you tell me what to do, and I can help you."

"I was going to help, too," Lynne said, "and Sloan is
as good a cook as anybody."

"Maybe, but turkey is not my thing. I'm going to the
garage and help Dad repair his fishing gear." He beckoned to her with his right index finger.

She put the pecans on the counter and walked over
to him, and he stepped with her into the dining room,
wrapped her in his arms and pressed his lips to hers. "I
was getting lonely."

"I'm sorry, but I want to stay where your mother can

keep an eye on me so she'll know I'm not engaged in any hanky-panky with you."

A dark frown followed his stare, and then he erupted into laughter. "My mother is a dyed-in-the-wool romantic. I can't believe she'd bother wondering whether and where we were making out."

"I'm sure you're right, but I'm taking no chances. She won't love me if she doesn't respect me."

There was no amusement in his eyes and nothing casual about his demeanor when he held her away from him and gazed into her eyes. *He's dead serious,* she thought, and he verified it when he asked her, "Why do you want my mother to love you?"

Irritation replaced the tenderness she felt for him a second earlier until she realized that his question was a legitimate one. "Because I love her son," she said. "Isn't that reason enough?"

When he rubbed the back of his neck, she knew that he was hunting for a response, and that his answer wouldn't be frivolous. "I'll keep this conversation in mind, Lynne." Suddenly he shrugged first one shoulder and then the other. "How long do you think you'll want to continue playing after you're number one?"

She knew what he was asking, and she also knew that he deserved an answer. "I want a family, Sloan, and I'm not going to sacrifice motherhood in order to become the best tennis player in the world. I'll be disappointed if I don't make it, but I gave myself two years, which means two tennis seasons in which to reach it, and as my life is shaping up now, I won't reconsider. Does that satisfy you?"

He folded her body to his. "Yes, it does. Did you start

seeing any other man while we were on the outs?" he asked her.

"It didn't cross my mind. I was fed up with men."

"Getting a substitute didn't cross my mind, either. I'll do everything I can to help you reach your goal. Now back into the kitchen with you. You wouldn't want my mother to think we're standing ten feet from her making out, would you?"

"You're a nut, Sloan, but that's one of your best attributes."

He stared at her for a second before a smile rearranged his facial contours and slowly dissolved into a roaring laugh. As if he'd read his mother's mind, when Lynne walked back into the kitchen, Lucille McNeil said to her, "Go see what Sloan's doing. I'll bet anything he's looking for something to do. That child was always such a loner."

"He was?"

"Yes, indeed. The only thing he did that required a playmate was play tennis, and he did that with his schoolmates in his athletics class."

"Didn't he play basketball?"

"Good heavens, no. When Sloan was a teenager, he thought there was a stigma attached to basketball playing. He used to say, "The players are always a bunch of tall black guys. I'd rather play tennis."

"Hmm…. He's good, too. Well, if you don't need me for anything…"

The woman stole her heart when she smiled and said, "I know where you'd rather be, and if I were in your place, I'd want the same. Thelma is equal to two people in the kitchen. We'll get along fine."

Spontaneously she kissed the woman's cheek. "I hope

Sloan knows how fortunate he is to have you for his mother. Somehow, I think he does."

She found him sitting in the garage holding a fishing rod while his father threaded it. *My Lord, that man has a sexy body,* she thought. *Just look at those legs and that chest.* When she realized that Connor had caught her ogling Sloan, she shifted her gaze to her feet. But Sloan's father winked at her and said, "It's allowed. Guys do it all the time." She was about to be scandalized when she realized that the comment was his effort to put her at ease, and when he laughed, she saw the humor in it and laughed with him.

"Am I missing something?" Sloan wanted to know.

"Yeah," Connor said, "but that's life. If you're walking on Apple Street, you miss what's happening on Beetle Street. You know what I'm saying?"

Sloan's eyes narrowed. "Sure. You're not telling, but I'll worm it out of Lynne."

"You will not."

"Wanna bet?"

She wanted so badly to kiss him, and she might have done it in his mother's presence, but not in front of his father. She had to be satisfied with moving over and sitting beside him on the old alligator steamer trunk. She noticed that Connor didn't miss that move or its significance, for he looked at her and nodded his approval.

I like this family, she said to herself. *Sloan is like both of his parents.* But Brad would turn up his nose at this three-bedroom wood-frame house, in spite of its attractive setting, style and interior. She hadn't seen much of the living room, and although the kitchen wasn't sparkling with chrome, it was large, modern and attractive with all the necessary features. A Persian-style carpet covered most of the dining room floor and the chairs, table, hutch and cupboard were made of walnut— "contemporary modern"—circa 1960 or 1970. They were not posh furnishings, but those of a knowledgeable and careful shopper of average means. *You never know a man until you meet his parents.* She recalled having heard the saying, and she concurred.

"We're going to fish for our supper," Connor said to her. "From the pier, not the boat. You want to come along?"

She was getting the message that both of Sloan's parents wanted them to be together as much as possible. "I'd love it. Thanks. I'd better change into long pants and a long-sleeve shirt. I'm not too fond of the sun."

She got up with the intention of entering the house through the kitchen, but she felt Sloan's hand on her arm steering her toward the front door. Inside the foyer, he penned her between his body and the wall and began nibbling on her lips. He kept at it until she began to squirm, her body eager for more than he was giving.

As if he had warmed up a motor until he was sure he could drive the car, he let the fingers of his right hand dust her cheek slowly and lovingly. "What is it that guys do all the time?" he asked her.

He had her so besotted that she could barely recall her name, not to speak of a conversation half an hour earlier. "What? What do you mean?"

"My dad said to you, 'Guys do it all the time.' And you knew what he was talking about. What did he mean?"

"Oh, *that!* He caught me admiring your body, and I must have had a lustful look, because he winked at me. I couldn't get the kiss I wanted, so I went over and sat beside you. That's when he made that smart remark."

"You could have kissed me."

She stared at him. "Not in your father's presence.

Your mother, maybe. He's a shrewd one." A thought occurred to her, and her face clouded into a frown. "You
mean you were being so sweet a minute ago only to get
me to tell you... Shame on you, and to think I fell for it.
Aren't you ashamed of yourself?"

His face lit up in a smile that tugged at her heart. "No.
I enjoyed every second of it."

"Men! I'm going up to change."

He didn't care if his father knew that Lynne wanted
him. In fact, he didn't care who knew it; he took great
pride in it. Heaven forbid he should fall in love with a
woman who didn't want him. He went back to the garage to help repair the fishing gear, but his father had
finished the task.

"So you wormed it out of her, did you?"

"How'd you know?"

"From the looks of you, I knew it had to be either that
or she agreed to marry you, and I don't think you're that
far along. When a peacock spreads his plumes, he makes
sure everybody sees him."

Sloan's lower lip dropped, and then he laughed.
"Sometimes I forget how shrewd you are, and that's a
pity because I've always enjoyed it. I'm going to make
a habit of coming home more often."

"I'm glad to hear it. Thelma is very fond of you. I
get the impression that she'd mother you to death if you
let her."

"She's been a widow for thirty-five years, and her social life died along with her husband. Her son was killed
while on active duty in Afghanistan. She's been very
much alone. She's Lynne's neighbor, and that's how I
met her. She's good to us, and we're good to her."

"Well, she certainly is likable, and Lucille's enjoying her. I'm glad you brought her."

He hadn't planned to ask, but the words fell off his tongue anyway. "Do you like Lynne?"

Connor rested his right elbow on his right thigh and rubbed his chin with the fingers of his right hand. It was a pose that Sloan was familiar with since he was old enough to observe his surroundings, one that he knew presaged serious words.

"You're asking me if I like Lynne? Well, I assume you want my answer. She's a beautiful, warm, sensuous woman, and she loves you. She's also intelligent, modest, independent, self-confident and goal-oriented. She's what a man wants in a wife, and if he's smart, she's what he would look for in the future mother of his children. You know whether she is loyal. If I were looking for a wife, I'd stop the search the minute I got to know her."

He had expected a simple yes or no, but instead he had practically been told that Lynne was the woman for him and that he should marry her. "I'm glad you like her, Dad. I think I would have been unhappy and disappointed if you didn't."

A half laugh slipped out of Connor. "I can't imagine that you gave that much thought. Surely you know you've got a gem."

"I know it. She's…she's so important to me, and until we split up a few weeks ago, I didn't know how much. The incident taught me never to rush to judgment." He looked around. "Where is that woman?"

When they sat down to supper that night, he felt like a whole person, a man with his house in order. "This is the best snapper I've ever eaten," Thelma said. She looked at Lynne. "What the corner of your garden needs is a grill."

Sloan deliberately waved his fork at Thelma. "Do not plant any seeds in her head, Thelma. I don't want her to get too comfortable in that house."

"Never mind," Thelma told him. "Lynne isn't stupid. She's got better sense than to laugh in God's face. When the Lord gives you something, you show your appreciation by taking good care of it."

"I've always wanted to be able to talk in parables," Lynne said to Lucille, "but after listening to this, I see that I should have been striving for something else. And I think that if they're going to talk about me, they should leave the Lord out of it."

"Oh, no," Connor said. "In this house, we don't leave the Lord out of things. Out there in the garage, maybe, but not in the house, and especially not at the table. Preach on, Sister Thelma."

"Amen," Lucille said.

He knew his father was engaging in a little leg-pulling and that, as usual, his mother encouraged her husband in his foolishness. He looked at Lynne to see how she was taking it and discovered that she could give as good as she got.

"You know, Mr. McNeil," she began, "for several years back, some power or other spent a lot of time laughing in *my* face." She looked toward the ceiling. "You don't think it was...uh...anybody up there, do you? If it was, I'm entitled to do a lot of laughing myself." She didn't look at anybody when she said it. "I hope you know how to set up a grill, Thelma, 'cause I don't, and I have a feeling that SM doesn't think much of the idea."

"Oh, don't worry," Thelma said. "I'll bake him a pie.

Anyhow, he's such a sweet gentleman, he wouldn't want us to struggle with something that he could do as easy as snapping his finger."

Connor leaned back in his chair and roared with laughter. "Son, if they set you up like this regularly, I don't envy you."

"They're just showing off," he said. But he didn't know when he'd felt surrounded with so much love. *She's not getting away from me,* he vowed silently. *She fits in like my gloves fit my fingers; I'll never let her go.*

He marveled at the ease with which the three women prepared Thanksgiving dinner the next day. Ordinarily he and his father would have helped with the preparations, but his mother explained that five people couldn't work in that kitchen without stepping on each other. As he observed Thelma from time to time, he thought he had never seen her so happy and so animated. He saw in the woman evidence that loneliness could sap a person's enthusiasm for life, destroy their vigor and change their personality. He meant to see that his parents didn't dry up for lack of contact with people, and as long as he lived near Thelma, he would visit her as regularly as he could.

At dinner that afternoon, he watched his father carve the turkey and thought how thankless the job of perfectly roasting the big bird was only to dismember it as quickly as five people could devour it. He saw in his mind's eye a similar table with himself at its head, Lynne sitting opposite him and their children sitting around them. After Thelma served the pecan pie with a flourish, he and his father cleaned the kitchen and they all assembled in the living room to listen to Connor's favorite jazz recordings, drink coffee and liqueurs and tell tales.

Several times, he caught Lynne watching him, but

he couldn't think of a way to get her alone. Just before sundown, he said to her, "If you love to see the sunset, come with me." She got up immediately.

He drove over the Pelican Island Causeway and on to Seawolf Parkway until Galveston Bay was all that they could see. He parked. "Please humor me and sit there until I open your door," he said. She stepped out of the door and into his open arms. "Just look at that," he said of the yellow, orange and purple streaks that surrounded the great red disc that was the sun on a quiet journey to its rest. As it was about to disappear, the sky above it darkened to a midnight-blue, the perfect backdrop for the sinking sun. She gasped as the sun slipped out of sight.

"That was…so beautiful that it was almost frightening, as if something so beautiful and so precious could slip away—" she snapped her finger "—just like that."

He wrapped her in his arms. "Are you telling me that you're afraid we'll lose what we feel for each other?"

"I just don't see how anything so perfect could last."

"It will last because you and I want it to last. No more negative thinking."

That Sunday afternoon when he parked in front of Lynne's house after taking Thelma home and making sure that her house was in order, he asked her, "When are you leaving for Australia? You understand that I can't be with you because I have to get things working smoothly at Castle Hills. Ben will be the manager there, Jasper will replace Ben at the San Antonio service center and I have to hire and train a man to replace Jasper. That means I'll be taking calls a full day rather than mornings as I've been doing. I know how important this is to you, and it distresses me that I can't be with you."

"I'm leaving January 5. From now until then, I'll be training and practicing rigorously."

"We'll see each other, and regularly. I'm not about to let this part of my life go to pot. Do you remember my introducing you to Drake Harrington and Pamela Langford at a meeting of my university alumni?"

"Yes. Why?"

"I have an invitation to their wedding on December 29. He lives in Eagle Park, Maryland, near Frederick, and the wedding's to be in Frederick. You and I would be guests at Harrington House, the family home. I'd like you to go with me. It'll take up the better part of a weekend. Can you manage it?"

"I'll be glad to go with you. Would you please check the dress code for me?"

"Sure. Lynne, this weekend was precious. It exceeded anything that I imagined, and my parents are enchanted with you. They liked Thelma, also, and they want her to visit with them whenever she feels like it."

"I like your parents, too, and I don't know why, but I felt as if I were at home. It was wonderful."

He leaned toward her and pressed a kiss to her mouth. "I'm not going in because I have to get up no later than five in the morning, and if I walk into your house, I can kiss that notion goodbye. I'll see you tomorrow."

As he drove home, his mind took a route that hers took earlier. *Could the happiness he felt possibly last?*

Chapter 10

The question of Sloan's place in her future plagued Lynne, although not because she had any quandary about her feelings for him, but because he seemed to be in a hurry, and she wasn't. She knew the reason was that she had experienced marriage and found it lacking, while Sloan had never married and looked forward to it as a way of making his life complete. She also knew that if he gave her an ultimatum—marry him or he was out of her life—she wouldn't hesitate to marry him. He hadn't said so, but she was certain that he wanted a family, and so did she.

She walked from one end of her bedroom to the other and back, and then repeated her steps. Sloan would be a good husband and father and he loved her. She went to the bathroom, turned on the lights and faced herself in the mirror. "If it's a choice between being number one and having a family, there's no contest—I'll choose a family. And if the choice is between life with Sloan and life without him?" She stared at herself for a long time. "He's got the music that makes you dance, kiddo," she said to the image before her. "So you'd better get busy and make yourself ready for the next tennis season starting with the Australian Open, because if you don't make it to number one, you'll always be dreaming of what might have been and always staging comebacks." She hadn't faced the question whether she'd choose life with Sloan or life without him, but she knew the answer.

"You were so mad with me that you chose to go somewhere else for Thanksgiving," Brad said to her when she called him the next morning. "We've always been together for Thanksgiving."

"I gave you my reasons, Brad, and I'm sorry if you prefer not to accept them. I had a wonderful time with Sloan, his parents and a neighbor who went with us. I'm glad I went, because I liked his parents very much, and I think they liked me."

"What the hell are you talking about? Why do you have to like his folks? Worse, why do they have to like you? You're taking this nonsense too far. Next, you'll tell me you're…you're fornicating with this mechanic."

"I wouldn't be that crude. Talk with you later." She hung up because she wasn't in the habit of disrespecting her brother, and she had come close to doing that.

Two weeks later when he asked if he and Debra could expect her for Christmas, she said that they could, and immediately regretted it because she would have preferred to spend the holiday with Sloan and his parents. Her schedule of training and practicing left too little time for Christmas shopping, so, from museum catalogs, she purchased cut velvet scarves for all the women she knew and silk scarves for the men, except Sloan. She would give him the leather case that she purchased in Seoul at a time when she thought he might never receive it.

"We can spend Christmas Eve together and fly to see our families Christmas morning," Sloan suggested, and she welcomed the idea.

For their Christmas Eve dinner, he chose an elegant restaurant that served mainly American-style food. When she opened her door and looked at him, so handsome in a gray pinstriped suit, white shirt and gray-and-red paisley tie, she wanted to put a sign on that read, This Is The Property Of Lynne Thurston. The thought amused her, and she laughed.

"Tell me," he said. "I'm in the mood to laugh, too."

"I don't think I'd better. I had a moment there when a streak of possessiveness nearly got the better of me."

"Possessiveness about what?" he asked and bent down to kiss her. "You're so beautiful. I'm a proud man, Lynne."

She fixed her face with a serious expression. "Thanks. Uh, would you be annoyed if I hung a sign on you? I conjured up a picture of you wearing two, one in the back and one in the front."

"And that's what made you laugh?"

"Uh-huh. I was laughing at what was on the signs."

"Well, if the sign read, This Man Is Mine, I'd be pleased."

"It was something like that." She was glad she'd worn a red dress and her red sandals with the three-inch heels. Sloan didn't consider himself elegant, but anybody who looked at him would.

After a traditional Christmas dinner of turkey and

all the trimmings, he took her to the lounge above the restaurant. He reached across the table for her hand and rubbed her right thumb. "What would you like to drink?"

"I think I'll stick with white wine. I'll have enough trouble dealing with Brad tomorrow without the added handicap of a headache."

"Let's not talk about Brad." He signaled for the waitress and gave their orders. "I have a score to settle with him, and I'm not prepared to like him until I do."

"After what he did, I don't blame you. I don't want to think about those three weeks. I was so unhappy."

"So was I, but thank God, it's behind us." The band struck the first chords of a Ray Charles hit that she couldn't identify by name, and Sloan stood and extended his hand to her. "Dance with me. I want you in my arms, and right now, this is the only way."

He held her loosely enough so that he could look down into her face. "One of these days, I'm going to love you, really love you the way I know I can. I'm not talking about the physical—I'm talking about what's in here." He pointed to his heart.

"Me, too. When I'm alone I don't have doubts, but I have questions…about myself, I mean. When I'm with you, I'm so sure."

His arms tightened around her. "Do you doubt that you love me?"

"Never. Somehow, I'm convinced that after the US Open next year, my life will straighten itself out."

The movement of his hand down her back sent tremors throughout her body, and she knew that he felt them because he moved backward just enough to gaze into her eyes.

"Do you want to leave?"

He knew her well, so she didn't bother to be demure, but merely nodded. They rode in silence until he stopped the car in front of her house and looked at her. "I'd like to come in."

"I expected that you would. It's Christmas Eve, and I can't imagine saying good-night to you in this car."

He reached into the glove compartment and took out a small bag, then went around and opened the door for her. "Thanks for not beating me to it," he said. "I know you can open the door, but it gives me pleasure to do it for you."

She didn't comment because her hand was on the door handle when he opened it. Inside the house, he locked the door, and she decided that if she was to have the kind of Christmas Eve with him that she craved, she had to set the scene.

"It's a little chilly," she told him, "so I think I'll light the fireplace." She did and then flipped the switch that lit the Christmas tree beside the fireplace. The effect was nearly ethereal, if she did say so herself. With no other light in the room, the setting was as in a dream world. "Have a seat and excuse me for a minute." Upstairs, she brushed her teeth, freshened up her body and dabbed some perfume behind her ears.

"Would you like a drink? Coffee? A liqueur?"

He shook his head and patted the seat beside him on the sofa. "Merry Christmas." His arms locked her to him and his lips opened over hers. She parted them to take him in, and knew at once that he was demanding all of her. With his tongue deep in her mouth and his hands roaming over her, a yearning to have his penis buried deep in her pulsating vagina took hold of her, and the memory of how he made her feel as he possessed her did the rest. She grabbed his hand and dipped it into the bosom of her low-cut dress. As he pinched and rubbed her nipple, liquid accumulated in her mouth, and she had to have more. Recklessly she used his hand to make her nipple accessible to his mouth and pressed his head with her other hand. Her groan split the air when his warm mouth covered her nipple and began to suck it vigorously.

"I want you inside me. Oh Lord. I'll die if you don't get in me." She tried to remove his jacket, but he resisted.

"Upstairs," he whispered.

"No. Here. Now. Right now."

He stared at her for a second, then flung off the jacket and his shirt, unzipped her dress and slid it off her body. She didn't try to still her dancing hips as he kicked off his trousers and shoes, placed her on the floor and stood over her staring down at her body, bare but for a red G-string.

"Oh, shit," he said. And then he was in her, wild and furious as he stormed within her. Almost immediately, the sensitive walls of her vagina began their pumping and squeezing and then locked themselves to him, holding him prisoner.

"Honey, I'm going to die. I'm... Oh Lord," she screamed, and he shouted in sweet agony and gave himself to her.

Later, Sloan sat with his back against the sofa, drained of energy. "That lasted five minutes," he said, "but I've never been so exhausted in my life. It seems as if everything went out of me."

"I feel the same way. What happened?"

He released a half laugh. "Sweetheart, abstinence is no good for us. We're going to have to do something about this."

"Don't I know it. Would you please look in the bathroom over there and get me a towel?"

"What for?"

"Because I'm not going to walk around here with no clothes on."

He knew better than to laugh. If he hadn't seen it, she didn't have it. He got the towel, handed it to her and smothered a laugh as she managed to wrap it around herself while sitting down. She walked over to the Christmas tree, got a package and brought it back to him.

"I hope you like it," she said.

He opened the beautifully wrapped package and stared at the brown gold-initialed leather kit that was meant for his personal items. "This is magnificent. I've never had one, and I really appreciate it. It's a very thoughtful gift." He planned to make good use of it. "This isn't what I would have preferred to give you this Christmas," he said. "It's a substitute."

She opened the box and gasped at the lustrous strand of eight-millimeter cultured pearls. Her eyes widened, and her gaze traveled from him to the pearls and back to him. "I've never had anything like this. These are beautiful." She flung her arms around him and pressed her lips to his. The towel fell away.

"Hold it," he said, "unless you want to start something again."

She looked down at her bare breasts and pulled up the towel. "Sorry."

Both of his eyebrows shot up. "Well, I'm not. And I'd better get out of here if I'm going to get that nine o'clock flight to Galveston."

"My plane's leaving at eight-thirty. Pity me," she said.

"Remember we're having dinner with Thelma on the twenty-seventh."

"I haven't forgotten." He dressed hurriedly and, still wrapped in the bath towel, she told him goodbye at the door. "I love you, sweetheart," he said, and that was one thing of which he was certain.

"And I love you."

On December 29, Sloan pointed out Drake Harrington, who waited for them in the Baltimore International Airport. "There he is, Lynne. Over there."

"It's great to see you, brother," Drake said, opening his arms and embracing Sloan. He looked at her. "As lovely as I remembered. I'm glad you could come. Pamela was hoping that the two of you were still an item. I had confidence that my man here is too smart to let you get away."

Sloan grasped the shoulders of his longtime friend. "Truth is, Drake, I'm still stunned that you're taking the plunge. You've always been so goal-oriented that I figured you wouldn't get married for years to come."

Drake grinned. "That's what I thought, too, but, man, when this thing hits you, you can fight it all you want to, but you don't stand a chance of winning. Might as well give in and let nature take her course. And the minute you cave in, you've never been so happy in your life. The sun shines bright, the air is sweeter and everything changes."

Sloan inclined his head slightly and smiled. "Tell me about it."

Drake looked at Lynne. "Don't let up. In fact, my advice is to increase the pressure. My car's this way."

"It's a good thing I don't mind what you're telling Lynne. How're your brothers reacting to your getting married?"

"Don't ask, man. They're relieved. They got married and couldn't stand the fact that I was single. Actually, they were right about Pamela." For a minute, he became reflective. "That woman makes my soul sing."

"Where will you and Pamela live?" Lynne asked him.

"I've started building a house on Harrington property not too far from my ancestral home, where you'll be staying. My brother Russ got married last year, and we've just finished building his house. My and Pamela's house will be about a third of a mile from his. It's a lovely area and in the summer, the view will be spectacular with the trees green and all the wildflowers in bloom."

When they arrived at Harrington House, Alexis Harrington, tall, willowy and beautiful, met them at the door. "I'm so glad to meet you, Sloan." She turned to Lynne. "And I've been rooting for you during each of your matches. By this time next year, you'll be number one. I'm so glad you could come."

Lynne thanked her. "I'm happy to meet you, Alexis, and especially since you believe I'll reach my goal. Australia will tell the tale."

"No, it won't," Alexis told her. "Only the end of the year will tell. Come on in and meet the rest of the family. This evening we'll have the rehearsal and after that, the bridal toast. Tonight's supper here at home will be promptly at seven. Drake, please take Lynne's bag to the guest room and Sloan's to Russ's room." When she looked, her face bore a sly smile. "I'm sorry to have to put you two so far apart, but others have managed to cross that bridge."

"Are you coming to the wedding?"

Sloan looked down into the little girl's eager face. "Why yes, I am."

Alexis patted the child's shoulder. "This is my daughter, Tara. Tara, our guests are Miss Lynne and Mr. Sloan."

The child glanced at Lynne. "Welcome, Miss Lynne." Then she smiled up at him, her preference for men obvious to anyone who cared to notice it. "I have a little brother, too. My dad put him in my mummy's tummy."

Apparently accustomed to Tara's glibness, Alexis said, "They know how it's done, Tara."

The little girl looked up at her mother with a perplexed expression on her face. "They do? Who told them?"

He laughed because he couldn't help it, but he also couldn't help wondering if and when he would have a daughter or son who would look at him as lovingly and trusting as that little girl looked at her mother.

"It's something that adults know," Alexis said, and the child smiled, content with the answer. He let his gaze sweep Lynne's face and caught his breath at the expression of longing in her eyes. Helpless to do otherwise, he opened his arms and drew her close to him.

Sloan sat beside Lynne on the Harrington side of the First Presbyterian Church in Frederick, Maryland, wondering when his own day would come. He had never seen Lynne so beautiful; she might well have been the bride. Gowned in a long, figure-hugging royal-blue sleeveless silk dress with its own jacket, she dazzled him. Her only jewelry was the string of pearls that were his Christmas gift to her. He squeezed her fingers, and she smiled in that special, intimate way of hers. Then, she whispered, "I love you," and he thought his heart would fly out of his chest.

The first strains of the organ brought his attention to the business at hand. Drake Harrington—elegant in full dress and white tie as was his brother, Telford, beside him—was about to wed Pamela Langford. He turned and looked back to see Tara—a small vision in pink— and a handsome boy near her age, also in full dress, walking up the aisle as Tara strew pink rose petals. The Harrington women, resplendent in gowns of a pinklike color, followed them. He thought the maid of honor had the most regal bearing of any woman he'd seen walk. He wondered what kind of work she did.

Finally the organ pealed forth the first bars of "Here Comes the Bride," and the audience stood and turned to see Pamela Langford escorted by her father, as proud a man as he'd ever seen. She wore a traditional white satin gown and veil, a single strand of white pearls, white el-bow-length gloves, a seed-pearl tiara, and her long white-satin train swept behind her.

I can imagine how you feel, man, he said to himself when he glanced at Drake and saw the smile that spread over his face and the look of pride that accompanied it.

When at last Pamela stood beside Drake, he faced his bride and, throughout the ceremony, he looked only at her. By the time the minister pronounced them husband and wife, tears cascaded down both their faces. They gazed at each other, seemingly in a world of their own, until the minister said for a second time, "You may kiss your bride." He didn't press a quick kiss to her lips, but wrapped her in his arms with a sense of urgency, and kissed her as if he was alone with her in the moonlight, bringing first a gasp and then a prolonged applause from the congregation.

Sloan looked at the woman beside him and saw that she, too, was unable to hold back the tears. He put an arm around her and drew her close to him. And he prayed silently that their day would come.

At the reception that followed, the obvious love of the Harrington family members for each other touched Sloan deeply, for it was so profound and so profuse that he felt enveloped in it.

"This is a wonderful, happy family," he said to Henry, who stood nearby.

"And it ain't just for show," Henry said. "I've been with the Harrington family since Russ over there was four years old. I raised these boys to love each other, and they were smart enough to find loving women. You married to this lady on the other side of you?"

"No, but—"

"She's got good manners and fine taste," Henry said. "If everything else is in place, I'd go for that one. She makes a man look good."

"Thank you, Henry," he said. "I'm working on it, and I appreciate your goodwill."

Lynne stepped out of the airport in Sydney, Australia, and was tempted to run back inside; not even in San Antonio had she experienced such stifling heat. She knew that January was Australian summer, but the import of that didn't sink in until she experienced the blazing sun. There for the Medibank International Tennis Tournament, a warm-up for the much more prestigious Australian Open, she told herself that heat was a part of the tennis player's lifestyle, and she would grin and bear it.

"How's it going?" Sloan asked her when he called after her second match. "The tournament's not broadcast over here."

"I won the first two matches relatively easily, but

the day after tomorrow Patty Lanier ought to be tough. How're things at Castle Hills?"

"You'll play rings around that girl. Putting a service center there was a good move. We're busy nonstop from opening to closing time, and Ben is a born manager. I'm lucky to have an honest and capable man like him. I'm already scouting for a site on which to place a third center two or three years down the road. I want McNeil Motor Service to be a household name in this part of the country."

"And it will be. I'm confident that you'll accomplish whatever you set out to do."

When he didn't respond, she said, "Surely you don't disagree with me."

"I take it you're aware that my prime goal right now is you, and that I'm out to get you for myself. You still think I can accomplish anything I set out to do?"

"Sloan, in a telephone call with half the world separating us is no time to discuss such things. But as in everything else, I'm on your side in that, too."

After nearly a minute of silence, his laughter greeted her. "That is the damnedest and most convoluted answer I ever heard. But, baby, I'll take it. If you're with me in this, I can't lose."

As Sloan predicted, she won against Lanier in straight sets, 6–1, 6–1. However, the following morning, she awoke with what appeared to be a strained back. She sent for a trainer, had her back taped and was advised to skip practice that day and rest. Gary spread the word about Lynne's back, mostly to psych her fourth-round opponent into thinking that the match with Lynne would be an easy one. He needn't have bothered. They played the first set to a tie, which Lynne won after an hour of play, and then she walked away with the second set with six points to none for her opponent.

She won over the crowd with her doggedness, for she chased every ball for every point, thrilling the onlookers. However, during her next match, her first semifinal since her return to tennis, she had to retire after the second game, a victim of the heat.

"I'm so sorry to hear that, but you were wise to quit. You might have had a sunstroke, and that is a serious thing. How do you feel about playing in the Open less than a week from now?" Sloan asked her.

"I'm told it should be a bit cooler in Melbourne. In any case, I'm going for it. I finally made it to the semifinal, even if it is a smaller tournament, and I'm feeling pretty strong mentally right now."

"I don't have to tell you that I wish I was there. If you need me, call me, and I'll be there as fast as planes fly."

"I know, and it's one of the reasons why you're so dear to me."

"I owe you one for that. Blow me a kiss, sweetheart." She did, and he returned it. "I'll be waiting for you when you get back here. Stay away from those Australian cowboys."

What might have been a laugh came out as a giggle. "I'll try." She listened for the words that she suddenly had a need to hear, and as if he knew what was in her head and her heart, he said, "I'm in love with you, Lynne. I love you."

"I'm glad, because I love you."

She checked into the elegant Crown Towers Hotel in Melbourne, grateful that the heat there was less intense than in Sydney, and began unpacking. The phone rang, and she rushed to answer it, certain that she would hear Sloan's voice.

"I figured you'd be more receptive if I came all the way here just to talk with you."

She stared at the receiver, stunned by the sound of Willard's voice. "Why are you calling me here? I don't want to talk with you."

"But you have to face the fact that no matter what man does, God has his laws, and what he put together, man is not supposed to tamper with."

"You came all the way here to…where are you right now, Willard?"

"The Ridges River Walk Hotel. I want to see you this evening, and I'll be at your hotel around six."

She laughed because Willard hated for anyone to laugh at him. "If you come here, I'll have you arrested for harassment. My passport says I'm divorced, and I'll report you to the U.S. Consulate and to the local police. I'll do the same if you call me again. You're here to ruin my chances of winning, but you can forget that. All you are is a nuisance. I don't need you."

"I'd like to know where you got that mouth. You're with some man, I'll bet, but I'll put a stop to that."

"You don't worry me, Willard, because I now realize that you're a coward, and I no longer respect you or fear you. Hang up before I call the police." He didn't hang up, so she placed the phone in its cradle, pulled off her clothes and went to the shower.

She breezed through the first four matches, slaying her opponents as if they were of no consequence.

"You can beat Sharapova," Sloan told her before her semifinal match. "You're faster. Give it all you've got. You know I'll be rooting for you."

She didn't tell him that Willard had annoyed her. "I mean to give it my best shot. She's great, and I have over ten years on her, but I'm intending to win."

She lost the first set in a tie and won the second one. How good it was to have the crowd behind her, to hear the screams of "Come on, Lynne. You can do it, babe. Go, Lynne."

"Sure I can do it," she told herself. "If I won that second set, when she played like a demon, I can beat her." But in the end, she lost the match in a long and hard-fought tiebreaker. The Russian champion didn't give up a point on her serve, and Lynne couldn't help but admire the woman's level of play. At the net, she told her, "You're as good as they get."

"Thanks, but the way you played today, I don't know."

"You can beat anybody playing today," Gary told her. "She was lucky that that ball fell back on your side of the net."

"I'm disappointed, but I played my best, and pretty soon, I'll be holding up one of those trophies."

"You outplayed her until you choked during the last game. You're on your way," Sloan told her that night. "I was sitting on the edge of my chair. You played a terrific match. I'm proud of you."

The plane landed, but it seemed to him that years passed before the passengers walked into the waiting room. His gaze captured each one as he sought the face of the woman so dear to him. The anxiety, the groundless fear that she wouldn't be on the plane evaporated when she walked through the door, saw him and hurried toward him with a happy welcoming smile. He rushed

to her, picked her up and twirled her around, before setting her on her feet and pressing his lips, firmly but
fleetingly, to hers.

"I think it's been years since I last saw you," he said.
"You're a shade darker and twice as beautiful. Let's go."
He took her bag in one hand and grasped the other one
as he walked with her through the terminal and out to
the parking lot. "Did you miss me?"

"Did the sun shine in Australia? Every minute."

"Let's stop by my place and get Caesar. He's been
rather antsy these past few days. I think he decided it was
time you came home." Full grown now, Caesar greeted
her with such eagerness that she had to calm him before
he jumped on her.

As they drove to her house, he told her about the new
service center. "I've had to hire another man, and Ben
thinks we ought to stay open all day Saturday and close
at six-thirty rather than at five-thirty. I'm willing to try
it for a couple of weeks, and if I think it's profitable, I'll
set a new time schedule. It will mean either overtime pay
or shuffling working hours for the men. I'll see which
they prefer."

"I'm glad business is good," she said. "It seems you
located in the right place. I hope you're as fortunate with
the next one."

"Thanks, but I don't depend on luck. I believe in mar-
ket research, and I'll work at that for the next eighteen
months."

He parked in front of her house, let her out of the
car and then took Caesar's leash. "He's so excited that I
don't trust him to walk alone to that front door," he said.

"Are you coming in?" she asked him.

"Long enough to get my kiss. Woman, I've been badly neglected these past three and a half weeks."

She stepped inside and put her arms around his waist. "You poor baby. Kiss me."

He hadn't intended to launch a heavy petting scene, but the feel of her soft and pliable in his arms and with her luscious lips turned up for his kiss, he gripped her to him and plunged his tongue into her waiting mouth. All that he felt for her and all that he longed to experience with her dropped down on him with the force of a wrecking ball. "Oh, Lynne. What have you done to me? I need you so."

She stepped back and looked at him as if better to assess the import and meaning of his words. "I don't mean merely the physical," he said. "I need you period."

Her pleading expression nearly caused him to lose his composure. "Please be patient a little longer," she said. "There's no one else, and there won't be. Only you."

He brushed his lips over hers as she stroked his cheek. "It isn't easy, but I know it's the best thing for us. May I see you tomorrow night?"

"I'd like that. Call me tomorrow morning, and let's plan something simple."

"Right. Meanwhile, I'll tell Thelma you're back, but I'll discourage a visit, because you were traveling al- most twenty-four hours." *Lord, I'd better get out of here before I do something stupid. She's got to be tired after that long flight from Australia, getting to the airport and maneuvering once she got there.*

"Look, sweetheart, I'd better go. See you tomorrow evening." Once more, he let himself know the sweetness and the torture of her kiss, turned and streaked down the walkway to his car. If he so much as glanced back, he'd make a fool of himself.

Lynne awoke early the next morning, refreshed and eager for the day. While still in bed, she telephoned Sloan. "Hi. It's such a pretty morning, and the breeze blowing through here is so refreshing, that I had to share it. Where are you?"

"Hi. I'm sitting out on my deck drinking coffee. You're right, this is great weather, and the breeze makes me feel as if I could run for miles and miles. It's a great morning. You're still in bed, aren't you?"

She hadn't intended to be suggestive. "Uh, yes, but I'm getting up after we talk."

"Yeah? If I didn't have to go to work, I'd be there before you had time to dress, and if I think about it, I'll do it anyhow."

"I'm getting up as we speak," she told him. "I don't ever want to get between you and your goals."

"Look, baby. I told you—you are my goal."

"I definitely did not forget. See you this evening. Bye, love."

"Bye, sweetheart."

After working in her garden all morning, she put together a light lunch of lettuce, tomato and a thin slice of ham on whole wheat bread, made a cup of tea and took it out on her deck. She was falling more and more in love with the garden, the thicket of tall oak and cedar trees beyond it and the bluebonnets that grew wild all around her. But she had to mark time while she waited for the end of the tennis season. She had to contend with the possibility that Texas might not become her permanent home.

Caesar sprang up and growled. "What is it?" she asked the dog, as if he could answer. He growled again and scratched at the back screen door. Warily she got up, opened the door and followed him to the front door.

"Who is it?" she asked, and hooked the leash on the dog's collar. "I said, who is it?" She watched Caesar, for although he didn't growl, his tail was straight out, and that meant he was especially alert.

She stepped to the side, peered through the plate-glass insert and stepped back, stunned. What was Willard Marsh doing at her front door? She unhooked the chain, unlocked the door and opened it.

"What are you doing here?"

"I came to repair my relationship with my wife. God is not pleased with what you're doing."

"Be careful," she said. "My dog doesn't like you, and if you make one false move, he'll rip you apart."

When Willard stared down at Caesar, the dog growled. "Come in," she said to Willard, "provided you're willing to risk it."

He walked in, but he didn't take his gaze off the dog. "You're fooling around with a criminal, and I'm surprised at you. I know all about the fellow you're consorting with. But let me tell you, you'd better be careful."

When both of her hands went to her hips, Caesar growled. "What the devil are you talking about, and who are you talking about?"

"You know who I'm talking about. It's that tall fellow who works at a garage in San Antonio. He was indicted for ripping off an old woman who took her Lexus Sedan to him, and when she got it back, he'd substituted Ford parts. That's against the law."

"You're lying, and you know it."

"I'm *what?*" He gasped the words. "Have you forgotten who you're talking to?"

"Oh, I know who you are. You're a liar, that's who you are." Feeling as if she would explode, she went into the kitchen, knowing that Willard wouldn't move for fear of exciting Caesar, and used the wall phone to call Sloan. "Since he's assassinating your character, I thought you might like the opportunity to straighten him out."

"I'll be right there, and don't let him out of the house, not even if you have to keep him there with Caesar's help."

She didn't believe Sloan was guilty of that or of any other crime, but she had suddenly realized that Willard was a coward, that he would attempt to intimidate a woman—he did that to a church full of women every Sunday morning, keeping them so scared that they always remembered to pay their tithes—but would probably not confront a man.

Caesar's bark alerted her to the fact that Sloan's car was in front of her house, but when the doorbell ran, the dog didn't run to greet Sloan but stood his ground, watching his prey. She opened the door, kissed Sloan and took his hand.

"Sloan, this is Reverend Willard Marsh from whom I've been divorced one year and two weeks. Thank the Lord."

She looked at Willard. "Willard, this is Sloan McNeil. I suggest you besmirch his character to his face instead of attempting to harass me. Have a seat." It didn't escape her that Caesar did not sit beside her as usual, but sat in the foyer. One could get out of the front door only with Caesar's permission.

"What possessed you to tell Lynne a lie about me?"

Sloan asked Willard, cutting to the chase. "You know nothing about me. I do not work at a service station. I own the service station, plus another one. Furthermore, my reputation as a service provider is spotless. If you can't show me a legal document that says I was indicted for anything, anywhere at any time in my life, I'll sue you for all you're worth."

Willard seemed to shrink in size. "I was told—"

Sloan didn't let him finish. "You made it up, but you're playing with the wrong man. I detest unscrupulous people, but to find a preacher guilty of it is sickening. Your problem is that your wife woke up to her rights and to your incompetence and meanness and divorced you. You want her back. Well, buddy, you can forget that. Lynne Thurston is mine. She belongs to me, and neither you nor any other man is going to do anything to change that. You had six years, and you blew every damned one of them. Continue to harass her, and you're going to jail. If you know what's good for you, you'll get your ass out of here and stay as far from San Antonio as you can get."

Lynne had never seen Sloan so angry and, although she believed he could control it, she wasn't satisfied that Willard wouldn't do or say something reckless. She got up. "I'd like you to leave, Willard. This minute."

Willard pursed his lips, and his face had all the serenity of a thundercloud. "You'll be—"

Again, Sloan interrupted Willard. "Don't tell her she'll be sorry. That's a threat, and I won't sit here and listen to you threaten her. Do you understand?"

She hadn't ever seen Sloan so edgy, seemingly ready to pounce—although he spoke in a calm, modulated voice—but she knew that a powerful anger surged within him. "If you're smart, Willard," she said, "you'll leave while you can go under your own steam."

True to his arrogant nature, he stared at her, but this time, she had the trump card and didn't hide her glee when she said, "You'll either catch it in here or at the door where Caesar is waiting."

Sloan took his time unfolding himself from the lounge chair in which he sat. "And let this be the last time you say anything to Lynne Thurston."

Willard started toward the front door, stopped and looked back at her, opened his mouth and closed it without speaking. She smothered a laugh, and went and stood beside the dog who reclined in the foyer.

"Let yourself out, Willard."

The door closed behind Willard Marsh, and she hoped it had closed for all time. Without Caesar and then Sloan, he would have attempted to intimidate and abuse her as he had during their marriage. Good riddance! Nonetheless, she was neither engaged nor married to Sloan McNeil and, therefore, she hadn't given him the right to tell anybody that she belonged to him. "We're nipping this in the bud right now," she said to herself and headed back to the living room to let him know he'd overstepped his bounds.

"Where'd that Joe get the nerve to come here acting as if you're his wife?" Sloan asked her.

"Willard is stupid, but you are not. I want to know who gave you the right to announce that I belong to you? I certainly didn't."

He stared at her with a puzzled expression on his face. "I remember telling you twice that you belonged to me, and you didn't dispute it. In fact, you informed me that, in that case, I belonged to you. That gave me the right to tell that jerk to stay away from my woman, that you belong to me. What I didn't tell him was the consequence he could suffer if he didn't leave you alone."

Her anger had begun to dissipate, but she wouldn't give in. "That didn't mean you should broadcast it—that was between you and me. Anyhow, I'm my own woman."

"You're mine. If you don't believe it, come here."

"I'm not going anywhere," she huffed, but he spread his legs, leaned back in the chair and gazed at her. All she could see was his masculinity, his strength and his tenderness. She tried to shift her gaze from his, but his eyes darkened to obsidian, and she could feel the man in him jumping out to her, heating her, and the longer he did, the hotter she got.

He leaned forward slightly and extended his arms. "Come here, baby."

She didn't remember moving, but within seconds, she was in his lap, on her knees facing him, and his arms were locked around her. She opened her mouth for his tongue and he thrust into her. In the back of her mind, she thought, *I haven't finished my lunch*. But then, his erection bulged against her pelvis and she undulated helplessly against him.

"Do you want me? Do you?"

"Yes. Yes."

He stood and carried her up the stairs to her bedroom. She thought he'd taught her everything there was to learn about the feelings a woman can have with a man, but his lips seared every centimeter of her, front, back and sides, and then he claimed her with his tongue, before thrusting into her and bringing her to orgasm again and again. When, at last, he spent himself with a shout of surrender, he looked into her face.

"I'm deeply in love with you. Does any man other than me have the right to say that you belong to him?"

With barely the energy to answer, she said, "There's no one, and I have never loved any man but you."

"Do you belong to me?"

"In my heart, yes, but not legally."

"After the US Open, I hope to change that. For now, can we each agree not to see other people? I asked you this before, but now, I'm asking for a commitment."

"All right. I agree."

He smiled so beautifully and so sweetly that she tightened her arms around him, closed her eyes and whispered, "You're so sweet."

Within seconds, she felt him harden inside of her, and when her eyes widened, he grinned, kissed her and, within a few minutes, they flew to the sun.

"I'd like to go with you to Paris for the French Open," he said. "I haven't been there since I finished college."

"You've been to Paris? I've never been there. I'd love for you to come. That will be a tough tournament, though, because clay is definitely not my best surface. Give me a hard court and after that, I'll take grass."

After Sloan left with the agreement that they would see a movie together that evening, she pondered her agreement to allow Sloan to accompany her to Paris. Brad would certainly know about it and, if she knew her brother, he'd show her, and perhaps Sloan, his worst side. Well, her commitment was to Sloan, not Brad. She'd deal with it as it came.

Chapter 11

During the weeks that followed, Sloan trained new workers and began grooming Jasper for the responsibility of managing the third service center when and if he opened it.

"Whenever I'm not here," he told his employees at the San Antonio service center, "Jasper is in charge." To Jasper, he said, "Whenever you need me and can't reach me, check with Ben. I'm expecting you to manage my next service center. That probably won't happen for the next eighteen months to two years, but it will happen."

"I can't tell you how much I appreciate your confidence, Sloan. You know I'll go the extra mile for you any day."

He expected that within the next nine months, he should begin to realize a profit from his investment in the Castle Hills center. So, with the assistance of a marketing firm, he investigated sites in several communities within forty miles of San Antonio. He didn't want to locate a center farther away, because Jasper would have to move his family to another town, and he knew him well enough to know that the man wouldn't want to take his children out of school, no matter what the move would mean for him personally.

"I've been fortunate in having a good bunch of men working with me," he told Thelma that evening as he sat on her back porch enjoying pecan pie and espresso coffee. After he taught her how to make espresso, she served it to him each time he visited her. "I hope my luck holds with the next shop I open."

"There's a long stretch of highway between here and Austin," she said. "Why don't you check out Marcos, or someplace around there? You can put up signs that read, Last Service Stop Before Austin or Last Service Stop Before San Antonio."

"You're a peach, Thelma. I hadn't been looking in that direction, and it's close enough to San Antonio. I'll look into it."

"Where's Lynne?"

"She's practicing on several different clay courts getting in shape for the French Open."

"Why don't you go to Paris with her?"

"I'm going to do precisely that."

On May 31, they walked out of Charles de Gaulle Airport in Paris and got into the limousine that awaited them. "We could had taken a two-bedroom suite," she said. "That way, we'd be together, and we wouldn't be shacking up."

He moved so that his back was in the corner and he

could look directly at her. "I won't ask you to repeat that because I'm afraid you might. I thought we had separate accommodations because you considered it inappropriate for us to share a room. You don't want to drift into an affair with me. Right?"

"Yes, but if we had a suite, we wouldn't be sleeping together."

He rested his right ankle on his left knee. "The hell you say. There's not one thing saintly about me, and if I knew you were sleeping in the suite with me, you weren't sick and your parents weren't present, I'd get into whatever bed you happened to be in. I'd do it even if you were mad with me. Let's get this straight. I want you, and not just occasionally, but all the time."

"That's what you say, but if I asked you not to do that, you wouldn't."

"Maybe you know me better than I know myself."

"I know how you treat me, and that's what I'm going on." She shifted her position, leaned over and kissed his cheek.

He put both hands behind his head and leaned against the back of the car. "You could at least have kissed me on the mouth," he said, his tone plaintive and his manner woebegone.

Although she was fairly certain that he was putting her on, nonetheless she stifled a laugh, stroked the right side of his face, urged him to her and kissed his lips. "What are we going to do when I'm not either playing or practicing?"

"We can visit some museums, take a ride down the Seine, go to the opera, listen to some jazz, go to the Lido, the Moulin Rouge, Montmartre. You can't get bored in Paris, and you'll never have to wonder what to do. Paris is great for people-watching. If none of that floats your boat, come next door to my room and we can make beautiful music."

"How long did you stay here?"

"Till my money gave out. If I hadn't promised my dad that I'd leave Paris with a hundred dollars in my pocket, I'd have stayed longer. I never want to see another canned sardine."

"When you got back home, what did you do with the one hundred dollars?"

"I gave it back to my dad. He wanted to be sure that I wouldn't be broke and stranded in a foreign country, so he gave me that money and extracted that promise from me."

"Did you have a really good time here?"

"Lynne, I was eighteen and right out of high school. I had the time of my life. Before I left home, I promised Mom that I would stay sober, stay out of trouble and avoid disease, and that's about all I can take credit for. Two months on my own in Paris. It's a memory I'll cherish forever."

"Can't you tell me what you did?"

"Uh...I did all the things tourists do, and I doubt Paris has changed in that respect. I met lots of females from sixteen to sixty, and French women are so frank about sex that I was shocked, though I welcomed the rewards. I sat in cafés, drank coffee and read books and newspapers. In the process, I discovered that what I wanted most was to be my own boss, to go and come as I pleased without having to account to anyone for my time."

"Wait until I tell Brad about this," she said to herself. "This will bring him down a peg or two."

The limousine arrived at Hotel Belle Époque on the

Champs-Elysées around noon. "Knowing the French, they'll probably make us wait until check-in time, and that may not be until four o'clock this afternoon," he said as they arrived at the registration desk.

The clerk raised an eyebrow at their request for separate rooms. "Are you traveling together?"

"Yes," Sloan said.

She handed them their keys. "Four-sixteen for madame and four-eighteen for monsieur." She handed Lynne an additional key, surprising her, and Lynne's eyes widened. "For the door between the two rooms," the registration clerk said, her expression that of one disgusted with such ignorance.

"Uh...thanks...I mean, *merci*," Lynne said, wishing she could disappear.

She appreciated Sloan's silence as the elevator took them to the fourth floor, although she would have loved to wipe the smirk off his face. They reached her room first, and he waited until she slid in the card and opened the door.

"If you decide you want to see me," he said, "be sure and knock, because I have a habit of walking around undressed, and I wouldn't want to offend your sensibility."

"You wouldn't..." She looked up at him, saw the glint in his eyes and punched him in the belly. He gave in to the mirth then and nearly doubled up with laughter.

"You're not nice," she huffed. "How was I to know what the darn key was for? This is the first time I've checked into a hotel in the company of a man."

He sobered. "Didn't you stay at a hotel on your honeymoon?"

"Are you serious? Willard was too cheap to spring for a hotel room. We stayed at his sister's summer house on the Eastern Shore of Maryland. I don't recommend cooking in a strange kitchen when you're supposed to be deliriously happy."

"Are you going to let me in my room through the magic door, or should I keep walking?"

She opened the door, stepped inside and looked back at him. "How can you look so innocent when you're so wicked?"

He looked down at her, his eyes sparkling and his teeth flashing his charismatic grin. "I'm straight. If that reads innocent to you, I can't help it. And I'm getting tired of standing out here. Can I come in, or can't I?"

She stepped aside and walked in behind him. The man could turn her to mush with a flash of his smile. "You shouldn't laugh at me," she said, lowering her lashes in a shameless flirtation.

"I'm the one who's more likely to be laughable in this setup," he told her, and she suspected that he meant it, because he displayed no humor whatsoever.

He leaned against the wall and looked around at the king-size bed, sofa and chairs upholstered in the same olive-green and rust color that made the carpet, bedspread and draperies warm and inviting. A bouquet of yellow snapdragons sat on the coffee table, and from somewhere came strains of Gershwin's "Love Walked In."

"You'd better set the rules right now," he said, "and if you walk in your sleep, I'll reserve the right to do the same."

She walked back to where he stood near the door. "I've never walked in my sleep, but there's a first time for everything."

"If I walk in my sleep, there's been no one to tell me, so I can't say I won't and swear to it."

A feeling of contentment and of pure joy stole over her and she locked her arms around his waist. "Asleep or not, you'd never do anything to upset me. Who knows? I may be the one to knock on the door and ask to come in. Let's play it by ear. Do you need to rest? Flying all night, even in first class, is not for me. I want to sleep for a couple of hours and then see some of Paris."

With his arms enveloping her, he placed her head on his shoulder and stroked her hair until a restlessness washed over her and she moved back and looked up at him.

"Do you think this is going to work?" she asked him.

For an answer, he bent his head and covered her mouth with his until she opened it, took him inside and let him sear her body and soul.

"It will work," he said later. "One way or the other."

She found the key and opened the door between their rooms. "I've got a small bistro table and two chairs in front of my window," he called back to her.

"I have, too, and I just found a little nook with a marble countertop, refrigerator, sink and a coffeemaker."

"I have the same. Come here," he called.

She rushed to him. "What is it?"

"Look at that. I can see the Eiffel Tower looming over all of Paris." He stood behind her with an arm around her shoulder, and she turned to him, aware of him as the man in whose arms she had known boundless pleasure.

"What is it? Are you all right?" he asked her.

She moved away and blew out a long sigh. "I guess so." She wished at the moment that she could get used to him, that his nearness wouldn't heat her like a boiling cauldron. "I'm going to get a nap. I'll knock in a couple of hours."

"Sure you don't want some company?"

"No, I'm not sure, but if I don't rest right now, I won't be worth a nickel when I go to practice tomorrow morning."

"Right. See you later."

After a quick shower, she dried off, treated herself to the soothing effect of her favorite lotion and slipped her nude body between the sheets. There was something about sleeping only a few feet from Sloan with an unlocked door between them that gave her a wanton feeling. She fell asleep remembering their last time together, when his mouth and tongue had caressed every inch of her.

She awakened distracted by her unfamiliar surroundings, made her way to the bathroom and brushed her teeth. Oops! With five o'clock hard upon them, it was probably too late to go sightseeing, but she could put her feet on the sidewalks of Paris. She dressed quickly in a white waffle piqué skirt and jacket and a kiwi-green tank, put on a pair of black loafers, combed her hair and knocked on Sloan's door. After knocking several times and getting no answer, she opened the door and called to him. However, when she saw from a reflection in a mirror that he was in bed, her alarm buttons went off, and she ran to the bed and shook him.

"Sloan. Sloan, wake up."

He turned over on his back, opened his eyes and gazed up at her through a sleepy haze. "Oh, Lynne." He turned over and went back to sleep.

It would be cruel to awaken him, she thought, *but if I don't, what will he think?*

She sat on the edge of the bed and was about to pull the covers off him when she realized that he was nude.

She stared down at him, and her mouth watered as the thought of stripping off her clothes and getting in that bed began to tantalize her. She swallowed hard as the heat settled in her loins.

"Sloan," she whispered. "Get up before I do something outrageous."

"Huh?" He opened his eyes and looked up at her, and at that moment, she knew with certainty that she was forever his and his alone.

She leaned over and kissed him quickly on the mouth. "It's past time for you to get up," she said.

He stretched lazily and invitingly. "Why didn't you join me?"

She explained to him how she happened to be in his room and added, "I would have joined you if I hadn't been dressed when I came in here. Come on and get up."

"Okay, but something tells me you'd rather I let you leave first."

"Right," she said, although she would love to see him in splendid nudity, standing tall like Michelangelo's exquisite "David" in Florence, Italy's Galleria dell'Accademia.

She winked at him. "This is a case in which honesty is not always the best policy."

He rolled over on his belly. "Keep at it, and you may find yourself spending the rest of the afternoon differently from the way you planned." Then with a mild yawn, he said, "I've done nothing to deserve this punishment… I have always been a moral person. Here I am, a thirty-six-year-old man, healthy and virile, sentenced to spend two weeks of abstinence in a hotel room with a woman whose moves in bed make my jaws lock. Is there any justice anywhere?"

"You poor baby. I'm leaving so you can get up."

She closed the door behind her, went to her bathroom and put a cold wet washcloth on the back of her neck. "This man is not to be played with." For want of diversion, she flipped on the television and immediately wished that she was more fluent in French. The swift pace of the dialogue was too much for her, and she switched to CNN, which broadcast in English. Within fifteen minutes, she heard his knock on her front door.

"Why didn't you use the connecting door?" she asked him.

"I'm keeping it between the lines. The first time I knock on *that* door, I will definitely mean business." He took her hand and walked with her to the elevator. "Let's go to the Lido. I know it's touristy, but I have this memory of the dancers kicking up their heels as they did the cancan, and I want to know if it seems as naughty now as it did when I was eighteen."

They walked down the broad avenue, holding hands and laughing. "I knew you didn't have on anything in that bed," she told him.

He hugged her as they walked. "Wasn't I even a little bit tempting?"

"I refuse to incriminate myself."

"The Lido's over there," he said, pointing to his left. "Let's sit on one of these benches and watch the people."

A woman, who she guessed to be about fifty, burst out of a food delicacies shop gesticulating wildly and shaking her fist at a man of about twenty-five who wore his hair jet-black and spiked. The man spread his arms wide, but she continued to shake her fist at him and, if the words Lynne caught from the woman's rapid speech were evidence, she also called him a vile name. The Parisians went their way as if they saw and heard no one, but the woman raved on, her voice becoming increasingly shrill. Finally the young man knelt and in a prayerful mode, said, *"Ah, ma petite chou, comme je t'aime."* Ah, my little cabbage, I love you so.

"Oh, Pierre. Pierre," she said, opening her arms wide, and he dashed into them. Arm in arm, they went back into the shop.

"Well, I'll be doggoned," Lynne said.

Sloan shrugged. "They probably play that scene half a dozen times a day. People here ignore it."

They ate dinner at a small bistro, and when she refused the wine, she swore that the waiter looked down his nose at her. When he returned to take their orders, she ignored him and let Sloan tell him what she wanted. Later, he brought the food, served hers with the greatest care, bowed and asked her, "Would madame care for anything else?"

"No, thank you," she said.

"I noticed that he didn't ask me if I wanted anything else," Sloan said, "but I can't blame the man for wanting to please a beautiful woman."

She didn't bother to tell Sloan that the poor Joe was correcting his error in the hope of getting a big tip. After their dinner, they strolled a few blocks further down the Champs-Elysées to the Lido, where Sloan bought their tickets, and they entered the dark, almost blackened theater. A man sat on the other side of her, and immediately Sloan exchanged seats with her, so that she sat at the aisle.

"I'm taking no chances," he said. "I didn't come to France to get locked up."

The curtain rose and a row of women dressed in

white bonnets, black-and-red skirts and red ruffled petticoats, black stockings and high-top buttoned shoes milled around and caroused on stage. The curtain fell, and someone in the audience shouted an obscenity.

"Looks as if the stagehand made a mistake and raised the curtain too early," Sloan said. And then the famous cancan music began, the curtain rose and the chorus of dancers brought the audience to its feet, until all the dancers fell to the floor one after the other in their famous split. The deafening applause reminded Lynne of the sound of the fans screaming and applauding her on center court.

I've got to get back to the top, she said to herself, *and I have to keep my word to Sloan and retire after the coming US Open.* She hadn't used the word "retire" to him, but she had let him believe that after that tournament, she would be ready to begin life with him.

"Was it all that you remembered?" she asked Sloan as they left the Lido.

He rubbed his chin and gave her fingers a gentle squeeze. "It was very entertaining, and I'm glad I saw it with you. But somehow, petticoats don't have the same appeal." A short laugh escaped him. "I've seen undergarments from a better vantage point."

"That's incontestable," she said. "When I'm preparing for a tournament and when I'm playing in one, I try to go to bed by nine-thirty. Do you mind?"

"Of course not, and you should also have an afternoon nap. I'm here to support you, sweetheart, so tell me what your program is, and I'll do all I can to help you through it."

"I'd like you to sit in my box with Gary and Clive. Will you?"

"Thanks. That's where I want to be. The media will play it up, you know."

"I don't care about that. I'm proud of my relationship with you. And if anyone asks me, I'll be glad to tell them who you are and who you are to me. Any objections?"

"On the contrary. I'll be delighted."

The sports photographers rushed Lynne when they arrived at Roland Garros for her first match two mornings later. He'd told himself that he was prepared for anything, but he hadn't counted on the pushing and shoving, the clicking of cameras and the seeming lack of concern for Lynne's safety. However, when she seemed unperturbed, he realized that it wasn't an unusual situation but, thinking that she needed a bodyguard, he stuck close to her.

"Who's this handsome gentleman?" a female reporter asked Lynne. He hoped she would say that he was her bodyguard but, as she had promised, she answered truthfully.

"Sloan McNeil."

"And is he a special friend?"

"Very, very special," Lynne said. "Now, unless all of you want me to lose this match, may I please pass? I promise an interview later, win or lose."

To his amazement, the reporters parted, and they walked through like Moses crossing the Red Sea. "You handled that well," he told her.

"And I have to answer all their questions later whether or not I feel like it."

In Lynne's box, he greeted Gary and introduced himself to Clive, who began biting his nails as soon as Lynne walked onto the court. Her opponent had a good record, but he had confidence in Lynne's ability to beat her.

"What the hell!" Sloan exclaimed, jumping up when Lynne missed a line drive.

"Not to worry, man," Gary said. "Save your nerves for later. If she gets past the quarters, she's got Sharapova waiting for her. Then, you can get nervous."

But watching her play in person was so much more draining than seeing her on television. However, he settled down as she began her first service game with two straight aces. Still, he couldn't banish the anxiety until she won the match fifty-eight minutes later.

"How do you stand this?" he asked Gary as Lynne took her bows to the crowd's wild applause.

"I don't have a choice, Sloan. I work with her as best I can, but when you get right down to it, it's up to her. She's good, and she's headed back toward greatness."

"See you later," he said to the two men, and headed for the entrance to the clubhouse, where he waited for about twenty minutes in the company of the reporters. "Are you two an item?" one of them asked him.

"I don't give interviews," he told them. "Ms. Thurston said she would give you an interview, and I'm sure she will."

Minutes later, she appeared and, with her arms outstretched, rushed to greet him. Hang the reporters, he thought as he lifted her and twirled around with her locked in his arms. Then he brushed her lips with his own. "You were wonderful, but I was a wreck when that gal won the first game she served. I'll get out of the way and let you talk with these reporters."

He watched as she impressed him with her deft answers to their questions, some of which were personal.

No, her ex-husband didn't want her to play tennis. No, that is not why they divorced. Yes, she was involved with Sloan McNeil. No, he had not asked her to marry him. Would she if he asked her?

"He's standing right here," she replied. "Don't you think he deserves to hear the answer to that in private?"

"Is he going to ask you?"

She nodded toward Sloan. "There he is. Ask him."

"He doesn't give interviews," one replied.

She shrugged. "Ask him again in September at the US Open."

"And not at Wimbledon?" the female reporter asked.

"That's only three weeks hence," she replied. "Now, I'm pooped, so I'd better go."

Their applause startled him, and later, he asked her if it was common for reporters to applaud an interviewee.

"Not in my experience," she said. "But most won't give that long an interview after a match. What are we doing this afternoon?"

He looked at his watch. "It's a quarter past eleven. After you rest, and we have lunch, it should be around two o'clock. If you like art, we could go to the Louvre or to the Musée Auguste Rodin. I love his statues."

"I'd like to see *The Kiss*. I've seen pictures and small reproductions, but it would be nice to see the original."

"It's life-size. Maybe we can do both."

They got into the limousine that awaited them, and she sat shoulder to shoulder and thigh to thigh with him and rested her head on his shoulder. With his arm snug around her, he kissed her gently and closed his eyes. *All this, and heaven was yet to come.*

After lunch, they went first to the Musée Auguste Rodin at 77 rue de Varene to see the famous Rodin statues, and she lingered at *The Kiss,* the one in which a man adores a woman's body, walked around it several time before she said, "It's beautiful," in a whisper of a breath. He realized that he was learning much about her that afternoon.

"You don't seem fond of *The Mona Lisa*," he said of Leonardo da Vinci's famous painting. "Why?"

"She doesn't look feminine, and it's a much smaller painting than I had imagined. Da Vinci's *St. John the Baptist* is a much more arresting painting."

"Strange," he said. "When I first saw them hanging together, I thought the same thing. Now, I'm not so sure. Want to take a look at those twenty-two famous paintings by Rubens?"

"Sure. I may not get another opportunity."

They strolled through the Louvre looking at paintings, sketches and sculptures until closing time. "I enjoyed that," she told him. "I wish I knew more about art."

"One day, we'll go to Florence and immerse ourselves in some of the world's best. We'll get some art books and study them, so we'll understand what we're seeing. What do you say?"

Her eyes shone with anticipation, and a smile seemed to attach itself to her face and linger there. "I'd love to see Italy with you. The art would be a bonus."

The wheels of his mind revved up like an engine given a shot of gasoline. If all went well with his second service station, he'd be able to take her there if and when she married him. *I'm getting ahead of myself. Must be this idyllic city.*

Her play seemed to improve with each match, and after each one, she greeted him at the clubhouse gate as if she had been waiting years to see him. In his joy, he forgot to telephone Ben and Jasper, but when he finally did so, their reports relieved him of any worry. Lynne breezed through her round-four match against one of the hottest players on the tour, and he began to hope that she could win the tournament.

"I take each point as it comes," she told him. "I don't even look ahead to the next game."

He marveled that she showed no interest in anything except that which he suggested, and that wherever they went, she didn't indicate an interest in leaving until he suggested that they go. Perplexed, he asked her, "You're not even a tiny bit feisty. Is that because you're contented? Are you happy?"

They strolled along Saint-Germain-de-Pres holding hands like so many couples that they met. "I'm spending all of my free time with you. Why wouldn't I be happy?"

"I get the urge to kiss you at the damnedest times," he said.

She smiled up at him. "If you were French, you wouldn't hesitate."

He saw an old Peugeot parked half on the sidewalk and half on the curb, leaned his back against it and pulled her into his arms. When she pressed a kiss against his mouth, he flicked his tongue across the seam of her lips, demanding that she open to him. What a mistake! She sucked him into her mouth, began to feast hungrily and he had to push her away, lest he have an erection in public.

"Try to remember that I'm practicing abstinence these days," he said with as much of a smile as he could muster.

The afternoon of Lynne's semifinal match arrived, and after telling Lynne goodbye at the club gate, he took his seat in her box and told himself to relax, a difficult thing to do with Clive sitting beside him chewing his fingernails down to the quick. She won the first set, but lost the second in a close final game. The third and final set went to a tiebreaker with six games each. Finally, a determined Sharapova stepped up to the plate and unleashed two consecutive aces and began hitting the corners.

"Go to the net," Sloan yelled.

Lynne raised the level of her own game, and evened the score at seven games apiece. Her opponent made it 8–7, and Lynne began to rush her serves and to make unforced errors, and lost to the number one player by a hair.

She'd had it within her grasp and let it slip away. Years earlier, she had learned not to count her chicks before they hatched, and that's what she did, thinking ahead to the finals and losing her concentration. She shook hands with the winner, bowed to the tumultuous applause and headed for the dressing room. After that match, no one could say that she wasn't one of the top players.

"You're number five in the world now," a reporter said as she entered the clubhouse. "How does it feel?"

She forced a smile. "Not quite as good as number two. I should have won it."

"You played a great three sets. What's you favorite surface?"

"Hard court, then grass."

"That's what I remembered," the woman said. "Good luck at Wimbledon. I wouldn't be surprised if you won it."

She thanked the woman, took a quick shower, dressed

and rushed to meet Sloan. He was there, and that was what she cared most about. She sprang into his arms, taking all the love he could demonstrate in the presence of thirty or more photographers.

"Looks as if you lost your concentration in that last game," one French female reporter said, and then she looked directly at Sloan. "Not that I blame you. I don't see how you could concentrate at all with this guy waiting for you."

Annoyance flared up in Lynne at the woman's blatant flirtation with Sloan. "I managed," she said, "because I knew he was waiting for *me*." If there was anything she had learned in Paris, it was that as far as French women were concerned, every woman was a competitor, and every man was fair game. She answered a few questions, and then asked to be excused.

"I'm sorry you didn't win," he said. "I thought you had it in the bag, but you seemed less focused in that last set."

"In the last two games, I was. I made the mistake of thinking about the finals and wondering whether I'd meet Davenport or Serena Williams. But that's over, and I'm proud of the way I played. The girl I played is number one, and I almost beat her. Next time, I will."

"I thought you outplayed her until the very end. You had more aces and more winners. You've really made a lot of progress. I suggest you get some rest, and we'll get together around six. Okay?" The limousine arrived at their hotel, the driver handed him her duffel bag and a reporter blocked their way as they approached the door of the hotel.

"You played a great three sets, Miss Thurston," he said. "Would you answer a couple of questions, please?" He wanted to tell the man to buzz off, but that was

Lynne's prerogative. "Are you and Mr. McNeil living together? Are you sharing a room here?"

"No and no," she said. "And I'd appreciate it if you would allow me to pass. This minute." The man, obviously from the United States, snapped a picture and ducked out of the way. He didn't doubt that the accompanying story would bear no resemblance to the truth, but he didn't share that thought with Lynne.

"Try to rest, and I'll check on you at six," he said when he reached his room door. He handed her the duffel bag, and pressed a quick kiss to her lips.

"Right. But I wanted to take a boat ride down the Seine. Can we do that tomorrow?" He nodded as the light of her smile quickened his heart. "See you later, love," she said.

Something had changed since they arrived in Paris. He had the feeling that she loved him more deeply, that he was dearer to her. He hoped so, because she had become everything to him, his life.

Lynne showered, dried her body and crawled into the bed. Exhausted. She hadn't let Sloan know that she was worn out. She had used all of her energy and skill in an effort to win that match. Yes, she lost concentration near the end, but the broiling heat had also depleted her strength, perspiration soaked her clothing and dripped into her eyes, and she'd been barely able to see. Maria deserved to win because she let down in the end, while Maria capitalized on every opportunity.

"I'm not going to sweat it," she told herself. "I played well, and the next time I will win."

Seconds after she stretched out her tired frame and sank her head into the pillow, she heard the telephone

ring. Thinking that the caller would be Sloan, she rolled
over on her stomach and answered.

"Hello," she said, her voice soft and seductive.

"What the devil do you mean by traipsing around
Paris with that guy? You ought to be ashamed of yourself. You're all over the papers and the TV." She held the
receiver away from her ear as her brother, Brad, ranted
on. "I dare you to tell me he isn't after your money. Mechanics don't earn enough to hang out in Paris at five-
star hotels and eat in top restaurants."

"How are you, Brad? Apparently you haven't been
watching me play or reading about my tennis matches,
for if you had, you would certainly have congratulated
me on what I've achieved." She hung up, dialed the op-
erator and told her she didn't want any more overseas
calls. No point in mentioning it to Sloan; he had a big
enough grievance against her brother.

That night, they dined at a small family restaurant
on the Left Bank. She had no idea how he found it but,
although the place lacked ambience, she had rarely enjoyed a meal so much. They strolled along the banks
of the Seine, crossed it at Pont des Arts and moseyed
along the quay until they came upon a bench and settled
themselves there.

"I could live like this forever," she told him as lovers strolled past them. An old woman stopped and gave
Sloan a pink flower, the stars twinkled and moonlight
drenched them as they gazed at each other, blissfully
unaware of the world around them.

They reached the hotel around eleven o'clock, took
the elevator to their rooms and lingered at Sloan's door.
His kiss was more brief than usual, and his eyes projected an unmistakable and urgent need, but he said,

"See you at nine in the dining room, and thanks for a special evening."

"Thank you, too," she said as she stood on tiptoe to kiss his cheek, then hurried off to her room. After a quick shower, she brushed her teeth, applied lotion to her body and slipped on a short nightgown that Victoria's Secret would have been proud of and got into bed. She flipped on the television and an advertisement of the cancan at the Lido brought her to reality.

I'm miserable, because I want to be with him, and he made it clear that while we're here, I'm the one calling the shots. She grabbed the robe that matched her peach-colored silk nightie, decided to carry it instead of wearing it and knocked on his door.

"Come in."

She opened the door gingerly and, when she stepped inside, he stood by the window wearing green boxer shorts, but he didn't move. "I got lonely," she whispered, and he rushed to her.

"I'm so glad you came. I was standing there thinking that, after what we shared this day, if you could get in that bed and go to sleep, knowing that I was on my way out of my senses wanting you, something had to be wrong."

"I almost did, then I remembered that you left it up to me and I made tracks, and fast."

"I've never seen you like this," he said of her nearly transparent gown. "You're so beautiful that I have to pinch myself sometimes."

"I could say the same about you," she said and raised her arms to him. Within minutes he threw the gown from her body and began to worship her, starting with her feet, licking her legs, thighs, pausing long enough to anoint her vagina with his surging tongue until she cried out, and moving up to her belly.

"Honey, put me in the bed," she moaned.

He lifted her and placed her in his bed, rid himself of his shorts, climbed beside her and locked her body to his. She held her breast for his kiss, and when he sucked her nipple into his warm mouth, her hips twisted and she reached down to hold and caress him, but he wouldn't allow it.

"If you touch me, I'll explode."

"I want you to explode inside of me," she moaned. "Get in me."

He handed her a condom and she rolled it on him, caressed and stroked him as his talented fingers massaged her most vulnerable spot until the liquid flowed over them. She locked one hand around his and, with her other hand on his buttocks, forced his entrance as she raised her hips to receive him.

"Don't do that. You'll make me hurt you," he groaned.

"Nothing this good could hurt," she said, and swung up to meet his thrust. It didn't last long. They were so hot for each other that as soon as he began his powerful strokes, tremors raced through her, and then he was in her, on her, beneath her and all around her. He sucked her nipples, put his hand between them and rubbed until she screamed from the pleasure that he gave her. Heat seared the bottom of her feet, and lights flashed behind her closed eyes before the pumping and squeezing began in her vagina and she could feel herself locking to him, gripping him, squeezing him until she thought she would die. All of a sudden, the bottom fell out of her and she screamed as he thrust her into ecstasy and his shout of "You're mine. This is mine, you hear?" reverberated through the room. He kissed the tears of joy from beneath her eyes, and she fell asleep in his arms with him locked inside her.

The following morning, around eleven o'clock, they boarded the Batobus at Quai d'Orsay and got seats at the front of the boat. "It's like a tour of the major Paris sights," she said, sitting snug in Sloan's arms as the glass-covered boat moseyed down the Seine past the Notre Dame cathedral.

"We ought to go in there," he said.

"All right, but Thelma said it's the outside that counts. She thought the inside was dreary, but it's always best to see for oneself."

"Do you want to go?" he asked when the boat docked on the quay.

"Not really. I'd rather get a sandwich and a soft drink, go to the Bois de Boulogne or the Café de la Paix at the Place Opera and watch the people while we eat. After that, I'll need to pack."

"Have you called Gary?"

"I forgot. You get in the way of everything else, buddy. I'll call him when we get back to the hotel."

Later, at the hotel, she called her coach, but he had checked out of his hotel. Then, she called Thelma. "I lost in the semifinal, but next time I'll win."

"You should have won yesterday. I was wondering where your mind was when you played those last two games. How's Sloan?"

"He's super."

"Well, at least you've got that under control. I hope you're coming home tomorrow. I just made two blueberry crumb pies, and there isn't a soul to eat them but me."

Lynne enjoyed a good laugh. "You'll have two additional mouths tomorrow."

"Good, then you both can come over here for supper. You need some real food after over two weeks of half-done duck breast, snails and goose fat."

"Oh, Thelma, you can make anything sound ridiculous."

"Sloan's mother called and invited me to come down to Galveston for a couple of weeks. She said Connor would drive up and get me. I told her I would as soon as you and Sloan got back from Paris."

"Maybe we'll take you, unless my coach decides to work me to death, and he might. Wimbledon is three weeks away. Anyhow, I'll see you tomorrow."

"Safe journey, you hear?"

Sloan brought Lynne home around five the next afternoon, and they spent a pleasant evening with Thelma, but the next morning, she faced Clive and Gary, both of whom laid out a rigid program for the next three weeks.

"You could have won," Clive told her, "but the heat got the better of you, so I want you to run five miles every morning and two miles after your practice session with Gary."

"You should have won," Gary told her later, "but you lost concentration, and we're going to work on that starting now."

"All right. I get the message," she said.

They could do and say whatever they pleased, but she was not giving up Sloan, as if he were just so much fat to be excluded from a diet, and she told both of them so.

"No problem," Gary said. "But watch the sex. If it

weakens men, it's gotta do the same for women." She didn't answer him.

Two weeks and five days later, she kissed Sloan good-bye at the San Antonio International Airport and headed for England and the prestigious Wimbledon tournament. At least she'd be playing on grass instead of clay. She skipped the grass court warm-up tournament at East-bourne, England, because she didn't want to exhaust herself, and she figured that playing four hours a day on grass for two solid weeks with a great male tennis player was warm-up enough.

She entered the court with her confidence high and her hopes on a par with her belief that she would win the prize. As she waved to the crowd, her adrenaline began pumping, and she was, at last, the Lynne Thurston of six years earlier, fearless and intimidating. She won the first set with six games to none for her opponent, as the crowd yelled, "Come on, Lynne. Go, Lynne." But at the first change of sides in the second set, she tripped over her chair, sprained her ankle and sustained a gash in her thigh.

Tears streamed down her face, and she sobbed into the towel as the trainer taped her ankle and wrapped her thigh. "You can't continue," the doctor told her. "If you do, you may risk your career." After signaling to the referee that she would retire from the match, she stood, waved to the crowd and left the court in a wheel-chair. If only Sloan had come with her this time! Gary and the limousine driver assisted her to her hotel, and a housekeeping assistant helped her pack. She changed her ticket and prepared to return home the next morn-ing. She didn't think she had ever been so unhappy, and she could not sustain an interest in anything.

"Hello," she said, answering the telephone.

"Hello, sweetheart, I won't ask how you are, because I know you must be miserable. How bad is your ankle?"

She perked up at the sound of his voice. "Thanks for calling. I… It's swollen, but it doesn't hurt too much. I wanted to continue playing, but the doctor said that I would risk my career, so I took her advice."

"You did the right thing. When are you coming back?" She told him. "I'll be there to meet you. Try not to be depressed. For one set, at least, you gave some great tennis lessons."

"Thanks. I felt so good out there, as if I was invincible. I wasn't, I know, but it was wonderful to feel that way again."

"Give me a kiss," he said. She made the sound of a kiss, and he returned it. "See you tomorrow," they said in unison.

She hadn't thought to order a wheelchair escort for her arrival in San Antonio, but Sloan did, and when she reached the baggage-claim area, he rushed to greet her, lifted her out of the chair and kissed her. "I'll get your bags," he told her. To the wheelchair escort he said, "Take her right out front, and I'll get my car and meet you there."

She looked at the man who'd taken her heart and made it his own as he strode through the crowd, and pride suffused her, pride that of all the women he knew and had known, he wanted her alone.

"That's quite a man you got there," the woman who escorted her said. "He thinks a lot of you, too. You going to marry him?"

"More than likely," she said, acknowledging it for the first time.

"You're crazy as hell if you don't. If I had time, I could give you a couple a dozen reasons not to let that brother go."

"Don't worry. I know a few myself."

"Ha. Ha. I bet you do."

Sloan lifted Lynne and put her in the car, gave the escort a tip and headed for Lynne's house. "I'm going to stay with you until you can take care of yourself," he told her. "The important thing is for you to stay off that foot. If I have to leave you for any reason, Thelma will be there. I don't want you to put any weight on that foot until the doctor says it's okay."

"I can—"

"This isn't debatable, Lynne. If you want to play in the US Open, you can't abuse that foot. Where can I sleep?"

"I have a guest room."

"Good." He carried her up to her room and sat her on the bed. "I'll be back in a minute, and by then you ought to be in bed."

When the telephone rang, she assumed that Thelma was the caller. "Hi, I just got home."

"So I gathered," Brad said. "How badly are you hurt?"

"Well, the gash in my thigh isn't very deep, but my ankle is swollen, and it doesn't feel too hot."

"I figured you didn't pull out of that match for fun. I'll be down there day after tomorrow to see how things are with you. Stay off that ankle. See you in a couple of days."

She was at the point of telling him not to come when it occurred to her that meeting Sloan would shock Brad, and that it was a lesson he needed.

Chapter 12

Lynne pulled off her clothes, welcomed the feel of her hard mattress against her back and closed her eyes in blessed relief. Almost immediately, she felt her foot lifted and elevated on a soft, but firm, object.

"How does that feel?" Sloan asked her.

"Wonderful, and the pain seems less sharp. Thanks."

He dragged the boudoir chair to the side of her bed, sat down and took her hand. "This is what I have in mind, and I hope it's okay with you. I'll stay here, get your breakfast and lunch, check in at the service center for about four hours, shop for whatever we need and be back around six or six-thirty. Thelma will be here during the afternoon. I spoke with Clive, and he said you are not to put any weight whatever on that foot. None. *Nada.* Okay?"

"Yes, thanks, but I don't like to take you from your work. You're needed at your service centers."

He patted her hand, rose and stood gazing down at her. "Whenever and for as long as you need me, I'll be here for you. I'll be up shortly with your supper." He started out of the room, turned and walked back to her bed. "Did Thelma call you a minute ago?"

"No. That call was from my brother. He said he'll be down day after tomorrow to see about me."

He rubbed his chin with a good deal of vigor. "Did you tell him I'd be staying here with you?"

"I didn't consider that his business. He'll find out when he gets here." She wasn't sure she cared for the pose that Sloan struck, belligerence being the best way to describe it, so she tried to cool him off. "And it still won't be his business."

She could see Sloan's muscles relax. "Just checking," he could be heard saying, loping down the stairs.

Wasn't that the same smart-ass brother who had him investigated? He couldn't wait to show the man how he felt about him. He put together a quick supper of deviled shrimp, buttered noodles and sautéed spinach, with melon for dessert, and prepared two trays. What was he to do about Nick? The man had been insubordinate, refusing to take orders from Jasper because he felt that he and not Jasper should have been promoted. Sloan didn't like firing a worker who had a good record as well as a family that depended on him. He had spoken candidly to Nick and warned him, but the man had a personality that literally trampled his good judgment, and he would act out even when he knew he was wrong.

"I'll take him in hand when I have to," he said to himself and headed up the stairs with the trays.

"The interesting thing about this situation," he told himself while cleaning the kitchen after they ate supper, "is that I enjoy taking care of Lynne, and I don't mind the menial part of it."

"Thelma changed my bedding," she told him when he returned from work the next day.

He kissed her quickly. "I'm glad she did. I had wondered if it was appropriate for me to do that. Would you like to sit on the deck while I get supper?" His niggling conscience mocked him, for he knew he wanted an excuse to get her into his arms, and the surest way would be to take her downstairs.

"I'd love it. I'm tired of this scene."

"Don't be impatient, sweetheart. We're after the prize, and you shouldn't forget that. Where's your robe?"

"Hanging on the inside of the bathroom door." He brought it, helped her into it and carried her down the stairs and out on the deck where he seated her and propped up her foot.

"This is heaven," she said, sniffing the scent of roses and inhaling the fresh evening air. After a supper of steak burgers, hash brown potatoes, string beans and pecan pie, Sloan cleaned the kitchen and they sat on the deck, holding hands and talking long into the night.

"What do you want after the US Open is over in September?" he asked her.

She didn't hesitate, and he liked that. In her usual forthright way she said, "If I'm fortunate, I'll be able to look forward to starting a family."

"Won't you have to get married first?"

"That would be preferable."

"All the more reason why we have to get you in shape. Maybe I should take you to the doctor tomorrow to get that foot X-rayed." He didn't intend to mention their future together until she was in a position to let him know whether she would keep her word. If she belonged to him as she had admitted, that would be the time for her to prove it.

"Could we go day after tomorrow instead? Brad's coming tomorrow. He's been a royal pain recently, but I still love him."

"Of course you do—he's your brother. But that doesn't mean I won't take him on if he gets out of his place with me. I hope you understand that."

"Oh, I do." A grin settled on her face. "He's going to deserve exactly what he gets."

To his delight, Brad arrived at Lynne's house shortly after he returned from work. He had wanted to be there when the man came so that he could show his status and his right to behave in accordance with it. The doorbell rang shortly after he brought Lynne downstairs and made her comfortable on the deck. When Caesar growled, he knew the caller wasn't Thelma, to whom the dog had taken a liking. He rushed to the door and opened it.

"I'm looking for Lynne Thurston," the man said.

"I'm Sloan McNeil," he said, "and you must be Lynne's brother. Come in."

He had the upper hand, and he could see that Brad was taken aback, for both of the man's eyebrows shot up. "Come on in," he said. "Lynne's out on the deck."

"Do you always answer her door?" Brad asked in a tone barely short of insulting.

"Why shouldn't I?" he asked. "Especially since she can't walk."

"Then how did she get outside?"

Sloan stopped walking and looked down at the man from his advantage of two good inches. "I picked her up out of bed, took her in my arms and walked down the stairs and out on the deck. It was as simple as that."

"Hmm. You've got a sharp tongue."

"It's sharper than you think." He headed for the back door and stopped when he heard Caesar's ferocious growl. "Wait here. I'd better go pacify Caesar."

He shortened the dog's leash and called Brad. "Come on out."

Brad embraced his sister, but before he asked her how she felt, he pointed to Sloan and said, "What's this all about? Surely you're not planning to continue with this?"

Sloan could hardly believe he'd heard correctly. The man had the temerity to insult him in his presence. He sat down in the chair he'd placed beside Lynne, took her hand, crossed his knee and got comfortable.

"You're asking your sister to choose between us, Thurston, and that isn't smart. You had me investigated, making me the subject of speculation by my employees and, even though you couldn't have discovered one negative thing about me, you've got your nose up in the air. You have a law degree. I have a master's degree in mechanical engineering. You work for a law firm—I work for myself. I own two service centers that bear my name, and I'm proud of what I do and what I have accomplished. I don't have to apologize to you or to any man."

"Look, you—"

"After I finish, you may say whatever you like. I have treated your sister honorably, and I demand that you and every other man do the same. She belongs to me, and I to her, and nothing that you say or do is going to make a damned bit of difference. I am staying here while she's recuperating, because I am going to take care of her until she can walk without damaging her foot and her career. Your being here won't make any difference in that respect, either."

Brad sat down and looked at his sister. "What do you have to say about this, sis?"

She lifted her right shoulder in a quick and, he thought, dismissive shrug. "Nothing. He's told you the truth."

"Excuse me while I get us some supper," Sloan said. He looked at Brad. "Would you like lemonade, wine or beer? There's no hard liquor in the house." Brad didn't answer.

He wasn't eavesdropping, but he left the kitchen door and window open in case a few words might drift within earshot.

"Are you living with this guy?"

"Right now? Yes, but we're not sharing a room. We're not shacking up, but if I want to sleep with him, I definitely will. You and Deb lived together for two years before you got married, so I'd rather not hear stuff about morals. I love Sloan, and he loves me. Furthermore, he's the only man who *has* loved me. Willard doesn't have a clue as to what love is." She changed the subject. "How long can you stay?"

"That ought to put him in his place," Sloan said to himself, as pride suffused him.

"A couple of days," Brad said, in answer to her question. "Where did you meet this guy?"

"On Route 35. He told me I was a smart-ass. Can you believe that?"

"Oh, yes, I definitely can. He's got the courage to say anything that pops up in his head."

"Back off, Brad. It ought to be clear to you by now that you misjudged Sloan. And another thing—you look down your nose at people who work with their hands, because you think they're not polished, not in your class. Well, that's silly. You wouldn't know a Rembrandt from a calendar, but Sloan can identify a Rembrandt by sight, a Reardon, a Rubens and many other painters. When did you last go to a symphony concert? How many operas do you know from memory? Not even *Carmen* or *Porgy and Bess,* I'll bet. And did you know that Duke Ellington wrote both classical and religious music? Sloan's well versed in all these things."

He could tell from the tone of her voice that she was enjoying putting her brother in his place and doing it with an air of innocence. "I don't expect ever to see him wear anything with a designer label stuck on it, but let me tell you when that man puts on a tuxedo, he looks good enough to eat."

"All right. All right. I get the message. Are you going to marry him?" Sloan felt the hair on his neck stand up.

"He hasn't asked me, but when he does, I'll let you know what I say to him."

"One thing is certain—the man's good for your ego. Your personality has definitely changed, and you've become very assertive."

"Right. So, Brad, please lay off Sloan. You hurt me when you say mean things about him, and there's no basis for them."

"I have to admit, he's a helluva surprise. By the way, is he really cooking?"

"Yes, and he's very good at it."

"What's he cooking?"

"I only know what my nose tells me."

"Damn. Don't ever tell Debra that he cooks."

Sloan went back to the deck. "Dinner's ready." To Lynne, he said, "I'll take you inside." Then he picked her up, carried her into the dining room and sat her in the chair at the head of the table. He served a meal of prosciutto-wrapped melon, broiled, bacon-wrapped scallops, buttered and parsleyed new potatoes, steamed yellow zucchini glazed with parmesan cheese, a green salad and pecan pie.

"Man, this is food for the gods. Where'd you learn to cook like this?"

"I live alone, and I like to eat. Necessity is the mother of invention."

Lynne gave silent thanks when Brad and Sloan shook hands as Brad was about to leave. "I'm relieved to know that my sister isn't alone down here, and I hope the two of you take care of what you have," Brad said to Sloan. "Do you plan to marry her?"

"If she'll have me. You bet I do."

"Then I'm sure we'll see each other again. Thanks for the great food."

The next morning, Sloan took Lynne to the hospital to have her foot X-rayed. "It's healing nicely and should be as good as new in another three weeks," the physician said. "It was only a hairline fracture, but that, too, takes time to heal. I want to see it again before you put your weight on it."

The days passed slowly and, true to his word, Sloan stayed with Lynne and took care of her. But she became increasingly concerned that, by spending so much time with her, his business could be suffering.

"I brought you some papers," Thelma told Lynne when she came over one afternoon to bring her a bowl of vegetable soup and a pecan pie for Sloan. "I don't know where you found Sloan McNeil, but I didn't know they made 'em like him anymore," she added. "Look at this." She opened the *San Antonio Sentinel* and pointed to a short column at the bottom of page sixteen. "Don't jump to conclusions, now."

The heading read: McNeil Motor Service Sued For Improper Service.

Lynne blotted out everything else from her thoughts, petrified as she read the brief notice.

"I don't believe it," she said. "This will ruin his business."

"Yeah," Thelma said. "I'll stay with you as long as you need me, but you send him back to his job even if you have to tell him you hate him. He's a good man, and whatever's going on there is happening behind his back."

Fortunately the next morning, Clive told Lynne that he wanted her to have her foot in a whirlpool mineral bath several hours every day, and she could only get that service at a live-in clinic, so she didn't have to concoct a tale in order to force Sloan to leave her.

"How are things at the shop?" she asked him when he visited her at the clinic that afternoon.

"I have some problems, but I'll work through this."

"What kinds of problems? Remember, we are open with each other, and we have no secrets from each other."

He told her what she already knew and added, "Local business is definitely down. I'm getting mainly travelers."

"I'm sorry, love. You deserve better. What are you going to do about Nick?"

"I fired him. I should have done it as soon as he made the first bad move, but I always try not to fire a man who has small children."

"Take out an ad in the *Sentinel,* and get on that morning talk show. Want me to make the call?"

"No, but thanks. I know Zack, and that's a good idea."

Later, when Clive and Gary visited her, she asked them to give Sloan their business, and to send their friends to him. It plagued her that Sloan had been away from his shop because of her, that if he'd been there, it wouldn't have happened.

At the beginning of the second week of July, the clinic released Lynne, and her doctor gave her permission to resume training and practicing. Overjoyed, she was unprepared for the brunt of Sloan's displeasure when he came to her house one evening.

"It has just occurred to me that all this wonderful new trade I'm getting at my San Antonio service center is coming from tennis players and other sports figures. You're behind this, and I want it to stop. I am not relying on you or any other woman to make my way, and I don't want a woman begging her friends to help me."

Annoyed and ready to pounce on him, she gazed up at the face she loved, its eyes stormy with the passion of disapproval, a passion so much like the heat that emanated from him when he wanted to make love with her. It had the same fierce intensity as the clouds that heralded a coming storm and darkened with the moments. She stared at him, poleaxed by his powerful masculinity, and he stared right back at her, his eyes getting stormier by the second. His nostrils flared as his libido battled with his anger, and she could feel the blood rushing to her loins. For in spite of her annoyance with him, the man in him leaped out to her and she wanted him, wanted to feel his powerful strokes as they drove her to ecstasy.

When he took a step toward her, she knew he wasn't responding to his own anger, but to the desire that had gripped her, and that was mirrored in every move she made and in every breath she panted. As of its own volition, her tongue rimmed her upper lip, and with two quick steps he had her in his arms. She opened her mouth and sucked his tongue into her. She had never wanted him so badly, and as she pulled his tongue deeper into her mouth, their groans echoed throughout the living room. He stopped, backed off and looked at her, panting, his feet wide apart. She grabbed his belt and would have jerked him to her if she could have, if he hadn't stood his ground.

"You're mine," she said. "I want you, and I'm going to have you. So don't you think for a minute that you're going anywhere and leaving me like this."

As if against his will, he reached out to her, picked her up and carried her up the stairs, not to her bedroom, but to the room he occupied while he stayed with her.

It would be raw sex, but she didn't care. She unhooked his belt and would have taken it off him, but he stilled her hand, looked at her for what seemed like ages, pulled her to him and bent to her mouth. She parted her lips, but he refused her his tongue, and when she put his hand on her breast, he ignored her.

Frustrated, she caressed his penis, catching him unawares, and he nearly buckled.

"I want your mouth on my breasts, all over me," she said.

He yanked the T-shirt over her head, jerked off her skirt, lifted her and clamped his mouth on her left breast. Screams tore out of her as he suckled her, and she felt the love liquid stream down her leg.

"If you don't get in me right now, I'll…I'll…"

"You'll what? I'll do it when I get ready."

She reached down, unzipped him and caressed the length of him.

"Oh, hell, baby." He put her on the bed, stripped himself and mounted her. She wrapped her legs around his back, took him and plunged him inside of her and began to move. But he forced her to his rhythm. And within minutes she erupted all around him, crying out his name. He pumped hard and followed her into ecstasy, screaming as he gave her the essence of himself. "Lynne. Oh, my Lord, Lynne."

He held her face in the palms of his hands, stared down into her eyes, kissed her, separated them and fell over on his back. "I've never done anything like that," he said. "I was so hurt, so mad at you and so damned crazy for you."

"I know. I didn't know what got into me, and I didn't question it. One minute I was annoyed—no, I was furious—and the next I wanted you badly enough to ravish you. And then you got me on your terms and sent molten lava shooting through me. My entire body convulsed into orgasm. I wasn't myself. I didn't know who I was or where I was. It was fantastic."

"Tell me about it. For a few seconds there, I thought

I'd died and gone to heaven." He sat up and braced himself on his elbows. "The bad thing about this is that, after
this unbelievable experience, I'm still upset with you,
and you're displeased with me for chewing you out."

"Are you going to get over it?" she asked him.

"In time, but right now, I think we need some breathing space."

"Are you serious?"

"Yes. I'm taking Thelma to Galveston with me this
weekend, and…well—"

She interrupted him. "Isn't your business doing well?
Would you rather have gone belly-up? Aren't we supposed to help each other? At least that's the line you've
been handing me." She crawled over him, got out of the
bed and asked him, "Why did you bring me in here instead of to my bedroom?"

"Animal instinct, I suppose. It was my room, and I
wanted you on my terms and in my kingdom. I'd prefer
to make love with you in my house."

"What am I supposed to do, ring your bell and ask if
I can come in so you can make love with me?"

He got up. "We're having a fight, and I don't want
that. I'll be in touch when I get back from Galveston."

He didn't want to break it off with Lynne; in fact, he
couldn't. He loved her, but she had to understand that he
would not accept largesse from her friends. How could
he and have his self-respect? She meant well; he didn't
doubt that, but certain things a man had to do for himself, and one of them was to get himself out of any trouble he happened to get into.

He shook his head vigorously as he put the car in
Drive and started home. He'd give anything to know

what had gotten into Lynne back there. He'd been mad enough to shake her, and she was getting irritated with him, and then she suddenly went into sexual overdrive. The sexual tension in her would have been obvious to a child. She challenged him as no woman ever had, or, evidently, had considered doing. Challenged him, yes, and proceeded to use her woman's advantage, getting him where she knew he was most vulnerable. Was there a man anywhere who didn't respond to his woman if she told him she wanted him and meant to have him?

He balled up his left fist and pounded the steering wheel when he thought of the way she went at him, not merely responding to him, but driving for what she needed. Hell! That woman was as different from the Lynne he'd first met as chalk was from cheese, and mad as he'd been, it made him proud, because he was the man who taught her. He scratched the side of his head. Damn, but she'd nearly blown his mind when she'd erupted around him like a violent storm thrashing everything in its way, wringing everything out of him. He'd been sexually active since he was thirteen, and he'd never experienced anything like it. Lord, but it was heaven!

Yet, after that eyeball-blistering sex, they were still mad at each other. He couldn't figure it out. Yeah, he'd connected with her on as deep a level as he ever had, maybe the deepest—and that was saying something— so how could he still be angry with her?

When he got home, he phoned his father. "I'll be there tomorrow night and Thelma will be with me," he said after they greeted each other.

"What about Lynne? I was hoping she'd come, too. Nothing wrong between you two, I hope."

"Nothing that a few hours together won't straighten out. Lynne is training for her next tournament."

"Give her our love, and tell her that your mother and I will be rooting for her."

"I'll do that. Give Mom a hug for me. See you tomorrow."

"Will do."

He hung up and flopped down in his favorite chair that sat beside the massive fireplace in his den. It pleased him that his parents liked Lynne, but he didn't want them to like her so much that it constituted a kind of pressure. He slapped his forehead with his right hand. Oh, what the hell! He'd be miserable if they didn't like her. And he wished Lynne would apologize for meddling in his business, so they could go back to being real friends.

In the meantime, Lynne's anger had begun to subside, and what she felt was a stinging hurt. The only experiences with the male ego that she'd had as an adult were what she'd come to realize as weaknesses in her ex-husband and in her brother, self-satisfaction that sprang from low self-esteem. But Sloan knew who he was and had the self-pride that went with accomplishment. Yet, he gave so much of himself and from the depth of himself and that, along with his unselfishness in caring for her when she could not take care of herself—as he'd done twice so far—had deepened her love for him.

"But he's not going to lose his temper with me and chew me out," she huffed. "I love him, but I've learned the hard way to stand up for myself." She went to the refrigerator, got a glass of lemonade, took a sip and dumped the remainder in the kitchen sink. It hurt. Oh Lord, it hurt. But she'd hurt before and that hadn't killed her. Neither would this. She had to win the US Open, and she intended to dedicate herself to that.

"I'm not tired, Gary," she told her coach several days later. "I've got to win the US Open, and the only way I'll do that is to train and practice."

"Maybe you're not tired," he said as he panted, "but I am. Six hours of practice daily for four consecutive days would kill a horse, and it's too much for you. How many hours a day are you training? Two, when I recommended one. What are you trying to do to yourself?"

"I'm tired of losing. I'm better than that."

"All right. Tomorrow, we'll practice your serve for two hours, and you will put it where I tell you to put it, but I am not going to see you destroy yourself practicing. Where's McNeil? Is that what this is all about? I haven't seen him this week."

"We had a tiff, but I don't think it's serious. I'm giving him some space."

She was doing more than that; she wanted him to know that he'd hurt her, and that she needed an apology as much as she suspected he did. *Love is not the be-all and the end-all, Lynne Thurston.* Still, she missed him. "When I'm tired and aching after seven hours of training and practicing," she said to herself, "that's when I wish he was here to hold my hand and tell me that he loves me and that I'm as good a player as I ever was."

Gary threw a ball at her to get her attention. "If I'm your coach, you have to do as I suggest, Lynne. No one wants you to get back to number one more than I do. You've made it to number five in a year's time. Take my advice and you'll reach your goal. If you overdo it, you'll sprain or break something, and you'll be so plagued with injuries that you'll never reach it. Hasn't Clive warned you about that?"

"Yeah. All right, I'll train one hour and practice four."

He patted her shoulder. "Good gal. You're already as fine a player as any of them. See you Monday. Same time."

She dragged herself to the house and into the shower. She knew that Gary was right, that she'd been overtaxing her body, but she wanted to win the Open, to reach her goal and then, if Sloan asked her to marry him, she'd be able to... "I'll cross that bridge if I ever get to it," she said to herself. "Nobody can ever tell what a man will do."

Her thought applied especially to her brother, Brad, who called her almost as soon as she got out of the shower. "Hi, Brad," she said. "How's everything?"

"That sounds like a dust-off," he grumbled. "I just wanted you to know that I think I might have been wrong about McNeil. That guy's no pansy."

"You're telling *me,* he's not!" she said.

"All right. Don't get your back up. He's pretty sure of himself, but I get the impression that he earned the right."

"Brad, I don't mind if you tell me that you were wrong about Sloan, and that you will stop judging people on the basis of one of your biases."

"Aw, sis, don't be so rough."

That was his way of capitulating, but she didn't mind. He was her precious brother, in spite of his faults. "I'm not, but you've given me a hard time about Sloan, and you were wrong."

"Okay. I was wrong. When is your next tournament?"

"Three weeks."

"Good luck."

After Brad hung up, she sat on the edge of her bed

pondering whether she should call Sloan. She missed him, but she hadn't forgiven him, and if he had forgiven her, wouldn't he call?

She dressed, took Caesar and walked over to Thelma's house. "Come on in," Thelma said when she opened the door. "Sloan just left here. He brought me back from Galveston half an hour ago. His folks wanted me to stay awhile longer, but I'm not one for wearing out my welcome. Sloan drove down early this morning to pick me up and bring me home. There isn't a thing I wouldn't do for that man. Don't you tell him, but I'm going to change my will with him in mind. What's wrong with you two now? I'm beginning to think you're both crazy and I told Sloan that. Why in the name of angels can't you two get together and *stay* together?"

"Did he tell you what happened?"

"Yes, and I told him that if he was ten, I'd paddle him. He said he'd never been paddled in his entire life. Lucille sent you a bag of apple turnovers, and she said you should come to see her. Sloan's parents are wonderful people."

She barely heard Thelma's words. Caesar began whimpering the way he did when a storm was imminent, so she rose and started for the door. "According to Caesar, we're going to have a thunderstorm, so I'd better get home before it starts." She told Thelma goodbye, took the bag of turnovers and left with Caesar close to her side. In the distance, she could hear the sound of thunder, and Caesar tugged at his leash, so she increased the pace of her steps to a trot.

"Hello," she said after racing to the phone.

"Hi, this is Sloan. Are you all right? We're having a storm here."

"I'm okay, Sloan. Thanks for thinking about me. The storm hasn't hit here yet, although I hear it coming."

"How are you?"

"I'm a little tired, because I'm preparing for my next tournament."

"When is it and where?" She told him. "I'll be with you in spirit." They talked for a few minutes about nothing in particular.

"I'll call you tomorrow," he said, "and you can call me, too."

For the next two weeks, he called her every evening, and they talked like good friends, neither saying what the other wanted to hear and both of them making the calls because they had to hear the other's voice.

One night, she said to him, "I'm leaving tomorrow morning for the Rogers Cup Tournament in Toronto. The top players will be there, and I'm going to give it my all. Wish me luck."

"You know I do, Lynne. I want the tournament for you more than you want it for yourself."

Sloan sat glued to his television set as Lynne walked out on the tennis court followed by her opponent. "Here she comes," the announcer said of Lynne. "She's recovered her old form, and if she plays this match as she's played the previous matches in this tournament, never dropping a set, she's a shoo-in to win the championship, her first since returning to the game."

He got up and made a pot of coffee. Not even when he put his last penny down on his first service center had he been as nervous as he was then. But with her first serve, Lynne gave notice that she planned to win and she wasn't going to take long to do it. For fifty-eight minutes, Sloan paced the floor, sat down, got up and paced again, punished his left palm with the brunt of his right fist and rubbed his chin until it burned.

With two points away from the championship, she hit the ball into the net, and his groans echoed through the house, but on the next point, she sent the ball to the corner out of her opponent's reach.

"Match point," the referee said, and Lynne tossed the ball up and hit it down the middle for an untouchable ace.

He jumped up and pounded his right fist into his left palm. She won. She had won her first tournament. He wiped the dampness from beneath his eyes. Thank God! She won! Now, if she could do the same at the US Open that began in two weeks, he could begin to deal seriously with their future and whether they would live it together or separately.

The next evening at eight o'clock, he stood at the gate as she disembarked from the American Airlines flight. Her face bloomed when she saw him, and he rushed forward and opened his arms to her.

"I was so happy," she said, "and you weren't there. Oh, Sloan, I missed you so."

He didn't need words. The feel of her, soft and responsive in his arms, told him that she still belonged to him. He brushed his lips over hers, and the sweetness of it tantalized him. He wanted and needed more, but he couldn't have it in that public place, so he merely squeezed her to him.

"I was with you every time you struck a ball," he told her. "I may have worn out the carpet in my den where I paced from the TV to the window and back. When you hit that last ace, I jumped straight up. Sweetheart, I'm tired of being away from you. I've hated every minute of it."

"Me, too. Are you going home with me?"

"Of course. If you'll let me."

She reached for his hand and walked with him to the luggage carousel where he retrieved her bags. "Stay here with the bags," he told her, "while I get my car."

With great difficulty, he controlled the urge to surpass the speed limit in order to get to her house where he could be alone with her at last. As he drove, he thought back to the last time he was in her house and to the blistering sex that passed for lovemaking between them. As good as it was, he meant to erase it from her memory with the sweetest loving they had experienced.

"It seems as if decades passed since I was last here," he said later as he sat on the stool in her kitchen drinking lemonade, "and I want to make you forget that night. I'm sorry that I didn't accept your kindness, but we'll have to talk about that at another time. Not taking from women is deeply ingrained in me. I hope you can forgive me."

"I have." With a hand on each of his knees, she leaned forward and kissed him.

She wanted them to make up, and she was stubborn enough to want it on her terms, but she knew he was not going to allow it, that he wanted them to make love as equals, not as onc dominating the other.

"Have you forgiven me?" she asked him, although she still didn't think she'd done anything wrong.

"It'll be out of my system as soon as I have a chance to tell you why I was upset, but I'm no longer hurt or angry. If you need the words, yes, I forgive you."

She had to put an end to the awkwardness, so she put

an arm around his shoulder, sat on his lap and pressed her lips to his. Anxious for all that he could give her, she parted her lips above his, placed his hand inside her blouse and gave herself up to his ministrations. His fingers toyed with her nipple, teasing and exciting her while she twisted and turned on his lap. Finally, desperate for the feel of his warm, moist mouth on her breast, she straddled him and rose on her knees to give him easy access. She felt him then, as he rose hard and heavy between her legs, and she would have lowered herself on him, but he lifted her away from him.

"I want more for you and for me," he said as he lifted her and carried her to her room. She understood that he wouldn't be satisfied by physical release alone when he began to kiss her eyes and her cheeks while he unbuttoned her blouse. At a slow and maddening pace he undressed her, kissing the places where his fingers trailed.

"I love your beautiful body," he murmured as he slowly slid her panties from her hips and replaced the garment with his tongue, trailing it over her flesh until he reached the place where she was most sensitive to him, twirled his tongue around it and then sucked it until she screamed. She didn't see how she could stand it any longer, and her hips began to sway uncontrollably. He put her on the bed then, knowing that she was going mad for him, and stared down at her while he took his time stripping off his clothes.

"Now. I want you now," she said, turning her head from side to side, embroiled in the heat of desire. But he let her know that he was charting their course when he thrust his tongue into her mouth, slid his hand slowly down her body until he reached his goal, parted her folds and let his talented fingers work their magic.

"I feel so full," she moaned. "Sweetheart, please, I'll die if I don't burst wide-open. Now. I need it."

"As soon as you're ready. Do you love me?"

"Yes. Yes. I love you. I'm crazy for you."

"Who do you want?"

"You. I want you. Honey, I'm…I need relief. I want you to get inside of me."

He moved from her, and she held her breath for his thrust. "I want this, too," he said as he spread her legs and let her feel the tip of his tongue. As he moved up her body, she felt the liquid flowing from her, grasped his penis and, as he mounted her, she thrust it into her as a scream of pleasure tore from her. She thought a volcano had erupted inside of her as he stroked her.

"We belong together," he murmured, "and don't you forget it." Then, he increased the power of his thrusts.

"Yes," she said. "Yes!

"I'm going to… Oh Lord," she yelled. She felt his power then as he drove within her. Heaven and hell must have broken loose inside her as she trembled uncontrollably from head to foot. "I'm dying," she moaned, just before he plunged them both into ecstasy.

She thrust her arms wide and gave herself to him completely and without reservation. Almost immediately, he braced himself on his elbows and looked down into her face.

"I love you, and don't you think for a moment that I'm going to let you out of my life. I won't ask if you were satisfied, because it was like spontaneous combustion, and believe me, I felt it. I could stay this way with you forever, but I want us to talk." He separated them and rolled off the bed.

They dressed and walked down the stairs holding

hands. "My father taught me that I am responsible for my woman and my family, that I take care of them and that, unless I am ill or badly disabled, I should never let a woman take care of me, that I should solve my own problems. You got me out of a terrible bind. One of Gary's friends got a local journalist to write a favorable story about me for the *Sentinel*. My business is better than ever, but I couldn't take credit for it.

"I appreciate your concern, your caring and, yes, your help. But if there's a next time, please talk with me about it first. I promise not to be pigheaded, which is what Thelma and my parents have accused me of in this instance. That's all I have to say. What about you?"

"All right. Next time I will discuss it, and I hope you'll remember that just as you need to help me when I'm down, I have the same need where you're concerned." She nodded. "Is this behind us now?"

His smile nearly unglued her. "Yeah. Want to finish what we started an hour ago?" She kissed him, reached for his hand and started toward the stairs.

Two weeks passed swiftly, for they spent every evening together. On Saturday, September 6, at eight o'clock in the evening, Lynne Thurston walked into Arthur Ashe Stadium carrying a bouquet of red and yellow roses, symbolic of her status as a finalist at the US Open. She hadn't had an easy time getting to the finals, because she had faced three top-ten players and played two tough three-set matches, including the semifinal that she won the previous morning. And her opponent in the final was the world's number one player, the woman who'd beat her in the Australian Open in January.

As she entered the brightly lit court to the roar of

the crowd and shouts of "Lynne, Lynne," she looked up at the star-filled, moonlit sky and then glanced toward her box and waved to Sloan, Brad, Gary, Clive, Thelma and Sloan's parents. "Lord, if I can just win, I'll be able to have peace and happiness in my life at last. But my game is on," she reminded herself, "so Maria will not beat me tonight."

After Lynne won the first set in a grueling, half-hour tiebreaker, she looked at her box and pumped her right fist when she saw Sloan jump up and shake both fists. The flow of adrenaline accelerated, and she could hardly wait out the five-minute rest period when it would be her turn to serve.

"I know she's not going to give me a single point," Lynne told herself, "so it's up to me to win." Tied at four games each, she finally broke Maria's serve, led five to four and began to serve for the match. Twice, she tossed up the ball for her serve and twice she let it fall to the ground.

"Steady, girl," she said aloud, and the crowd in the stadium echoed, "Steady, Lynne."

She took a deep breath and served the ball down the middle for an ace with a speed clocked at one hundred and twenty-six miles an hour. Maria sent her next serve into the corner for a point, and they were even. "I'm going for broke," she said to herself. "She can't hit 'em if she can't reach 'em." Ten minutes later, she sent an ace to Maria's left, tossed her racket, spread her arms and jumped for joy. She'd done it. She had won the US Open.

With tears streaming down her face, she raced to the net, shook her opponent's hand as gracefully as she could, turned and raced into the stands, jumping over knees and stepping on bottles of cola and beer as she headed for her box. Sloan met her halfway, picked her up and kissed her.

"I'll be waiting for you at the clubhouse door," he said. "You were unbelievable out there." She blew kisses to the other occupants of her box and raced back to the court. Minutes later, she held the coveted trophy in her hands once more.

"You're world number one now," the tour president told her, "and we've never had a finer champion."

"Maria pushed me to my limit," she told the crowd. "I gave myself two seasons in which to climb to where I am now and win this tournament, and I'm satisfied. Thank you for your support." She held up the trophy for the benefit of the photographers, grabbed her duffel bag and raced to the dressing room.

After showering and dressing in record time, she stuffed her belongings into the duffel bag and raced to the entrance where she knew Sloan waited for her. As she stepped through the door, his arms went around her.

"I've never been so happy," he told her. "I sweated every bead of sweat right along with you."

"And you're here," she said, as if in wonder. "You're here to share this with me."

He tightened his arms around her, bent to her lips and savored them. "I'm having a party for you at 21 Club just as I promised last year when you played here. I hope you feel up to it."

"Absolutely," she said with a vigorous nod of her head.

"Good. If you'd like, I'll take you to your hotel so you can change, and—"

"And I'll check out and spend the night at your…uh… where are your parents staying?"

"Two floors above me at the Willard, and Thelma's in the room next to them. I want you to stay with me."

At the Mayflower, she changed, packed and was leaving the room to check out when he knocked on the door. She looked through the peephole, saw him and flung open the door. "Come in."

She thought she detected diffidence in his manner as he stood before her holding a bouquet of pink, purple and lavender calla lilies. Her fingers shook, but she managed to take them and hold them. But when he knelt before her, she nearly swallowed her tongue, and her heart lunged in her chest.

"I've waited almost two years for this minute, Lynne. I love you, and I want you to be my wife. Will you do me the honor of marrying me? I'll be a good husband to you and a good father to our children. My family will come first in my life, and I'll always be there for you and for our children as long as I live."

So shaken that she couldn't speak, she knelt with him as tears of joy cascaded from her eyes. When at last she could force out the words, she said, "Oh, yes. I'll be honored to be your wife, Sloan. This is why I wanted so badly to reach my goal tonight. I love you. I've never loved anyone else."

He rose with her in his arms and brushed her lips with his own. "I can hardly believe this is happening to me. To us. Can we tell them tonight at the party?" he asked her.

Laughter poured out of her. "Sweetheart, I'd like to phone the Associated Press with the news," she told him. "I want to tell the world. I want everybody to know that you belong to me."

An hour and a half later, she followed the maître d' to a private dining room at the 21 Club, conscious of

Sloan just behind her. When they entered the candlelit room, his arm clasped her close to him, and she looked up to see his face wreathed in smiles and joy sparkling in his eyes.

"Let me introduce the world's number one tennis player and the woman who has just honored me by agreeing to be my wife." He kissed her then, blotting out the sound of applause. Then, as she looked into his eyes, she told him, their families and their friends, "This is the happiest day of my life."

* * * * *

REQUEST YOUR FREE BOOKS!

2 FREE NOVELS PLUS 2 FREE GIFTS!

KIMANI™ ROMANCE

Love's ultimate destination!

YES! Please send me 2 FREE Harlequin® Kimani™ Romance novels and my 2 FREE gifts (gifts are worth about $10). After receiving them, if I don't wish to receive any more books, I can return the shipping statement marked "cancel." If I don't cancel, I will receive 4 brand-new novels every month and be billed just $5.19 per book in the U.S. or $5.74 per book in Canada. That's a savings of at least 20% off the cover price. It's quite a bargain! Shipping and handling is just 50¢ per book in the U.S. and 75¢ per book in Canada.* I understand that accepting the 2 free books and gifts places me under no obligation to buy anything. I can always return a shipment and cancel at any time. Even if I never buy another book, the two free books and gifts are mine to keep forever.

168/368 XDN F4XC

Name	(PLEASE PRINT)	
Address		Apt. #
City	State/Prov.	Zip/Postal Code

Signature (if under 18, a parent or guardian must sign)

Mail to the Harlequin® Reader Service:
IN U.S.A.: P.O. Box 1867, Buffalo, NY 14240-1867
IN CANADA: P.O. Box 609, Fort Erie, Ontario L2A 5X3

Want to try two free books from another line?
Call 1-800-873-8635 or visit www.ReaderService.com.

* Terms and prices subject to change without notice. Prices do not include applicable taxes. Sales tax applicable in N.Y. Canadian residents will be charged applicable taxes. Offer not valid in Quebec. This offer is limited to one order per household. Not valid for current subscribers to Harlequin® Kimani™ Romance books. All orders subject to credit approval. Credit or debit balances in a customer's account(s) may be offset by any other outstanding balance owed by or to the customer. Please allow 4 to 6 weeks for delivery. Offer available while quantities last.

Your Privacy—The Harlequin® Reader Service is committed to protecting your privacy. Our Privacy Policy is available online at www.ReaderService.com or upon request from the Harlequin Reader Service.

We make a portion of our mailing list available to reputable third parties that offer products we believe may interest you. If you prefer that we not exchange your name with third parties, or if you wish to clarify or modify your communication preferences, please visit us at www.ReaderService.com/consumerschoice or write to us at Harlequin Reader Service Preference Service, P.O. Box 9062, Buffalo, NY 14269. Include your complete name and address.

KROM13R

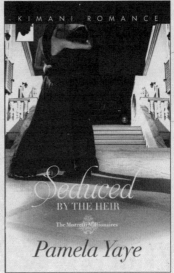